To Lust or Love?

"The wedding bed is the only way you shall ever have me."

He eyed her in speculation, "I could take you by force and no one would think harshly of me. I am master of Malvern and of every living creature on the plantation!"

"You could, though it might not be so easy. But that is not your way, Malcolm Verner. To your credit, you are a true gentleman."

He brooded. "You believe you know me that well?"

"I'm beginning to."

"Perhaps you think so, but I would not depend overmuch on it, my dear."

For a moment Hannah was afraid she had gone too far, at least broached her bold proposal too soon. *No,* she told herself fiercely; *I'm right, I know I am! The other way, I would have to settle for becoming his mistress, and he would soon grow tired of me and I would indeed end up a tavern whore . . .*

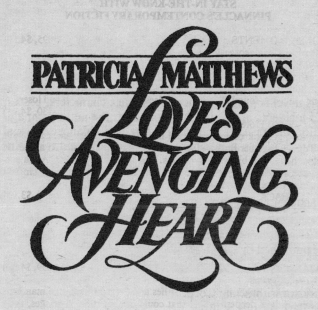

PATRICIA MATTHEWS

LOVE'S AVENGING HEART

PINNACLE BOOKS
WINDSOR PUBLISHING CORP.

PINNACLE BOOKS

are published by

Windsor Publishing Corp.
475 Park Avenue South
New York, NY 10016

Seventeenth printing: November, 1989

Printed in the United States of America

LOVE'S AVENGING HEART

PART ONE

Hannah McCambridge

Chapter One

On a summer morning in July, 1717, early risers in the village of Williamsburg, Virginia, were treated to the sight of a short, pudgy, ill-kempt man pulling a tall, buxom, red-headed lass of perhaps sixteen along the dusty streets, by a rope around her shapely neck.

At the end of the rope, Hannah McCambridge, head held as high as the cruel tug of the rope would permit, fought back tears, and tried to ignore the stares and the snickers. Her hands were lashed together behind her back.

The tears that scalded her eyes were caused mostly by anger. Of all the indignities that she had suffered at the hands of her stepfather, Silas Quint, this was the worst; the final insult, the most crushing blow of all. To be sold as a bond servant; to be dragged through the streets like a black slave ...

Hannah remembered once seeing female slaves, black flesh naked and shining in the sun, auctioned on the block, prospective buyers fondling and pinching their flesh, looking at their teeth as they would at the teeth of a horse. At the time, her heart had gone out to them, and now she felt that she knew the full depth of their degradation and shame.

Silas Quint, gleeful over the stir they were creating, jerked hard on the rope, causing the rough fibers to bite into the flesh of Hannah's neck, and once bringing the girl to her knees in the mud.

As they turned onto Duke of Gloucester Street, Quint halted and turned to her. "Look sharp now, missy. Yonder's the Cup and Horn."

Hannah stared with distaste at her stepfather's red face. Silas Quint could not, by any standards, however charitable, be called an attractive man. He had a huge, veined nose—a toper's snout it was—and his cruel black eyes were buried in lumps of flesh, like shot embedded in suet.

"But just look at you. Filthy, as though you'd been wallowing in a pig sty. Ye don't look so high and mighty now, my girl."

Hannah raised her chin and fixed him with a hard green glare that would have shamed a man with any sensitivity. She said not a word. Arguing with him would only please him, she well knew.

"Clumsy, ye always was clumsy as a cow. You'll have to do better than that at the tavern, missy, or Amos Stritch will be taking a switch to those fine legs of yours." He stared at her slyly, relishing her anger and helplessness.

"But wait now...." His usually lusterless eyes glittered, and his thin-lipped, mean little mouth took on that wet, loose-lipped smile that Hannah had seen all too often of late upon his face. "I see you've torn your dress, missy. Might as well make some use of it. I always say it's a sharp man that turns things to his own advantage."

Before Hannah could guess his intention, he swooped down on her, a sausage-fingered hand hooking in the high-necked bodice of her dress. She felt the pressure of the material pulling against her back, and heard the tearing sound of the fabric as the material came away, shift and all, almost baring her right breast.

Quint's face grew redder still, and he wet his lips with his tongue as he stared at the soft, seductive swell of his stepdaughter's plump breast.

She was a tasty morsel, to be sure, Quint thought, and the feeling of heaviness in his crotch reminded him of his thwarted desires toward the girl. He reached out again and fondled the soft skin, pushing the torn flap of fabric away from the rosy nipple, savoring the silken feel, and enjoyed the girl's quivering flesh under his touch as she vainly endeavored to draw back.

Hannah felt the bitter taste of vomit rise in her throat. The man's hands were grimy with filth, half-moons of dirt under the broken nails. But it was the thought of what she knew was in his mind that made her sick with loathing and disgust. For the last few months, ever since her body had flowered into an almost embarrassing opulence, she had observed the expression on his face every time he looked at her. And although she was young, and a virgin still, Hannah knew what those looks meant. The small hovel that she, her mother, and her stepfather called home allowed almost no privacy for any of them, day or night.

Silas Quint was a sorry provider for Hannah and her mother. He worked no more than he had to, mostly at jobs clerking in the Williamsburg shops. The rest of his time he spent drinking and gaming in whatever tavern would grant him credit.

Since the Crown would not allow the Colonies to mint their own currency, ready money was always scarce; it was not uncommon for a shopkeeper to grant extended credit. A yearly settling of accounts was the usual thing. Most often the settling was done in the form of barter—warehouse receipts for part of a year's tobacco crop, for example. But Silas Quint didn't own a tobacco plantation; he didn't even own the miserable hovel they lived in.

Now Quint released Hannah's breast and stepped back. "Mayhap ye are clumsy, and not as hard a worker as might be desired, but old Stritch, elder that he is, still has an eye for young maids. One look at your breasts and his breeches will swell, to be sure, and he'll care not how good a serving wench ye be. So come along, missy."

Quint was exulting in his good fortune as he pulled Hannah along at the end of the rope. He had been mystified that Amos Stritch would allow him to build up such a large account. He hadn't questioned his good luck, but had continued to take advantage of it.

A week ago he had finally been given an explanation when Stritch had demanded payment. If the account was not settled at once, Quint faced

4

debtor's prison. Of course Quint didn't have a shilling. Stritch suggested another means of payment. He suggested that Quint indenture his stepdaughter to him for a period of five years—then the debt would not only be canceled, *some* additional credit would be forthcoming, contingent on how well Hannah worked out.

Quint had seized the chance. To him, Hannah was another belly to fill, and his own lecherous thoughts had been troubling him for some time. He knew that some night soon he would creep into Hannah's bed and have her. God knew he hadn't held off this long from any moral scruples. Even though he was a bully, he knew that the girl's mother was capable of killing him if he touched Hannah. Also in the back of his mind had been the thought that a girl as comely as Hannah might be sold in some fashion, but that a man able to pay a good price would want a virgin. Turn Hannah into spoiled merchandise, and she would not be worth a farthing.

The Cup and Horn was a narrow, two-story, steep-roofed building of brick, with sleeping quarters for rent above, and an ordinary below. Since it was early in the day, the tavern was empty of customers. A young boy of twelve or so was busy in front of the tavern with a bucket and mop. He gaped at the sight of the man towing the girl on a rope.

Trudging wearily along behind Silas Quint into the dank liquor-stench of the tavern, Hannah felt her strength ebbing fast. She had not eaten that morning. And her throat felt parched and sore. At least the dark tavern was blessedly cool after the burning of the hot morning sun. She was ready to drop wearily to the floor when the bulk of Amos Stritch, the tavern owner, loomed up before them.

Stritch was a large man of fifty or so, with a bald, wigless pate and a round, protruding belly under a stained waistcoat. The vast belly protruded so far that Hannah was reminded of a woman quick with child. He was limping, favoring his right foot.

His popping gray eyes bulged even more than usual at the sight of Hannah's *dishabille*. "What's this, Quint? She looks like some strumpet dragged in off the street!"

Despite his words, Hannah noticed that his gaze did not move from the mound of her breast, half exposed by the torn bodice of her dress.

Quint pulled off his soiled cap and made a knee. "She were reluctant to come along, Squire Stritch. Had to use a bit of rope to bring her along, I did. Has spirit, this missy!" Quint smirked. "Not some milksop female with no blood in her veins. I know ye like wenches with a bit of spit and fire to 'em!"

The tavern owner licked thick lips with a tongue stained brown with tobacco, and his eyes burned on Hannah's flesh like flaming faggots.

Quint chortled, reached over, and grasped the remaining shreds of Hannah's bodice. The rest came away easily, and Hannah's firm young breasts popped free. "Just like young melons, they be," he said, as he squeezed and fondled them, making the nipples stand out like thimbles. "Do ye think the lass will do?"

Amos Stritch, his color almost apoplectic now, swallowed and nodded, unable to get the words past the lump in his throat. By George, the maid

6

was a ripe one, for all that she was sixteen! Suddenly he shot a sharp, inquiring look at Quint, who was still fondling Hannah's breast.

Hannah, mind numb now with shame and shock, tried to still the trembling of her lips and keep the tears from her eyes. She refused to give them the satisfaction of seeing her cry. But would there never be an end to it? Would the degradation, the scalding anger, and the cold despair never be finished? She tried to use her thoughts to shield herself from the touch of Quint's hand on her flesh.

But Quint, reading Amos Stritch's thoughts correctly, quickly pulled his hand away and stepped aside. "Now, now, not to fret, she's all yours. Just as we agreed."

Stritch cleared his throat. "You swore the girl was a virgin. Yet you handle her most familiarly . . . I want no damaged goods. Tell me straight now, Quint, is the girl untouched?"

Quint bobbed his head and assumed a humble expression. "On my oath, she is. Would I lie to you, sir, after all ye have done for me? No, I've not touched the girl, though 'tis often enough I have wanted to. It's just that I couldn't resist, so to speak. You can see for yourself, Squire, how tempting a lass she is."

Hannah, wishing only that it would end, paid scant heed to the exchange between the two men.

Stritch grunted, for the moment appeased. He did not necessarily believe Quint. He knew that the man was a liar, a drunkard, and a blackguard, but he would find out the truth for himself soon enough. He shifted position, wincing with pain as all his considerable weight came down on the gouty foot. He said, "Bargain it is, then." He jerked his head. "Up those stairs with you, wench. Up to your quarters. Your stepfather and me have business to decide."

Quint removed the rope from around Hannah's neck, then untied the lashings around her wrists.

Staggering slightly, Hannah obeyed Stritch's command, rubbing her wrists to restore circulation. Clutching the narrow bannister, she went up the steep, winding stairs. Stritch limped along behind her. Once he placed a hand on her haunch. She hurried on ahead, and Stritch laughed, a whistling sound like a pig's squeal.

On the second story, he prodded her on down the hall. "Not here—this is where I bed down the paying guests. Up the ladder with you."

Hannah, calling upon the last of her strength, climbed the ladder, which was little more than strips of wood nailed to the wall. She again heard Stritch's lewd laughter and belatedly realized that he was peering up under her skirts. She was too weary and dispirited to be angry.

The moment she had pulled herself through the trap door, Hannah heard it slam shut. The bolt was driven home.

It was a poor room, not much larger than a horse stall. The steep slant of the roof made it possible to stand upright only along the inner wall. It was stifling, airless, except for what little air seeped in through the rough planks forming the outside wall. The only light came from one small window set in the slant of the roof. It was dirty, and Hannah saw no way to get it open. She crouched before it, wiping away as much dirt as she could to peer outside. All she could see was a small slice of blue sky and the roofs of nearby buildings.

Shoulders slumped with discouragement, she looked around the room. The only furnishings were a trunk in one corner, empty, the lid thrown back; a pallet on the floor; and a chamber pot. The bedclothes were filthy and looked bug-infested. The rough plank flooring had at least an inch of dirt on it.

Gingerly, she sat down on the pallet. In one respect it was little worse than where she slept at home, except that she and her mother tried to keep their house reasonably clean.

Her mother, her poor, work-worn mother. Hannah could scarcely remember her real father, even though she'd been eight at the time of his death. Every time she thought of him she visioned blood and violent death, and a shutter seemed to come down across her mind.

Her mother had married Silas Quint not long after her father's death. Since that time they had known nothing but hardship and privation. Aside from keeping house and looking after Hannah, her mother took what work she could find in the households of the gentry. Most of the money she earned was taken away from her by Quint. She was only able to hide enough coins to provide Hannah with a few extra tidbits of food and a new garment from time to time. Sometimes Quint would stumble onto her pitiful hoard of coins, beat her unconscious, and then spend the money for drink and gaming.

There was only one bedroom in the house they inhabited. Hannah slept on a pallet on the kitchen floor, which at least had the advantage of being warmer than the rest of the house in the cold of winter. Only a few feet separated her from the room where Silas Quint bedded with her mother. The walls had cracks wide enough to peek through. Not that Hannah ever had, but she could hear every word spoken in that room. Hannah heard their couplings, heard the slap of a hand across her mother's face when she attempted to deny Quint what he called his "husbandly rights." She heard their almost nightly quarrels, and afterwards, Quint's drunken snores and her mother's heart-wrenching sobs.

It was from one of these nocturnal conversations that Hannah first learned of Quint's proposal to indenture her to Amos Stritch, the tavern owner. . . .

"I won't hear of it, Mr. Quint," said her mother. "She's my daughter! My own daughter made little more than a black slave!"

"Your daughter she may be, woman, but to me she's another bell to stuff. Times is hard. I work me fingers to the bone, 'tis never enough. I should think ye would be gladdened. She will have food to eat, a place to sleep and clothes on her back. It's only until she comes to age twenty-one. By that time some young buck'll be willing to wed her." Quint's voice had a wheedling note unusual for him to use when speaking to his wife.

"They'll work her from dawn till midnight. And only the ruffians and street trash come into those taverns."

"Trash, am I?" There was the sound of a slap, and her mother cried out.

"Sorry, wifey. You got me riled a bit, ye did.

But it's the only way, you see. Squire Stritch will count all accounts settled and grant me credit."

"'Tis for the drink you are in debt, Silas Quint! And now my poor girl will be selling herself for more drink and gaming debts for you!"

Hannah, listening closely, held her breath. It was rare for her mother to speak up so, the spirit having been beaten out of her long ago. Then Hannah realized that the only times she remembered her mother speaking back to Quint were on her behalf.

But Quint held his tongue this once. "A man has to do something besides work from daylight to dark. And it'll be for the girl's own benefit, don't ye see, woman? She'll learn a useful trade if nothing else. There's always a good place for a tavern wench worth her salt. At the end of her indenture, she'll come into fifty shillings, if naught else. 'Tis in the indenture agreement."

"No, I will not allow ..."

Again there was the sound of a slap. "You will allow what I say! Now it's settled. Stop your tongue, woman. It's sleep I need."

In a moment the only sounds from the other room were Quint's snores and her mother's muffled weeping.

But the following day her mother changed her mind. Or so it seemed. To Hannah she said, "Perhaps it is for the best, daughter. Better you be away from this house. I have seen the looks from Quint. . . ."

She broke off abruptly, clamping her lips shut, but Hannah knew all too well what her mother meant.

Suddenly Mary Quint took her daughter into

11

her arms, and Hannah could feel the wetness of her mother's tears on her face. The woman heaved a sigh. "The lot of a female is surely a sorry one. Sometimes I wonder if the Lord above made us women just to punish us for something. . . ."

Hannah smoothed her mother's rough hair with her hand, scarcely listening now. She was off again, alternately beseeching God and blaming Him for her lot. Hannah well knew that her mother was right; the plight of womankind was not easy. . . .

And now, after this morning's humiliating experience, Hannah felt that she knew the full bitterness of a woman's lot. Still, perhaps her mother had been right in saying that she was better off away from Quint. Matters could be little worse than at home. She could clean the attic room, and she would probably get more food to eat. Even the scraps from the tables would be better than what she was accustomed to at home, and her mother had told her that sometimes a man, when in his cups, might leave a coin or two in gratitude for services rendered.

But then she thought of Amos Stritch—the look in his eyes, the creepy feel of his hand on her hip as he followed her up the stairs. He was nigh as repulsive as Quint, and it seemed to her that he had the same intent toward her. And besides, she was now an indentured servant. Her status was now not much better than that of the blackest slave brought over in chains from Africa. It was the thought of that bondage that had caused her to fight coming here, battling to the point where Quint had finally been forced to drag her on the end of a rope.

It happened to men, true. It had happened to

12

the boy mopping up down below. But a man could, if he had the spirit for it, escape, run away. He might be caught eventually and brought back in chains and perhaps placed in the stocks and publicly whipped, but a few did make good their escape.

But a girl, a girl didn't have a chance. If she tried to run the first chance she got, Hannah knew she wouldn't get more than a few miles before she'd be brought back. A man could skulk through the woods, he could live off the land. If he met a stranger, he could merely say he was passing through; he would probably be believed.

But a strange woman, alone? Immediate suspicion would be aroused.

Hannah sighed. She had no choice but to make the best of it. At least she would be free of Silas Quint here, and perhaps she was wrong about Stritch. Perhaps he would be kind to her if she worked hard and made no trouble.

Had Hannah been privy to the conversation taking place between her stepfather and Amos in the taproom downstairs, she would have had far more reason for concern.

The two men were having tankards of ale in the empty taproom. Stritch, gouty foot propped up, was drawing on a foul-smelling pipe, and Quint greedily sucked at the ale. He would have liked something stronger, but he didn't dare ask until their agreement was final.

Stritch was saying, "You sure the girl is a virgin, now, Quint? If she ain't, any bargain is off."

"On my oath, she is, Squire Stritch. Not a man has laid a finger on her." Quint grinned evilly. "If there be no blood spots on the sheets the first time ye take her, I will not hold ye to our bargain."

"Watch you curb your loose tongue, man," Stritch said sternly. "You know 'tis against all custom and the law for a master to tumble his female indentured servants." Then he smiled, smacking his lips. "Still, she is a juicy wench."

"That she is. Juicy as a peach." Quint's lewd grin broadened. "I've sneaked a peek or two whilst she was at her bath."

Stritch's bulging eyes glared.

"I told you! I ain't touched a hair of her head, on my oath!" Quint assured him hastily. He assumed a righteous air. "But I will have to tell ye, honest man that I am—you will have to keep a sharp eye on 'er. She's a worker when ye can keep her at it, but she moons about considerable if she ain't watched sharp."

"That's no worry," Stritch growled. "I've handled the moony ones before. A few whacks of the lash on her backside and she'll jump to it. By the king, she will!" He took some papers from his pocket. "Here are the articles of indenture. Just make your X by the place where I've writ your name."

Quint made his X. Then he drained the tankard, thumped it down on the table, and grinned companionably, saying, "Maybe now we could have a tot of something stronger to seal our bargain?"

Chapter Two

Quint was drunk when he came home, even though it was only midday. Mary Quint was not at all surprised. Seldom did she see her husband sober. He had gotten drunk on the day they had wed, had fallen sodden into their wedding bed, and had been drunk, it seemed to Mary, most of the time since.

Leaning against the door jamb, he sneered at her, eyes red and swollen by the drink. "Well, 'tis done, wife. Hannah will learn what it means to earn her keep."

Mary said nothing, just stared at him with dull eyes.

"Ain't you nothing to say?" he taunted. "Ye had plenty to say when I broached the matter."

Mary pushed work-reddened fingers through her

15

graying hair. "What's to say, Mr. Quint? Like you say, it's done."

"That's right, it's done. And we're the better for it." He lurched toward the bedroom. "I'm going to sleep a little. 'Twas hard work, dragging that stubborn bitch. Worse'n a mule, she was. See to it that ye keep yourself quiet."

Mary watched without moving as he made his stumbling way into the bedroom. She didn't move until she heard the bed's protest as he sprawled across it. His raucous snores started at once.

Finally she went about cleaning the hovel, careful not to make any unnecessary noise. As long as Quint slept, she could think her own thoughts and have a bit of peace. Not that the cleaning did a great deal of good—a regiment of house cleaners could have gone through the place and never have gotten the accumulated dirt off the floors and walls—but it was a habit now. It gave her something to do with her body and hands.

It seemed to Mary that her six years of marriage to Silas Quint had been spent doing nothing but cleaning, and cooking, when there was something to cook, and doing what she could for Hannah. She had married Quint to give the ten-year-old girl a father. And a fine father he had turned out to be—selling his own daughter into what amounted to little more than slavery!

She caught herself up short. Not *Quint's* daughter, Sweet Jesus, no!

Mary's thoughts, as happened so often of late, escaped into the past.

In a legal sense, Hannah didn't have a father; Mary had not been legally married to Robert McCambridge. Although she had loved him with

16

desperation, and he her, Robert had steadfastly refused to make her his legal spouse. The son of a Scotch plantation owner in South Carolina and a slave mother, Robert had been given his freedom on the death of his mother. In truth, his mother had not been a full-blood African, either; her father had also been white, which made Robert a quadroon. Although his skin had been olive, he had inherited his father's aristocratic features, and had been able to pass for a Spaniard or any other dark-skinned Caucasian if he hadn't been scrutinized too closely. But plantation gentry were close-knit, and too many people had known what he was. For a black or a mulatto to marry a white woman could mean banishment from the Colonies forever—for both. And there were instances on record where both parties had been hanged. For that reason, Robert had refused to marry her.

They had moved north to a spot near the border of Virginia, where no one would know them, and had found a small abandoned farm with a dilapidated cabin. Robert had started farming it. . . .

They were hard times, there was never any extra money, and most of the time very little to eat; still, they were happy. Hannah was born a year later, and Mary did not think she could bear such happiness. At times she was even happy enough to forget for a little the fact that she was living in an unmarried state, living in sin.

Robert adored Hannah, and father and daughter were inseparable. From the time she could toddle Hannah followed her father everywhere. They lived in virtual isolation—there were no near neighbors—and Robert always went alone to the small village twenty miles away when it was necessary to trade for supplies. It was unspoken between them that having friends would be a mistake, and this applied to friends of either race.

Ironically, it was a Negro who killed Robert, not a white man. A runaway slave from the McCambridge plantation stumbled into their cabin late one night. He was badly wounded and half starved, a pitiful remnant of a man. They took him in, tended him, even hid him when the bounty hunters came by. The slave, Isaiah by name, was their guest for several weeks, sharing their meager fare and poor quarters.

When he began to mend, Isaiah started eyeing Mary. She noticed it, and arranged to keep out of his way as much as possible. Robert seemed oblivious to what was going on, and she didn't dare tell him, for although he was a gentle man, his temper, when aroused, was terrible.

Then one afternoon, when Robert was working in the fields with Hannah, now eight, playing nearby, the runaway slave pounced on Mary in the cabin and tumbled her to the floor, tossing up her skirts. When she fought him, he cuffed her viciously across the face. She revived from a near faint to find him between her spread thighs, his breeches down around his knees, preparing to violate her. Mary's shrill screams echoed in the small cabin.

The next thing she knew, Isaiah was gone before he had penetrated her, plucked from her body as though a hovering angel had come to her rescue.

Mary sat up and saw Robert, dark face drawn with fury, his eyes blazing fire. This gentlest of men, this man who had never struck her, or even so much as raised his voice to her, was now a tower of rage.

Then he spoke in a voice of thunder, and she remembered and looked toward the corner of the cabin where Isaiah had been flung like a sack of grain.

"You who call yourself Isaiah came to us nigh onto death. We gave you shelter and food and tended your wounds. We took you in as a brother, and in payment you attack my wife!"

Isaiah was sliding up the wall, pulling up his breeches. "Your wife! Your woman, you mean, your white woman!" The black man sneered. "You knows what the white man says. One of his women fucks a nigger, she a nigger, too. And just 'cause you got white blood, *Squire* McCambridge, don't save you. You still a nigger, nigger, and what do that make her?"

Almost trembling in his wrath, Robert moved toward him. "I am going to kill you for that, Isaiah."

"You gon' kill nobody, nigger."

Then the knife was out, the butcher knife from Mary's kitchen, glittering evilly in Isaiah's hand.

He must have hidden it somewhere on his person, Mary thought dimly, and then she screamed Robert's name as Isaiah advanced in a weaving crouch.

Robert stood loose and ready, hands curled into fists at his side. Then suddenly both men moved with the speed of fighting cats, coming together with an impact that shook the small cabin. Robert had one huge hand wrapped around the wrist holding the knife. They wrestled back and forth, knocking over furniture. Mary was on her feet

19

now, crouched against the wall, petrified with fear and concern for Robert. He was bigger than the other man, but Isaiah was younger and quicker.

They stormed back and forth in straining silence. Then Isaiah brought a knee up into Robert's crotch. Robert yelled in agony and loosed his grip on the knife wrist, doubling over.

Quick as a snake, the knife struck, and struck again, and again a third time, each time coming out stained scarlet with Robert's blood.

Now Robert began to fall. He fell on his face on the floor and lay still.

Breathing harshly, eyes wild as a cornered animal's, Isaiah stood over him, waiting. Robert didn't move.

Finally Isaiah looked around dazedly. His eyes found Mary, and he took a step toward her. Mary screamed.

And Isaiah whirled and ran from the cabin, the blood-dripping knife still clenched in his fist.

Mary ran to Robert McCambridge. With a great effort she rolled him over onto his back. His belly lay open, his intestines spilling out like a mass of worms. Blood came from him in great gouts.

His eyes fluttered open, trying to focus on her. He whispered, "Mary, my love. Mary ..." And he died.

Mary knelt there, desolated, dying inside. Her reason for living had been snuffed out in an instant of shocking violence. She remained on her knees, mumbling prayers, useless words repeated over and over. God had scorned her, for some undefined reason. Was it because she had been living in sin, cohabiting with a man to whom she was not churched? If Isaiah had left the knife beside the body, in that dark moment she would have plunged it into her own breast.

"Mommy, Mommy, what's wrong with Daddy?"

The note of hysteria in Hannah's voice brought Mary to her senses. There *was* someone she had to live for. How could she have forgotten Hannah?

She leaped to her feet and hurried to intercept the girl as she came into the room, enfolding her against her skirts.

"Daddy's hurted, ain't he? There's blood, blood all over everything!"

"Yes, child, he is hurt," Mary said, in as steady a voice as she could manage. "There's been a ..." She swallowed in an attempt to gain control of her voice. "Your daddy's gone away, he's gone away forever. You will have to learn to . . ."

Hannah slid from her encircling arms, slipping to the floor in a faint.

Mary was grateful for God's mercy in granting her that boon. She picked the girl up in her arms and toted her into the small bedroom. Then, in a flurry of strength she didn't know she possessed, Mary dragged Robert's body outside and quickly put him into the earth. Afterward, she came back inside and scrubbed the blood from the floor, for no reason that she could think of, except to give her body something to do while she thought about what to do next.

She had already decided that she couldn't stay here. Isaiah might come back and kill them both. She didn't dare report the crime. She couldn't, not without admitting they had been harboring a run-a-way slave. And besides, she wouldn't be able to run the farm by herself.

By that evening they were gone. She threw their

few possessions onto the cart and hitched up the spavined horse that Robert had used for plowing. Hannah sat slumped on the seat beside her. The girl had been in a dazed state since reviving from the faint.

Mary had no money. She traded a few of their meager possessions for food along the way, and finally made it to Williamsburg, where she sold the horse and cart. She found cleaning work in some of the fine houses springing up around Market Square.

And then she found Silas Quint. Naturally she had never breathed a word to Quint about Hannah having Negro blood. . . .

What was going to happen to Hannah now? Since Robert had been his son, the plantation owner had seen to it that the boy had had some education, and Robert had been teaching Hannah her numbers and how to read. But Mary had had very little education herself, so she had been unable to teach the girl more. . . .

"Old woman!" came Quint's roar from the bedroom. "I'm hungry. Put some food on the table!"

Mary sighed and went about preparing what little food they had in the house.

She was scarcely forty, and yet she was old. And Hannah—Hannah too would become old before her time.

Chapter Three

At that moment Hannah was on her hands and knees scrubbing the rough taproom floor. An hour ago Amos Stritch had unbolted the trap door and told her, "Get yourself downstairs, girl, and to work. The taproom floor has need of scrubbing before the night's business begins. Now you do good work or I'll cane your backside good. I can't watch over you ever' minute. I'm off to bed with this damned gouty foot. It pains me sorely to be on it. But mind the floor's clean when I come down."

Hannah had cultivated a trick that made the time pass more easily while performing drudge work—the trick that had caused Quint to scorn her for being moony.

She remembered the few times she had accompanied her mother to work in some of the fine houses around Market Square. How wonderful it would be to live in a house like that! How much *more* wonderful to be its mistress! The fine white linens, the gleaming silverware, the great chandeliers, the highly polished furniture, so polished it mirrored her features. And the clothes, the fine clothes the ladies wore! Silks and velvets and satins. Hannah wondered how the soft fabrics would feel against her own skin. And the scents, so strong as to almost cause her to faint, smelling like a hundred gardens in bloom.

There were many such houses being constructed in Williamsburg now. Much of the work was done by skilled artisans, but there was common work to be had. Yet whenever her mother mentioned this fact to Silas Quint, he had the same plaint: "My back, woman! You know I hurt it something sore years ago. I cannot do the hard labor needed for such tasks."

Hannah pulled her thoughts away from the unpleasant subject of her stepfather and continued her dreaming. She would never forget riding on that creaking cart on the way to Williamsburg all those years ago with her mother. The trip had taken almost a month, and during that time her father's death had receded a little in her mind; or, rather, she had drawn a mental shutter around the memory, blocking it out of her conscious mind.

She remembered the great plantations they had passed on their slow way—the fine houses set back beyond green, rolling grounds, and the fine ladies and gentlemen, sometimes seen for an instant. She remembered the green fields of growing tobacco tended by slaves, their ebony skins glistening with sweat as they labored in the sweltering heat. . . .

Many of them were naked. It was the first time Hannah had seen a man's unclothed body. She stared in awed curiosity at the male genitals, swinging as the men worked.

Mary Quint saw the direction of her stare and swung her daughter's face forward. She said tartly, "'Tain't fitting for a girl of your years to be looking at such."

"But why don't they wear clothes, Mommy?"

Her mother was silent for so long Hannah thought she wasn't going to answer. Finally the woman said bitterly, "Because too many folks have no respect for their black slaves. To them, they're a . . . a *thing*, no more human than this old horse here. So why go to all the bother of giving them clothes?"

The plantation house Hannah remembered best of all was the one only a quarter day's ride from Williamsburg. It was white, two-story, shaded by great trees, and it sat on a knoll overlooking the James River, with vast green lawns on all sides. Surrounding the main house were the dependencies, or outbuildings. To Hannah it seemed like a small village.

Over the gate opening onto the sweeping driveway leading up to the main house hung a sign. The sign had one word. Hannah, not yet able to make out all her letters, asked her mother what the sign said.

" 'Malvern,' it says," her mother replied. "Many of the fine gentry have names for their plantations. Putting on fancy airs, you ask me."

Later, Hannah was to learn that the plantation belonged to Malcolm Verner. And she knew that he lived there alone nowadays, except for his many servants and field hands. His wife had died some years back of the fever, and his only son, Michael, had been lost at sea the year before. With all his wealth and property, she thought, he must be a most unhappy man.

To be mistress of such a great plantation would be more wonderful than anything she could dream of. Of course, it was just a dream; it could never be more than that. But even to be indentured to such a household would be infinitely better than this. ...

"You be the new one?"

Startled, Hannah jumped to her feet. Weariness and hunger combined brought on a sudden dizziness. She swayed and started to fall.

She was caught in strong arms and cradled against an ample bosom smelling deliciously of baked bread and other good food. A deep voice said, "Gracious, child, what's troubling you? You gone pale as a ghost!" A rumbling laugh sounded. "Lawd knows, I ain't that." The huge bosom shook with laughter.

Hannah opened her eyes and looked into the blackest face and the kindest eyes she had ever seen. The face was so black it seemed almost blue in the dim light. There was a smudge or two of something white, like flour, on the broad cheeks.

Embarrassed, Hannah stepped back. "Thank you," she said shyly. "I'm sorry. I ..."

The black woman waved away her apologies. "I'm Bess, child. Old Stritch calls me Black Bess, when he ain't riled up. When he *is* riled, which is most of the time, he calls me things ain't fittin' for a child's ears to hear." Bess looked at her soberly. "You be Hannah. Now, what made you so fainty?"

She slapped her forehead, leaving another smudge of white. "But I knows! You hongry, ain't you, child? And scrubbing away here in all this heat. Come with me."

"But Mr. Stritch said . . ."

"Bother with that old devil Stritch! 'Sides, he ain't gonna be moving out of that feather bed of his'n before this day's over, if'n then." Bess grinned with a flash of white teeth. "Not with that old gouty foot, he ain't."

Bess led Hannah out back to the kitchen, separated from the main building by several yards. Hannah knew this was so that the heat from cooking fires wouldn't heat up the tavern.

She stepped into the building behind Bess and was almost overcome by the combination of smothering heat and the odor of roasting meat.

Her gaze quickly scanned the room, and, in awe, she realized that it was larger than the whole miserable place where she and her mother lived.

One wall was dominated by an enormous fireplace, almost large enough for a person to stand in, and its cooking equipment. A large haunch of venison was turning slowly on a spit, and, for a moment, the sight of it so overwhelmed Hannah's thoughts that she felt herself begin to salivate. Bess followed the direction of her gaze. She gestured to a small table by the door. "You set there, child, where it's cooler, whilst I hustle up something for your belly."

The black woman waddled to the hearth, stopped the clock jack turning the spit, and began to slice strips of roasted meat from the haunch. She put the meat onto a large pewter plate while Hannah watched in disbelief, not daring to think that such food was going to be given to her to eat.

Bess started the clock jack up again, and then picked up the plate and placed it on a large center table. Out of a nearby food safe she took a big loaf of bread. She cut a thick slice and put it next to the meat.

White bread. They never had white bread at home. Hunger squeezed Hannah's insides as she watched Bess add a pat of butter to the plate and then pour a mug full of fresh, foaming milk.

Bess motioned Hannah over and set the food before her. Hannah, despite her resolve to behave in a ladylike manner, fell on the food like a starving savage. Bess watched in approval for a moment, then turned away.

The meat was crisp on the outside and dripping with juice, the bread tender and fragrant, the milk cool and delicious. When Hannah finally slowed her eating, she saw that Bess had already set down another plate. It held pieces of crisp, pungent gingerbread, a slice of baked Indian meal pudding, and a large, ripe, rosy peach.

She looked up at Bess gratefully, unable to speak. The big woman smiled in understanding, then returned to her cooking chores, letting Hannah finish without embarrassment.

When Hannah's appetite was appeased and she had a chance to look around, her wonder increased. Such a wealth of pots and pans she had never seen. It was surely a modern kitchen. She could not even guess at the uses of the utensils and pieces of equipment she saw hanging over the fireplace and on the wall racks; and the spit that turned the roasting meat by itself was a real wonder.

Finally sated, she sat back in her chair, feeling drowsy and somewhat bloated by the unusual amount of food she had consumed. She watched Bess move ponderously around the kitchen, working slowly but with scarcely a wasted motion. She kept up a constant stream of chatter as she worked. The woman's girth was so huge that Hannah wondered how she could bear the heat.

". . . That old devil Stritch comes down ever' fortnight or so with a case of the gout. Fills his belly with too much of my cooking, he does. Some day that belly of his gonna bust wide open!" She laughed richly. "Now that'll be the day I surely hope I lives to see! You'd better be glad of that, child, old Stritch's gout. He won't be hopping around much for the next few days."

She paused to give Hannah a compassionate look, but Hannah was too drowsy to really notice.

Bess went on about her work, still talking. "Know who they named me after, honey? That there queen the white folks had over there in England. Queen Elizabeth. Queen Bess, they called her." She gave her rolling laugh. "My old mammy, she found many things funny, even though slaves we was, and she thought it funny to name me after the white folks' queen."

Hannah gave her head a sharp shake and tried to show some interest. "Bess, how long are you indentured to Mr. Stritch for?"

"Indentured!" Bess swung around, face grave for once, hands on hips. "Lawd, child, I ain't indentured to old Stritch at all! He done bought me body and soul, for life! Less'n he ups and sells me."

29

Hannah's breath caught. "Ah-h, Bess, I'm sorry!"

"Now honey, no need you wasting your breath feeling sorry for ole Bess. I been a slave all my natural-born life. You gonna have enough to be sorry about your own self. . . ."

In that moment the boy Hannah had seen earlier scrubbing out front came timidly into the kitchen.

Bess swung around on him. "Come for a bite, have you? You done finished up out there?"

"Yes'm." The boy bobbed his head.

"This here child is called Dickie, Hannah," Bess said.

Hannah smiled at the lad. "Hello, Dickie. What's your family name?"

The lad ducked his head, staring down at his bare feet. He mumbled, "Got no other name, m'-lady."

Bess rumpled the boy's long mop of hair. "Dickie's an orphan child, honey. Ain't neither kith nor kin that he knows. He was shipped over from across the water, from that there England, and indentured to old Stritch." Then she stepped back, her voice roughening. "Before you get something in your belly, boy, you got to fill the kettle with water from the well house."

Dickie nodded and took a wooden bucket from the corner, going outside with it.

Bess turned to Hannah. "You, child, you badly needs a good washing. I'll heat a kettle of water and you can wash in that tub over there. And we gotta find another garment for you—that one's rags and tatters."

Remembering, Hannah clutched the torn bodice

to her breasts. "It ... it got torn on the way over. ..."

"I seen. I was watching when that man came dragging you on a rope," Bess said grimly. "Should be stocked, he should. Doing his own child that-away!"

"He's not my father, he's my stepfather!"

"Don't matter none. 'Twas a shameful thing."

Dickie returned with a bucket of water and filled the huge black kettle suspended over the hearth. Bess stoked up the fire while Dickie made several more trips, emptying the buckets into a wooden tub in one corner.

Finally Bess said, "That'll do it. Here ..." She piled food on a plate. "Now you go outside, Dickie. Don't you be peeking in here. We gonna wash this child up good."

She shooed Dickie out, then turned to Hannah. "Now you get yo'self undressed, honey. Right down to the hide."

Hannah hesitated, embarrassed. She had never stood naked before anyone but her mother.

Bess, sensing the girl's embarrassment, turned her back, going on with her chatter. "We'll burn that rag you got on. Couple of dresses around that the last girl wore should fit you. She jest ended her term of ..."

She faced around again just as Hannah stepped out of her ragged shift. Hannah stood frozen.

"Lawd, Lawd, child, you some sight!" Bess pursed her lips in a silent whistle. "You purty as any of them quality ladies."

Hannah felt herself blushing. "You think so, Bess? Quint says I'm too tall for a woman. He says I'm a great cow."

31

Bess snorted. "Don't you ever listen to what *that* kind of a man says, honey. He nothing but trash and don't know nothing about quality. You listen to old Bess—old Bess says you is a beauty."

Bess's black eyes took in the long, copper-colored locks framing the heart-shaped face. The green eyes were like emeralds. Hannah's breasts were high, proud; her belly was slightly rounded above the rust-colored fleece covering the pout of her womanhood. Her legs were long and lovely. There was a promise of great beauty about her, Bess thought, once the touch of baby fat was gone. And what she had told the girl was true. Standing there with a proud stance, she could put most of the quality ladies to shame. Even the smudges of dirt on her hands and face took away not a whit of her beauty. And there was a touch of singular grace about her, a manner of the queenly. Her skin was soft and rosy-gold, like the skin of a ripe peach.

Suddenly Bess reached out and took one of Hannah's hands. Although work-marked, the hand was shapely and well formed. Bess let the hand drop and patted Hannah on the head, distressed by what she had seen. Somewhere back there in this child's blood line was an African queen, she thought, but she was certain that the girl had no inkling of this fact.

Looking at Hannah's ripe body, she could surely see why that old devil Stritch had jumped at the chance to indenture this one! The poor child, if she only knew what was in store for her!

She gestured brusquely. "Into the tub with you, child."

Hannah obeyed, stepping in with one foot, then the other. "Oh! Bess, it's cold!"

"'Course it is, honey," Bess said in a scolding voice, coming with the steaming kettle. "Now you tell me when it hots up enough for you."

She poured hot water from the kettle as Hannah stood in the tub, strangely unembarrassed by her nakedness now. In a moment warmth began to creep up around her legs. She sank down into the tub, knees drawn up.

"Warm enough?"

Hannah nodded, and Bess handed her a bar of rough soap and a washcloth. "Mind you scrub good, now."

She needn't have worried, Hannah thought, luxuriating in it. At home the best she could manage was a washcloth bath. This was sheer heaven! She washed slowly, listening idly to Bess's chatter.

"Most taverns have a dozen to help around, slaves and indentures both. But old Stritch, he too tight in the purse. Just you and me and Dickie and three to serve in the ordinary and clean the upstairs. And Nell."

"Who's Nell?"

"Nell's the other barmaid. She's a mean 'un, Hannah, honey, and common as cat shit. Don't let her bother you none...."

At first Hannah had been shocked at hearing such language from a woman, but she was growing used to it now, and she knew that she was going to like Black Bess, coarse language and all.

"One thing you can be thankful for, child. Prob'ly won't be too busy for a few weeks—give you time to catch on. It's during Public Times, when that there House of Burgesses sets, it's busy. Fine gentlemen from all over Virginny come. That's when we all get wore right down to the nub. All

33

the beds upstairs full, excepting old Stritch's own, and men eating and a-drinking at all hours . . ."

A shout from the tavern upstairs interrupted her. Bess went to the door. "Yassuh, Massa Stritch?"

"You hustle your black tail up here with some victuals, blast you!"

"Yassuh, Massa Stritch. In a shake."

Bess, turning, caught Hannah's glance. She grinned widely, and winked. "That the way old Stritch like to hear me talk. To his way of figuring, a black mammy talks no other way. He's real tetchy, these gouty times, so I never cross him. Old Stritch a mighty mean man at any time, but when he riled—whoo-ee!" She bustled about filling a platter with food. "You just stay right there until I gets back, honey. Won't be but a minute or two. I'll bring along a dress for you. I'll feed him some of this rich duckling, mebbe it'll keep him bedded down all night. Old Stritch ain't the sense to know his eating keeps him in bed." Bess went to the hearth before a small roasting oven shaped like a half cylinder, and squatted down to check the bird roasting within. She began slicing off pieces of meat.

Hannah found that Bess was right on three counts. Stritch didn't put in an appearance; the taproom, while busy, was not overly crowded, and Nell, the other taproom serving maid, was foul of temper and common as dirt. In fact, she was none too clean about her person, and had a rank odor about her. Older than Hannah, nearing the end of her indenture period, she was somewhat buxom, and wore a low bodice out of which generous breasts threatened to spill every time she stooped

34

over, which she did frequently while serving men their drinks.

The dress Bess had supplied Hannah with had been a trifle too large, but Bess had fussed with it until it fit well enough. It was of a soft material, in a light green that suited Hannah's coloring. Then Bess had brushed Hannah's hair until it glistened. Afterward, Hannah had admired herself in a bit of looking glass that Bess had brought from one of the cupboards. She had never felt so fine and fair, nor smelled so good. She was fresh and sweet-smelling from her bath, and from some essence Bess had liberally sprinkled her with.

The taproom was nearly empty when Hannah came in to work, and Nell came over to her. With contempt in her snapping black eyes, she surveyed Hannah from head to foot, and she sneered openly. "Well, if you ain't the fine lady! All dollied up like one of the gentry from the big houses. I'll wager you'll not be so fine-looking before this eve's past. Better not bounce that tail of yours so saucily, or it'll soon be pinched black and blue!"

Hannah was too flustered to reply, but had she had a fitting answer at hand, it would have availed her nothing, for, having delivered her verbal barrage, Nell flounced off.

Since everything was new, and she had never been inside a taproom before, Hannah was too absorbed for a while in what she saw to give much thought to Nell.

Even the street outside was thronged with people now—tradesmen conducting business; fine gentlemen in knee breeches, fine hose and buckled shoes, and powdered wigs, conversing quietly; and the common riffraff weaving in and out. Hannah knew that taverns, especially at night, were the center of much activity.

But it was the inside of the tavern that she found most fascinating.

The taproom was relatively small. There was a large fireplace set in one wall, the hearth cold now in summer. Two armchairs flanked the fireplace, and there were a number of small tables with chairs, and several benches along two walls. There was a chess set on one table, and Hannah had not been there long before two gentlemen began a game. She served each a tankard of ale. At another table a boisterous trio were tossing dice from a cup. As the taproom filled up, most of the other gentlemen sat talking quietly, but sometimes voices were raised in argument. Many of the men smoked fragrant tobacco in long-stemmed clay pipes.

In one corner was the bar, a short mahogany affair with a stout barricade of wooden bars that could be let down from the ceiling, locking it safely away from the rest of the room. Hannah later learned that there was a trap door behind the bar and a ladder leading down into the wine cellar below, where all the liquor was stored.

Bess had told her that Stritch himself usually stood behind the bar, not trusting anyone else overmuch, but since he was unable to put in an appearance tonight, one of the black butlers who served food in the ordinary, the dining room, had taken his place this night. This, Hannah soon realized, was fortunate for her, since she was totally ignorant of what to do, and the butler was patient with her, explaining her duties in a soft voice and showing her which drink was which. Hannah suspected that Bess had had a quiet word with him earlier.

One object on the bar Hannah did find curious. It was an odd little contraption containing pipe tobacco. On the lid was the word HONOUR. The patron was supposed to drop a twopence into a slot in the side, raise the lid, and take one pipeful of tobacco. The patron was on his honor to take no more.

Bess had told Hannah, "It galls old Stritch something fierce to have that box there. He trusts nobody. But 'tis the custom in all taverns. Many taprooms don't use serving maids in the public rooms, only to serve the victuals in the ordinary. But old Stritch figures that a comely wench draws the trade. Other taprooms use indentured boys like Dickie to trot back and forth with the drinks, trusting the men to pay at the end of the evening, or put it on their yearly accounts. 'Course old Stritch gives credit, has to. 'Tis also the custom. But he keeps a sharp eye out."

Hannah wondered if Silas Quint could be trusted to drop his twopence into the tobacco box. But then Quint didn't smoke, saving all his money for drink and gaming. Fortunately Quint did not put in an appearance this night; Hannah had been worried lest he might.

The variety of drinks was not large. Most of the patrons asked for ale or wine, a few demanding French brandy, or rum, or punch.

After the initial encounter, Nell didn't speak to Hannah again during the evening, although Hannah caught the girl's gaze on her from time to time. She noticed that Nell's behavior was openly wanton. She seized every opportunity to lean far over and display her ample bosoms, and was not averse to bumping a well-rounded haunch against a man. This maneuver was usually greeted with much raucous laughter and many ribald comments.

The men seemed wary of Hannah as she moved between the tables with that queenly grace of hers. Perhaps it was because she was new, but few lewd remarks were directed at her. Twice she was pinched on the leg, and once a broad hand slapped her on one buttock. She ignored it all, pretending it hadn't happened.

The next time she passed that particular table, the man who had slapped her bottom reached out and caught her hand. Before she could pull away, she felt something being pressed into it. A moment later she opened her hand and looked—a whole shilling! The chess players also gave her coins, two farthings each as they left.

The taproom was clearing out now, soon it was empty. The ordinary had long since closed. Hannah and Nell went about cleaning the tables and washing the tankards and glasses. Dickie came in and began sweeping the floor while the man behind the bar returned the liquor to the cellar below.

Hannah was weary, but there was a feeling of uplift about it, a feeling of accomplishment. And she had a few coins in her pocket—the first money she'd ever had of her own in her life.

The good feeling didn't last long. As the two girls left the tavern and headed for the kitchen, where Bess was keeping a bite of supper warm for them, Nell suddenly seized Hannah's hand and whirled her around.

"All right, me fine lady!" she said with a hiss of

breath. "I was a-watching you like a hawk. I saw them three give you something. It's share and share alike. Gimme!" She held out her hand, palm up.

Angrily, Hannah tore her arm free. "I will not! They gave the coins to me!"

"Don't matter. Anything we get in there, we share. If Stritch sees us get anything, he demands it for himself. So if you don't give me my share, I'll tell him and he'll take it all for himself!"

"No! They were given to me!"

Nell sneered. "Mayhap you promised to meet 'em under a tree later on?"

Without thinking, Hannah swung her hand up and around, delivering a stinging slap to the other girl, sending her reeling back. Appalled at what she had done, Hannah stepped back. She stuck one hand in the dress pocket where the coins were, clutching them protectively.

Face wild, Nell came at her, screaming, "You barnyard bitch! Swat me, will you? I'll mark you good!"

Fingers like claws, she swiped at Hannah's face. Hannah ducked, barely avoiding being scratched.

Nell halted, a cunning look coming over her face. Suddenly she moved again, grabbing at Hannah's hand in the dress pocket. The dress tore, and the coins spilled out onto the ground.

All the rage and frustration that had been building in Hannah that day boiled up all of a sudden. She flew at the other girl, and in an instant they were rolling over and over in the dirt, pummelling and scratching. Hannah sank her fingers into Nell's long hair and began to pound her head against the ground. Nell screamed shrilly.

A voice above them said, "Here now! That be enough!"

Strong hands grasped Hannah under the arms and hauled her upright. Nell, face pale with fright now, scrambled crab-wise for a few feet, then got up and ran, skirts flying.

Bess chuckled richly. "Don't think she'll be bothering you again, honey. You gave her what for." Bess released her. "And don't be fretting about her telling old Stritch. Does, she'll have to be admitting she's been squirreling away what them men give her. He learn that, he'll give her a good caning."

Dickie approached them shyly, hand held out. "Tain't lost, Miss Hannah. I found them, found them all."

Hannah accepted the coins. Then, on impulse, she held out one of the farthings. "Here, Dickie. That's for you."

Dickie gaped at her in astonishment. He reached out tentatively, as though fearful she would snatch it back. Having it safe in his hand, he said breathlessly, "Thankee, m'lady," and took to his heels, bare feet pounding the earth.

Hannah gazed after him somewhat wistfully. She said, "Did you know that nobody ever called me 'm'lady' before, Bess?"

"Poor lad. He's not used to hearing a kind word. . . ."

A window banged open on the second story and a voice bawled, "What the devil's going on down there? Sounds like two cats caterwauling!" Stritch's head was poked out the window, bald pate covered with a flannel nightcap.

"Just some funning, Massa Stritch."

40

"No time of the night for funning. Now see it's quiet or I'll put a cane to the lot of you!"

"Yassuh, Massa Stritch."

"Man can't even be ailing in peace...." The head withdrew, the window slamming shut.

Shaking with silent laughter, Bess put her arm around Hannah's shoulders. "Come along, child, I got a plate of supper warming for you." Just before they entered the kitchen, she sobered and stopped to glance up at the second story. There was an odd note in her voice as she said, "Old Stritch sounds like his old self. He'll be up and about afore long, Lawd help us!"

Hannah learned what Bess meant two nights later.

On the next night Stritch still did not appear in the tavern, and everything went well. Nell carefully avoided her, and Hannah knew pretty much what her duties were now. She didn't receive any coins from the patrons, but she knew she couldn't expect that every night.

There was only one unpleasant note. Silas Quint came into the tavern. Hannah didn't speak to him, even avoiding the bench where he sat, and he had to go to the bar for his own drinks.

Once, on his way back, he intercepted her, seizing her arm in a cruel grip. "Don't ye even have a good word for your old father, missy?"

Hannah tore her arm out of his grip. "You're not my father. Besides, why should you want to talk to me? You have sold me."

Quint scowled blackly. "I hear that Master Stritch has been a-bed these past days. Wait until

41

he's up and about—then ye won't be acting such the fine lady, missy!"

The tenor of the tavern changed drastically when Amos Stritch appeared behind the bar on the third night. He watched everything with a sharp eye. Once, when a departing patron had left Hannah a farthing, Stritch demanded it when next she came to the bar.

"Anything left on the tables here belongs to me, my girl. See you don't forget. I have a sharp eye—it misses nothing. I catch you filching what's mine, it's the cane for you!"

When the tavern closed and the girls were about to leave, Stritch called from behind the bar, "You, girl! You, Hannah! Come here."

She approached the bar apprehensively.

But Stritch was all smiles now, red face creased in a gargoyle's grin. "Hurry you out to the kitchen and tell that Black Bess to fix my supper. Then bring it up to my room."

"Me, sir?"

"Yes, you. And look sharp now. I'm weary of waiting."

Heart fluttering with a dread she could not put a name to, Hannah went out to the kitchen. To Bess, she said, "Master Stritch wants I should bring his supper to his room."

Bess stiffened, eyes narrowing. "Does he now? Dirty old lecher, that he is." She turned away, muttering. "Wished I had some saltpeter, that would fix *him*."

"What, Bess?"

"Never mind, honey, never mind."

While Bess prepared a platter for Stritch, Hannah snatched a bite or two for herself. Bess seemed to dawdle forever. Hannah wished she would hurry. She was bone-weary, longing for her pallet.

Finally the platter was ready. Bess gave it to her without a word, face averted. Puzzled by Bess's behavior, and slightly hurt, Hannah left the kitchen.

Had she looked behind her, she would have seen two huge tears form in Bess's eyes and roll down her cheeks. She would have seen Bess looking heavenward, muttering a prayer: "Help that poor girl, please Lawd. She's just a child, innocent as a little babe."

Except for the one room to the right at the top of the stairs, which Stritch kept for his very own, the entire second floor was a series of four connecting rooms, with no doors between. All available space was taken by beds; heating was provided by a central fireplace. During Public Times, or any other busy times, Hannah had learned, Stritch rented out the beds, sometimes sleeping three in a bed, strangers or no. There were no accommodations for ladies, of course. Rarely did a man travel with his wife. If he did come to Williamsburg with his spouse, he made prior arrangements for her to stay with friends. It was not the custom for taverns, or inns, to provide lodgings for ladies.

Hannah knocked timidly on Stritch's door.

It opened at once. There he stood in that flannel cap and a long nightgown reaching to the floor. He looked so funny that Hannah wanted to laugh. But she knew she didn't dare.

"Well, girl, it took you long enough!" he growled. "Come in, come in!"

Hannah went in, shying aside from him.

"Set it on the table by the bed."

43

The bed was a huge four-poster, high off the floor. Hannah looked at it askance as she placed the platter on the table.

She spun around as she heard the lock turn. Stritch was grinning at her, bouncing the long brass key in his hand.

"What is this about, sir?"

He came toward her, leering, face red as a cooked beet. "I'm about to have you, girl. I'm going to claim my rights."

"What rights, sir?" Hannah exclaimed with a sinking heart. "I was indentured to work in the tavern."

"Did not Quint tell you? Well, no matter. I can find any number of wenches to work below. I need one to warm my bed. And a virgin." His face darkened. "You *are* a virgin? Quint swore to me . . ."

Hannah said in a quavering voice, "Yes, Master Stritch, I am a virgin. And I wish to remain so."

His face cleared. He came on toward her. Hannah's eyes darted about nervously, seeking an escape. Her heart thundered in her breast. But there was no escape. The heavy wooden door was the only way out of the room. Even if she could get past Stritch, the door was now locked. Even as she thought this, she saw Stritch drop the big key into the pocket of the nightgown.

Her mind darted frantically, seeking some means of escape. She could scream, but she knew that none of the servants would dare come to her rescue, not even Black Bess.

Stritch was close now, so close she could smell his fetid breath. His eyes, glazed with lust, seemed to be popping from his head.

He reached out a hand for her, but Hannah

ducked nimbly under his arm and raced for the door, light-headed with panic. She tried the knob, but it would not turn. Blindly, she began to beat on the thick door with her fists, not even feeling the rough wood against her hands. Then Stritch was behind her, fingers buried in her hair. He jerked brutally, and she fetched up against the far wall so hard the breath was driven from her body and her wits were totally muddled. He was on her before she could recover. He was still favoring his right foot, yet he seemed to get around well enough.

"Quint was right about one thing. You got spirit, you have. Now on the bed with you, girl! I want those garments off you so I can see what you look like. I don't like to buy a pig in a poke."

He gave her a hard shove toward the bed. She careened across the room, ending up half on, half off the soft feather bed. But her mind had cleared a little, and before he could reach her, she was off the bed.

Stritch came after her, breathing hard. He cut a ridiculous figure in the cap and long nightgown, but Hannah was too terrified to even think about laughing.

For some minutes she managed to duck around him, running from one side of the room to the other. He kept limping after her, relentlessly, his unattractive face growing redder and redder. *Maybe he'll have an attack of apoplexy*, Hannah thought hopefully. She was becoming exhausted herself.

"Damnation, girl," Stritch rumbled, "I'm getting my fill of this!"

And then, suddenly, he had her crowded into a

corner. There was nowhere left to run. Stritch caught her by the arm and slammed her up against the wall. His other arm drew back. His fist smashed into her face, and blackness descended on Hannah like a merciful blanket.

Stritch stood back as the girl crumpled in a heap to the floor. He waited a moment until he could breathe more normally. Then he stooped and caught her under the arms, and hauled her across the floor to the bed. It took much effort to heave her up onto the bed. *Damme, she's a big one,* he thought. Finally he had her stretched out on her back.

Without wasting another moment, he methodically stripped the clothes from her body.

He stood back and looked her over from head to toe. What a fine-looking wench! He had never looked upon one so well built. His gaze lingered long upon the copper-colored moss curling at the fork of her thighs. The heaviness in his own loins was urgent, and he could barely restrain himself from jumping on her.

But she might come to while he was at it, and strong as she was, she could easily toss him to the floor. That would never do. Hastily he turned aside and reached into the bottom drawer in the chest for what he kept stored there for just such occasions as this.

Hannah revived to the feel of hands stroking her body. Her head throbbed horribly, and for a moment she thought she was sick with the fever, her body burning and her head hurting, and her mother was bathing her with a cold cloth, crooning to her.

Then memory returned with a rush of horror,

and her eyes flew open. The cold cloth was the clammy hands of Amos Stritch, and the sound came from his drooling lips.

His hands were on her body, everywhere, and she was stark naked!

Hannah tried to throw herself off the bed, and found that she could not move her arms and legs. She raised her head, and saw with consternation that she was bound to the bedposts, each hand and foot tied with leather thongs. She was spread-eagled, stretched tautly like pictures she had seen of people bound to the torture rack.

"Ha, girl! You are finally awake. I wanted you to be. . . ."

Stritch raised up on his knees and hiked the nightgown up over the mound of his huge belly.

Hannah averted her face from the red, odious thing projecting from beneath the pendulous belly. Then his full weight came down on her. She tried to avoid what she knew was about to happen, but it was no use. She was pinned there, for him to make use of in any way he cared to.

"Now, my feisty beauty, I'll have you!" Stritch shouted.

Hannah felt a brief, searing pain—but even worse, she felt his flesh inside her flesh. She cringed and tried to sink deeper into the feather bed.

The pain, dulled now, kept on. He snorted and slobbered on her as he plunged and plunged again.

Fortunately it did not last long. He gave a shrill, whistling cry like the squeal of a shoat and collapsed on top of her.

Hannah lay rigid beneath the malodorous mass of flesh that was Amos Stritch's body. It was plain he did not bathe over often. Hannah was wet with his sweat, and his limp weight on her chest made breathing difficult. She willed her body to be still, to endure for now, but in that moment a hate was born in her, a loathing for this man and for all men like him—a hate she knew would never know easement until she somehow managed to gain vengeance against Amos Stritch.

Finally he gave a windy sigh and reared back on his knees, letting the nightgown fall into place, hiding the obscenity of his gross, hairy body.

He bent to peer at the bedclothes. He snorted in satisfaction, a gloating triumphant sound.

"For once Quint was truthful. The proof is there. 'Tis a virgin you were, girl! A good bargain I made!"

Chapter Four

Bess didn't need to see the blood spots on the sheets from old Stritch's bed to know that Hannah had been a virgin. When the girl whose chore it was to clean the tavern upstairs came tittering to her with the sheets, Bess snapped, "Never you mind that, girl! Ain't none of your business—and don't be tattling it 'bout all over the tavern!"

Little good the warning would do, Bess knew. The empty-headed girl would go whispering to everyone within earshot.

In truth, Bess couldn't understand all the fuss about virginity, why the white folks put such store by it. She had lost hers at twelve in much the same manner—at the hands of a brutal white man.

But she knew that among white folks a maiden-

49

head was highly prized both by a young girl and the man who first had her.

Bess carefully avoided Stritch the next day, fearful of what she might say to him, but she could imagine him strutting about, prideful as a rooster in a barnyard of hens.

And Hannah ... the poor girl said not a word about what had happened. She had a lump the size of an egg on her cheek, and she dragged about with eyes cast down, as low in spirits as a snake's belly.

Bess desperately wanted to say something, to try and console the poor child, but she sensed that it would be the wrong thing to do.

She finally tried in a roundabout way to let the girl know she was aware of what had happened.

Since Hannah's arrival, Bess had been shooing all the others out to eat their dinners in the yard, leaving just Hannah and Dickie in the kitchen. The others did not object, since it was cooler in the yard.

That afternoon, as Hannah and Dickie ate, Hannah merely picking at her food, Bess began a rambling, seemingly pointless tale. "You know, that old devil Stritch is a mean man, real mean. Nothing's too mean for him to do. When he first bought me, some ten years back, I was put in here as a scullion. In them days he had no clock spit. He used turnspit dogs. Know what a turnspit dog is, honey?" She looked directly at Hannah.

Hannah said, dully, dutifully, "No, Bess." She wondered, not caring, what Bess was getting at. She didn't want to talk, to listen—she just wanted to sink into her own apathy, down into the pit of abject misery where she had dwelt since last night.

"Well now, if you'd ever seen one, one who'd turned a spit for a long spell, you'd know right enough. They was long, with legs as crooked as a rabbit's. You see, a turnspit dog was put on a wheel fastened to the turnspit, which turned the roasting spit as long as that old dog kept running. To make sure he did, a burning coal was placed on the wheel with him. If'n he stopped running, his paws got scorched. . . ."

Hannah roused herself enough to gasp. "Why, that's awful!"

Bess smiled slightly. "Nothing too mean for old Stritch to do. Anyways, this old dog, whichever one 'twas, soon learned his lesson. It was hard work, since sometimes the roast weighed twice the dog, and it took three-some hours to roast a haunch to a turn. 'Course, sometimes them old dogs would smarten up and run hide around about roasting time and couldn't be found, hide nor hair. Then it was left up to me to turn that devil-blasted spit for three hours. I finally worked old Stritch around to getting a clock spit. You chillun know how I did that?"

It was Dickie who answered, "How, Black Bess?"

"I got at his purse—only one way to get to old Stritch. I told him that feeding them dogs cost him more over a stretch of time than 'twould for him to buy a clock spit." Her laughter rumbled. "'Course I stretched it a little. Them dogs usually got by on scraps, but old Stritch, now, he pretty stupid 'bout some things, almost as stupid as he is mean."

Suddenly, Hannah started to weep. Choking back sobs, she got up and ran from the kitchen.

Bess stared after her sorrowfully. Dickie gaped in astonishment. "What's troubling Miss Hannah?"

"Never you mind, boy. You wouldn't understand, being a man. Close to being a man, anyways."

Hannah hurried through the empty tavern and up to her attic room. She hated for anyone to see her cry. The attic room was stifling, and still almost as dirty as when she'd first seen it. She had made little effort to tidy it up. What did it matter if she lived in filth? Nothing could be as filthy as what had happened to her last night. And would happen again tonight, she knew, and keep on happening.

There were only two choices open to her that she could see. She could flee—but she knew she would be caught and brought back, and that would only make it worse for her. If she ran home and hid, Quint would only beat her and drag her back again. So there was really no choice. She had to stay and endure. She wiped the tears from her eyes with the back of her hand.

But she was grimly determined about one thing. She would not submit easily. Old devil Stritch liked spirit; well, she would show him spirit!

Again that evening as the tavern closed down, Stritch directed her to come to his room with his supper. Hannah flushed when she saw Nell nearby, watching with a knowing sneer.

Going up the stairs with the plate of food, Hannah thought about what had happened last night after Stritch was finally done with her.

He had clambered out of bed and pointedly ignored her, falling on the cold food with a trencherman's appetite. She had gotten dressed in her torn

52

clothing and crept painfully from the room, with never a gesture or word from him. She had felt like a rag, used for some disgusting purpose and then tossed aside.

Tonight, he again opened the door in the nightgown and cap and locked the door behind her. Hannah forced him to chase her around the room again—not to oblige or tantalize him but simply to make him exert the effort, hoping against hope that he might tire and leave her alone, or, failing that, succumb to an attack of apoplexy.

But in the end, he had her spreadeagled on the bed, her cringing body bared to his lustful stare. He was panting from exhaustion.

"On my oath, girl," he growled, "I'm going to dampen that spirit of yours, the last thing I ever do. By God, I will!"

Hannah struggled against him. Even tied down as she was, she fought him, making it as difficult as possible for him to effect entry into her body.

And when Stritch was finally at it, at the very height of his laboring lust, she raised her head and spat full in his face.

He collapsed, rolling off her. "Before God, I have never seen such a wench. You are the devil's spawn, you are! Now get out, get out of my sight!"

"I cannot," Hannah said calmly. "Not so long as I am tied up in this manner."

Stritch untied one of her hands, then fell back onto the bed. "Now finish the rest yourself. If I was not weak as a puling brat, I would beat you until you could not walk, damme, I would!"

Hannah quickly untied herself, hurried into her clothes, and left. Stritch was snoring behind her.

Did she dare hope that this was the end of it? Had she won?

Her hopes grew the next evening when closing time came and went, and Stritch said not a word to her.

Hannah slept well and dreamlessly that night. The next morning Bess raised an eyebrow at her revived spirits as Hannah went about her work humming. She was tempted to relate it all to Bess, but she was still too shamed and humiliated by all that had happened. Perhaps later on she would feel up to telling about it.

That night her hopes were dashed. As they closed, Stritch beckoned to her. His ugly face wore a mean look. "I want my supper brought up, girl. And see you be quick about it. Tonight we shall see what we shall see!"

Much to her dismay, Hannah could not keep her hands from trembling as she set the supper plate down on the table in Stritch's room. As Stritch locked the door and started for her, she ran around the bed.

He stopped, a savage grin stretching his thick lips. "Oh, not tonight, my beauty. This eve, we have a lesson to learn."

He strode to the chest of drawers against the wall while Hannah watched fearfully. She had learned that this was where he kept the thongs he used to bind her to the bedposts. From a middle drawer he took a long, thick, knobby stick. With that same evil, savage smile, he hefted it in his hands.

"And now, girl, we shall see who is the master and who is the servant. When I am finished with you this night, you will plead on your hands and knees to lay down with me!"

Hannah watched in fear and trembling as he advanced on her. For a moment her resolve wavered, and everything in her cried out to bend to his will. What did it matter if he had her again? The damage had already been done. Her body was already cringing away from the expected thump of that fearsome stick.

Then she stiffened. She would die and rot in everlasting hell before she would ever accede willingly to his foul desires!

As he neared her, Hannah gathered herself and darted around him. But she was not quick enough. As she flashed past, the stick whistled through the air and struck her a stunning blow on the shoulder. She cried out in anguish and stumbled, and he was on her, the stick descending again and again on her back and shoulders and buttocks. Finally she was driven to her knees, half-fainting from the pain. He struck her twice more across the back, driving her face down on the floor.

Then Stritch stood back, breathing hard, gloating down at her. Her gown was ripped and torn, her back seeping blood in many places. *Now*, he thought gleefully, *now you are mine, all mine! No more will you fight and spit like a cat!* The beating had aroused him fully; he was ready.

"On the bed, wench," he said harshly. "On the bed with you, on your back!"

Hannah heard his voice through a red haze of pain. She obeyed his command by instinct, the instinct of an animal beaten to a threshold of pain so severe there is no resistance left, only an eagerness to obey.

With great difficulty she dragged herself to the bed and painfully climbed onto it. Stritch offered not a hand to help her. He waited until she was on her back on the bed. Then he clambered on it, hiking up his nightgown. He did not bother to remove her clothes; his need was too urgent. He shoved her dress up over her belly, brutally ripping aside all undergarments, and drove himself at her.

Hannah was only dimly aware of him. She felt the pounding weight of his heavy body, each impact sending searing waves of pain across her back. But at the last moment, when that whistling sound of release came from him, she roused enough to raise her head. She worked saliva into her dry mouth until she had a mouthful, and spat a huge glob directly into his face.

And then, remembering that her hands were free, she slashed out at him with one hand, nails raking down across his cheek, his flesh gathering under her fingernails like mush. She left four parallel gouges. Each began to bleed at once.

"Sweet Jesus! Lawd, Lawd," Bess muttered in great anger as she rubbed a pungent ointment over the wide stripes of torn and bloody flesh across Hannah's back. "A pig, a snake, a demon right out of hell, is that old devil Stritch. Lawd, child. Your poor back! I could kill that man, and the Lawd would bless me for it!"

"No, Bess," Hannah said faintly. "If you did that, they'd hang you."

"Anyways, I'll give him a piece of my mind!"

"No, not that, either. You know what would happen then. He'd beat you, too. But thank you,

Bess, for caring." She patted the woman's hand. "You're the only one who ever has, aside from my mother and ... and my father. It's my predicament—I'll survive somehow." She smiled grimly. "Master Stritch hasn't mastered me yet."

But *would* she survive? How could she endure more humiliation and abuse?

She had told Bess about the caning. She had no other choice. Her lacerated and bleeding back had been an agony all night, allowing her no rest. And she knew that an infection could set in in the wounds if something wasn't done to them, and she couldn't tend them herself.

So she had come to Bess.

Bess said, "But honey, you can't keep on this way! Oh, I'm not talking 'bout him bedding you. That means nothing, a woman can stand that till a man wears himself down to the nub, till that thing of his won't stand up. But fighting back, scratching, spitting ... he could beat you to death, that mean old devil." A chuckle escaped her. "But Lawd God, I would have liked to have seen it, I purely would. Such a sight would warm old Bess's days for the rest of her natural life!"

Dickie burst into the kitchen, skidding to a stop when he saw Hannah nearly naked. Bess hastily covered her up.

"What you mean running in here like that, boy?" Bess scolded. "Ain't I told you never to do that? Next time, you make yo'self known first!"

"What's the matter with Miss Hannah?"

"Never you mind. Now what's all the scurry?"

Dickie had to think for a moment. Then his face lighted up. "Blackbeard's men are in the village, walking about as bold as you please!"

"Lawd God," Bess breathed.

"Who's Blackbeard?" Hannah asked.

"Teach, the pirate, child. Blackbeard, they call him. He's been a-plundering and murdering folks all up and down the coast. A mean devil, they say."

"How can they come in here so bold?"

"Ain't supposed to, but who's to stop 'em? Less'n the governor calls in the militia. By that time they be all long gone. You be careful in that tavern tonight, honey. Them pirates ain't a-feared of God nor man. They get full of old Stritch's liquor, they be capable of anything!" She snorted scornfully. "Against the law to sell to them, to serve any sailors off the ships, 'cause they runs off without paying, most times. Most taverns won't open this night. But old Stritch, he'll do anything to fatten his purse. He'd serve the devil himself had he the coins to pay!"

Amos Stritch was a sorely puzzled man.

He was very busy getting the taproom ready for business, pressing everyone except Black Bess into serving. Blackbeard's men would make him rich this night. He would be the only tavern open to them. He was not afraid of what they might do; they would get drunk and rowdy, but they would do no harm to his place, he was reasonably certain, because they would want to be welcome again another time.

He saw Hannah come into the taproom, walking with her back held stiff. He grinned with relish, remembering the caning. Then he fingered the scabbing scratches on his cheek, and the grin faded away.

She was what sorely puzzled him, the bitch! Never in all his life had he encountered such a stubborn one. He had been sure that last night's caning would break her spirit. Then, at the very height of his passion, she had spat another gob into his face, and dared to scratch him in the bargain!

All day he had been the target of sly questions. He had passed them off with a remark about a cat jumping on him in the dark.

Damnation, there had to be *some* way he could tame her spirit. Never had he been so sorely tried. He was even tempted to send her back to Quint, but be damned if he would admit defeat at the hands of a mere child!

Suddenly he cocked his head as he heard two voices chanting outside:

"This is the tree that never grew,
This is the bird that never flew,
This is the ship that never sailed,
This is the mug that never failed."

As the shanty ended, a rough voice said, "This is it, me hearties. The Cup and Horn. Old Stritch will make us welcome!"

Blackbeard's men! A broad grin stretched across his face as an idea sprouted in Stritch's devious brain, and he knew how he would finally break Hannah! When this night was done, she would be happy to hop quick as a flea into his bed when he had need of her. Oh, indeed, she would!

Quickly he hurried across the room to her. He took her arm and said in a low, ingratiating voice, "Come along with me, girl."

Without giving her a chance to demur, he hustled her toward the stairs. Halfway up, she hung back. "Not now, sir, please. My back is terrible sore. . . ."

"It's not that, you ninny. I'm doing it for your benefit." He put on a concerned manner. "'Tis not safe for you to work the taproom this night. These pirates of Blackbeard's have been at sea for months, without a female in sight. When they get full of ale and see a comely young lass like you, they might drag you outside and jump you. 'Tis looking out for you I am."

Hannah gave him a dubious look. This sudden solicitude did not ring true, but she went along with him. Upstairs, he shoved her into his room and closed the door. "Now take off all your garments."

She shrank away. "No! You said . . ."

"Not that, you silly girl," he said in fatherly, unctuous tones. "I have to be downstairs in the taproom. It's just that you have such spirit, you might get out of the room." He put some admiration into his smile. "Now give me your garments and I'll return them when all Blackbeard's men are gone." He held up his hand. "You have my oath on it!"

Hannah gave him another dubious glance, but she finally turned her back and took off all her clothing. Stritch took everything from her and went out quickly. He locked the door and slipped the key into his pocket, ignoring her cries at the sound of the lock turning. He tossed her clothing onto the window seat on the landing, smiling to himself at the cleverness of his plan.

Rubbing his hands together gleefully, he hurried

downstairs and got back behind the bar. The taproom was quite lively now, full of men—seafaring men in jerkins and wide-bottomed trousers of common sailcloth, all coated with pitch thick enough to withstand the points of daggers, or even blunt the edge of a sword. They were a strange breed, these buccaneers; many were bearded, with long, shaggy hair. They wore caps or tricorner hats; some of them had gold earrings dangling from their ears. Many of the faces were scarred and disfigured from battle, and their loud talk rang with salty oaths. Since they came from all parts of the world, many tongues were spoken, but they all had money and were free with it. Coins and currency from every nation passed over Stritch's bar. He accepted it all, and gladly.

None of his regular patrons were here tonight, Stritch noted, but that was all right; they would return when Blackbeard had put out to sea with his men again.

Stritch kept a weather eye out for just the right man. And finally, when the taproom was thick with smoke and loud with voices, he saw him. Tall, broad of shoulder and narrow of waist, garbed in finery fit for gentry, he stopped in the doorway of the taproom and sent an imperious glance around, broad nostrils quivering as though he had smelled a barnyard stench. He wore a thick beard, black as night, and from one ear swung a golden earring in which some precious gem twinkled. He was dressed in fine broadcloth, knee britches, and buckled shoes. He wore no sword, nor had he any weapon in sight, but Stritch was sure he carried a dagger concealed somewhere on his person.

It was not Blackbeard himself, Stritch knew, even if the beard much resembled Teach's own.

Now he was making his way through the crowd toward the bar. From the respectful glances sent his way by the other pirates, Stritch knew that this one was of some importance, clearly one of Blackbeard's lieutenants. He walked with a singularly catlike grace for such a tall man. And he moved with arrogance and disdain, as though the others in the room did not exist.

"Do you have French brandy, innkeeper?" His voice was deep and full; he had the manner of an educated man.

Stritch knew that many men of gentry turned to piracy. There was an old rumor that Governor Spotswood himself had gained much of his fortune through a partnership with a pirate....

"Are you deaf, innkeeper?"

Stritch came to with a start. "My apologies, sir," he said with fawning mien. "French brandy? Yes, indeed I do!"

"The best, mind. No slop."

"Oh, it is the best, not long off the ship from France."

Stritch poured the brandy. The man with the beard picked it up, sniffed deeply of the liquor, then nodded and drank. He did not move away, but lounged with one elbow negligently on the bar, his disdainful glance sweeping the room.

Stritch waited a moment before leaning close to whisper, "Would the gentleman like a wench, sir?"

The brilliant black eyes swung around. "A wench, is it? Likely some alley slut, with the French disease."

"Oh, no, sir," Stritch assured him hastily. "The

wench is young, not diseased, my oath on it. Saucy, full of spirit she is, and fresh as a new rose."

The man with the beard did not speak for a long moment, weighing the proposition carefully. Finally he said, "It is not my custom to buy my pleasure, yet I have been at sea these many months."

"Your pleasure will be of the greatest, sir. My oath on it."

"Then I will buy your wench's favors."

Stritch said slyly, "Since she is fresh and a great beauty, she does not come cheaply."

The man with the beard reached into his pocket, took out a large coin, and tossed it onto the bar with a contemptuous flick of his wrist. "Enough for your wench, innkeeper?"

Stritch picked up the coin with a hand that trembled slightly. A Spanish gold piece! He yearned mightily to test it with his teeth, but managed to refrain. He said, "You are most generous, fine sir."

"And the brandy?" The man across the bar tossed off the rest of the brandy. "That enough for both your wench *and* your brandy?"

Stritch hesitated, wondering if he dared ask for more. But the look in those black eyes stayed him. He said hastily, "Oh, yes, sir. Enough!"

"Now where is this wench of whose charms you sing so highly?"

Stritch took the brass key from his pocket and held it out. "Up the stairs and the first door on your right, sir. Here is the key."

The man eyed him askance. "What manner of wench is this to be locked up like some wild beast in a cage?"

"Like I said, sir, she has spirit. But I am sure a man such as yourself will have no trouble taming her."

"I do like a lass with some fire, and I daresay I have tamed more spirited wenches than she."

He took the key from Stritch's palm and started toward the stairs.

From Stritch's room, Hannah could hear the sounds of revelry below. In a way she longed to be down there; she had never seen a pirate. It might be interesting to serve them. Yet Stritch had said they could be dangerous.

Stritch's concern mystified her. It was unlike him to be so concerned for her welfare. . . .

The key turned in the lock, and Hannah whirled, facing the door as it swung open.

A tall man with a black beard, a stranger, strode in. He stopped short at the sight of her naked body. His black eyes lit up as his insolent gaze raked her from head to toe. Hannah felt herself coloring.

"Who are you, sir?"

"I am called Dancer, madam." He dipped a knee gracefully, a mocking smile on his full lips.

"But how did you get the key?"

"Why, your master downstairs sold it to me for Spanish gold. He sold me the use of your favors for an hour's dalliance."

"Dear God, no!" Hannah's hands went to her face, and she cringed away, turning her back.

She heard an indrawn breath from him. "God in Heaven, girl, what happened to your back?"

Hannah did not answer.

"Did the innkeeper do that?"

Hannah nodded wordlessly.

"A villain I took him for on first sight, and a villain he is—most villainous indeed!"

Hannah heard his footsteps approach, and she tensed herself to spring away.

"Have no fear, madam." His deep voice was compassionate, his touch on her shoulder gentle. "I will not harm you. I will not touch you. A blackguard I would indeed be if I forced myself upon you in your condition. I bid you good night, madam."

Hannah listened to his footsteps recede and the door close with a great feeling of relief. It did not occur to her to wonder why a pirate should show such consideration.

Her mind was grappling with this latest example of Stritch's perfidy. After she had been so certain that she had experienced the ultimate in degradation and abuse, she now knew there was more, and worse, still to come.

Now Stritch was selling her—like a tankard of ale across his bar!

The man who called himself Dancer paused for a little outside the door, wondering if he should lock it or leave it open so she could escape, if she so wished.

He was in the grip of a great rage. That a man should so abuse a woman, alley slut or not, was monstrous! His inclination was to charge downstairs and run the man through with his sword. Then he remembered that he had come ashore weaponless, except for a dagger concealed at his waist. But even if he had had his scabbard buckled to his waist, he knew he would have done nothing, no matter how much the blackguard deserved it. He could afford to attract no undue attention this night. In a short time he had an important rendez-vous to keep, and if he got involved in anything that might attract attention to himself, not only would that rendezvous be jeopardized, but he might be placed in danger himself.

He sighed and turned the brass key in the lock. He muttered under his breath, "My apologies, madam. But whatever your sorry situation, you must be at least in part to blame."

He lingered for another few minutes on the landing, so as not to arouse the innkeeper's suspicions, and then went downstairs. He strode to the bar and tossed the key to the man. He could not resist a parting remark. "You were wrong, inn-keeper. I have seen kittens with more spirit than that one." He went on out of the taproom.

Stritch stood gaping after him, frozen in aston-ishment. How could he have finished with the girl so quickly? Had she not fought him? Stritch's ris-ing anger almost choked him. Had she submitted to this one because he was handsome, with the cut of a gentleman?

Well, by the hand of God, he would fix her!

Key clutched in his hand, he peered squinch-eyed around the taproom, searching out the most villainous-looking one of the lot. . . .

As the door crashed open, Hannah whirled about. Her first thought was that the man named Dancer had changed his mind.

Then she saw how sorely mistaken she was, and her heart almost stopped beating.

Standing in the doorway was the hugest man Hannah had ever seen. He filled the doorway from jamb to jamb, and his face was a horror. He was beardless, but a cutlass scar zigzagged down across his face like a lightning streak. The cutlass had sliced away a part of his nose and cut a gap in his upper lip, so that stubs of blackened teeth protruded.

He was roaring drunk. Staring at her naked body with bloodshot eyes, he shouted, "So you be the wench old Stritch sold me! You be a fetching sight, aye, that you are!" Due to the slash in his upper lip, he spoke with a slight lisp, but his presence was so formidable that the lisp did not seem at all amusing to Hannah—it only made him the more terrifying.

Hannah watched in near panic as he lurched toward her, slamming the door so hard the room shook. She began backing away from him.

"But where's the spirit Stritch spoke of? Methinks you be more like a frightened mouse! But no matter, you be comely enough. I'm going to pleasure myself, by Teach's beard, I am!"

He was close enough now for Hannah to smell him. It must have been months since he had bathed. Even over the liquor stench, she could smell the rank odor of his body.

She tried to evade his groping hands, but even drunk as he was, he was quick. He clamped a huge hand on her shoulder and flung her toward the bed, staggering after her, roaring with laughter, showing a mouthful of rotting, broken teeth.

The backs of Hannah's knees struck the bed, and she lost her balance and fell. He was on top of her in an instant, falling like a great tree, smothering her with his weight and smell.

Her struggles were useless. He placed an arm like an iron bar across her throat, choking off her

67

breathing. With his other hand he fumbled with his breeches. Hannah felt herself swooning.

Then he was at her, rough hands mauling her breasts, gross body rising and falling. He was bruising her with every movement. When she tried again to squirm away, he bore down harder on the arm across her throat, and darkness imploded behind Hannah's eyes as she sank into unconsciousness.

When she regained her senses, the arm was gone from her neck, but his weight still held her pressed down into the feather bed. He was asleep, his snores like a donkey's bray.

Hannah gathered all her strength and pushed against his insensate bulk. At first it seemed she would never move him, but finally she shoved his great weight off. He rolled onto his back on the other side of the bed; he never once stopped snoring.

Exhausted and revolted by the stench of him on her body, Hannah lay for a little, waiting for her strength to return.

Then she remembered—the door, he hadn't locked the door! She was up in a flash and across the room. Yes, the knob turned in her hand. She opened the door a crack and peered out. There was no one in sight on the landing. She hesitated, looking down at her bare body; then she crept out, closing the door softly.

And there, a miracle surely! In a heap on the window seat were her clothes. In trembling haste she dressed herself. The taproom downstairs still rang with the sounds of drunken merriment. How long would Stritch wait before he came up to check on the pirate in his room?

Hannah tiptoed down the narrow stairs, carrying her shoes in her hand. She turned right at the bottom. If she went out the front way, she would have to pass the open door of the taproom. She went through the ordinary, which was empty—no food was being served now. Cautiously she let herself out the back door; then she hesitated, looking toward the kitchen. Should she speak to Bess?

No, Bess would only try to dissuade her, and her mind was firmly decided.

She was fleeing this place. The horror of the past half hour was more than she could bear; no more could she endure it here. She was going to run away. They would have to put her in chains to bring her back! And even if they did bring her back, she would find a way of killing herself.

The night was balmy, but Hannah's body was bathed in cold sweat as she unconsciously headed south, the way she had come into Williamsburg with her mother. She still carried her shoes in her hand. She was accustomed to going barefoot most of the time, and the soles of her feet were toughened. She could move faster, and more quietly, without shoes. She didn't think there was much danger of being seen so long as she stayed off Duke of Gloucester Street, which was still thronged with Blackbeard's men. All the houses on the other streets were dark and shuttered tight. Clearly everyone was abed, or cowering in the dark in terror of the pirates.

In what seemed to Hannah a very short time, she was out of town, hurrying along the south coach road. It was a dark moonless night, and she remained on the road, terrified of going into the trees that grew thick and close to the roadway.

Once she flung herself off the road to lie trembling in the weeds as a coach and four rumbled past. And again, an hour later, she heard the thunder of hooves and hid in the high weeds until a horse and rider had gone by.

By this time she was almost spent with exhaustion. She had no idea how far she had come, but she knew it must be several miles. She stumbled on, step after weary step, feet and limbs growing numb, carried along by will alone. She fell occasionally, but always got up again to stagger on.

Then she stumbled over a rut in the road and fell headlong, landing partially dazed in the dust. This time she gave up and curled herself into a ball, falling into an exhausted sleep.

Hannah did not hear the approach of a handsome chariot drawn by two prancing black horses. The chariot was lined with coffy, beautifully carved and painted, a glass across the front. The single seat inside, which could accommodate two persons, was embroidered with silver, and there was a silk fringe around the entire seat. One man sat alone on the chariot seat, hands crossed over the silver head of a cane braced against the floorboards.

The Negro driver sat on an elevated seat separated from the main body of the chariot. Two huge candles burned with flickering flames in enclosed globes on each front corner of the vehicle.

Suddenly, the driver muttered under his breath and began sawing on the reins, pulling the snorting horses to a halt.

The man inside the chariot, thrown forward, demanded in a loud voice, "What the devil is about, John?"

"A body in the road, master. Looks to be female."

The man in the chariot became animated at this sudden diversion. "Well, hustle down and see if she is living. If she is, fetch her here."

Hannah awoke to a rocking motion. She opened her eyes cautiously. She was in some sort of coach, which was in full motion. Was she caught already?

She looked to her left and saw that there was a man on the seat beside her. He was dressed splendidly in a square-cut coat stiffened with buckram and whalebone, a satin waistcoat over a ruffled cambric shirt, and close knee britches. His stockings were blue, with elaborately embroidered clocks. Small silver buttons fastened velvet garters just below his knees, and the buckles on his shoes also looked to be silver. He wore a powdered wig with full, long curls puffed at the sides and a long queue at the back.

At a sound from Hannah, his face swung around, and she saw that he was old, his face lined and filled with melancholy. Now she noted that he was also very thin, almost to the point of emaciation.

His lips moved in a shadow of a smile. "Well, my dear young lady, I am delighted to see that you have been restored to us."

"Who are you, sir?"

"Malcolm Verner, madam. At your service."

Hannah glanced fearfully about the chariot. "Where are you taking me?"

"Why, to Malvern, my dear. To my plantation."

Chapter Five

A short time later, the coach rumbled up before the main house of Malcolm Verner's estate, but Hannah was too exhausted, too low in spirit, to really take notice of the beauty of Malvern.

She was only dimly aware of Verner shouting for the servants; then she was being helped, almost carried, up a wide sweep of stairs and into a bedroom. She stood passively while gentle hands undressed her and laved her bruised and weary body with warm water and soft cloths. Dark faces grouped around her, clucking at the scars and fresh lacerations on her back. A sweet-smelling ointment was rubbed on her back, and for a moment she thought of Bess. Then, almost asleep, she was led to a large four-poster bed and pushed gently back upon a feather mattress that softly received her tired body. Her last awareness, before sleep took her, was of the smell of clean linen and the scent of lavender.

Hannah awoke with the sun streaming into the room. Through mosquito netting she saw lacy curtains moving in a slight breeze from the open window. Drowsily, she listened to the sounds of activity that came from outside. Somewhere, a child laughed. Hannah felt disoriented, unsure of where she was; last night was only a vague memory. Before she could collect her thoughts, she was asleep again.

When she awoke a second time, there were two dark faces beside her, one on each side of the bed, watching her with curious eyes. The mosquito netting had been removed. Hannah awoke slowly, half sitting up to obtain a better look at her nursemaids, who began to giggle, softly, as soon as they saw that she was awake. As Hannah sat up, there was a sharp rap on the door, which swung open immediately to admit Malcolm Verner. All at once, the memory of last night returned to her in full clarity, bringing with it a flood of apprehension and fear.

In the same instant, she realized that she was naked under the bed coverings, and pulled the quilt up around her breasts.

Verner's face was stern, and Hannah's apprehension mounted. She expected the worst, without knowing quite what that might be.

"Madam, the servants tell me that you have lash marks on your back," Verner said in a harsh voice. "Is that true?"

Hannah nodded mutely.

"Who did this monstrous thing?" His voice was

74

cold and controlled, but she could sense a true anger in him.

For a moment she didn't answer, blinking, pretending to be still befuddled from sleep, but she fully understood the question. Her mind was racing. How much should she tell this man? If he learned that she was a runaway indentured servant, would he return her to Amos Stritch?

For the first time in her life, Hannah was aware of having a choice in her own destiny. Should she use guile and lie? Or should she be bluntly truthful? More important, which course would be to her ultimate benefit?

As she thought, Hannah watched Malcolm Verner from under lowered lids. The night before, even in her distraught condition, she had recognized some inexplicable sorrow in this man. Now she also sensed a gentleness, a kindness, a depth of understanding. In an instant, she decided to risk the truth.

"I am a bond servant, sir," she said simply. "When you found me on the road, I was running away."

Verner seemed at a loss for a moment. "I do not hold with indenturing as such," he finally said. "But a contract must be honored. I do not hold with slavery, either, yet I own many slaves." His mouth held a bitter twist as he glanced directly at the two black girls by Hannah's bed. "Jenny, Philomne, you may go. Leave us." After the girls had left, Verner said to Hannah, "Now, who indentured you, girl?"

"My stepfather, sir."

Verner seemed taken aback. "Your stepfather! Why, may I ask?"

Hannah lowered her gaze. "He is a poor man, sir, with many debts, and a strong liking for drink. A cruel man, too, who would have used me badly himself, except for the fact that my mother was there to protect me. . . ."

And then it all came pouring out, beginning with her mother's marriage to Silas Quint, and ending with her indenture to Amos Stritch and her brutal treatment at his hands. "It was not the lash with which he beat me, but a knobby stick he sometimes carries. Amos Stritch suffers sorely from the gout. . . ."

Malcolm Verner listened, aghast, his outrage mounting. Somewhere during the telling he had sat down on a footstool beside the bed. And soon, without his fully realizing it, he took Hannah's hand in his and patted it from time to time, as a father might pat a weeping child.

Hannah was indeed weeping by the time she was finished, weeping weak tears, nearly drained of emotion from reliving the ordeal she had gone through.

Listening closely, watching her, Verner did feel a paternal concern for her, and yet at the same time he had to admire her beauty. Even with her hair in a tangle and her eyes red from weeping, she was remarkably attractive. From time to time, in the agitation of her tale, she allowed the quilt to slip below the swell of her breasts, and Verner felt a stirring in his loins that he had not known for some years. *Passion,* he thought, *after all this time and at my age?* And then he answered his own question. *Just because I'm past three-score years does not have to mean that all passion is dead!* Immediately ashamed of himself, he forced his thoughts into other channels.

He was horrified at her story. "This Amos Stritch is a blackguard, a proper villain indeed!" he said stormily. "He must be made to pay for what he has done to you. He should be soundly thrashed, and I would see to it myself were I not in failing health. The lot of an indentured servant is a sorry one, I know, but there are laws to prevent cruel mistreatment, and the penalties are severe. Many indentured servants do not know of this. But I am not without some influence in Williamsburg, and I shall see to it that this Amos Stritch pays dearly!"

Hannah's first inclination was to agree with him wholeheartedly. She would dearly love to see Amos Stritch punished. The very thought of him suffering filled her with a fierce joy. And yet . . .

She hadn't failed to notice Verner's interest in her, the glitter of his brown eyes, the languid droop of his eyelids, and the sensual curve of his full mouth. Even though her experience with the ways of men had been meager, she had already learned how easily their passions could be inflamed by a beautiful female body. Quickly she calculated just what she could gain from Verner's reaction to her beauty.

She said guardedly, "Just what are the penalties, sir?"

"Why . . . usually fines. Sometimes the courts may levy heavy fines on an offender. They have that power. And I shall see to it that their power is fully exercised."

Hannah recalled how tight-fisted Amos Stritch was. The fines would hurt him sorely. But . . .

"But what then will happen to me, Mr. Verner? Will I be returned to him to serve out my indenture?"

Verner looked startled. "Why, yes ... I suppose that would be the court's decision, my dear. But I believe you may be confident that he will not so abuse you again."

"Not that, anything but that! You don't know this man. If I'm returned to him, I will only run away again. Or kill myself!" She sat up straighter in bed. Acting on an impulse she could not explain, she allowed the quilt to fall below her breasts. Tears she could not help stood in her eyes. "Please, Mr. Verner, isn't there some other way?"

"Now, my dear, don't upset yourself unduly."

Verner touched her shoulder, then jerked his hand away as though he'd placed it on hot coals. Face flushed, he averted his eyes. "I will endeavor to think of something."

"Mr. Verner, could you manage it so that I could serve out my indenture here?" Hannah said eagerly. "I am a good and faithful worker. I understand you have nothing but slaves in your household. Perhaps I could work as a housekeeper, overseeing them? If you think I couldn't be trusted for that, I'd be willing to work as a kitchen slavey." She seized his hand and pressed it between hers. "I would go to any lengths not to go back to Stritch's tavern!"

Face flushed even more, Verner gently removed his hand from hers. "I will think of something, my dear. My promise on it." His gaze swung her way again. "Uh ... perhaps you should, uh, cover yourself."

"I'm sorry, sir. I didn't mean to embarrass you.

It's just that the thought of returning to that dreadful place, to that terrible man . . ." She pulled the quilt up, but slowly, so that he could have his fill of looking. She was beginning to enjoy this game, this feeling of power. Verner's breath came harshly. This time he did not look away, and sweat beaded his brow.

"Mr. Verner?"

Malcolm Verner started. "Yes, my dear?"

"I believe I know a way. You say that he might be fined severely if you hale him into court. Amos Stritch is a miserly man. If you went to him and told him that you knew of his mistreatment of me, then perhaps you could *threaten* to take him before a magistrate, where he would have to pay a large fine. That would frighten him far more than the threat of a thrashing, I am sure. Then if you . . ." She hesitated, casting her eyes down. "If you offered to keep quiet about it in exchange for his signing over my articles of indenture to you . . ."

Verner expressed shock. "But that, madam, would be blackmail! A gentleman does not stoop to such methods!"

Hannah gave him a wide smile. "I remember my mother telling me once that the only way to deal with a villain and a blackguard is on his own level."

Verner's indignation did not abate. "What you suggest, madam, is out of the question! I would prefer that we not continue this discussion. Perhaps you will be more . . . rational when your, uh, fever subsides." He got up and made a knee. "Your leave, madam. Mayhap you are hungry. I will have food sent in." He left the room quickly.

Hannah was not dismayed. In her new shrewdness, she perceived that Malcolm Verner was not so outraged as he pretended. She lay back on the soft pillows, feeling very pleased with what she had begun.

Through the open door, she heard Verner giving the two servants instructions. His tone was not sharp, not as domineering as that of the many slave owners she had overheard ordering their chattels about.

The two young black girls came hurrying back into the room, not in fright but giggling, exchanging roguish glances, and Hannah guessed that they were anticipating her sharing the master's bed.

An idea formed in her mind, or rather an extension of the proposal she had made to Verner. As they tended her, she questioned them: How harsh a master was Malcolm Verner? How hard was their lot?

"Oh, missy, the master, he good," said the older one, Jenny. "He never beat us, not less'n we steal or lie to him."

"He much better than most masters," Philomne said. She couldn't be much more than sixteen. "He never tries to bed us. He . . ."

"Silly girl! 'Course he don't!" said Jenny, aiming a slap at the other, which was avoided easily. "But he good, is the master. I hears that he's never sold one of us'ns once he buys us. The other niggers say this has never happened. He never beat man or woman, never sell the chilluns, never hires out the best bucks for breeding. . . ."

The girl ran on, but Hannah ceased to listen. She'd heard all she needed to hear. She retired into her own head, scheming on how she would work it. . . .

Malcolm Verner was in a state of confusion as he unlocked the door to the downstairs room he called his office—a small, stuffy room where he had a chair and desk, a bottle of brandy always at hand, a box of cheroots, and shelves of books. This was the room where he worked on the account books of Malvern.

He got himself a cigar and tumbler of brandy and sank down into the room's one luxury, a thickly cushioned chair with a footstool. The chair was turned to the room's one large window so that Verner could take advantage of the light from outside. Nowadays the plantation practically ran itself, and he had much idle time. The only time he found it necessary to do much overseeing was during harvest and curing time—and then he personally attended the tobacco sales, of course. Harvest time was a month or more away. . . .

He was kind to the slaves on Malvern, and he could trust them to do a full day's work without his standing over them. Besides, his overseer, Henry, knew as much about raising tobacco as he did, if not more. Malcolm Verner was the only tobacco grower in Virginia with a black overseer, and the other planters said he was a fool. Yet Henry had never once given him cause to regret the trust he placed in him.

The one possible bad result of this was too much leisure time. Time to brood, to read, to drink. In the beginning, Verner, a reasonably well educated man, had intended to devote the spare time to reading the many books he had accumulated. But nowadays the books mostly gathered dust, remaining unread, and he spent the time in here brooding and drinking glass after glass of brandy, until he often had to be assisted up to bed.

It hadn't always been this way, of course. Verner had purchased his first fifty acres of land twenty-three years ago, and had erected a small, crude cabin and settled down with Martha. Michael had been born in the cabin that same year. Verner had been in his prime then, just past forty, robust, energetic, able and willing to work around the clock if necessary.

In England he had been of the gentry, if impoverished (at least by country-squire standards), and had known little of hard work and nothing at all of plantation life. But when he'd received a small inheritance, Verner had come to this raw, new land with the belief that with hard work and determination, a man could become wealthy. He had had determination, and had applied it to good advantage.

He had been one of the first to realize the full potential in tobacco, and had planted it to the exclusion of everything else. He had also been one of the first to realize that the constant planting of tobacco on the same land rapidly wore it out. The theory of the rotation of crops had been the cornerstone of English agriculture since the Middle Ages, but the theory had seemed little known in the new land.

Verner had soon learned that land was good for about seven years of good crops before it was worked out, that it should then be allowed to lie fallow for fifteen years or so. This meant the constant acquisition of new land. His original fifty acres had grown to a hundred and then to several hundred, until it was one of the largest plantations in Virginia. This foresight and acumen had paid dividends.

At the end of seventeen years, he had been able to build Malvern, a house destined to become a showplace in the Williamsburg area.

Verner had intended to throw a ball to celebrate the completion of Malvern, a grand ball on such a scale that it would be talked of for many years to come. But they had scarcely settled into the new house when Martha had sickened and died of the swamp fever. . . .

The tragic and totally unexpected death of his wife threw Verner into a slough of despond from which he supposed he had never completely recovered. Certainly he had never enjoyed Malvern as much as he had anticipated he would, although he was proud of it.

Michael had been short of seventeen when his mother had died, a tall, strapping, handsome youth. Verner had had his son to live for, at least, and he later came to think that that had kept him from going completely to pieces—even, perhaps, from going mad. . . .

There was a rebellious streak in Michael, however, that both puzzled and angered Verner. The boy had a reckless, impulsive nature, and showed little interest in plantation life. It was natural for a father to expect that his only begotten son would take over the reins of the family estate. In England, it had been the accepted thing.

Michael balked him at every turn. When Verner forced the lad to accompany him on tours of the plantation, he went along sulking and silent, absorbing very little of what there was to learn.

He would much rather spend his time in Williamsburg gambling and, Verner suspected, woman-izing. By the time he was twenty, he was away for days at a time. Verner could understand hot blood in a youth and he tried to be tolerant, confident that in time Michael would settle down.

But this did not happen. He spent money fool-ishly, lavishly, and Verner learned that he was gaining a reputation as a rakehell around Williams-burg. Verner didn't mind the money; he was a wealthy man and not a miser by any means. It was the black mark against the Verner name that he objected to.

It all came to a head on Michael's twenty-first birthday. Verner planned a lavish ball, inviting neighboring planters. It was to be the grandest oc-casion Malvern had ever seen, the ball that had been aborted by Martha's untimely death. The household slaves, as well as the field hands, were in a joyous mood, and Verner allowed them to have a celebration of their own.

Wine flowed freely at supper, and afterward dur-ing the dancing in the ballroom. Even with his reputation, Michael was considered a prime catch by all the mothers with marriageable daughters, and he danced many a dance that evening. But as the evening wore on, he became intoxicated and lapsed into one of his dark moods, becoming arro-gant and rude to the guests.

Since it was his son's birthday, Verner was willing to overlook his cloddish behavior—up to a point. But when some of the guests departed in a huff and one indignant woman, enormous breasts sailing before her like the prow of a ship, came to him protesting that Michael had taken liberties with her daughter in the darkness of the veranda, Verner knew it was time he took matters in hand.

He found Michael refreshing himself from a bottle of brandy at the punch table in the ball-room. He wanted to reprimand his son for his excesses. With an effort, he curbed his tongue and draped his arm around his son's shoulders. He said, "Michael, I think it's about time for you to receive your birthday present."

Michael muttered something inaudible under his breath.

"What, son?"

"Never mind ... Father." Michael tossed his head, a dark lock of hair falling over his forehead. "Birthday present, I believe you said?"

"Yes. We'll have to go outside."

Verner knew that it wouldn't be much of a sur-prise by the time they reached the stable. Michael loved horses—they were, in fact, the one feature of plantation life that he did like—and he was an ex-cellent horseman.

A few weeks back they had been invited to Sun-day supper at a neighboring plantation. The owner of this plantation made a hobby of breeding and raising fine riding stock. One horse in particu-lar Michael had taken to at once—a high-spirited black stallion, that had just attained his maturity. The huge beast was as black as the absence of light, except for a small white star between his eyes. His name was Black Star.

Michael's features had lit up with delight at the sight of the great horse, and for just a moment Verner had been reminded of the endearing lad Michael had once been.

Michael had approached Black Star's stall, crooning, "Oh, you black beauty! You darling!"

"Careful, boy," Bart Myers, their host, had said. "He's a spirited beast, and I fear he has a vicious streak bred into him. Not a fortnight ago he bit me, sinking his teeth into my arm almost to the bone."

Heedless, Michael had continued on to the stall, crooning, hand held out. The horse had whinnied, snorting through flaring nostrils, and then had reared up, great hooves slashing the air.

And yet, within seconds after Michael had bellied up to the stall door, the horse had been nuzzling his outstretched hand.

"I'll be Billy-be-damned!" Bart Myers had said in awe. "Anybody else, the beast would either be chomping or stomping on him. That son of yours must be a witch, Verner!"

"He does have a way with horses," Verner had said with some pride. *A very rare moment of pride it was*, he thought, and was instantly ashamed of such disloyal thoughts.

Later, he had bargained with Myers to buy Black Star. He had sensed that Myers was eager to be rid of the animal, yet he had paid the man a good price just to escape the haggling.

Now, as he pushed open the stable doors at Malvern, candle-lanterns flickered on. John and another slave had been alerted to watch for their approach.

Down the line a horse neighed, a great black head tossing, a proud mane flying. "Black Star!" Michael broke into a run.

Verner followed more slowly, smiling indulgently. In his mind's eye he had a vision—Michael

Verner, his son, riding the plantation astride this great stallion! Mayhap his choice of a birthday present had been wiser than he knew. The gift could be just the thing needed to bind his son closer to hearth and home.

Michael was stroking the animal's neck, murmuring to him, as Verner approached the stall.

Michael faced around. "Thank you, Father," he said simply. His eyes glistened in the dim light with what could have been tears. Then he motioned imperiously, the moment gone forever. He called, "John, a bridle and saddle! I must ride him! At once!"

"But, son!" Verner said in dismay. "Now, at night? We still have guests!"

Michael's eyes flashed. He tossed his head in disdain. "Guests! A gaggle of giggling females, not a thought in their empty heads but being wedded to the son of the master of Malvern! And the men ... they talk only of crops, of the price of tobacco. Father, that is not enough for me, can't you see? There's a whole other world out there." He flung a hand wide. "I must see some of it. I must!"

Verner was silent. He thought of forbidding Michael to ride out like this. But he procrastinated, waiting too long. John, taking his silence for permission, already had a bridle on the black horse and was leading him out of the stall. The other slave helping, they threw a saddle on Black Star, cinching it tight beneath the great belly. The horse stood surprisingly docile, liquid eyes fixed on Michael, as though in hungry anticipation of speeding through the dark night with Michael astride him.

Grinning, Michael took the reins from John. In

one mighty leap he was astride the horse. Except for the white ruffled shirt, Michael's clothing was all black, making him one with the animal. He pulled back on the reins, and the horse reared. Verner thought, fleetingly, of a centaur, and then dismissed the thought as fanciful.

The ground shook as the hooves of the horse came down. Lightly, Michael tapped the black, gleaming flanks with his bootheels.

Verner took a step. "Son, wait! Where are you . . . ?"

He was too late. Already Black Star was bolting for the open stable door, Michael riding him with practiced ease.

He twisted his face toward Verner, teeth flashing whitely. He shouted something, but the words were lost in the thunder of hooves, and horse and rider vanished into the night.

Verner moved to the stable door and listened to the sound of hooves diminishing, listened until the sound existed only in his mind.

Finally, with a heavy step, he turned toward the house, trying to think of an excuse for his son's sudden disappearance to give the few remaining guests. . . .

In the past, Michael had often been gone a night, perhaps two or more. But after a week passed and no word came from him, Verner grew uneasy. He took the coach into Williamsburg. Most people averted their faces when he inquired about his son. Finally he located him, at cards in one of the village's lowest taverns at the worst end of Duke of Gloucester Street. The men he played with were lowly fellows, mostly riffraff, and Michael's face was loose with wine, unshaven, his clothing wrinkled and soiled.

Verner noticed, in passing, that his son had a stack of winnings before him.

He paused for a moment, unnoticed by the players. He knew that he had spoiled Michael. Was it so unnatural for a man to spoil his only child, and a son at that? But Verner had always told himself that the boy would grow out of it. Now it appeared that he had been wrong.

A black rage grew in Verner, a rage such as he had never known. He stepped to the table.

Michael saw him and leaned back. He smiled, a taunting, somewhat cruel smile. "Well, Father?"

Verner was still so angry that he didn't trust himself to speak. Finally he found his voice. "Michael, could I speak with you?"

Michael gestured carelessly. "Speak away, Father."

"Alone, if you please."

They locked stares briefly. Then Michael shoved back his chair. "By your leave, gentlemen. I shall return shortly."

Verner turned on his heel and strode outside. He didn't look to see if Michael had risen, but he could hear footsteps following.

On the cobblestones outside, Verner wheeled about. "When are you coming home, boy?"

"Boy? I'm past twenty-one, Father. Remember?" Michael cocked his head. His breath was sour with wine. He said with studied insolence, "I have given some thought to coming home. I have yet to make up my mind."

"Is it your intention then to remain here roistering?" Verner's voice trembled now.

"It has its attractions. After all, Father, I'm a man now. It's my life to do with as I wish."

"How will you live? You will receive no money from me!"

"I could survive quite easily by gambling. I find that I am good at it."

"My son a gambler, a rakehell! I will not abide it! It's disgraceful!"

Michael's smile grew. "Are you sure it's not the good name of Verner you're fearful of having disgraced, Father?"

"You belong at Malvern!"

"You mean I should be there working like one of the field slaves—working myself to death as Mother did?"

Verner gaped, stunned by the accusation. "Your mother died from the fever! If she worked hard, it was of her own choosing."

"At Malvern, Father, you are master." Michael was openly sneering now. "Nothing is done but at *your* choosing."

"That is not true!" Malcolm Verner was beyond anger now, shocked and deeply hurt. Was it the wine in Michael speaking, or had he harbored such feelings in his bosom these long years? Verner held out his hand in a beseeching gesture. "You cannot believe that, my son! Please tell me that you speak in jest!"

Michael half turned away, gesturing indifferently. He took out a thin cigar to roll between his fingers. "No jest, Father. I speak of what's in my heart."

Verner was dimly aware of men lounging nearby, no doubt listening avidly. Pride came to his rescue, straightening his spine. "If you persist on this course, I have no choice but to disown you. ..."

"Too late, Father." Michael cut him off with a motion of his hand. "I here and now disavow the name of Verner."

Without even thinking, Verner lashed out with his open hand and slapped his son across the face, knocking the cheroot from his mouth. The blow was enough to send Michael staggering back a few steps. His black eyes flashed fire, and his fists clenched at his sides. He took a step forward, and for a moment Verner thought he was going to strike out. Then he made a gesture of contempt. Without another word he turned and strode back into the tavern.

Malcolm Verner stood for a time with shoulders slumped. Despair welled up in him. He felt as though he'd aged ten years in just a few minutes. Finally he raised his head and looked about. Men still lounged nearby, staring at him. He glared, and their glances dropped away, and most of them slouched off. But he knew that word would be abroad in Williamsburg before nightfall of the quarrel between the Verners, between father and son.

Wearily Verner trudged to the coach and returned to Malvern.

Three days later Black Star arrived. The man paid to deliver the animal also had a short letter for Verner. It read:

Sir: Since I am no longer considered your son, I thought it beholden on me to return your birthday gift to me. I shall be leaving Williamsburg shortly. Michael.

A rumor reached Malcolm Verner within days that Michael had indeed left Williamsburg. And this year past, word had come to him that his only son was dead at sea.

Now there was no son to carry on the Verner name. He had considered marriage so that he could sire another son—God knew there were many women eager to marry the master of Malvern. But somehow it had never come about. Instead, he sat in here and drank himself into a stupor. . . .

A timid knock on the door broke through his bitter reverie. His head came up. "Yes? Who ish . . . who is it?" He realized that he was very drunk.

"Mr. Verner," a female voice said hesitantly, "could I talk to you, sir?"

It was the girl . . . what was her name? Hannah, Hannah McCambridge.

"No!" he shouted. "Go away! Leave me alone!"

After a moment he heard her retreating footsteps. He let his breath go with a sigh.

What was he going to do about her? By just keeping her here without informing the courts or this Amos Stritch, he was breaking the law. But Verner knew that he wasn't going to inform anyone. Not right away. Just the thought of those marks on her back made him shudder.

Her suggestion that he blackmail Amos Stritch was distasteful to him. At the same time, there was an ironic justice about it that appealed to his sense of humor.

Then he remembered the effect that the sight of her uncovered breasts had had on him, and he felt a wash of shame. Why had she suddenly appeared in his life, upsetting a patterned rhythm, sterile though it might be?

He closed his eyes briefly. Across the screen of his mind danced erotic images of himself locked in a carnal embrace with her. And what a son she could produce for him. . . .

No!

Damn the girl, anyway!

With a muttered obscenity he flung his glass against the wall. It shattered, shards falling to the floor, a brown stain appearing on the wall.

Immediately he got up to look for a new glass to pour full of brandy.

Chapter Six

Hannah was overwhelmed by Malvern.

On that long-ago day when she and her mother had passed the plantation, she had dreamed of someday seeing the interior. Now that she was there, it far surpassed her expectations.

The thought of her mother made Hannah feel guilty. She knew her mother would be worried and heartsick at Hannah's unexplained disappearance, but she also knew that if she tried to contact her mother, Silas Quint would learn of it, and would report immediately to Stritch. Hannah could only hope that her mother, who had borne so much, could bear this, too, at least for a while longer.

Such thoughts only caused Hannah pain, so she put them from her mind, and turned to exploring the great manor house.

Although she had been inside the fine homes of the Williamsburg gentry with her mother, those houses, which she had thought so grand at the time, were nothing to what she saw here.

Malvern had been constructed more recently than many of the plantation homes. Many of the others had been created piecemeal, room being added to room as the need arose. But Malvern had been designed by a man who had studied architecture, and had been built to exact specifications. The tall white columns that framed the entrance doors were unusual at the time, and the wide, sweeping staircase leading up to the second floor was very different from the narrow, twisting stairways that many of the older manor houses still had.

Malvern boasted an entryway that extended through the center of the house, dividing around the stairway like a stream around a boulder, and when both front and rear doors were open, it provided a refreshing breeze, even in the heat of summer. And the giant oaks that surrounded the house on three sides gave cooling shade.

Hannah never tired of exploring the many rooms, which held furnishings the like of which she had never seen. She loved her own room, the room she had been allowed to use. She felt luxuriously pampered in the great four-poster bed with its velvet valances, fine linen sheets, and silken coverlet. There was a beautiful, green, Turkey-worked carpet on the floor a little way back from the large open fireplace, and a beautifully finished, ornately carved chest for her clothing—except that she had none to put in it.

One of the rooms she loved most was the music

room. It was a rather formal room, containing a virginal, two fiddles, a hand lyre, a recorder, and a flute. Although Hannah was unfamiliar with all save the fiddles, she loved to handle the musical instruments, and when no one was about, she learned to pick out a passable tune on the keys of the virginal.

She also explored the grounds of Malvern. Besides the formal gardens, which Hannah loved, there were the dependencies, or outbuildings, which housed the kitchen, the smokehouse, the spring house, and the necessary. Most of the outbuildings were connected to the main house by covered walkways so that travel back and forth could be accomplished without discomfort in inclement weather. It all represented life on a grander scale than Hannah had ever imagined.

Although the wide expanse of lawn and gardens reaching down to the James River about two hundred yards distant pleased Hannah's innate sense of beauty, it was the inside of the house that fascinated her the most. The house raised a great many questions in her mind. Despite its luxuriousness and its elegant appointments, Hannah had a feeling that this was not a happy place. A faint aura of sorrow, like the lingering scent of faded funeral flowers, hung in the empty rooms. For empty they were except for herself and the house slaves who cleaned them—cursorily.

The large withdrawing room was covered with a patina of dust, the furniture draped with muslin. Hannah could not help but feel that the house was sleeping—waiting for someone, or something, to bring it to life again.

Besides the withdrawing room, or parlor, there

97

were a book-lined library downstairs, all leathery and masculine; the small study into which Malcolm Verner locked himself daily; and a large dining room on the one side of the entryway and stairway. On the other side, Hannah soon discovered, was a magnificent ballroom.

When she first found this room, the door seemed to be stuck, but with determination she managed to open it, and she gasped with surprise and delight.

A grand ballroom!

Hannah had heard of them, but had never seen one. Although the air was thick with dust, it could not hide the intrinsic beauty of the ballroom. Lining the long walls were rows of chairs, now swathed in muslin. At one end of the room was an ornately ornamented virginal, a large harp, and several music stands. It did not take much for Hannah's imagination to picture the musicians there playing their instruments while dancers glided gracefully about the polished floor. In the center of the room, a huge crystal chandelier, its sparkle dimmed by dust, hung from an iron chain; it was rigged so that it might be lowered to light the candles. It was flanked by two smaller, but no less beautiful, chandeliers, one at each end of the ballroom.

It was a pity that such a beautiful room, capable of giving so much joy, should remain dusty and unused, thought Hannah.

At the first opportunity, she asked Jenny when the ballroom had last been used.

Jenny got a frightened look, darting a glance toward the closed door to Verner's study. "Not since Master Michael left, missy."

"Mr. Verner's son?"

Jenny nodded. "It was only used just the once, that room. I hear tell that the master was gon' give a big fancy ball and invite all the gentry when this house was built. But then the mistress die, and it never happen.

"Then, when Master Michael, he reach twenty-one, the master open up the room, and they have a grand party. Oh, I do hear tell it was something to behold, that party.

"Then Master Michael, he left, and the master, he close up the room, and say it never gon' be used again."

With a bob of her head, Jenny ran off.

Hannah stared after her for a moment. Then she crossed the hall and opened the door to the ballroom.

In her mind's eye she saw the musicians at their instruments. They were playing a minuet, a melody that Hannah had known as long as she could remember. She knew it had been taught to her by Robert McCambridge, for her mother had told her so.

In her short life, Hannah had never danced with a man, but her mother had taught her a few steps, and her inborn ear for music and her natural grace, helped her to move gracefully across the floor now.

Eyes closed, her hand in that of an imaginary partner, her waist supported by his strong arm, she glided and turned across the huge empty room. Dust, stirred by her feet, rose into the air until Hannah seemed to be moving in a soft golden haze as ethereal as her own dream.

A harsh voice brought her daydream to a crashing halt. "Hellfire and damnation, girl, what do you think you're doing?"

Hannah's eyes flew open. Malcolm Verner stood in the doorway, swaying slightly himself, as though to the music in her own head. His buckled shoes were dusty, his shirt and trousers stained and rumpled. His hair was unkempt, his face covered with a gray stubble, and his glaring eyes were bleary and bloodshot. It was the first time she had seen him since that first day, a week past now.

"I ..." Hannah began a stumbling explanation. Then she drew herself up sharply. She had vowed to herself that she would never be cowed by a man again. "I am dancing, sir. 'Tis a ballroom, is it not?"

"Damned sacrilege," Verner muttered. "I gave instructions this room was not to be used." He seemed to focus on her more clearly. "And what manner of garment is that you're wearing?"

Hannah's head went back. Jenny had taken it to wash and iron and mend, but it was still little more than a rag. "It's the only dress I have, sir."

"You look a disgrace in it. Martha ... my wife was about your size. I'll tell Jenny to see what can be done. I never gave her clothes ..." He swallowed, his glance falling away. His voice roughened as he continued, "My wife's clothes are packed away in a trunk. Now, come out of there. This room is to stay locked."

Hannah went past him, head still high. He closed the door firmly behind her and then went across the hall to his study without another word.

A short time later Hannah tiptoed back and tried the door to the ballroom. He hadn't locked it, and she knew in her heart that he would not. So long as she closed the door after her, she could enter the room as often as she wished, with his tacit consent.

The clothes that had belonged to Martha Verner smelled musty and had to be aired for a day and a night. The dresses were somewhat small for Hannah, but there was enough material so that they could be altered to fit. There were many fine dresses, and Hannah felt like a queen when she finally started wearing them. Jenny was a good seamstress, but she had never served a mistress before, and she knew nothing of paint and powder, or doing hair, so in that respect Hannah was unchanged. But for the moment, the clothes were enough.

Hannah still had no hint as to what Verner intended to do about her. Not one word of her eventual fate had passed his lips, but so long as she was allowed to remain here, Hannah believed she would be content.

After several more days had passed, however, she became restless. She was now thoroughly familiar with the main house and the outbuildings—there was nothing left to explore. She felt useless and badly needed an outlet for her energies; she wasn't accustomed to idling away time. She made an effort to help Jenny and the other house servants, but she soon realized that she was only embarrassing them.

At last she decided to confront Malcolm Verner. He had had time enough to make up his mind about her.

She had to know. Though she flinched away from the thought, even being forced to leave Malvern would be better than not knowing.

She took a bath, washed her hair, and brushed it until it shone. She put on what she thought was the best of Mrs. Verner's gowns that Jenny had made over for her, a dress coppery in color, a close match for her hair. The dress dipped daringly low in front, revealing the swell of her breasts. In Mrs. Verner's trunk she found a sachet of scented lavender. It was so old that the scent was nearly gone, but she dusted lavishly between her breasts with it.

As prepared as she would ever be, Hannah went down the stairs and to the door of Verner's room. Taking a deep breath, she rapped on the door. This was the only room in the house she hadn't been in. She had no idea of his condition, or if he would even admit her.

Hannah had suspected from that first day what Malcolm Verner did in that room. Finally she had put it bluntly to Jenny.

Eyes fearful, Jenny had told her in a whisper, "Master has these bad spells. He liquors up. Since'n Master Michael is dead, master drinks terrible sometimes. This time ..." Jenny drew a deep breath. "This time worse'n any t'others."

Hannah knocked again, louder this time.

"Come in," Verner said clearly. "It isn't locked."

Hannah opened the door and went in. The room was thick with cigar smoke, hot and close with the window shut.

She choked on the fumes, and tears came to her eyes. Without awaiting his permission, she marched past him and threw the window wide, letting a breeze in. Then she turned, looking at him fully for the first time. To her surprise he seemed in command of himself today. His clothes were clean and freshly pressed, his shoes polished, his eyes clear. His features were firm, although clearly ravaged after his long spell of tippling.

"You seem to take a lot upon yourself, girl. Marching into my private office in such a manner and throwing wide the window." But there was little rancor in his voice. "What is it you want of me?"

"It is not so much what I want of you," Hannah said steadily, "but what you want of me. I mean, what is to happen to me?"

He sighed, scrubbing at his freshly shaven chin. "I have given much thought to your situation. In fact, it was on my thoughts just now."

"And what have you decided?"

"It seems I have little choice but to follow your suggestion." He shrugged with a wry smile. "By dallying these two weeks, I have placed myself in jeopardy. There are laws against harboring runaway indentured servants—it is as much a violation of our current laws as harboring runaway slaves. So, as repugnant as your suggestion may be, I seem to have little choice. I will take the coach into Williamsburg this very day and confront your Amos Stritch. . . ."

"I want to beg more of you than that." Hannah paused to take a breath, then plunged recklessly into it. "At the Cup and Horn are two people, one a slave, the other indentured like myself, a mere lad. In addition to myself, I ask that you bring them here also. If Amos Stritch is frightened enough, I am sure he will part with them for very little. . . ."

Malcolm Verner straightened, his eyes growing angry. "You do indeed take much upon yourself, madam, making such demands upon me! Do not forget your situation. You are still an indentured girl!"

Hannah refused to let him weaken her resolve. "You need a cook here, a good cook. The food served at your table is often little better than the slop fed to swine. Perhaps in your condition you don't notice...." She stopped, realizing that she was going too far.

Verner stirred, eyes becoming hard. But he subsided, waiting her out.

"The slave I mentioned, Black Bess, is a wondrous cook. Her dishes are a marvel. She would be worth any price. And the lad ... Dickie is a fine lad, a hard and willing worker." Her eyes sparked. "Amos Stritch canes him something fierce when he is in a temper, for no reason at all. Before his indenture time is served, the boy's spirit will be broken. He will have no more gumption than a whipped cur."

Verner studied her quietly for a moment. "And that is all? Are you certain you have no more demands I should meet?" His voice had a sharp edge of sarcasm.

"They will repay whatever they cost you, sir, twice over. I swear 'tis true! And handled right, I know old Stritch will let them go to you for a mere pittance...."

"Enough, girl!" Verner snapped, slashing the air with his hand. Again he studied her—that fine, ripe body straining at the confines of the too-tight dress. He recalled that moment in the bedroom and the faint stirrings of lust. There was fire and spirit in this girl, and suddenly he knew that he wanted to bed her. Voice sharper than he intended, he said,

"And what services may I expect from you, madam, should I do as you ask?"

There was something different about his manner now, Hannah thought. His eyes had a sleepy, hooded look, and for a little she was at a loss, not sure how to respond, a little frightened by what she had read into his words. Then she drew a deep breath, causing her breasts to swell over the bodice of her gown. Watching his gaze fix on them, she said, "You need a housekeeper, someone to see that your house is running smoothly. Jenny and the other house slaves are willing and hard workers, but they need a firm hand."

"And you, a tavern wench of sixteen, can provide that firm hand?"

"I'm a quick learner, sir. I will manage—you will see."

"And that's all I get in return for this hard bargain you're driving?"

"What else, pray, sir?" she said innocently. "I am but a poor bond servant, as you say, uneducated for anything else."

Verner's head snapped back. "Do you mock me, madam?"

Hannah widened her eyes. "I know not your meaning, sir."

Verner stared at her hard, eyes narrowed and brooding. Then he gestured abruptly. "Be gone with you, girl. Leave me alone."

"But you haven't yet told me what your intentions may be."

"I'll think on it. Now be gone!"

Hannah made a small curtsy and swept out.

Behind her, Malcolm Verner sat without moving until the door had closed. Then he got up and shot the bolt home. He took out the brandy bottle and started to pour. With a muttered curse he changed his mind. Lighting a cheroot from the candle he kept burning for that purpose, he stood at the window she had opened. He stood for a long time, smoking and staring unseeingly into the distance. He was unsettled in mind. He knew what he *should* do. He should return Hannah McCambridge to her master. Her very presence in this house was devilishly upsetting.

Amos Stritch had been almost out of his mind with rage when he'd discovered that Hannah had run away. He hadn't known she was gone until the tavern had closed and he'd limped up to his room, preening over his shrewdness, sure he would find her cowering in his bed, shamed and broken in spirit, willing to do his bidding from this time henceforth. . . .

His first intimation that anything was amiss came when he found the door to his room unlocked. He threw it open, and instead of Hannah, there in his bed was the great drunken hulk of a pirate, snoring lustily. Hannah was nowhere to be seen.

Stritch fell upon the pirate with his cane until the poor man came awake. He leaped out of bed with a yowl, scooped up his clothes, and fled the room.

Stritch threw open the window and bellowed down into the courtyard.

Black Bess was the first to appear. "Yes, Massa?"

"That wench, Hannah, is not in my room! Get your black ass up to the attic and fetch her! And be quick about it!"

A short time later Bess knocked on his door. Stritch flung it open. "Well?"

"Miss Hannah not there, Massa." Bess stood placidly with her hands folded over her great belly.

Stritch was sure that he detected a gloating smile on her face. "What do you mean, not there?"

"Like I say, Massa, she not there. She purely ain't."

Stritch raised his cane, of a mind to strike her. Then he lowered it. He had long since learned how much wasted effort it was to beat on her. Bess endured it stoically, without a whimper, and went her own way regardless. Somehow, it always seemed to Stritch that he came away the loser in such encounters.

"Then turn everybody out. Search the tavern, search the grounds. If she's run away, I'll have the dogs after her!"

"Yassuh, Massa Stritch."

It didn't take long for it to become apparent that Hannah was not to be found. Stritch whacked Dickie on the shoulder with his cane. "Run and fetch Silas Quint. He'll be abed, no doubt, but you tell him I'll come after him myself if he don't hurry here."

Stritch was sitting at a table in the tavern, a lone candle sputtering at his elbow, when Silas Quint hurried in. Clothes rumpled, face unshaven, eyes bloodshot, breath stinking like a rum-pot, he reminded Stritch of a gutter rat flushed from his hole.

He thumped his cane on the floor and roared, "That girl of yours . . . she's run off! She come running home?"

107

"I ain't seen her, Squire." Out of breath, Quint sank into a chair. "I swear she ain't come home. Had she, I'd've fetched her back, ye can be sure. Could she be hiding somewheres around here?"

"Damnation, no! You think I'm stupid? I've searched everywhere!"

"I could use a tot of something, Squire," Quint whined, eyes darting about. "Indeed I could. Woken up out of a sound sleep near morn, my head is muddled. . . ."

"Your head is always muddled, you dung-heap!" Thump went the cane on the floor. "And no more do you partake of drink in my tavern until the girl is found!"

Quint reared back in alarm. " 'Tis not of my doing she ran off. I swear I had naught to do . . ."

"She's your daughter, ain't she?" Stritch growled.

"Stepdaughter. She's no whelp of mine, not a drop of my blood in her!"

Stritch grunted. "That's clear enough to any but a blind man. If she'd been of your blood, I would never have bought her from you."

"Master Stritch, just a tot . . ."

"No!" The cane thumped. "Could it be your spouse, her mother, knows of this?"

"Mary?" Quint's eyes widened. "I'm sure not, but I'll hurry home and ask her." Still he didn't move, staring wide-eyed at Stritch. "What are ye going to do, if she ain't to be found? Set the slave hunters and their dogs after her?"

Stritch grunted again, without answering. He had already considered that course of action. But it would be an expense, whether or not they tracked the wench down—either way, it would cost him. And he remembered the way she had fought,

108

wounding him sorely, and for just a moment he wondered if he really *wanted* her brought back.

"Damme to hell, yes! She's my property, she belongs to me!" This time he whacked the table with his cane.

Affrighted, Quint leaped to his feet. "Squire Stritch? What . . . ?"

Stritch glared at him. "I thought you were away home to question your spouse?"

"I'm away, Squire Stritch. I'll find out." He made a fist. "I'll beat it out of her, if need be."

Silas Quint scurried from the room. Stritch sat staring long after him, his thoughts dark. He had no thought that Hannah had run home. Quint would have known and would certainly have told him. Quint was happy as a pig wallowing in a full trough to be able to drink his fill here without paying. Stritch made a sound, half grunt, half sigh. Quint would be hanging around now, whining for drink. Stritch was of firm resolve—if the girl was not returned to him, Silas Quint could go begging for drink somewhere else.

Finally Stritch dragged himself up the narrow stairs to bed. The night's activity had aggravated his gout. His foot pained him something terrible.

He did not send hunters and dogs out. The only action he took was to post a notice in the square offering a small reward for word of the whereabouts of his runaway indentured girl, Hannah McCambridge. And he questioned everyone who came into the tavern. None had a word for him.

After nearly two weeks had passed, he had about given up. He was sorely puzzled. How in Satan's name could a slip of a girl like Hannah, without a farthing to her name, manage to escape through the countryside without notice? He had a dark suspicion that someone was hiding her. If he ever found out who, the culprit would be haled into court and be made to pay dearly. . . .

Early one afternoon he was in the barroom. It was a warm, drowsy day. There were only two men in the place, at a table, each with a tankard of ale. Stritch leaned on his elbows on the bar, half asleep. Suddenly Dickie burst into the barroom, startling Stritch awake.

The lad announced breathlessly, "A coach outside, Master Stritch. The passenger has business with you. Malcolm Verner, he says he is."

Stritch gaped. "Verner? Malcolm Vernor of Malvern?"

"So he say."

"He wishes to speak to *me?*" Stritch thumped himself on the chest.

Then he was suddenly fully awake and roaring at the two ale drinkers at the table. "Out, you louts, out! I have business with Malcolm Verner himself, and gentry such as he will not care to conduct business before the likes of ye!"

The two men hastily drained their tankards and took their leave. Stritch reached across the bar for a handful of Dickie's shirtfront, jerking him hard against the bar—hard enough to drive the breath from him. "You conduct Master Verner in like the gentry he is, and then stand guard in the doorway. Let no one in until our business is done. Do so at the peril of your life. Do you understand me, boy?"

"Yes . . ." Dickie gasped out. "I will guard the door with my life, sir."

Stritch released him, and Dickie ran out. Stritch

put a bottle of his finest French brandy on the bar. Suddenly he realized the state he was in. His wig was upstairs, his shirt and trousers were stained with splatters of wine, and he had neglected to shave this morning. Was this any way to receive the master of Malvern? In a panic he took two limping steps toward the staircase, then stopped, knowing it was too late for that. And for the first time it occurred to him to wonder—what did Malcolm Verner want with *him*? He knew of the man, of course—everyone in Williamsburg knew Malcolm Verner was the most successful planter in all of Virginia—but Stritch had never so much as passed a word with him.

Before he could think on it further, Malcolm Verner was there, pausing just inside the door. He was splendid in a square-cut coat, a satin waistcoat over a ruffled shirt, and knee breeches. Gray stockings were embroidered with clocks, and his shoes had brass buckles. He wore a full, powdered wig. Stritch couldn't remember ever seeing a man dressed so fine in his tavern.

He hurried toward Verner, a servile smile on his face. He bowed. "Welcome to the Cup and Horn, Squire Verner. I am honored, indeed I am!"

Verner looked about the tavern with some disdain. He was not a frequenter of taverns, preferring to do his drinking at Malvern. But the few he had been in had been, in the main, at least clean. This one smelled of spilled wine and ale, and he was sure that he detected the sour odor of vomit. He wrinkled his nose, and stifled the urge to put a handkerchief to his nostrils.

And this specimen of manhood before him. Obese, with tattered and stained clothing, his red

111

face wearing an obsequious grin. The very thought of this man in bed with Hannah, copulating with her, beating her, forcing her to labor in this foul place, sent waves of anger through Verner. It was all he could do to refrain from lashing out at him with his stick.

"I have important business with you, innkeeper," he said icily.

"Of course, sir. I am at your service." Stritch motioned toward a table by the fireplace. "Perhaps a tot of brandy while we talk? I have the finest of French brandy...."

Verner made a face, motioning with the cane. "I think it best we talk without the aid of brandy. I must warn you that this isn't a friendly visit." His glance swept the tavern. "Do you not have an office, offering us some privacy?"

Stritch had no office. An office brought in no income. Every foot of available space in the building was devoted to earning money.

"My office is being, uh, painted, Master Verner," he lied. "But we will not be bothered here. My oath on it. The boy at the door has orders to bar anyone from entering."

"The boy, yes. Nice-looking lad," Verner said, tapping his toe with the walking stick. "What might be his name?"

"Why, Dickie, sir," Stritch said, puzzled.

"Dickie? No surname?"

"None that I know. Nor does he." Stritch laughed. "A bastard child, knows not his father's name. Sent over from England, he was. Indentured by the woman who bore him."

"I understand you also have a girl indentured to you, a Hannah McCambridge."

112

"Hannah?" Stritch gaped. "What do you know of Hannah?" he added eagerly, "If you know where she is, I have posted a reward. She ran away, did the ungrateful wench!"

"Ungrateful? For what should she be grateful, pray? For the canings until her back was a running sore? Grateful for your taking her by force, using her most foully? Grateful for your selling her into whoredom to pirates against her wishes?"

Mouth agape, Stritch backed up, dropping onto the bench by the fireplace. "I know not where you heard such, sir. But 'tis a lie—all lies, black lies!"

"Is it indeed?" Verner said coldly. "And what say you, innkeeper, if I lay claim to proof?"

Stritch opened his mouth, then closed it. A horrible suspicion sprouted in his mind. He said angrily, "You! That McCambridge bitch, you're hiding her!"

Verner gestured carelessly. "That is of no concern to you."

"No concern? No concern!" Stritch squeaked. A righteous fury boiled through him. His gouty foot twinged. "She belongs to me. I have the articles of indenture on her! 'Tis a crime to harbor a runaway bond servant!"

"Do not take me to be stupid, Amos Stritch. There are also laws to protect bond servants. You think I do not know this? If I hale you up before the magistrates and expound on the offenses you have committed against this poor girl, you could be liable for heavy fines. Perhaps so heavy that you will have . . ." He waved his stick around the tavern. "So heavy that you could well be forced to sell your inn to pay."

And how is that for blackmail, Hannah, my

113

dear? Verner was thinking wryly. Strangely enough he felt elated by it. This seemed the first, strong, affirmative action he had taken in a long while, even though it was not the sort of thing a gentleman would do.

For his part, Stritch's thoughts were tumbling wildly about in his head. He looked at this finely turned-out gentleman, threatening his very livelihood, this pale, emaciated man who looked not long out of a sickbed. For a mad moment he thought of rising up and caning him out of the barroom. Then he remembered, in time, who Malcolm Verner was, and knew he could not do it.

As though reading his thoughts, Verner said, "And if you are thinking who the magistrates would believe, do not forget who I am. They will believe me, you may be sure. I am a man well thought of, a man of some influence in Williamsburg."

This was true. Stritch knew it was all too true. Who would take the word of a tavern keeper against such a fine gentleman?

He said sullenly, "What do you wish of me?"

"First, you will turn over to me the girl's articles of indenture. In return for that, however much it galls me, I will keep quiet about your vile treatment of her."

Stritch pretended to give it deep consideration, but he already knew he would agree to whatever Verner proposed. "Agreed," he finally said. Besides, probably he was well rid of the bitch. If he had her back, she might very well sneak up on him in his sleep and hack away at his male appendages.

"And in addition you have two other people in

114

service here," Verner said crisply. "The bond-servant lad, Dickie, and a slave called Black Bess . . ."

Stritch reared back in indignation. "That is asking too much of me, sir! That pair cost me dearly!"

"Hear me out, if you please. I am not asking you to *give* them to me. I am willing to pay a fair price. But their sale to me is an additional penalty you must pay for my silence."

"A fair price? What do you deem a fair price?" Stritch sat up, prepared to haggle, but only half-heartedly. The woman, Black Bess, had always been trouble, and he would probably be well rid of her as well. As for Dickie . . . a mere lad, costing him a nominal sum initially. If he could get a fair price for them . . .

"The woman is well past her prime and the boy is too young to perform more than menial chores. Yet I am prepared to offer you their market value. But do not try to rook me, innkeeper. I know well the price they would command on the market!"

To salvage at least something from the encounter, Stritch bargained a bit. But in the end, when they settled on a price, it was a price that Stritch knew was more than fair.

He heaved his bulk up, wincing as his weight came down on the gouty foot. "I will fetch the articles of indenture. . . ." He started off, limping toward the bar. He kept all papers of value, as well as his hoard of money, hidden away in the wine cellar, behind a loose wall stone.

"Stritch . . . one thing more!"

Stritch halted, turning back. "Yes, Master Verner?"

"I will not shame you by relating the details of

115

our arrangements. In return, I expect the same silence from you. If questions are asked of you, you may boast that you sold the three to me at great profit. I will not dispute you on it."

Since Stritch had no intention of ever revealing the details of what had happened here, he was only too happy to agree.

Verner lit a cheroot from the coals in the fireplace and stood smoking while the corpulent tavern owner made his way through the trap door, wheezing and grunting. Verner was weary. His distaste for the proceedings just concluded only increased his weariness. Even if the circumstances had been different, he would have felt some contempt for himself. To buy or sell human flesh like cattle always distressed him. He knew that the economy of Virginia in its present state would flounder without slavery and the use of bond servants, but that knowledge did not lessen his distaste for it.

Tired and dispirited as he was, he refused to sit down in this place. He leaned heavily on his cane, waiting.

A timorous voice spoke behind him. "Sir? Master Verner?"

Verner glanced around. The lad Dickie stood a few feet away. He was visibly trembling, from either fear or anticipation. Or perhaps both, Verner thought. He smiled. "Yes, lad?"

"Pardon me, sir. I did not mean to, but I overheard what was said from my post in the doorway. Is it true, sir? Have you bought Black Bess and me? Will we be living with you and Miss Hannah?"

"You will indeed, lad," Verner said, still smiling. Then he made his voice stern. "But not a word of what you overheard here to Hannah. Do I have your solemn oath on that?"

"Oh, indeed, sir! Not a word will I breathe!"

And then, to Verner's great discomfiture, the boy seized his hand. He bowed his head and kissed it.

Releasing the hand, Dickie moved back a step and looked up, eyes awash with tears. He whispered, "Thankee, sir. Ever' night in prayer will I bless you before our God."

"There, there, lad." Impulsively Verner reached down and tousled the boy's mop of hair. Then he drew himself up and said briskly, "Now, why don't you hasten with the news to Black Bess? Collect your belongings, both of you, and be prepared shortly to leave with me in my coach for Malvern."

Dickie bobbed his head and ran out of the room, skidding and almost falling in his haste.

Verner drew on his cigar with more vigor, smiling broadly.

All at once, he felt much better about the entire transaction. Perhaps it had been a worthwhile afternoon's endeavor, after all, methods be damned!

Chapter Seven

Now, almost overnight, it seemed to Hannah, a great change came over Malvern. It became a happy house. From the moment Black Bess's rumbling laughter sounded through the rooms, the change began.

There was even a change in Malcolm Verner. No longer did he stay locked in his small room, attempting to dull the emptiness and pain of his life with brandy. Instead, he was out early every morning, riding the plantation, getting back in touch with his property and with the people who provided his livelihood.

In the evenings, now, the dining room was in use, bright with candle flame and shining silver, light reflecting off the crystal and fine china.

Hannah, in the beginning, had often wondered

if Verner ate at all, for she never saw him do so. Now he ate heartily of Bess's lovingly cooked, ample maels, and the gauntness was gradually leaving his face and body. Hannah thought that with each pound he gained, he seemed to grow at least a year younger in appearance.

Hannah was delighted with the turn of events. For the first time in her young life, she knew real contentment. . . .

Dickie and Bess were more than grateful for Hannah's intercession for them. The evening Bess alighted from Verner's coach, Hannah came running down the steps of Malvern, and Bess enfolded her in a smothering embrace.

"Gracious Lawd, child, I thought these old eyes would never see you again!"

Hannah saw tears in Bess's eyes. She realized that she had never seen Bess cry, and was touched.

" 'Tis a goodly thing you've done, honey, freeing us from that old devil Stritch!"

Hannah was surprised to find that she was crying too. She took hold of the other woman's hand. "Welcome to Malvern, Bess."

Stepping back, Bess rolled her eyes and clapped her hands. "And such a fine place it is. Never did I think I'd work in such a place as this. Why, I feel like I passed away and gone to heaven for sure, 'cause you purely look to me like one of them angels!" Her impish, rolling laughter sounded.

And then Hannah noticed Dickie, standing aside, a wistful expression on his face. She hugged and kissed him, too, until all three of them were laughing as if they were possessed.

Malcolm Verner, standing beside his coach, watched them, and a smile softened his usually melancholy features. He knew now without doubt that what he had done this day was right.

Bess went immediately to the cookhouse, taking command. That night those in the manor house dined on saddle of venison, a large dish of beef and bacon, fresh garden vegetables, sago cream, and apple pie.

Verner dined alone, Hannah as usual eating with the others in the serving pantry off the dining room.

Afterwards, Verner sat over a glass of brandy, smoking a cigar. When Hannah came in to clear away the dishes, he said, "You were right, my dear. Your Bess is a marvelous cook. I cannot remember when I have supped so well. I had forgotten what good victuals taste like."

Flushed from her exertions, Hannah brushed a strand of hair out of her eyes. A trifle smugly, she said, "I told you that you wouldn't be sorry."

"Yes," he said, staring at her intently.

A little flustered by his stare, Hannah picked up some dishes and started out.

"For God's sake, girl!" he said irritably. "Do not bustle about so. That is work for the serving girls. Sit down for a minute. I wish a word with you."

Fearful of what he had on his mind, Hannah perched tentatively on the edge of a chair.

He stared at her for a while longer, smoke curling up from his cigar. Finally he said brusquely, "From this day forward, I will expect you to dine with me every evening. A man does not take much pleasure from dining alone, no matter how delicious the food. Besides . . ." A wry amusement touched his full mouth. "It is only fitting that my housekeeper dine with me. Is that not so?"

121

"If you wish, sir," Hannah murmured.

"I do so wish."

Hannah started to get up. Verner waved her back down. He reached into his coat pocket and extracted folded papers. He held them out. "These are yours, to do with as you like."

Hannah took the papers, puzzled. She unfolded them. Her articles of indenture! Stunned, she looked across the table at him, unable to speak for a moment. She managed to stammer, "Th-thank you, sir."

"Yes." He nodded. "You are now a freed woman." His gaze became intent. "You may leave Malvern. Or stay. The choice is yours."

Hannah didn't even have to think about it. "Where would I go? What would I do?" She made a helpless gesture. "I choose to stay at Malvern. I love it here, sir."

"As you wish." His gaze dropped away now, as though indifferent to her decision. "But if I may make a suggestion, madam. I would not bandy it about that you are now a freed woman. People would not think kindly of you for remaining here of your own accord, serving as my housekeeper. A man alone, like myself . . . they might think . . ." He looked up, scowling. "It isn't for myself I care, you understand. I have seldom cared overmuch for the good opinion of my neighbors. It is your reputation I am concerned about, Hannah."

Hannah tossed her head. "Nor do I care what people may think."

"Perhaps not at the moment," he said drily. "But the time may come when you could well regret it."

"Malcolm . . ."

His head came up at this bold use of his first name.

She rushed on, "I want to thank you from the bottom of my heart for what you did."

He made no reply, but his gaze softened, the brown eyes becoming hooded.

Emboldened, Hannah said, "Can you not find it in you to also make Dickie free?"

He straightened, color touching his pale cheeks. "Do not presume on my good nature, madam! You push yourself too far!" Then he shook his head. "The lad will be better off remaining a bond servant. In the event I do as you ask, he might take it into his head to run away. The young are rash, never thinking of the consequences of their acts. If he remains here and applies himself, he can learn a trade, a trade that will be of value to him when he attains manhood and his term of servitude is ended." Looking suddenly weary, Verner waved a hand abruptly. "Now leave me. I believe I will retire. It has been a wearing day."

Hannah hurriedly left the dining room.

In the days that followed she dined in the evenings with Verner, feeling very much the grand lady of the manor. In her more thoughtful moments, she realized that this was far from true. She was still little more than a servant, if a freed one, playing the grand lady for a little while every evening.

And now she was greatly dissatisfied with her apparel. She knew she was expected to dress for supper, and she did the best she could. Yet she knew that the dresses, fine as they once had been, had been left behind by a dead woman, and did not truly befit her. She confided in Bess.

"Gracious, honey. I knows little about fine ladies' fixings. I never learned much about sewing and such like. I always been too busy with my cooking."

She cocked her head, hands on hips, eyeing Hannah critically.

"One thing I does know, though. All the fine ladies wears corsets, or stays. That's why they all so cinched in in the middle. Always fainting, and turning pale, 'cause they can't catch a good breath. Anyway, I think Master Verner, he likes you just like you are."

"I'm not even sure he looks at me," Hannah muttered. She looked down at herself. "Stays, you say?"

"Stays *and* hoops," Bess said, laughing. "You don't think those big old skirts puff out like that all by themselves, do you, child? Always was a puzzle to me how white ladies ever got with child, all the trouble it must be to get down to the meat of it. Some white ladies I knowed must wear 'em to bed!"

Hannah could not help but laugh. She could see in her mind's eye the tiny-waisted, full-skirted figures that she had occasionally seen going into the shops in Williamsburg. Mentally she compared her own, fuller figure with theirs, and was sobered. She must have stays.

Then she remembered the trunk full of Mrs. Verner's clothes. Surely there must be something she could use. Vaguely she recalled a peculiar contrivance of bone and white cloth that she had cast aside while trying on the gowns.

"Bess, upstairs. In the trunk. I think there are some stays in the trunk. Help me, Bess!"

124

Hannah, stripped to her petticoats, stood in front of the large pier glass in her room. After much fussing and muttering Bess had finally managed to get the contrary contrivance around Hannah's waist, and now she began to tighten the laces.

Hannah expelled her breath in a long gasp. "That's awfully tight, Bess!"

"Got to be, honey, got to be. That much I know. Hang onto that bed post there. It'll help some."

Grunting with effort, Bess pulled the laces so tightly around Hannah's middle that Hannah felt faint from lack of breath.

Finally Bess stood back, walking around her. "Reckon that's the way it's s'pose to be. Anyway, now you got a teeny little waist just like all the fine ladies. Now let's see if we can find those hoops."

Hannah stood quietly, still holding onto the post to her bed, trying to take small, shallow breaths, while Bess rummaged in the trunk, finally coming up with a strange contraption formed of slats banded together with strips of white fabric. This she fastened around Hannah's waist.

Hannah glanced down at herself. It looked as if she had a large bowl suspended from her waist, upside down.

"Now, put on your dress, honey."

Hardly able to move from the unusual constriction, Hannah struggled into the dress with Bess's help. Dress finally on, she looked again at herself in the glass. The dress, which she had so recently let out at the waist, hung loosely now. Her plump breasts, pushed up by the stays, threatened to spill over the confines of the bodice.

Hannah, looking at her image with critical eyes, attempted to estimate whether her looks had truly been enhanced by this fiendish contraption. The tiny waist did look well, and the full skirt, now swelled out by the hoop, looked graceful. She tried to walk around the room, but the skirt bumped and caught on every piece of furniture, and the stays still caused her to feel faint.

Bess was staring at her, shaking her head. "My, my, you must be a lot more ample in the bosom than Mistress Verner was, child. Why, with those stays, your top part ain't hardly decent."

"Dear God, Bess," Hannah said. "I do think that these things were invented by somebody who hated women. It's plain torture. I feel like I'm in an oven!"

Bess was shaking with laughter. "That's the price you has to pay to play the fine lady, child. We'uns better off, not having to wear such getups. The mistress, she goes around steamy as a bonfire on hot days. Leastways we don't have to wear such things like that!"

Hannah looked at herself once more in the mirror. "Damn it," she snapped. "Neither do I. My waist is small enough to suit me, and I don't intend to put up with this kind of torture every day. I guess I'll just never be a fine lady!" She looked off and added in a musing voice, "I doubt that Malcolm ever notices what I wear anyway...."

Malcolm, is it, Bess was thinking. She had wondered if the master of Malvern was bedding Hannah. She had been sure that he wasn't, not yet. Now she was not all that sure....

"Bess!" Hannah stamped her foot. "Stop standing there grinning like a fool and help me out of this infernal contraption!"

It was true that Malcolm Verner had little eye or concern for women's attire. If someone had asked him to describe the clothes Hannah wore to supper every night, he would have been at a loss. But he was very much aware of what was *under* the clothes. The tight fit of the dresses made him conscious of the ripeness of Hannah's body every time she moved. He had never been a particularly lustful man, never a womanizer. Since marrying Martha many years ago, he had never known another woman carnally. But now his dreams were fevered and lusting, and he was becoming increasingly uncomfortable in Hannah's presence.

Perhaps this was the reason he talked so much now at supper. He told Hannah of the early days in England, of his marriage to Martha and the early struggles to build the plantation into a paying proposition. He told of how he had mourned his wife's early death, and of how much he missed her.

But Hannah noticed that never a word passed his lips about his dead son. She had picked up bits of gossip from the house servants to the effect that there had been friction between master and son. She wanted very much to ask Malcolm about him, yet she knew that she dared not. She was knowledgeable enough now to know that it was a forbidden subject with him.

During the two weeks following the arrival of Bess and Dickie at Malvern and her own official installation as housekeeper, Hannah's days were very

127

busy. She had asked Malcolm's permission to use two more girls to work in the house, and she set the four of them to work. All the windows and doors were opened, letting fresh air circulate through the house. All dust covers were removed. Every item of furniture was dusted and polished, and the woodwork, the floors, and the walls were washed and polished, as were the chandeliers. The curtains were taken down and given a thorough washing and ironing.

Hannah flitted back and forth, supervising. She found that the role of mistress of the manor house came naturally to her. She seemed to know instinctively what to do next. She wasn't harsh with the servants, rarely scolded, but instead was lavish with praise and free with her help, and she allowed the four girls frequent rest periods. Soon they seemed to take pleasure in doing her bidding.

Once, during the cleaning of the ballroom, she sensed a presence behind her. Fearful that it was Malcolm Verner, she tensed and turned. Bess stood in the doorway, in that familiar stance—hands on broad hips.

"Gracious, honey, you looks and acts like you was born to this!"

Hannah flushed with pleasure. Yet in her heart she knew it wasn't true. It was all play-acting, just like the suppers with Malcolm. She was here on his sufferance. She had to keep running up to her room to take out the articles of indenture from the place where she had hidden them and look at them—she did this at least once a day. Verner had suggested that she burn them, but Hannah couldn't bring herself to do this. Not yet. It seemed to her that she held the essence of her life in those papers.

Each time she looked at the papers she thought of her mother with a pang of guilt. By now her mother must know she was alive and well, yet she had to be concerned. Hannah knew she should visit her, reassure her that her daughter was doing well.

She shoved the thought from her mind and went back to work.

When the house was finally clean and shining, however, Hannah could no longer keep herself occupied, and her thoughts returned increasingly to Mary Quint.

Malcolm Verner had to have noticed what was going on in the manor house. But he made no comment; he just came and went, spending most of the day in the fields.

One evening at supper, he made his first and only remark. "The house looks nice, Hannah." His eyes twinkled. "It seems I made a good bargain all around."

"Thank you, sir," Hannah said, her eyes lowered. Then she looked up at him. "Malcolm, I would like to go see my mother. She has to be fretting."

Verner toyed with his brandy glass. Then he nodded soberly. "Of course you should. I can understand why she might be concerned. I'll tell John to take you into Williamsburg on the morrow."

For a moment Hannah felt a quiver of apprehension.

Sensing her doubts, Verner said, "Are you perhaps afraid of your stepfather?"

Hannah gestured, and said with more bravado than she felt, "I'm not worried about Silas Quint. I can handle him."

"He is likely to be angry over what has happened. And from your tale of him, he is a vicious man. However ..." He gestured abruptly. "I do not think it prudent for me to accompany you. But do not worry, my dear. John will see to it that nothing untoward happens to you."

As Hannah started to get up, Verner added softly, "Hannah ... if your mother wishes to abide at Malvern, she is more than welcome."

Hannah felt the ache of tears. She swallowed. "I'll ask her. Thank you, Malcolm. You are a good and thoughtful man."

Verner motioned brusquely and took a cigar from his pocket, devoting all his attention to it, dipping the mouth end into the brandy before lighting the cigar.

Hannah had not left the plantation since coming there, and now that the time was here, she was full of doubts and fears. With Bess's help, she dressed carefully the next day, trying to look her best.

"Best take along a bonnet, honey," Bess said. "You be going in the open carriage. This sun can be something fierce."

"The open carriage!" Hannah echoed. "I thought the coach!"

"That John sent word in. The coach is down, a wheel off. It has to be the carriage."

The open carriage made it even worse. She would be on display to anyone they met on the trip. Hannah knew that gossip must be rampant in

Williamsburg and the surrounding area about Malcolm Verner and the young, beautiful bond servant living in his house.

Fortunately they passed few people on the road in, but the passengers in the few vehicles they did meet all stared openly. Hannah looked straight ahead, refusing to acknowledge their stares. As they clattered onto the cobbled streets of Williamsburg, she sat proudly, looking neither left nor right.

The streets in the section where the Quint house was located weren't cobbled. They were plain earth, and full of potholes that set the carriage to rocking, the wheels pluming dust behind. People came out of the hovels to stare, but Hannah knew it wasn't because of her. In this section people weren't neighborly; Hannah hadn't known any of their neighbors except by sight, and she very much doubted that any recognized her as Mary Quint's daughter now. They were staring because it was probably the first time they had seen such a fine carriage in this neighborhood. They lined up, staring openly.

Finally Hannah leaned forward, touching the driver on the shoulder. "There, John. The second one on the right."

With a flourish the driver drew the team of matched grays to a halt. He hopped down off the driver's seat to offer Hannah a hand down.

John was not a young man, but he was tall and broad, well over six feet, with large hands, and he was light on his feet for a man of his size. He looked splendid in his livery. Hannah knew why Malcolm had sent John; she did feel safe with him. There was an air of quiet competence about him.

He spoke like a man with some education. Curious, Hannah had once asked Verner about him.

"I employed a tutor to stay at Malvern and teach Michael. John asked me if he could sit in on the lessons. I couldn't see any harm in it." It was the only time Malcolm Verner had spoken of his son to Hannah.

Now she stood for a moment, looking at the house where she had spent so many unhappy years. Unlike the other houses along the row, there was no sign of life in this one. It struck Hannah as odd that her mother hadn't come running to greet her.

She sighed. "Well, I reckon I'd better go in and get it over with."

"Yes, ma'm," John said softly. "I'll be right here if you need me."

Hannah smiled. "Thank you, John."

She went up the short dirt walk to the house, holding her head high as she had seen the gentry ladies do. The door stood slightly ajar.

Without knocking, Hannah pushed the door open and went in, calling, "Mother? It's Hannah!"

The inside of the house was filthy. Hannah was astonished. Her mother kept even a hovel like this scrubbed and clean. Now it looked like a pigsty. Apprehension stirred in her breast.

She advanced a few steps and called again, louder. "Mother, it's Hannah! Where are you?"

She heard a stirring sound in the bedroom and she waited, eyes on the door. It opened, and Silas Quint emerged. His clothes were rumpled from sleeping in them, and stained with food and wine droppings. Even at this distance she could smell his foul odor.

At the sight of Hannah, his eyes widened. They

132

were red-streaked, almost as though they had been bleeding, and the pig snout that was his nose was redder than usual. "Well, lookee here! If it ain't the fine lady come to visit her old father!"

"I'm not here to see you. Where's my mother?"

"I've heard about the grand situation ye got for yourself out there at Malvern. I been thinking of coming calling. Times is hard for old Quint." That familiar whine crept into his voice. "Thinking mayhap ye could spare a coin or two."

"You'll get nothing from me, you understand? Nothing! And if you ever show your face at Malvern, Mr. Verner will run you off!"

"Ye'd let him do that to your poor old father?"

"You're not my father!" Hannah flared, temper sparking. "Now *where* is my mother?"

"Mary Quint is dead and buried these four weeks," Quint said, his glance sliding away.

"Dead? I don't believe it!" Hannah was stunned. She staggered, catching herself against the wall. For a moment she thought she would swoon.

Dimly, as through a thin wall, she heard Quint saying in an unctuous voice, " 'Tis sad but true. Me poor Mary, dead and buried in a pauper's grave."

Hannah rallied, focusing on that hateful face. "Why wasn't word sent to me?"

"Why, ye ran away and left your poor mother. I didn't think ye'd care to know." He was openly sneering now, no longer even pretending grief.

"I didn't run away from *her*.... How did she die? She wasn't ailing the last time *I* saw her."

Again Quint's glance slipped away. " 'Twas an accident. Going out back, late at night, to use the privy, she tripped on the steps and fell. Broke her neck like a twig. She was dead afore I got to her."

133

Something in his evasive manner alerted her. She straightened, iron in her voice. "I don't believe you! You killed her, I know you did! You were always beating my poor mother. You hit her—*you* broke her neck!"

"Don't be saying such things, girl!" Quint's glance darted about frantically. "Some'un might overhear. Not so, I swear! 'Twas an accident. On my word, it was!"

"Your *word!*" Hannah said scornfully. "Your word means nothing. You would always choose a falsehood over the truth. You killed my mother, I know you did. You foul murderer!" She knew her voice was rising, that she was on the edge of losing control. "And you'll pay. I'll see that you pay if it's the last thing I ever do!"

"Don't be screaming such things, girl! Hush, for the Lord's sake, hush!" He advanced toward her, making shushing motions with his hands.

Unheeding, Hannah screamed, "Murderer, murderer!"

Quint's face darkened, and he came on toward her, hands reaching for her throat, mouth working. "Shut up, ye addled bitch, shut your blathering!"

A measure of reason returned to Hannah, and, almost too late, she realized that she was in some danger. The thought of calling John crossed her mind, but even as she thought it, she saw a broom leaning against the wall. Seizing it, she gave Quint a sharp rap across the head. He yowled, hands coming up, and Hannah, both hands around the broom handle, used it like a sword, ramming the blunt tip into Quint's sagging belly—once, twice, rapidly. Quint gasped, now trying to protect his

134

belly. But at the same time he advanced, lurching toward her.

A little frightened now, Hannah groped behind her for the doorway. She found it and began backing out. Quint followed her just outside the door, where he came to an abrupt stop, staring past her.

Hannah glanced around to see John standing right behind her.

"This white trash giving you trouble, Miss Hannah?" he asked, face as still as though it was carved from black ivory.

"It's all right, John. I'm all right. Let's go back to Malvern."

She took a few steps toward the carriage, then whirled back. "You'll rue the day you killed my mother, Silas Quint! I'll see to it that you do. My promise on it!"

It wasn't until then that Hannah noticed she had an audience. People from the nearby huts were gathered on both sides, listening silently. Hannah hastened on, climbing into the carriage before John could help her. He got up on the seat, flicked the reins, and the carriage began to move.

Hannah rode with her head held high, staring straight ahead. She didn't give way to her grief until they were well out of Williamsburg. Then she broke down, the tears coming in a flood. She doubled up, harsh, racking sobs tearing at her. Her poor mother! Mary Quint had known nothing but toil and misery, except for those few brief years of happiness with Robert McCambridge. And now, when Hannah finally had a chance to take her out of that hovel and away from Quint, give her some ease and comfort in the remaining years of her life, it was too late. She was dead.

Hannah continued to weep. But underneath the tears, underneath the grief, was a hard core of rage, a rage for vengeance. Her heart ached with it. Some day, some way, she would see that Silas Quint suffered. And Amos Stritch as well. In some way, no matter how illogical it was, Hannah connected Amos Stritch with the death of her mother.

She had never received anything but rough treatment at the hands of men. Except Malcolm Verner. And why should he be any different? Maybe, being gentry, he was more sly about it.

She determined to be very wary. Any demands he made on her would cost him!

Silas Quint stood staring after the carriage long after it had vanished from sight. Finally he started to turn back into the house. It was then that he noticed the neighbors, watching him in silence, a silence that seemed accusing to Quint. How much had they heard? And how much did they believe of what that stupid girl had said?

A quiver of fear shot through him. He bared his teeth in a snarl. "What are ye gaping at? Get back to your own places and keep your noses out of a neighbor's business!"

They began to disperse, and Quint made his way back into the house. His head pounded, and his heart was racing. He badly needed a tot of something. He'd been blind, staggering drunk when he'd made it to bed last night, and he couldn't remember if anything had been left around the house.

He searched frantically through the house, finally discovering a cider jug with an inch or so left in it. He drank greedily. It was sour as vinegar. His belly rebelled, and for a little he feared he would vomit everything back up.

Lurching into the bedroom, he fell across the bed. In a little while the cider worked on him, and he began to feel a wee bit better. At least he could think again.

He hadn't meant to kill the stupid woman, damnation, he hadn't! It *had* been an accident.

He had come home that night, after learning from Stritch that Hannah had run away, and had rousted Mary out of bed.

"That stupid girl of yours has run away!"

Mary had blinked the sleep out of her eyes, beginning to show alarm. "Hannah? Hannah has run away?"

"Hannah? Yes, Hannah!" he had mocked her. "That's the name of your brat, ain't it? She's put me in a bad position, running away. . . ."

"Put *you* in a bad position?" Mary had wailed. "Have you no concern for her? She could be taken by savages and killed!"

"Woman, you be addled! Ain't been no red hostiles around in years. Squire Stritch thought ye might know of what happened. The more I think on it, the more it strikes me he's right. Where is she? Where is the ungrateful wench?"

Mary was crying now, silent tears coursing down her face. "I know not where she is!"

"You're lying, woman! She's your issue. Ye were dead set agin indenturing her from the start. Now, where have ye hid her out?" He backhanded his wife across the face.

The blow sent her reeling, but she was between Quint and the door. She ran into the other room, crying. Quint was right on her heels.

Mary Quint's long hair was loose and flying out behind her. Quint made a leap and just managed to tangle his fingers in that hair. Jerked up short like a rambunctious horse on a short bridle, Mary stopped in her tracks. Quint swung her about to face him, fist drawn back. She screamed.

"Stop your caterwauling and tell me where the little bitch is, or I'll give ye something to blubber about! I'll beat ye within a breath of your life!"

"I don't know, Silas. I swear I don't know!"

"You're lying, woman. I know ye are."

It was then that he hit her, without even thinking about it, flush on the point of the chin with his fist. She flew across the room, falling. Her head struck the wall with a dull, thudding sound, and she slumped to the floor.

"Woman?"

She didn't move. After a moment he stepped over and prodded her with his toe. She still didn't move. He knelt, pulling her away from the wall. Her head lolled brokenly. He felt for a pulse and found none.

Panic hit him. He stood up and backed away from her. He turned to flee the room, the house, but stopped just outside the door. He knew he was doomed if he ran away and left her like that. A touch of reason returned to him, and his crafty mind began to pick at the problem as he went back inside.

After a little he took her by the feet and dragged her outside to the back stoop. He arranged her body on the steps, head on the ground.

Then he went running next door to rouse the neighbors.

There had been little problem with the authorities. Quint's story of Mary tripping on the steps on the way to the privy in the dark was accepted at face value. People died every day in this section of town from sickness or accident. Nobody really cared enough to question it. . . .

Now, on the bed, Quint found himself weeping weak tears. Not for his dead wife—she had far outlived her usefulness. Of late, she had found it difficult to find work in the houses of the gentry and had been bringing in little income. The only thing of value she had had was the bitch, Hannah, and she had nattered at him day and night since he had indentured the girl to Stritch.

No, the tears came from self-pity.

What was he going to do now for food and drink?

The weeks since Mary's death had been hard. Amos Stritch refused him credit now, and wouldn't even let him set foot inside the Cup and Horn. What was worse, Stritch had refused to explain why Hannah was still at Malvern. Now that Stritch knew where she was, Quint was sure the tavern owner had sold the girl to Malcolm Verner. If such was the case, Quint figured he should be given something. Stritch steadfastly refused to discuss it, roaring at him to get out.

So what am I to do? Quint thought.

He couldn't find work. People in Williamsburg no longer trusted him to do an honest day's work. They had little sympathy for him, not believing his claim that his back was in such terrible bad shape.

And Hannah . . . would anybody believe her accusations?

Quint shook his head and sat up, in better spirits suddenly. Who would take the word of an indentured girl who hadn't even been present when the accident had happened? Even if she *was* now residing on such a fine estate.

And that was the key. Abiding there, she must have access to *some* money. After her anger and grief had subsided, surely she would be more amenable to his pleas. Surely she wouldn't let her poor old stepfather starve!

He stretched out on the bed, his devious mind scheming ways of wheedling money from her.

Chapter Eight

"Down south a ways once lived a man they called High John the Conqueror," Bess said. "Now he was what you'd call a *real* man. He was a slave on one of them bad plantations. White folks around there so mean snakes wouldn't bite them. Only bit the niggers. White folks there so mean they'd kill a nigger just to bet on whether the body'd fall front or backwards. If'n he fell the wrong way, they'd go whup the dead nigger's old mammy. . . ."

As she unfolded her tale, Bess sneaked a look at Hannah. All the children on the plantation too young to work in the fields were gathered in a semi-circle before Bess, who sat on the steps of the cook-house. Hannah sat with her arm around Dickie's shoulders, as rapt in the story as any of the children.

Bess was pleased by this. It had been two weeks

since the girl had gone into Williamsburg and found that her mother was dead and buried, and no word to her about it. Since that day Hannah had moped about, bursting into tears at unexpected moments.

In Bess's opinion, Hannah's mother's death could be a blessing for the girl. Quite likely the secret of Hannah's black blood had died with her mother. Certainly that no-account white trash, Silas Quint didn't know, or he'd never have married the girl's mother in the first place.

Bess realized from the puzzled looks on the faces looking at her that she had fallen silent. She cleared her throat.

One of the smaller children asked, "Why'd they call him High John, Bess?"

"Like I told you, child, 'cause he was a real man. Some tales have it that he was a *big* man, biggest man around. Some folks who've seen him say he no bigger than a ordinary man. Whatever, he stand high. I recollect one story they tells about High John real well. Seems the master on the plantation where High John was a slave was a gambling man, and he was allus getting High John into some kind of a thing where he could bet on him. Now, John usually wins for ole massa, but he had his own way going about it. Well, one day ole massa was talking to 'nother white man and they started swapping brags about their slaves. Other white man says, 'I got a nigger on my place can whup any other nigger alive!' John's massa says, 'Can't whup my John. I'll bet fifty pounds on him against yours.'

"Well, the other white man, he agree, and they settled that the fight would be held Saturday afternoon, in town, one month from that day. Folks,

142

they come from miles and miles around, making a regular fair day of it. Even the governor of the state, his lady, and they daughter, they come. Lots of heavy bets was made.

"The other plantation massa brought his nigger in early, 'bout two hours afore the fight was to start. The way the story goes, that was one big nigger! He so big he had to stoop to keep from bumping his head on the stars at night. Half dozen white ladies swooned dead away at the very sight of him. When John's massa saw this nigger, he knew he had lost his bet. *Nobody* was gon' whup this nigger!

"Now John didn't show up until a few minutes afore the fight was to begin. And where this other nigger was all stripped down, ready to fight, John came dressed up like he was king of the Colonies. He wearing black boots, bright red pants, white ruffled shirt, and a fancy hat, and carrying a gold-headed cane. He came a-whistling and a-smiling, tipping his hat to everybody, taking his time.

"Then he did something took everybody's breath plumb away. He walked right up to where the governor sat with his wife and daughter, and hauled off and slapped that girl child right across the face. Once, twice he slapped her. Now all them white folks was plumb horrified and probably would have hung High John on the nearest tree hadn't been for something else happened just then.

"This other nigger, the one he s'posed to fight, saw what High John did and took off a-running. He ran right on out of the country and was never seen anywhere around again."

Bess paused, waiting for the expected question.

It came from one of the children. "Why'd the other nigger run, Bess?"

"Why, child," she said, beaming, "when he saw what happened, he knew that if High John was bad enough to slap a white child lady, High John was bad enough to whup him any day of the week. Now when the white folks finally figured out that High John had outsmarted everybody, 'specially that other nigger, their mad went away. They all had a big laugh. The ones betting on High John was 'specially happy. John's massa was happy 'cause he'd won his fifty pounds, and he gave the governor half his winnings, so the governor wouldn't be so mad about High John slapping his child thataway. Yessir, massa was happy with High John—so happy that he didn't beat up on him for several whole days!"

As the group of children broke up, Hannah came to Bess and leaned down to whisper in her ear, "You tell the biggest lies I ever heard, Bess!"

"Gracious, honey, I be truthful as the day is long," Bess said with a solemn face. "You hurt old Bess something sore, saying such a thing!"

Hannah laughed, shaking her head, and turned away. She headed toward the stable. Before she had taken a dozen steps, she heard that deep rumble of laughter coming from Bess. Hannah continued on, smiling to herself.

She was in better spirits today than she'd been at any time since learning of her mother's death. The grief was still there, but she had finally stored it away in a secret corner of her mind. The anger at Silas Quint still blazed unabated, however. She was convinced in her heart that Quint had killed her mother. She had no proof, though, and knowing that no one would believe her, Hannah had kept it to herself. Yet she had vowed to herself that someday she would find a way to get vengeance on that despicable man for murdering Mary Quint!

Hannah entered the gloom of the stable. During the past few weeks she had spent much of her free time in here, when Verner wasn't about and Black Star was stabled instead of in the pasture. She had fallen in love with the animal. The first time she had come in and approached his stall, the horse had shied away from her, eyes rolling wildly. Whinnying, he had reared up on his hind legs, front hooves drumming against the stall door. Hannah had drawn back, frightened.

A quiet voice behind her had said, "Mustn't get too close to the beast, Miss Hannah. He's a mean 'un."

Hannah had whirled to see John. As well as driving the coach and carriage, John was in charge of the stable and the riding stock.

"Such a beautiful animal!" she'd exclaimed.

John had nodded gravely. "That he is. But nobody dares ride him. Not even the master. Master Verner tried a few times, but not even he can handle him."

"Then why is he here? Who does he belong to?"

John had studied her thoughtfully for a moment, apparently weighing his words carefully. Finally he'd said, "The master bought him for the young master's birthday years ago. The young master was the only one to ever ride him. Since his death, nary a man has been able to stay on his back. So mean is he that I dare not let him graze in the pasture with the other horses. Already he's killed one. Master Verner has talked of shooting him, but I doubt he'll ever do that."

"I hope not. It would be such a pity!"

"Best to steer clear of him. One blow from those hooves of his could split your skull."

But Hannah couldn't stay away. She kept sneaking in to see Black Star when no one was around. Gradually the animal had become accustomed to her, and now Hannah could reach into the stall and stroke his sleek neck. Black Star would toss his head at first, but in a little while he would quiet down. She'd begun bringing sugar out to feed him. Now he neighed the moment he saw her enter the stable, and crowded against the stall door, neck arching out to nuzzle her hand for the sugar. Her growing affection for the horse helped a great deal to assuage her grief over her mother's death.

Hannah had never been on a horse in her life. Now she desperately wanted to learn to ride. But she had the good sense to realize that she couldn't learn on Black Star, even if Verner would allow it, which she knew was unlikely.

One evening at supper she said, "Malcolm, I'd like to learn to ride. The house is running fine now. I'd like to be able to ride out over the plantation."

Verner's gaze was gentle across the table. He had been very solicitous of her since she'd come home with the sad news about her mother, and let her have her way in almost everything.

"I think that might be good for you, Hannah." They had fallen easily into the habit of first names now. "Have you ever ridden before?"

Hannah shook her head.

"Then we'll have to start you off with a gentle

horse. I'll instruct John to pick one out and watch over you until you know what you're doing. There is one thing, however. There isn't a sidesaddle on the place. Martha never rode—she couldn't stand to be near a horse."

"Pooh!" Hannah said with a shrug of her shoulders. "I don't need a sidesaddle. I can learn with a regular saddle."

A glint of amusement came into his eyes. "A lady riding without the benefit of a sidesaddle is considered shocking behavior."

"You think the whole countryside isn't already shocked by my just being here?" she said calmly. "Besides, you told me once that you cared little for the opinion of your neighbors."

"I did say that, didn't I?" Verner pushed back his plate, and took out a cigar, rolling it between his fingers, regarding her gravely. "It shall be as you wish, my dear." The amusement struck his eyes again. "You will, I suspect, have your way in any event."

But Hannah found that she had to make a compromise. The next day John saddled a horse for her, a gentle, swaybacked old mare.

Hannah looked at the mare in disgust. "My heavens, this one looks like she'll break in two once I get on!"

"My mammy had a saying, Miss Hannah: A child must learn to crawl before he can stand upright."

He gave her a hand up. When Hannah was fully in the saddle, it became apparent that something would have to be done about her skirts and petticoats. They fell over the mare's haunches and piled up in bulky folds upon the front of the

147

saddle. The bulk and the movement of the fabric caused the poor mare to show the whites of her eyes, and her laid-back ears clearly stated her fears and her displeasure at having this peculiar creature upon her back.

It was also clear that any forward movement of the animal would cause the fabric to blow back, exposing Hannah's limbs. Plainly, she could not possibly ride about the plantation in this condition, even if the mare could be persuaded to carry her.

A rumble of laughter came from the stable door.

"Damn you, Bess, don't just stand there laughing! Think of something! . . . I know—I'll wear a pair of men's trousers!"

"Naw, honey." Bess shook her head, still laughing. "That'd be even worse. You'd have ever'body's eyeballs bulging out on stalks. Git your butt down from there and let me think on it."

With John's help Hannah climbed down. The usually sober John was smiling slightly. Hannah started to snap at him, then changed her mind. It *was* funny.

In the end Bess devised a way. She doubled the dress under and tucked a fold of it up between Hannah's legs, pinning it in back. Then she pinned the skirt around each leg. She stood back, surveying her handiwork. She laughed.

"Now what's so funny?"

"I seen a picture once in a book showing one of them harem ladies over across the water. You look just like one of them in that getup."

But when John helped Hannah aboard the mare again, it worked. Maybe she looked a little ridiculous, but Hannah didn't care.

Holding the reins, John led the mare outside and to the nearby pasture. Hannah found the saddle very uncomfortable: it was rock hard, and try as she would, she couldn't adjust to the uneven gait of the animal. It seemed that every time she came down the saddle was coming up. She knew she would have a sore rear end. But she was determined to stick with it.

"You'll get used to the gait, Miss Hannah. You've got to learn to put your weight on the stirrups, and sort of lift yourself so that you and the saddle don't come together so hard. You keep at it and riding will be as comfortable as sitting in an old rocking chair." John handed up the reins. "Not much guiding you can do about this old mare—she'll set her own gait. When you want her to turn right, haul hard on the right rein. You do the same, you want to turn left."

For that day, and the next, John stayed close to her as Hannah learned the rudiments of horseback riding. She learned quickly, although she was impatient with the slow gait of the old mare. She could only be urged into a trot with great effort. And it was true that Hannah had a sore bottom for the first few days.

But it kept her out of the house for a couple of hours a day, kept her thoughts away from her mother. When she was in the house, Hannah was apt to break into tears at unexpected moments.

On the third day, John said, "I think it's safe enough now to let you ride out on your own, Miss Hannah." He smiled. "At the pace she goes you wouldn't be hurt much if you did tumble off."

So Hannah began to explore the plantation. Several times she saw Malcolm Verner riding at a distance, but he was too busy to bother with her. It was harvest and curing time now. Hannah found it all absorbing, and often she climbed down off the mare at the edge of the fields to watch.

She learned that ripeness was indicated by the leaves taking on a yellowish tinge, the bottom leaves first, and that the leaves, thickening as they ripened, had a leathery feel. Verner and Henry, the overseer, were everywhere in the fields. Moving from row to row, they turned up the leaves, folding the undersides between their fingers. If ripe, the leaf would snap or crack and retain a crease. In some fields the ripening was uneven, and Verner or Henry would indicate to the hands which leaves to cut and which to leave a few more days. All worms and suckers were carefully removed.

Henry, like the other slaves, was bare to the waist, his mighty shoulders shining like oiled mahogany in the sun. However, he wore a wide-brimmed hat, the symbol of his authority.

The field hands used knives to cut the tobacco leaves from the stalk. Some sang as they worked, the knives flashing in the blazing sun.

The tobacco was allowed to wilt slightly, then hung on stalks, placed on scaffolds, and left outdoors for a few days in the sun. Then the yellowing tobacco leaves were hung on poles in the firing house.

This was a long, high log cabin, the logs tightly chinked. The leaves were hung close together and allowed to yellow for a few days more; then firing was begun. A fire was built close to the ground directly underneath the tobacco. For the first two or three days the fires were kept low; hotter fires were then kept going until the curing process was completed—this usually took a week. Hickory and oak wood were used.

Next the tobacco was allowed to "sweat" for a few days, until the leaves and stems were pliable and could be handled easily without breaking. Finally, the tobacco was packed into hogsheads, a thousand pounds per hogshead, later to be rolled down to the river landing. From there it was taken by ship either to Williamsburg or on to England.

Hannah was to learn that Malcolm Verner was the innovator of open-fire curing, far ahead of his time. He had started a couple of years before. Most of the planters were contemptuous of this new method and still used dry curing or sun curing. A few, however, realizing the superior grade of tobacco Verner was producing by open-fire curing, were beginning to consider using his radical process.

Tobacco was, in effect, money. It was used to pay taxes and ministers' salaries, and most of all to establish credit with merchants in Williamsburg for purchases to be made during the coming year. Only a planter's surplus was shipped to England for sale; the planter would eventually receive letters of credit in payment.

For days, the redolent odor of curing tobacco hung over Malvern. Hannah found it repugnant at first. It clung to her clothes even when she went inside the house. But she not only grew accustomed to it, she came to think of it as a not unpleasant odor.

On this day, Hannah knew that all the harvesting and most of the curing was done. Last night at supper Verner had spoken of a good crop this year.

And this very morning he had taken the coach into Williamsburg to make arrangements with various merchants for the sale of the tobacco. So both Verner and John were gone, having given no indication of when they would return.

This was the best opportunity she would have to ride Black Star. Hannah knew that no one else on the plantation would try to stop her. She was sick of riding the slow, plodding mare.

She had watched carefully during the past few days while John saddled the mare, and she was confident she could do it on her own. She pinned the dress the way Bess had showed her and then approached the stall. Black Star whinnied, head reaching out to nuzzle her hand.

"No sugar today, beauty," she whispered. "Today we're going to ride!"

She had no trouble slipping the bridle on. Then she opened the stall door and led the horse out, looping the reins over a stall post. She went to the saddle rack for a saddle. The saddle was heavier than she had anticipated, and since the animal stood almost as tall as her head, it took much effort to hoist the saddle onto his back. Fortunately, Black Star stood quietly, almost as though he sensed what was coming and welcomed it. While she went about cinching the saddle tightly under his belly, he pawed the ground with one hoof, snorting softly.

Finally it was done. Hannah was perspiring freely. She pushed the damp hair out of her eyes, resting for a moment. Now she had another problem. Always before John had been there to give her a leg up. She took a deep breath, reached up to grasp the saddle, and tried to haul herself up.

She failed, falling against the horse. Black Star shied away, neighing.

"It's all right, beauty," she murmured, stroking his neck. "It's all right."

Along one wall of the stable stood a low bench, small enough for Hannah to move easily. She pulled it over to Black Star's left side. Standing on the bench, she was able to lift herself into the saddle. She made a sound of satisfaction and fitted her feet into the stirrups. With her knees Hannah urged the horse over to the stall post, and untied the reins.

Black Star didn't need any urging. Stepping high, almost dancing, he headed for the stable door. Then they were outside. Hannah held back on the reins, looking in both directions. There was no one about.

Hannah drew a deep breath, loosening the reins, and drummed her heels lightly on the animal's flanks.

"Now go! Go, beauty!"

Black Star sprang forward; he went into a full gallop within a few feet. He went like the wind. The exhilaration Hannah felt was like nothing she had ever experienced. The horse's hooves drummed like thunder. Hannah's hair streamed back in the wind created by their passage. But even with Black Star's size and at the speed they were going, Hannah found his gait far more comfortable than the mare's had ever been.

Before Hannah realized it, they were approaching the split rail fence surrounding the pasture. She started to pull back on the reins. But she was too late. Black Star gathered himself and cleared the fence in a mighty leap, without once breaking stride. The pasture was gentle, rolling land, mostly open with the exception of a few massive, spreading oaks, and these Black Star easily avoided. Other horses were in the meadow, all under the shade of the oaks, drowsing in the midday heat.

Hannah gave Black Star free rein, and he ran on. She let him run until his pace began to slacken, flecks of foam flying back into her face.

"All right, beauty, enough for now." Gingerly, she pulled back on the reins. "Whoa, boy, whoa!"

Black Star came to an easy, floating stop. His sides heaved like a great bellows. But Hannah knew that he wasn't anywhere near exhausted; he just needed to catch his breath and get a second wind.

She caressed his neck, slick as grease with sweat. "Ah, you are a beauty! Like some great, beautiful machine!"

Hannah was unhappy about one thing. She felt uncomfortable, restricted, in the tucked-up, pinned dress. She wanted to ride free and loose. The devil take anyone who might see her limbs!

It would be easier to unpin the dress on the ground, she realized. She gauged the long distance down dubiously, remembering how much trouble she'd had mounting Black Star in the stable.

Hannah stood up in the stirrups and found it easy enough to undo the part of the dress that ran up between her thighs and was pinned in the back. Then she leaned down to unpin the part of the garment wrapped around her right leg. She knew at once that this was going to be more difficult. Clinging to the saddle with one hand, she managed to remove one pin. Then her grasp on the saddle slipped. Frantically she tried to pull herself back up into the saddle. In so doing, she jabbed the pin deep into Black Star's hide.

The animal reared, snorting, then bolted. Hannah desperately tried to hold on, but her grip continued to slip. And then she was falling. She could see the ground flying fast beneath her. The dress caught on something for just an instant. Then she heard a ripping sound, and the ground came up to meet her.

She struck head first. The pain was deep and red before a merciful blackness took its place.

Malcolm Verner concluded his business in Williamsburg and returned to Malvern sooner than he had anticipated. He was content as John drew the coach to a stop in the driveway. His business transactions had been satisfactory. There would be ample credit with the Williamsburg merchants for the coming year, and a goodly surplus to ship to England for a letter of credit in return. It had been his most profitable year since he had been in Virginia. He felt a deep sadness that there was no one to share the good news with—no family, no Michael.

Getting out of the coach, he stood before the house for a little, chewing on a cigar, while John drove on toward the stable. He watched John unhitch the team and lead them into the stable.

Then he remembered Hannah with a rush of pleasure. Of late, she had become almost family to him. She seemed to show genuine interest when he discussed the affairs of the plantation with her. She would be most happy to share his good news, he was sure.

He started to turn away and was stopped in his tracks by a shout from the stable. He turned to see John running toward him.

"Black Star! He's gone!"

Verner frowned. "Gone? What do you mean, gone? Did he break out?"

"No, sir, his stall door is open."

"You mean someone stole him?"

"No, sir. I think . . ." John's gaze dropped away.

"You think what, man?" Verner urged. "What is it?"

Still without looking at him, John said in a low voice, "Miss Hannah . . . she's been fooling around with that animal."

"And you let her?" Verner seized the man's arm and started to shake him, then desisted. "No, I don't blame you. I should know. That damn willful female, when she gets something into her head . . . Do you think she's taken him out?"

John looked at him, nodding.

Verner swore. "She could be killed! Saddle my horse, John, and be quick about it!"

Verner didn't take time to go inside to change into riding clothes and boots. Instead, he followed John into the stable just as he was.

A few minutes later he rode out of the stable at a full gallop. Now that his anger had cooled a little, he was concerned for her. Damned woman could be killed riding that unruly beast! He recalled his thoughts of a few minutes ago, and he realized what a change Hannah had wrought at Malvern in the brief time she had been there. For the first time in a long while, Malvern was a happy house, and he was grudgingly willing to credit her with that.

156

He urged his mount on. The most likely place, at least a place to start looking, would be the pasture where the horses were turned out to graze.

Leaping off to open the gate, he led his horse through, closed the gate, then mounted up again, drumming his heels on the horse's flanks. Heart pumping, Verner let his gaze flick back and forth. Halfway across the pasture he saw Black Star, saddled, reins trailing, grazing unconcernedly.

But where was Hannah?

Then he saw a bit of bright color on the ground. He veered his horse toward it. Drawing near, he saw that it was indeed Hannah—lying crumpled and still.

Heart racing fast now, Verner reined in his horse and slid off. It crashed into his consciousness that he really cared for this woman very much. She was still half a child, yet . . . If she were dead, his life would truly be at an end, for not only had she brought life and laughter back to Malvern, she had brought *him* back to life as well.

Running toward her, he breathed a silent prayer. *Dear Lord, don't let her be dead!*

He dropped to one knee beside her crumpled form. She was lying in a somewhat wanton sprawl, the dress and petticoats rucked up around her waist. Her legs were long and lovely—breathtakingly lovely.

He averted his gaze and reached a tentative hand out to her. "Hannah? Dearest Hannah!"

At the sound of his voice she stirred. She half sat up, eyes fluttering open. "Malcolm?" She looked around dazedly, awareness slowly returning to her eyes. "Black Star?" Then she saw the horse grazing nearby, and her face lit up.

In sitting up, the upper part of her dress fell away, revealing a full breast. Somehow, in falling from the horse, that ridiculous getup he'd seen her riding in during the past two weeks had been almost torn from her body. Now Verner knew not where to look. To his shame, he felt his manhood stirring. He blurted, "Hannah, are you all right?"

"Why, I think so. I struck my head on something," she said slowly. She explored the back of her skull, and winced slightly.

Suddenly angry, he snapped, "You could have been killed! Hell and damnation, woman! Willfulness is one thing, but riding Black Star was sheer stupidity!"

"It wasn't Black Star's fault," she said quickly. "I was trying to unpin this damnable dress and I stuck a pin in his side by accident."

"Nevertheless, I forbid you to ride him again."

Verner got to his feet, then leaned back down to help her up.

"Now, Malcolm, I was doing fine. Black Star and I understand each other. He would never throw me on purpose."

"You still don't understand. You could have been killed!"

She smiled up into his eyes. "Would you have cared, Malcolm?"

"Of course I would have cared!"

"Would you?" she murmured. She swayed suddenly, as though swooning, and he caught her in his arms.

"Hannah?"

"I'm all right, just a little dizzy."

In his arms she tilted her head back. With a smothered groan he tightened his embrace, and then he was kissing her. He smelled not unpleasantly of sweat, tobacco, and a strong male odor. His kiss was gentle at first; then he became more ardent, his mouth bruising hers. Despite herself, she felt an answering warmth in her lower belly.

Hannah could feel the hardness of his manhood against her. Without thinking, she let herself go soft and pliable in his arms. Verner became more agitated, groaning deep in his throat.

He tore his mouth away, muttering, "I want you, Hannah." He darted a glance around. They were near a large oak. Arms still around Hannah, he began to urge her toward the shade of the tree. "No one will see us here. I need you, dearest Hannah."

It would have been so easy, so easy to let him lead her beneath that tree. So easy to lie beside him. Malcolm was a kind man. Perhaps it would be different with him; perhaps he could show her how love between a man and a woman should be. But then the sharp, ugly picture of Amos Stritch came into her mind, and she recalled her determination to be mistress of her own fate.

She freed herself from Verner's arms and stood back, brushing at herself. She smiled sweetly. "I'm sure you do, sir. And you may have me. But you have to wed me first."

"Wed you!" He glared, blinking incredulously. "Have you taken leave of your senses?" His face was red, and anger showed in his eyes. "A tavern wench, a servant girl, becoming mistress of Malvern? A child, a child of sixteen?"

"Seventeen I'll be on my next birthday, not yet a month."

He brushed her words aside. "Still a child. And

that does not erase what you have been! A tavern whore, you told me so yourself!"

" 'Twas not by choice, you well know that." Her smile did not waver. "At your age, do you expect a virgin, Malcolm Verner? Besides ..." Her smile widened. "You want a son. You think I do not know this? Would you want your son a bastard?"

"Only a tumble I had in mind, and here you have me wedded and siring a son!"

"Isn't that what you want, Malcolm? Search your heart for the answer. Anyway ..." She was serene. "The wedding bed is the only way you shall ever have me."

He eyed her in speculation, the bulge in his trousers still noticeable. "I could take you by force and no one would think harshly of me for it. I am master of Malvern and of every living creature on the plantation!"

"You could, though it might not be so easy. But that is not your way, Malcolm Verner. To your credit, you are a true gentleman."

He brooded. "You believe you know me that well?"

"I'm beginning to."

"Perhaps you think so, but I would not depend overmuch on it, my dear." He grew distant, formal.

For a moment Hannah was afraid she had gone too far, at least broached her bold proposal too soon. *No*, she told herself fiercely; *I'm right, I know I am! The other way, I would have to settle for becoming his mistress, and he would soon grow tired of me and I would indeed end up a tavern whore.*

Verner gestured. "You may ride back with me. I'll send John to fetch Black Star."

160

"No," she said stoutly. "I'm safe on Black Star. It was my fault, not his. I will ride him back."

His head swung around. His eyes were cold, without feeling. "Suit yourself, madam. But understand this ... I disclaim all responsibility if the beast throws you again."

"He won't."

He nodded shortly and turned away to stride to his horse and mount up. Hannah watched him ride away. She was still unsure whether she had done the right thing. She shrugged. Well, it was done now, for good or bad. Repinning her torn garments as best she could, Hannah approached Black Star.

Black Star raised his head. She stroked his neck, then gathered up the trailing reins. With the help of a large rock nearby, she mounted him. The animal turned at the tug of rein, and they went at a sedate pace back to Malvern.

For two days Malcolm Verner locked himself in his study, refusing to talk to anyone, eating little of the food sent in to him, demanding a bottle of brandy every so often. When one of the servant girls timidly approached to knock on the door, he would roar savagely at her.

The house was quiet, almost funeral quiet, the house servants speaking in whispers.

Even Bess stayed in her kitchen. Hannah told her what had happened.

Frowning, Bess shook her head. "I hope you knows what you're at, child. Master Verner be a gentleman, true, but he got a powerful temper in him, near as bad as that old devil Stritch."

Hannah didn't go near Verner. She spent most

of the daylight hours riding Black Star to the far reaches of the plantation. She rode well now, and there were no more falls.

On the afternoon of the third day, as she walked into the house after her ride, the study door crashed open before she could mount the stairs, and Malcolm Verner strode out.

"Hannah?"

She halted, waiting for him. He hadn't shaved for two days, and he looked worn and haggard. He was unsteady on his feet.

As he stopped before her, his glance dropped to the floor. "I saw you ride up." He gestured. "You should wear riding boots. Those flimsy shoes you wear are dangerous on a horse."

"I have none."

"Then have a pair made in town, for the love of God!" He looked up now, and suddenly he seemed at peace. "I have been thinking long and hard, Hannah. You shall have your wish, my dear. I will wed you."

Elation swept through Hannah. She had won! Careful to let none of her jubilation show, she reached out and touched his bristly cheek. "You'll not be sorry, sir. I promise. I will make you a good wife."

The old wry humor touched his mouth. "The question is, what kind of a husband will I make to you?"

"A fine one, I am sure." Then she took a step back, speaking in a stronger voice. "When? When will the wedding be?"

of the daylight hours riding Black Star to the far reaches of the plantation. She rode well now, and

Chapter Nine

The wedding date was set for one month away, a week past Hannah's seventeenth birthday—a time when the tobacco sales would be concluded.

Hannah had somehow envisioned a simple, almost private ceremony, thinking Malcolm would probably be ashamed of her.

This, she discovered to her great delight, was not to be the way of it at all.

"We Virginians," Verner said with his wry smile, "seize upon any excuse to make a grand occasion of any get-together. And what better excuse than a wedding? And . . ." He kissed her on the cheek. "I wish the whole countryside to know how proud I am, and will always be, of my beautiful bride."

He was a kind man, a man she could respect,

and Hannah grew more fond of him every day. Sometimes she experienced a fleeting guilt at how she had led him into his proposal of marriage, but the guilt never lasted long. She was too happy.

The days were busy for Hannah. There was never enough time.

At first she was appalled to learn that the wedding festivities would last two, perhaps three, days, and that every planter along the James River was being invited, along with many important personages from Williamsburg.

"Many guests will be arriving from far plantations, Hannah, some traveling for days," Verner explained. "We can't expect them to come all that distance for just half a day's festivities." He smiled, face lighting up. "This will be a great occasion, my dear. A great ball, musicians playing, dancing, gentlemen at cards. The cookhouse will be busy for days beforehand—food for many people must be prepared. I will have to order much liquor brought in."

All this Hannah soon came to find exciting. She was to be mistress of a great, three-day ball! Malvern would be alive, gay with talk and music and dancing.

But then dismay filled her on another account. Again she went to Verner. "Malcolm, I need someone to help me. I knowing nothing of dressing and such. I need dresses of my own."

He cocked his head. "You look fine, my dear."

"You! You know nothing of a lady's clothing! I could be wearing a sack for all the notice you'd take!"

"True. I do know little of such things." He was grave now. "And, of course, you will need garments of your own, not Martha's cast-offs. I should have thought of this. We will ride into Williamsburg this very day and you may be fitted for new dresses."

"But there is more," she insisted. "I don't know how to dance, and I need someone to teach me how to conduct myself. I'd rather not go into Williamsburg just yet, Malcolm. Not until I ... can't you have someone come out here who can do these things? I would be ashamed to go alone into the stores. The shopkeepers will think me an ignorant country girl!"

"My dear, you're asking me to go and fetch a regiment of females to Malvern! The house shall be overrun with them." But he was still smiling. He waved his hand. "I will take the coach into the village and see what I can do."

Hannah was quivering with anticipation all afternoon, running to the door to look up the driveway toward the road every few minutes. And yet, when finally she saw the coach approaching, her courage deserted her, and she fled upstairs. She hovered just out of sight of the entryway, listening intently. She heard the front door open, and she listened for female voices. How could she face a group of women who had knowledge of how a lady should look and act? What if they determined her a hopeless case?

Then she heard Malcolm's voice. "Hannah? Where are you?"

Timidly she approached the top of the stairs. "Up here, Malcolm."

"Come down here, my dear. I want you to meet someone."

Hannah stared. Instead of a group of women, there was only one person with Malcolm—a man.

And such a man!

She had never seen a gentleman so splendidly turned out. Coming slowly down the staircase, she stared at him openly. A rather small, slender man, he wore a camlet coat, the sleeves ending in lace ruffles, and a waistcoat of blue, adorned with patterns elaborately Turkey-worked. His breeches were made of expensive plush and were of an olive color. His stockings were of blue-dyed silk, and his highly polished red shoes were adorned with elaborate silver buckles. About his neck he wore a cloth of finest holland, and he carried in his right hand a lace handkerchief.

A tricornered beaver hat was on his head, and he doffed it, making a knee as Hannah reached the bottom of the stairs, revealing a queue wig, pissburnt in color, with a single queue bound in a bow made of a ribbon of bright blue.

A veritable peacock of a man! Hannah had heard of dandies, of fops, but this was the first one she had ever seen.

"Hannah, my dear," Verner said, "I'd like to introduce you to André Leclaire. Monsieur Leclaire, my bride-to-be, Hannah McCambridge."

"A great pleasure, milady," he said, again making a knee. The hand holding the handkerchief took hers and raised it to his lips.

For heaven's sake, Hannah thought; *it's scented!* A man carrying a scented handkerchief!

She could only stare, speechless, as he dropped her hand and stepped back. His face was heartshaped, with a rather large nose and a sensual mouth so red she had to wonder if it was painted.

His eyes were a clear blue, and managed to appear cynical, worldly-wise, and merry at the same time. His age was indeterminate. It seemed to Hannah that he must have a puckish sense of humor. His voice was a languid drawl, striking her as being affected.

"Monsieur Leclaire is a man of many parts, my dear." There was a light amusement in Malcolm's eyes that puzzled Hannah. "He is a dancing master, a language teacher, and, of late, in Williamsburg, the proprietor of Leclaire's Wig Shoppe."

André Leclaire spread his hands. "I am, alas, not much of a businessman, milady."

"And in his native country, France, Monsieur Leclaire was a couturier."

Hannah frowned. "A court-your—what?"

"A designer of ladies' garments, milady," André said smoothly. He gestured with his graceful hands, drawing a female figure in the air.

"I thought dressmakers were women."

"Here, in your Colonies, yes. They look with horror on a man performing such work." He smiled sadly. "But in my country it is different."

"I think, Hannah," Verner said, "that Monsieur Leclaire will be able to perform the duties you require of him, and ably." He nodded to André. "And now perhaps you would like to be shown to your room to freshen up?"

"By your leave, sir." André ruefully examined his hands. "The grime of travel collects quickly in your Virginia."

Verner called for Jenny, and gave her instructions to show André to a room upstairs and to fetch hot water for a bath. André made a knee, kissed Hannah's hand again, and followed Jenny upstairs.

Hannah had been suppressing her amusement. Now, as André passed out of hearing, she laughed. "He got dirty just coming from Williamsburg?"

"I fear our Monsieur Leclaire is somewhat fastidious, my dear," Verner said drily.

"But are you sure he can do all those things you say?"

"Oh, yes. André is a man of many talents, except, as he said, for business. As you know, shops carry their customers from harvest time to harvest time on their books, currency being so scarce. Poor André could not survive a full year. He was forced to close his wig shop some months back. Since then he has been eking out a poor living teaching and at whatever other tasks he could get people to pay him to perform."

"But his clothes! Malcolm, they must have cost a great deal!"

"If you should look closely, you'd see they have been mended carefully and repeatedly."

"But a man like that, used to the wonders of Paris, why should he leave, to come here, to Virginia? He seems so . . . so out of place."

"I suspect he fled here from France," Verner said with a wry smile. "A man of his, uh, nature, would find it easy to get into difficulty."

"But you *must* remove your clothing, dearest Hannah. Every stitch," André said, his hands in constant motion. "How else can I take your measurements? We must learn your measurements so that I can order the dress goods required for your gowns. If you were to visit a dressmaking

168

shop in Williamsburg, you would not be so reluctant to disrobe, I am sure."

Hannah felt herself flushing. "But you're a man, André!"

"Ah, yes. A man." He sighed. "That is perhaps unfortunate, but that is the way it is. Now, do we proceed?"

"Oh, very well then! If you insist!"

Quickly Hannah undressed until she stood in her skin before him; strangely, she did not feel the embarrassment she had expected.

Chin propped on his hand, André went around her several times, humming under his breath. "A well-formed body, dear lady. You should be proud. As should be Monsieur Verner."

Hannah snapped, "He hasn't seen me without covering. We're not yet wed!"

"Indeed?" André's eyebrows arched. "Most unusual, I must say. Though I suppose it would be considered admirable here. But in my country . . ." He gave a Gallic shrug, and made a clicking sound with his tongue against the roof of his mouth. "Such a waste! Such a pity!"

"What's a pity?" she demanded.

"For you to wed some plantation owner and destroy that lovely body with child-bearing and hard work. In my country, you could have been a great courtesan."

Curiosity prompted Hannah to ask, "What's a courtesan?"

"Why, a whore, dear lady. Oh . . ." He held up his hands. "One of class, to be sure. Pampered and spoiled and well provided for."

Hannah gasped. "What a thing to say!"

"Is it, dear lady? In my country, any lady would

169

consider it a compliment. But no matter." He shrugged negligently. "That is not why we are here, is it?"

He circled her again. "First, of course, the foundation ... we start with corset and stays. ..."

"No!" Hannah stamped her bare foot. "I will not wear one of those damned torture contraptions!"

"What is this?" He stared at her in astonishment. "You refuse to wear what every woman in Virginia considers essential, the very foundation on which one is supposed to construct a lady of the gentry?"

"I do. They pinch your ribs until you can't breathe, and in them you sweat like a horse. I will *not* wear one!"

André pursed his lips. "*Mon Dieu*! A woman of spirit and independent thought." He clapped his hands together. "I applaud you. To find, in this uncivilized country, a woman with spirit enough to defy convention! So ..." Again the Gallic shrug. "We will forget about the foundation garments and build from what nature endowed you with, dear lady."

He began to take measurements, touching her naked body here and there. She experienced no embarrassment at his seeing her naked, not even at his touching her. He went about it in such an impersonal manner, as though she were no more flesh and blood than a dress form. As André measured, she puzzled over this phenomenon.

Slowly, the truth dawned on her. Hannah had heard snatches of whispered gossip about men who enjoyed carnal love with other men; men who had no sexual interest in women at all. She had never

170

met one, and hadn't even been sure they existed. She supposed she should feel revulsion, yet she did not. She was beginning to like André. He represented a sophistication she had never before encountered, and he had a sharp wit that amused her.

Suddenly another thought occurred to her. This, then, was the reason for the strange look of amusement she had detected in Malcolm. He had known. Was that why he would trust her in the hands of this man? If André had been some other man, would he have been jealous? The idea of Malcolm being jealous intrigued and delighted her, bringing to her a flood of warm pleasure.

Now André was draping her with some old material he had found in Mrs. Verner's trunk. "Only to make a pattern, you understand. We will purchase new material and make it to fit the pattern." He stuck pins in the material here and there. All at once he said angrily, "*Merde!*" and stepped back, frowning down at his finger where a spot of blood had appeared.

Hannah said, " '*Merde*'? What does that mean?"

Without looking up, André said, "In your language, it means 'shit.' "

For a moment Hannah was shocked. Then she threw back her head and laughed heartily.

Fastidiously André took a handkerchief from his pocket and scrubbed at the blood. Then he looked at her, smiling. "Did I shock you? My apologies, dear lady. I sometimes speak before I think."

"I'm not shocked," Hannah said, still laughing. "I've heard the word before. I was raised on a farm."

André continued with his pinning and measuring.

171

"André . . . could you design a pair of riding breeches for me?"

"Riding breeches?" Now it was his turn to look shocked. "Even in my country ladies do not ride in men's breeches!"

"I don't care!" Hannah tossed her head. "I love to ride, and it's not easy in a dress."

"There are such things as ladies' sidesaddles."

"That's not for me, either. That would take all the joy out of it."

André shook his head, making that clicking sound again. "You do continue to astonish me. I believe I am going to enjoy . . ."

There was a knock on the door.

Hannah said, "Yes? Who is it?"

"Dickie, m'lady."

"Just a minute." Hannah made sure that she was fully covered by the draped material, then said, "Come in, Dickie."

The door opened, and Dickie came in, crossing over to them. "Miss Hannah, Bess says 'tis time to consider cooking supper, and she wants to talk to you about what to be serving."

Hannah shot a glance through the open window. The afternoon shadows were lengthening; she hadn't realized it was so late.

"Damnation! Bess doesn't need my help to . . ." She broke off suddenly. Had Bess been wondering what was happening up here and sent Dickie up to disrupt whatever *might* be going on? She smothered an impulse to laugh. Wait until she told Bess about André!

She stole a glance at André and saw that he was staring at Dickie intently.

172

"Dickie, you go back and tell Bess that she doesn't need me to . . ."

But Dickie wasn't listening. He was staring at André in awe, as though half blinded by the glitter of his finery.

André stepped toward the boy. "Dickie, is it?" He placed a hand on Dickie's head. In a dreaming voice, he said, "Such a handsome lad. A veritable Adonis he could be. . . ."

"Dickie!" Hannah said sharply. "Leave us! I told you what to do!"

"Yes, Miss Hannah." Dickie came to with a start. "Right away, m'lady." He darted out.

As the door closed behind him, Hannah wheeled on André in a fury. "You will not touch Dickie!" she said coldly.

He looked at her, his features shadowed with melancholy. "So you know, do you? Usually I am fortunate. Not many people in this backward country grasp the truth about me."

"Never mind that." She gestured. "Just leave Dickie alone! He's an innocent lad."

"You wound me deeply, madam." There was a sadness in him now, a sadness that ran deep, she sensed. Hannah was to learn that André Leclaire could feign a gamut of emotions during a few minutes of conversation. Later, she came to believe that he would have made a great actor. But in that moment she knew that she was seeing into the true soul of André Leclaire.

He was saying, "Do you think me so unmannered that I would so abuse your, and Monsieur Verner's, hospitality?" He spread his hands, face still melancholy. "I suppose you now wish me to leave?"

173

"I did not say that." Hannah turned her back. "Shouldn't we get back to work? The time grows short."

For a moment there was no sound, no movement, from André. When he spoke again, the old mocking note was in his voice. "Not only beauty and intelligence, but an understanding heart as well. A rare combination, dear lady."

Hannah felt a flush of pleasure at his compliment, but she would not tell him so.

Now he was busy again, pinning, measuring, talking. He talked more than any man she had ever known. He had been at Malvern four days now, and of course he dined with Hannah and Verner in the evenings. He kept them both laughing at his wit and conversation, hands never still, except when occupied with food. His wit flashed like light winking off a rapier blade.

And Hannah especially was fascinated by his stories of France, of the intrigue that went on in high social circles in that country, and in the court of the king. It appeared that André Leclaire had once moved in the company of the great. Either that, or he was a greater inventor of tales than Bess.

"A woman, especially a married woman, is little more than a chattel, dear lady, with scarcely more rights than the slaves Monsieur Verner owns," André was saying now as he worked. "It is an amazement to me that more do not show the spirit you seem to possess. I am reminded of a rather amusing incident in Williamsburg this month past. I was attending a wedding. During the ceremony, when the clergyman reached the first phrase stating that a spouse should obey her husband in all

174

things, the bride interrupted, saying, 'Not obey.' The clergyman continued as though the poor woman had not spoken. Twice more during the ceremony the clergyman came to the same phrase, and each time she responded in the same fashion: 'Not obey.' In all instances, she was ignored. Do you know that under English law, which is applicable here also, the wife can only inherit a third of her husband's estate? Do you also not know that a husband has the legal right to beat his spouse if she does not not accede to his wishes in all matters?"

"Malcolm wouldn't do that to me."

"And why might that be?"

"Because he loves me!"

"Ah, love!" André got up from bended knees. "And do you love him?"

"I . . ." Hannah hesitated. "I have great affection for him."

"Affection is what one feels for a friend, dear lady."

Hannah whirled on him. "How else could I get all this without marrying someone like Malcolm Verner?" She flung her hands wide. "You speak of whores, these courtesans, in your country . . . do you know what a whore is here? A whore works in a tavern. And that is what I did before Malcolm bought me from Amos Stritch! What else could I have ever expected to be? I have little education, only what my father taught me. If perchance I had ever had an opportunity to wed, it could only have been to some drunken lout who would certainly have beat me and worked me to death. The way my poor mother was."

"Ah, forgive me, dear Hannah. I did not know

175

of this," André said with a sober face. And then his eyes began to dance in that delightfully wicked way he had. "Now I see. Now I understand."

"Do you indeed?"

"Ah, yes. And my congratulations, madam." He seized her hand and bowed over it. "You are a lady after my own heart."

Hannah, passing the open door to the music room, heard the sounds of music swelling from the virginal. She went in.

André was at the virginal, supple fingers moving over the keys with consummate artistry. It was music strange to her. It was light and airy, yet with a powerful cadence. She listened, rapt, until he had finished.

Approaching the virginal, she said, "What music is that?"

He glanced up at her. "It is a French dance suite. It was the latest thing in Paris when I left."

"It is strange to me. But you play very well."

"*Naturellement.*" He gave that shrug. "André is also a musician."

"Do you know this one?" Hannah searched back in dim memory. "It's a song my father used to sing to me." She sang a verse of it.

André listened intently, head cocked, humming under his breath. "Again, please."

> "My love is like the vi-o-let
> That bloometh in a hidden place,
> And only I know where she lies,
> And only I may see her face.
> The bold rose in the garden grows,

And many men may find her there,
But I alone my true love know,
My vi-o-let, so sweet and fair."

As Hannah sang the verse again, André began to play, softly, but the melody was as she remembered. She sang the verse yet again, with more assurance this time.

When she was done, he applauded lightly. "You have a good voice, dear lady. Untrained, but true and sweet and clear. With proper training . . ."

"Will you teach me?" she said eagerly. "And teach me to play, too?"

"If you like." His gaze was intent. "But it will take time, more time than we have before your wedding."

"But can't you stay on, after the wedding? There are so many things I want you to teach me. To sing, to play—and learning, how to speak and write better. How to be a real lady!"

He said, "You were born a lady, my dear, dear Hannah."

As always, she felt her color rising under his unexpected compliments. She rushed on, "Malcolm said you were a teacher. There are so many things I need to learn!"

"I would be most happy to stay. But what will your husband-to-be say to that?"

Hannah tossed her head. "He will agree, if I ask."

André smiled. "Yes, I should imagine he would."

She took his hand and tugged. "Come on, into the ballroom. I have to learn to dance before the wedding ball!"

André stood up. "Is there anyone else here who can play music?"

"None that I know of."

"It would be far easier to teach you dancing with musical accompaniment...." The shrug again. "But André will manage."

"Don't worry." She smiled. "*I* won't need music. I'll dance to the music in my head."

He stopped and stared at her in astonishment. "In your head?"

"Of course," she said simply. "I hear music in my head when I dance."

"*Mon Dieu!*" André slapped his forehead. "Not only does the lady possess fire and spirit and beauty, but she's a little mad as well." He tapped the side of his head with one finger.

He made a mocking half bow, and gestured. "After you, madam."

PART TWO

Hannah Verner

Chapter Ten

A few guests began to arrive the day before the wedding—by horse, by cart, by coach, and some even on foot.

No one had come in to awaken Hannah on this morning of the day before she was to be wed, and she awoke with a start to the sound of a fiddle playing, and many voices. She flew to the window and peeked out. There, on the back lawn, several people were gathered around a man sawing away at a fiddle. A few couples were dancing on the lawn.

There was a knock on the door as she gaped at this display.

"Hannah? My dear, may I come in?" It was Malcolm's voice.

"Just a minute!"

Hannah quickly picked up her dressing gown from the foot of the bed and put it on. "You can come in now."

Malcolm Verner entered carrying a small, ornately carved chest in his hands.

Hannah motioned outside. "Who are all those people?"

"Why, our guests, Hannah." He moved to the window with her. "Early arrivals. A great many more will be here before nightfall, you may be sure."

He faced her. "Hannah ... I have something here I wish to give you." He hefted the tiny chest. "You may consider it your wedding gift, if you like. I bought them for Martha." A touch of sorrow shadowed his face. "She never got a chance to wear most of them. And she never cared overmuch for jewelry, anyway."

He raised the lid of the little chest, and Hannah gasped, gazing in open-mouthed awe at the sparkling display of jewels.

She knew little of jewelry and was reluctant to show her ignorance by asking, but in time she was to learn the names of the items in the jewel casket. It contained two pearl necklaces, one diamond necklace, and one amber necklace. There were both gold and silver earrings, a half dozen pairs of each, and rings in abundance—plain gold rings; one gold ring set with a large ruby, glittering like fire; another ring set with three stones, blue and green and yellow respectively; and another with eight diamonds of varying sizes. In addition, the casket contained a number of gold and silver bodkins for holding together and decorating the hair.

But even in that moment, knowing little of jewelry, Hannah realized that the casket of gems represented a great deal of money. "Dear God, Malcolm, all this must have cost a fortune!"

"That's not important." He made a negligent gesture. "It's all yours. Select from it what you wish to be married in tomorrow. And the rest is yours, to do with as you please."

A surge of affection seized her. She rushed forward and embraced him. "You are a dear, sweet man, Malcolm! Thank you, thank you!"

"It's only a small measure of what I realize you have come to mean to me, my dearest Hannah. I love you. I thought . . ." He cleared his throat. "I thought I would never come to love a woman again."

She kissed him, clinging to him with a passion she had not shown before. Verner's arms went around her, and his kiss became urgent, demanding. She felt him begin to harden against her, and Hannah abandoned herself to his fierce embrace. In a small corner of her mind she knew that she would, if he expressed such a desire, let him take her then and there.

Then, suddenly, he broke away with an embarrassed laugh. "I have heard that it is bad fortune for a man to kiss his betrothed just before the wedding." Formal now, he made a knee. "By your leave, madam."

He quickly left the room.

Hannah, her passions still stirred, stood staring after him for a moment. Then she spun around to the bed where the jewel casket reposed. With a child's delight, she ran her fingers deep into the pile of glittering gems and let them trickle through like large droplets of shining water.

Oh, how far, how very far she had come within a space of weeks! It all far exceeded her most cherished dreams.

Hannah got dressed and went downstairs. There were guests already circulating through the house. Gentlemen were at cards in the ballroom, and ladies were gathered in small groups, talking, gaily colored fans as active as their busy mouths. All wore stays and hoops, and elaborate wigs. Hannah had had another disagreement with André—she had refused to wear a wig.

"Damn it, André, with that thing piled high on my head—if I so much as nodded it would probably fall off!"

"But dear lady, you must wear a wig at balls and weddings! I can understand and sympathize about your not wearing stays and hoops, but a peruke is of a necessity!"

"Pooh! You just say that because you're a perukemaker and vain about the wigs you make. I will not wear a corset and stays, and will *not* wear a wig! My own hair is good enough, and that's the end of it!"

None of the ladies gave Hannah more than a passing glance, and she assumed that, dressed as she was, they dismissed her as a serving girl. That assessment wasn't far wrong, she supposed, but what a shock they were going to be in for on the morrow! Hannah suppressed a giggle.

She peeked outside. Many more guests had arrived. Tents were being pitched. So many people! For just a moment she felt a quaver of fear. Would she be capable of handling herself so as not to disgrace Malcolm?

Feeling lost and a little lonely, she wandered out to the cookhouse—and found bedlam. The huge kitchen was bustling, Bess supervising half a dozen girls at work. The fire in the great hearth was roaring, and the cookhouse was like an oven. Bess ignored the perspiration pouring off her in rivulets and moved ponderously about, keeping a careful eye on everything.

And the food . . . Hannah had never seen so much food at one time. Cured hams, venison, mutton, poultry, wild turkey and geese and pigeons. Several varieties of fish, including oysters and shellfish taken from the tidal basin. Hannah knew that Malcolm had gone on several hunting trips with the field hands over the past two weeks, and the results of their hunting was evident.

Pastries, pies, cakes, and puddings of every kind were cooling. Pots were filled with cooking vegetables—both Irish and sweet potatoes, and different kinds of peas, especially black-eyed peas. Ears of sweet corn were roasting on coals in the hearth, and much cornpone was being baked.

And Hannah knew that the springhouse was filled to overflowing with milk, butter, cheese, and several varieties of fruit, all being kept cool until it was time to feed the guests.

Malcolm had told her that the guests usually brought their own picnic baskets for the first day, but beginning tomorrow all the food eaten would be provided by Malvern.

Bess spotted her and hurried over, wiping at her streaming brow with her apron. "Honey, what are y'all doing in here?"

"I felt sort of lost, Bess. Everybody is so busy, and ..." She flapped her hands. "And me with nothing to do."

"Foolish child! You the bride—you ain't *s'posed*

183

to do nothing!" Bess scolded. "Gracious, you not even s'posed to be seen until it time to stand up before the preacher man! Now shoo—git on out'n here." She flapped her apron. "You just in the way here. Go up to your room and admire all them fine clothes you gonna be wearing. Scoot now!"

Hannah left the cookhouse, but she didn't go back into the main house. She wandered among the guests outside. She didn't see a soul she knew.

Malcolm Verner finally came upon her listening to the fiddle player on the back lawn.

"Hannah, what on earth are you doing out here?" he asked in genuine horror.

"I got lonesome, Malcolm. I don't know anybody, anybody at all! Aren't you going to introduce me to the guests?"

"Introduce you? My dear, that isn't the way it's to be. The bride does not meet the wedding guests until *after* the ceremony. You know the way it's usually done—if the bride has parents, the wedding is held in their home, if possible. If not, if it's in the groom's house, the bride isn't brought there until just before the ceremony. And in your case ... well."

"But what am I supposed to do until tomorrow?" she wailed.

"You will stay in your room from now on, until you come down for the ceremony. I will have food sent up to you."

"Malcolm, that's cruel! I'll go mad up there."

"I'm sorry, my dear," he said gently but firmly. "But that's the way it has to be. Now, run along."

So Hannah trudged up to her room. She sulked there for the rest of the afternoon, snapping at the girl who brought up her supper. Hannah thought that at least André would come up to see her. But, drawing up a chair by the window, she saw him on the back lawn, strolling among the guests, his hands in constant motion. He strolled from lady to lady, pausing to say a word or two, and leaving them in gales of laughter.

And when it grew dark, Hannah heard music start up in the ballroom, heard the virginal along with the other instruments, and she recognized André's playing.

They were dancing down there, and here she was stuck up here alone!

She listened as minuets, gigues, and reels were played, listened in envy to the sounds of music and gay laughter. The revelry went on far into the night. Malcolm had told her that most guests would not sleep at all, except the ladies for a few hours. After the ladies wearied of dancing and re-tired, the men would play at cards and drink for the remainder of the night.

Music poured through the window. Hannah got up and danced by herself, eyes closed. André had told her, "You learn quickly, dear lady. Already you are an accomplished dancer, even with only a few short lessons." That wicked smile. "Of course, André is an accomplished dancing master."

Hannah was sure that she wouldn't sleep at all, what with the excitement of tomorrow and the sounds of music from below.

But finally she fell across the bed, and she was asleep almost at once. She dreamed that she was riding Black Star, wearing her wedding gown. Black Star flew, and the wind rushing past her ears carried the sounds of music. . . .

The next afternoon, Hannah—Hannah McCambridge for the last time—came down the wide stairs on André's arm. Since neither Malcolm Verner nor Hannah had any living relatives, André was to be, at Hannah's insistence, the one to give the bride away.

Hannah went tense, a nervous tremor racing through her, as she saw the crowd of guests gathered at the foot of the stairs, staring up at her.

"Steady, dear lady," André whispered into her ear. "You are without doubt the loveliest lady present. But do not forget . . . much of the credit belongs to André. I feel much like Pygmalion must have felt. Pygmalion, dear Hannah, was a figure out of legend, a king of Cyprus who made a female figure out of ivory and brought her to life . . . with a little help from the goddess Aphrodite."

Hannah laughed, squeezing his hand, and whispered back, "You can always make me laugh, André. Thank you for that."

The wedding gown André had made for her was of ruffled blue velvet, dipping daringly low above the swell of her breasts. It was a very simple garment really, but due to André's artistry it fitted her figure beautifully, making her naturally small waist appear even smaller. Hannah had chosen only one piece of jewelry from the casket Malcolm had given her—the diamond necklace. And she had picked a plain gold band as her wedding ring; André now had it in his pocket.

They had reached the bottom of the steps now, and the guests parted, forming a lane into the ballroom, where the wedding ceremony was to take place.

Hannah couldn't help but overhear the comments from the ladies on each side, even though they whispered behind fans.

"Shocking, utterly shocking! No stays or hoop!"

"And look how low it is in front. Vulgar, indeed vulgar!"

"What else could you expect, pray? Didn't you know? She was a tavern wench and a serving girl. I don't know what ever possessed Malcolm Verner!"

There was a male rejoinder to that remark. "I can see what possessed him. Yes, indeed!" The low laugh following the remark was lascivious.

André tightened his grip on her arm, his mouth near her ear again. "Pay no heed, dear Hannah. The ugly in mind always envy the beautiful."

They were inside the ballroom now, and Hannah saw Malcolm already standing in place before the clergyman. Everything else went out of her mind in a rush. She was about to become his wife, the mistress of Malvern. What harm could vicious whispers do her now?

Malcolm Verner stood slender and erect, elegantly attired in white velvet knee breeches and a brocade vest, with silver buckles on his shoes. On his head was a white peruke that André had made for him. He turned as Hannah came toward him, and smiled. Hannah's heart went out to him. He was a wonderful man. She doubted that she would ever truly love him, but she had a great affection for him. She would make him a good wife, and she was determined never to do anything to hurt him.

She stopped by his side, still on André's arm, and the ceremony began. When the clergyman, a tall, dour man with a sonorous voice, reached the phrase instructing her to obey Malcolm Verner in all things, Hannah's thoughts flashed back to the story André had told her. A nervous giggle escaped her. The clergyman broke off momentarily, frowning, and Verner looked at her sharply. André squeezed her arm lightly, and she knew without looking at him that he wore that wicked smile.

Finally it was all over, and Hannah turned to Verner, face tilted up for his kiss. Before people crowded around with their congratulations, André brushed his lips across hers. "I wish you all happiness, dear lady."

Hannah noticed that few women approached to congratulate her, but she saw with secret delight that most of the men did. Soon the musicians began to play. The center of the ballroom floor was cleared. Verner extended his arm and led Hannah onto the dance floor. The musicians were playing a minuet. Verner held himself stiffly as he whirled her around the floor.

"I'm afraid I'm out of practice, my dear. It has been years since I've danced."

"It'll come back to you, darling." She smiled tenderly. "And I'll see to it that you dance more often from now on."

They had the floor to themselves for the first dance, the guests standing back politely against the walls. When the music ended, a splattering of applause went around the room.

Smiling, Verner stood back and made a knee. Then he took her into his arms as the music started up once more. This time, the others joined in, and the wedding ball had officially started.

André Leclaire claimed her for the next dance. He was an excellent dancer, of course.

Hannah said, "Malcolm, now you. I wonder if any of the other men will ask to dance with me?"

"I predict that you will be much in demand, dear lady. All the single men will pursue you, you may be sure, and I suspect that many if not all of the married men will too. Even though they risk the rough edges of their spouses' tongues later."

It was as he said. Hannah never lacked for partners. The men came to her one after another, many more times than once. Hannah danced until her head was awhirl, both from the dancing and the wine she consumed.

Various liquors were available at a long table along one side of the room, and Hannah kept her dancing partners trotting back and forth to fetch her goblets of wine.

Verner didn't claim her for a dance again. He was everywhere at once, supervising the service. Tables of food had been set up in the entryway, and the dining-room table groaned with food. There was to be no formal dining, since the dining-room table could not even come close to accommodating the vast number of guests, but people could eat whenever they wished.

The ball went on, the merriment unabated. Hannah danced, ignoring the murderous glances of most of the women. She drank more wine. Now and then she would step outside for a breath of fresh air, snatching tidbits from the table to nibble on. Usually a young gallant accompanied her outside, flattering her with compliments and bombarding her with what she was sure he considered witty remarks. She found most of them boring. Only the single men went outside with her; the married men, she realized, dared not go that far. Verner noticed her coming and going, but made no comment.

Once their paths crossed in the entryway, and he said with a gentle smile, "Enjoying yourself, my dear?"

"I'm loving it. I feel like a princess." She touched his cheek with her fingers, a lingering caress. "It's a marvelous ball. Thank you for everything."

"The hour grows late," he said, grave now, his eyes searching hers. "The ball will continue all night. But the guests will expect us to retire ere long. We are man and wife now. They would think it strange if we did not."

"Whenever you say, darling," she whispered. "I am yours now."

He came for her on the stroke of midnight. His eyes were slightly glazed, and he was unsteady on his feet. He had not been drinking earlier, so he must have consumed a great deal in the last hour.

Hannah had to wonder as to the reason. Was he afraid of what was to come in the bedroom? Remembering Stritch and the drunken pirate, she felt some amusement at the thought of a man being timid about bedding her. At the same time, it filled her with tenderness.

"Time to retire, my dear," he said in slurred tones.

"I'm ready, Malcolm."

As they made their way through the guests toward the stairs, Hannah expected some ribald comments aimed at them. The guests were strangely silent. Yet Hannah knew what they were thinking—a man taking into his bed a girl young enough to be his granddaughter. Hannah's head went back, and she took Verner's arm, ignoring the staring faces. Even the musicians had momentarily

190

stopped playing, and, with the absence of voices, the quiet was almost eerie.

But they were hardly inside the door to Verner's bedroom when she heard the music start up again. The bed had been turned down, and a small table had been set with a bottle of wine, two glasses, and two candles burning on it.

Verner, still oddly nervous, went at once to the table. "A glass of wine, my dear? To finish off the evening?"

"No, I think not, darling. My head is already dizzy from too much wine."

He had picked up the wine bottle to pour. Now he paused and looked around at her. "Perhaps you're right." He replaced the bottle and leaned down to blow out the candles.

Hannah was a little surprised at this. Perhaps he didn't consider it proper for a man and wife to undress together in the light? With a shrug she quickly stripped down to her skin, leaving her clothes where they fell. She made her way to the high bed, stepped upon the footstool, and climbed in.

She lay, somewhat drowsy now, listening to the rustling sounds of Malcolm undressing. He seemed to take an uncommonly long time to get undressed.

Finally she heard him approach, the bed sagging as his weight came down on it.

He groped for her. As his fingers encountered bare flesh, he jerked his hands away as though scalded. "Why, you're naked!"

"Shouldn't I be?" she said in a puzzled voice.

"But I ... you see, Martha ... she always wore a nightgown." He added hastily, "Not that I'm being critical. There is no reason on earth why you shouldn't be...."

Hannah reached out to touch him. "Malcolm, *you're* wearing a nightshirt!"

"Well, yes," he said uncertainly. "Would you rather I not?"

"Yes!"

He laughed suddenly, the most joyous sound she'd ever heard from him. "By the gods, you're right!"

The bed heaved as he struggled out of the nightshirt. Then he rolled against her, naked now. Hannah felt the prod of his manhood against her thigh, and she tensed, waiting for him to mount her.

Instead, he began to caress her, exploring tenderly, his touch feather light. He kissed her with gentle lips, kissed her breasts and nipples, and she felt them respond, the nipples budding, flowering, growing hard. As he continued to stroke and kiss her, Hannah felt a slow warmth diffuse in her body. It became a sweet ache. She wanted ...

She knew not what she wanted.

Malcolm kissed her mouth. Her lips opened to his, their breaths mingled. Her body responded without her willing it, her flesh where he touched and kissed it throbbing, leaping. A tingling sensation sped over her nerve ends, radiating out from her lower belly.

The music from below, faint in the roaring in her ears, seemed a delicious counterpoint to his lovemaking.

She had never felt this way before. Was this the way it was supposed to be? After all the terrible times with Stritch, was it going to be good for her?

These questions occupied only a small corner of her mind. All other thought was drowned out by the sensations he evoked in her.

His tender caresses continued for a long time, until Hannah lay in a wanton sprawl, in a rosy haze of pleasure that would build and then recede. To Hannah, it seemed that her body now had an existence of its very own, that it was waiting for the pleasure to reach an unbearable peak.

Then she felt Malcolm move, hovering over her. He probed gently, going into her, moving slowly, and Hannah's sensations of pleasure mounted.

Abruptly his breathing became harsh, quick, shallow, and he was moving hard, driving hard. Then a guttural moan came from him, and he shuddered briefly, collapsing atop her.

After a moment he brushed his lips across hers. "I love you, dearest Hannah. I know now that I will never regret wedding you."

He slumped over onto his back, and after a little was sound asleep, snoring softly.

Hannah lay still, a huddle of disappointment. Was that it? Would it always be this way? Her body felt feverish. The sweet ache was still there, less strong now, but she felt a vague discontent, a longing, a sense of something incomplete.

Fully awake now, she knew that she wouldn't be able to sleep. She got out of bed quietly, found a dressing gown, and moved to a chair by the window where she could listen to the music and the sounds of merriment from below.

For a daring moment she thought of getting dressed and going back down to the ball. Yet common sense prevailed. That would never do. Not only would it shock the guests, it would shame Malcolm.

Her thoughts strayed, and she found herself thinking of another man—a tall, graceful man, with a full black beard and fierce yet mocking black eyes. The pirate named Dancer.

Hannah came to herself with a start. Why on earth should her thoughts dwell on a man she had only seen once, for a minute or so, and under the most ignominious of circumstance?

To her astonishment, Hannah discovered that she was weeping softly, weeping for she knew not what.

Chapter Eleven

Silas Quint was shrewd enough not to approach the manor house directly. He lurked about like a chicken-hunting fox, hiding in the bushes and the fields.

This was the fourth time that he had come skulking around Malvern plantation. When he had learned that Hannah had become the wife of Malcolm Verner and the mistress of Malvern, he had been torn by conflicting emotions—envy, anger, and a certain gleeful anticipation. He was envious of her good fortune, and he was angry that such an ungrateful wench should *be* so fortunate. What stung him the most was that she hadn't invited him, her poor old stepfather, her only living relative, to the wedding! Oh, he'd heard what a fine wedding it was—all the food and drink a man could wish for. The three-day wedding celebration had been the talk of Williamsburg this month past.

But most of all, Quint was quivering with greedy anticipation. The wife of a rich man, the wench had to have access to money now. Surely she wouldn't refuse her poor old stepfather a few coins. If not from daughterly gratitude, if not from pity, at least—and here he grinned craftily—as payment to keep him away from Malvern!

During his reconnoiterings, he had learned that almost every afternoon Hannah rode a huge black stallion about the plantation. Quint noted that she usually started by riding through the large pasture stretching south of the manor house.

So, on a cool, cloudy fall afternoon when there was a mist in the air, he climbed over the fence and made his way toward the spot where she usually rode, carrying what was left of a bottle of rum. He eyed the few animals in the pasture warily. He had always been fearful of animals, especially horses. They were so unpredictable. He made it safely to the huge, spreading oak in the center of the pasture, settled down behind the wide trunk, and took a tot of rum to bolster his courage. He kept drinking from the bottle until it was empty, peering around the tree trunk from time to time.

Suppose the wench didn't ride out today? Or mayhap he had missed her. He had caught a ride out of Williamsburg on a farmer's cart that had moved at the pace of molasses in January, and he'd been a bit late.

Quint was dozing when he heard the thunder of hooves. He peeked around the trunk and saw the black monster thundering across the meadow, Hannah astride his back. They seemed headed straight for the oak.

Quint waited until they were a few yards away, then stepped out from behind the tree, emboldened by the rum. He stood right in the path of the horse, flapping his arms.

The horse saw him and plowed to a stop, neighing, rearing, hooves slashing the air. Hannah fought to stay on his back.

Quint squealed in terror and darted back behind the tree trunk.

In a moment he heard Hannah's voice. "You can come out now, Silas Quint."

Cautiously he edged out from behind the tree. The black horse was standing perfectly still, Hannah erect and at ease in the saddle, as though born to it. The sight made Quint angry, and he forgot his terror of a moment ago. He was his old sneering self again as he took a couple of steps toward her.

"Well, if it ain't the mistress of Malvern upon a big fancy beast like that. Very much the lady, ain't ye?"

Hannah's eyes flashed fire. "What are you doing on Malvern? Didn't I warn you never to come here?"

"I came to inquire why ye didn't ask me to the wedding. I thought maybe you'd forgotten old Quint."

"*Forget* you? Never—I'll never forget you," she said witheringly. "As for inviting you to the wedding, we do not allow white trash on Malvern!"

"We, is it? White trash, am I?" His anger boiled over, and he took another step toward her. The horse shied, eyes rolling. Quint darted back a few steps.

Hannah held tight on the reins. "Careful, Quint! If I let him go, he could easily run you down!" The horse pawed the ground, snorting, then stood still once more. "Now, tell me the real reason you are here."

"I figured that now you're the rich, fine lady, ye could spare a few coins for your poor old stepfather," Quint whined. "I need a few shillings, I need them sorely."

"I have already told you. You'll never get so much as a farthing from me."

"Just enough to keep me in food and drink, missy. Squire Verner will never miss it. Do that and I won't be a-bothering ye," he said slyly. "Mayhap ye could send a few pounds to me monthly. Do, and on my word, you'll not be bothered by me again."

"The answer is no—not a ha'penny. Not now, not ever!"

"Ye ungrateful slut! Does Master Verner know what kind of a wench he's wed to?" His lips drew back in a snarl. "Does he know that ye not only scrubbed tavern floors, was a serving wench, but also laid on your back at Stritch's bidding? What if I was to whisper them truths in his ear?"

For the first time Quint realized that Hannah was carrying a leather riding quirt. Before his rum-addled brain could grasp her intention, she slackened the reins, drummed her heels on the horse's flanks, and rode right at him. Quint stood frozen in his tracks, gaping. At the last instant she wheeled the horse slightly to the left, but she rode so close Quint got a whiff of the horse's rank odor. As she thundered past, Hannah leaned far out and down, the quirt slashing the air. The fringed quirt missed his face by a whisker, making a sound like a swarm of angry bees.

If she hadn't missed her mark, his face would have been slashed to ribbons!

He turned just as she wheeled the big stallion around and came charging back. The pair of them, as one, loomed larger and larger in his vision until it came to him that this time she had no intention of veering aside at the last moment. She meant to ride him down! If he was knocked down and trampled by the horse, he would be chewed up like sausage meat!

Desperately Quint threw himself aside. He hit the ground hard enough to knock the breath from him. On hand and knees, he scrambled toward the sanctuary of the oak tree. The horse pounded past, hooves thudding the ground where Quint had been standing only seconds before. He reached the tree and huddled behind it. Trembling with fright, he peered around it. The black horse was racing away south.

Quint waited until he was sure Hannah wasn't coming back before he stood up on quivering limbs, holding onto the tree for support.

Anger choked him like bile. The crazy bitch had tried to kill him! And he was helpless to do anything about it. Who would believe him over the mistress of Malvern? All Hannah would have to do was calmly deny that she had tried to kill him, and he would be called a liar and a villain for trying to blacken her name.

Calmer now, he thought of his next move. And then it came to him. He knew from watching her those other times that she wouldn't return for at least an hour. And likely Master Verner would be at the manor house.

Smiling craftily, he picked up the rum bottle and shook it. It was empty. With a curse he threw it away.

But he soon would have money to purchase another. He set out in the direction of the plantation house.

Hannah was furious when she learned that Malcolm had given Quint a handful of coins. "I told you never to give him money!"

"He said he was hungry and needed money for food. He *is* your stepfather, my dear."

"Food! He wants it to spend on drink!"

"At least it served to rid ourselves of him."

Malcolm Verner had changed during the month since their wedding day. For the first few days he had seemed happy with his new life and his new wife, but of late Hannah had noticed a difference in his manner. His energy seemed to have slackened off, and he smiled seldom. There had been times, when she had caught him unawares, when he seemed to have aged ten years, and his face wore the old shadow of melancholy.

She said sharply, "We are *not* rid of him, Malcolm! Your giving him money will only encourage him to come whining around for more."

He gestured indifferently. "It doesn't matter. What's a few coins more or less, no matter what his need is?"

"But it does matter. It matters to *me*! He killed my mother, I am convinced of it!"

His gaze sharpened. "Killed her? What do you

know of this? If this be true, something should have been done about it."

"I can't prove it, if that's what you mean, but I know it in my heart."

"What's in a woman's heart is scarcely proof to take into court, my dear." Some of the old wry amusement was in his slight smile.

"I very well know that. That's the reason I haven't spoken of it before. Malcolm . . ." She caught his sleeve. "Darling, I want your promise. If he comes here again, turn him away. For me?"

"You have my promise, Hannah. If it means so much to you. It's certainly of no importance to me. Now, by your leave, madam."

He turned away with a weary gesture and went into his study. Hannah heard the bolt snick home. That was another thing. For the past two weeks, he had returned to locking himself in his study. . . .

"And what seems to ail the master of Malvern, dear lady?"

Hannah wheeled at the sound of André's voice. "What do you mean? There's nothing ailing Malcolm!"

"Perhaps not, dear lady." André shrugged. "It just struck me that your husband is behaving rather oddly these past days. Being rather distant, shall we say?"

"Why oddly? Just because he chooses not to prattle away like a goose, like somebody I could mention?"

"Touché, madam." André's eyebrows rose slightly. "My, we are in rather a state, are we not? Your husband, dear lady, is your own affair. But it is time for your music lesson. . . ."

"I need a bath first. I smell of horse."

"You do surprise me, dearest Hannah. Most colonists I have met bathe once a month, if that; a few mayhap once a week. But none so often as you. Even in France, the most civilized country in the world, we do not bathe so often. Whatever purpose do you think perfume serves?"

"You could drown a pig in perfume and it still would not drown out his stench," Hannah said tartly, and she started up the stairs.

André stood gazing after her with an amused, and somewhat wistful, smile. He had never, in all his wide experience, encountered a woman with the varied talents, charm, and beauty of Hannah Verner. She had learned to dance exquisitely within less than a month, and if he wasn't careful she would soon surpass him at skill on the virginal. It was indeed a great waste; she would be prized as a great beauty in France, much sought after.

André sighed. At times like this, he even wished he were different. Never very strongly, of course, but it would be intriguing . . .

"*Merde*, André," he said aloud, with an ironic chuckle. "What the gods have ordained, man cannot change."

He turned away, striding into the music room.

Upstairs, undressing, Hannah's thoughts were still on Malcolm. She believed she knew what was troubling him. After the first week or so his vigor in bed had diminished. He still lay with her, made slow and tender love to her, and seemed to love her more than ever, yet there were times when he could not summon his manhood to the task at hand.

And, except for the sensations of pleasure she received from his preliminary lovemaking, Hannah had yet to experience the ultimate pleasure, and was always left with vague feelings of frustration.

However, what was really important, at least to Malcolm, Hannah was sure, was that she had not yet conceived. He desperately wanted a son and heir; he had finally gone so far as to admit as much to her. And her time of the month had come and gone, and still she had not conceived. Could he be blaming himself for this failure, as well?

Hannah had finally confided in Bess.

"He not young, the master, child," Bess had said. "Oftentime, age will weaken a man's seed."

"But I've heard there are remedies, love potions, many concoctions, that will make a man more potent."

Bess's laughter had rolled. "Conjure woman's tales, child! Do you not think I've tried them all? And I have no child. Lawd, how I've wished for children around my feet." For one of the few times since Hannah had known Bess, her face had taken on a look of sadness. Then she'd laughed again. "And don't you be thinking it ain't from lack of trying. I've bedded many a man and jollied in it. And most of them very same bucks went on to get other gals with child."

"Then what do I do, Bess? Malcolm so much wants a son!"

"He does lie with you?"

Hannah had felt herself blushing. "Oh, yes. Almost . . ." She'd swallowed. "Almost every night."

"Time, honey, only time will tell." She'd patted Hannah on the shoulder. Her face had been sober. "I hates to tell you this, honey, but it could be you. Ofttimes the Lawd somehow sees fit to make us women barren . . . like me."

That evening at supper, Malcolm Verner said somewhat gloomily, "I have to go into Williamsburg on the morrow. There is a slave auction, and I need to buy more. I have not purchased slaves in some years, and my field hands are meager. I have to clear twenty acres of land this winter for planting, and I need more hands."

André made a face. "Slavery is an evil institution, sir."

Verner's pale face flushed. "You think I do not know that? Yet it is a necessary evil, if Virginia's economy is to survive in its present form."

"It is not right to enslave a man, any man."

"Correct me if I'm wrong, my dear Leclaire, but I have heard some tales of the conditions of the serfs in your own *civilized* country. If what I've heard is true, they are little better than slaves. In fact, I would wager that the lot of some slaves here in Virginia is better than that of many of your own serfs. And your countrymen, they are besides . . ."

Hannah ceased to listen to the discussion and applied herself to her food, smiling slightly. Almost nightly, Malcolm and André got into a heated discussion on some subject. The discussions sometimes continued far into the night in Malcolm's study.

André was almost a permanent fixture at Malvern now; Hannah had found Malcolm quite agreeable to having André stay on indefinitely. She was sure she knew the reason for this: André was a stimulating conversationalist, and Malcolm liked to converse with him, even when they did not agree—which was certainly more often than not!

The next morning, early, Malcolm Verner embarked on his onerous chore. Driving toward Williamsburg, the group from Malvern comprised something of a caravan. First came the coach carrying Verner, with John at the reins. Beside John rode Henry, the overseer. Behind them came two carts driven by field hands; the carts would be used to transport the purchased slaves back to Malvern.

It would be Henry's chore to select the slaves that Verner would bid for against the other planters at the auction. It was something Verner could not bring himself to do. His stomach churned every time he attended an auction and watched a planter examine a slave on the auction block—feeling his muscles, inspecting his teeth as though he might be a horse. It was a humiliating thing to watch, and Verner could only imagine how humiliating and shaming it had to be for the slave on the block. Why, he had even seen a plantation owner once examining a male Negro's genitals, judging the penis for breeding purposes!

To get his mind off what would happen later that day, he turned his thoughts to his own predicament. For days he had been brooding about Hannah and his failure to get her with child. In his darkest moods he knew it had been a mistake to wed her. Not that he didn't love her; he loved Hannah more with every passing day. He knew that much laughter and many jests must have circulated among the wedding guests, and others since, about a man his age marrying a girl of seventeen. It wasn't unusual for an older man to marry a much younger woman—not in this country where the male population far outnumbered the female. But the age gap between them was too much. . . . It wasn't the lewd laughter and the crude jests that concerned him—it was his own failure in bed with her. In the beginning he had thought with joy that the male vigor he had once possessed had returned to him. It hadn't been long before he'd learned that he was in error.

Now he realized that it had been an illusion, a momentary thing. To his humiliation he was finding it more and more difficult to get an erection, and it was quite a strain on him when he did manage to perform the marital act. Afterward, he would be exhausted, his heart racing, sometimes paining him severely, and it often took him a long time for his breathing to return to normal. It reminded him that all men were mortal, and it frightened him.

None of that concerned him overmuch. After all, it was a well-established fact that women did not enjoy coupling; they merely endured it for the man's pleasure. But if only he could get her with child! Dear God, how sorely he wished for a son to take over Malvern after he was gone!

With that came another thought. What if he *were* to die suddenly? Today, while in Williamsburg, he must see a lawyer and have a will drawn, leaving Malvern to Hannah, or to his son, in the event such a miracle were to occur before or shortly after his death. He owed Hannah that much at least. If he died without a will, he well knew that the courts would be hard on her. A woman had few legal rights. With a will she would at least have some legal position. God only knew what would happen to the plantation. Certainly she could not manage it on her own. But at least if it were legally hers, she could sell it.

Verner muttered an oath under his breath, shaking his head. It had been said that when a man began thinking seriously of his own death, it would soon follow. Probably an old wives' tale, but still . . .

They were entering Williamsburg now. Verner saw that the coach was approaching the auction area. There was a carnival atmosphere, a festive air about the people gathered. Booths had been set up to sell food and drink. The men and women wore their finest garments, and children darted about in noisy play.

This was something else that Verner detested. A funeral atmosphere would be more fitting for such an occasion.

But he knew that few would agree with this opinion, and he had long since learned to keep such views to himself. His treatment of his slaves was already considered too liberal by many. The use of a black overseer was scandalous enough. But to use that same black overseer to make a plantation owner's decisions about which slaves to purchase was beyond the bounds of good sense!

Verner was grateful for one thing. The slaves auctioned here once or twice a year were usually not right off a slave ship from Africa, were not in chains, half starved, and frightened out of their wits by not knowing why they were here or even *where* they were. Most slave ships unloaded their unholy cargoes farther south, down off the Carolina coast. The slaves for sale here most often belonged to plantation owners who possessed too many for their own use, or to slave owners who had fallen on hard times and had to sell for economic reasons. Thus, most of them were from the immediate area. It was true that slave traders from the Carolinas and other southern colonies sometimes attended with a number of slaves for sale, but Verner had early on instructed Henry to select only the local slaves.

Verner sat in the coach on the edge of the square. He had no wish to mix and mingle with the other slave buyers. Perhaps they thought that strange. But since he knew they already considered him a strange breed of plantation owner, that mattered little to him.

Henry spent his time trotting back and forth from coach to auction block. When he recommended a purchase, Verner stood on the coach steps and shouted his bids from there. He had come prepared to buy eight slaves, all males in their prime. Since he was always willing to bid high, he had no difficulty in purchasing Henry's choices.

He had bought seven of the eight by midafternoon. He was glad it was almost finished. Soon the carts could start back to Malvern. He lit a cigar from the burning candle in its holder by the coach door, and sat back to smoke and relax for a moment. In a little while he craned forward to look out the coach window. He saw Henry talking to one of the few remaining slaves, who stood in line waiting to be led to the auction block.

The man Henry was conversing with was medium tall, but wide and powerful. He wore only a pair of ragged breeches, and muscles rippled like snakes across his broad chest. He looked to be in his prime. Then Verner noticed something that made him draw a sharp breath.

The slave was in chains—his legs were hobbled at the ankles, and chains bound his wrists together. He was either a runaway or a troublemaker. It was the only explanation.

In a moment Verner saw Henry break away and come toward the coach. Verner got down to meet him.

"Master," Henry said. "The big buck I was talking to. His name Leon. I think he make a good buy."

Verner drew on his cigar. "But the man is in chains, Henry. Why is that?"

"He been in trouble, Master Verner," Henry said somewhat uneasily. "He run away a number of times, but I thinks . . ."

"I've always trusted your judgment, Henry, you know that. But a runaway? He'd be nothing but trouble."

"But that just it," Henry said eagerly. "He say he tired of running, always being in trouble. I tell him you be a good master, better'n any around. He swear he willing to behave. He tired of being hunted down by dogs, tired being whupped and allus in chains. He say if you a good master, he work hard and not run away." Henry added slyly, "In chains like that, he come cheap, you bet."

"Henry, I just don't know. A runaway . . ."

"He brought up from down south a ways. His master tired of his running off, and figures nobody down there buy him. Most runaways I knows have spirit and don't take kindly to being treated cruel. They handled right, they make good workers. You buy him, I promise he make the best worker on the plantation."

Verner stared toward the chained slave, standing dejectedly, head hanging. If some other man bought him, probably the first thing he'd do would be to put the lash to him, try to break his spirit. Verner was moved to pity. He came to a sudden deci-

209

sion and nodded. "All right, Henry. You've always been right before. But I'm holding you responsible, you understand?"

Henry nodded, smiling, and hurried back toward the auction ring. The chained slave was now being led up onto the block. The auctioneer went into his spiel, extolling the man's prime condition and strength, carefully not mentioning the chains.

When he called for bids, Verner's was the first. "Five pounds!"

There was a murmur from the crowd, people glancing over at him.

Bart Myers strolled up. "Malcolm, you addled? You going to buy a nigger in chains? He has to be a runaway from down south."

"Henry recommended that I buy him."

"Henry!" Myers snorted. "You're a strange one, Malcolm Verner, trusting a nigger's judgment about another nigger!"

There was another bid from someone in the crowd, and Verner raised it.

"It's on your own head. But I think you're a fool." Myers moved off.

Verner finally bought the slave for fifteen pounds, a ridiculously low figure. "All right, Henry," he said briskly. "Load the carts and get started back to Malvern. I will stay awhile. I have more business to attend to."

After the newly purchased slaves were unloaded at Malvern, Henry kept them in a group, delivering a little speech. The one named Leon, his chains removed now, listened quietly, if skeptically.

"Now, you niggers listen close to what I tell you.

210

This ain't one of them bad plantations. Master Verner the best master anywheres around. We don't sleep on the ground here, and he let us have wood for heat in cold weather. We ain't fed slops. Food's good. We provided with good garments to wear, given good presents come Christmas. And we don't work from sunup to sundown, ever'day the week, except'n maybe harvest and curing time. All you have to do is work hard at what you s'posed to do. And we don't get whupped regularly. The only times Master Verner use the lash is for lying and stealing. If you find a woman of your own, you allowed a house to use." Henry smiled knowingly. "You don't have to sneak around to fuck some gal you take a fancy to. You find one you wants, come tell me. . . ."

Henry continued in the same vein for a little. Listening, Leon sighed. He was dubious, but he hoped that what he was hearing was true. Lord God, he was weary of running, of being hunted down like a wild animal, then chained up, starved, and beaten until he nigh bled to death. That had happened several times. More than once he had tried to run fast and far enough to escape up north, where he had been told that people of his race were treated at least *some* better. But he had always been caught before he could make it. Everybody was afraid to help a runaway, even other Negroes.

Yes, he was tired of running. He wasn't so young and full of fire and spirit anymore. True, he was still in his prime and could do a day's work to match any man's, but the years of running and the beatings had taken a great deal out of him.

If what this Henry was saying was true, Leon

felt that he might not run away again. He wouldn't be content, he would never be content being the white man's slave, but if he could find a place where he could do his work, eat regularly, and not be beaten every day, he would be as content as he ever would be.

There was one thing that looked favorable. This was the first plantation he'd ever heard of that had a Negro overseer. Maybe this white man, Malcolm Verner, was a notch above other slave owners....

He looked up, stream of thought broken, as Henry stopped speaking. Then Leon heard the drum of hoofbeats and saw that the others were all staring at a great black stallion approaching the stable. In the saddle rode a white woman with long, coppery hair, and easy, erect carriage.

Henry said, "That the mistress of the plantation, Mistress Hannah. She as good a mistress as the master...."

A vague memory nagged at Leon as he stared at the long, loose, coppery hair. Something about the woman seemed familiar. Then he dismissed it as his imagination. He had never been in this part of the country before.

Still he stared, frowning, scouring his memory—the slave who now called himself Leon, the runaway slave who had once been known as Isaiah.

Chapter Twelve

"Tell a tale of High John the Conquerer, Bess!" clamored the children gathered around Bess in the cookhouse.

A winter's chill had driven them all inside. It was late, nigh onto nine, and usually all the children would be abed at this hour. But it was December now, only a short time before Christmas, and work on the plantation had slowed. The only active labor being done at present was the clearing of timber from twenty acres for the new planting, so the young ones were allowed to stay up later. Bess had baked a batch of cornmeal cookies, and they huddled close to the heat of the great hearth, nibbling on them.

"Well now, let me think on it a minute," Bess

said soberly. "Could be I told you young'uns 'bout all the tales of High John I knows."

A groan went up from them, and several voices were raised in protest.

"Hush now, let me think."

Her gaze went past them as the cookhouse door opened and closed. The man entering was one of the new slaves, the one called Leon. Bess frowned, thinking of ordering him out. She didn't cotton to him. He was a good worker; Henry had told her that. But Bess had a feeling about him. He was a bad one, she felt it in her bones. Yet she decided to let him stay instead of fussing about it.

She didn't even utter a complaint when he filched a handful of cookies from the pan and squatted down against the back wall, crunching on them. Maybe he was hungry. Bess sighed. Goodness knows, most of the new slaves had been starved and couldn't believe their good fortune at the plenitude of food at Malvern. Plain fare, of course, not fancied up like that provided for the manor house, but ample and filling. And Bess could never deny a hungry man food, no matter what bad feelings she might have about him.

She began her tale. "Like I tole you afore, High John was allus making money for the massa when he bet on him. One day massa finagled High John into running a foot race with a nigger from another plantation. High John run half a day, run that other nigger right into the ground, and won fifty pounds for massa. Now, High John figured he wouldn't have to go back to the fields that day, winning all that money, but massa sent him to the fields anyway. High John was feeling mighty abused, so that night he snuck into the barn and

214

broke up all the hoes and other field tools. The next morning ole massa suspicioned 'twas John's doing. He accused John of it. 'Sho did,' John says, grinning all over his face.

"Massa says, 'I'm gon' kill you for that, John.' High John only laughed. 'You does, massa, and I'll beat you at making money.' Now of course ole massa didn't believe *that*. So he shoved John into a sack and drug him down to the river. Just as he was 'bout to throw the sack in the river, he remembered he'd forgot to tie weights to the thing. So he goes back to the barn for some. Now John had a knife, so he sawed his way out'n that old sack, filled it up with rocks, and tied it back up again.

"When massa came back with his weights, he throw just a sack full of rocks into the river. 'Course he didn't know that. By that time John was in his bed, asleep.

"Come morning, John was up early. He took his old muleskin and went into the village to tell fortunes for money. High John could do that, using a muleskin. He could foretell when a man gon' die and when a baby gon' be born. He could cast all kinds of spells. Why, if'n he wanted to, he could make birds sing at midnight!

"Anyways, John went into the village and came back that afternoon with pockets jingling with coins. Massa almost swooned away when he sees him. 'John, is that you? Can't be you!'

"John, he just laughed and jingled his money. 'Tole you if'n you killed me I'd beat you at making money!' Still gaping, ole massa says, 'You think if I let you kill me, I could make some money?' High John laughs fit to kill. 'Massa, I *knows* you could!'

"So massa let John tie him up in a sack. John tied weights to it, rolled that sack down to the river. Just before John pushed the sack into the water, massa calls out, 'John, you sure now I'm gonna make some money?' With that big laugh of his'n, John says, 'Massa, I *knows* you is!'

"High John rolled the sack into the river, and that was the last of ole massa!"

Laughter rumbling, Bess shooed the children out of the cookhouse and on their way to their beds. Leon lingered behind. When the cookhouse was empty except for the pair of them, he came toward her.

Bess stood up. "What you want, you Leon? More cookies? You been stuffing yo'self like a pig!"

Leon was shaking his head. "No, old woman. I just been listening with a head full of wonderment. What kind of stuff you filling them chilluns' heads with?"

Bess shrugged massive shoulders. "Just tales to help them pass the time."

"That ain't it. You know you preaching rebellion, telling how this High John fight back at white folks, killing his master, and getting way with it!"

"Just a tale to while away the time," she said stiffly. "I ain't preaching nothing."

"The hell you ain't, old woman," Leon said softly.

"Don't you go swearing at me!"

"I just wondering how you get away with it, is all."

Bess tossed her head. "Miss Hannah, she take joy from my tales her ownself."

Leon shook his head again. "Then I reckon

what I been hearing about this plantation must be true. This Miss Hannah . . . what y'all know about her?"

"What I know about Miss Hannah is none of your business, nigger!" Bess glared. "She the mistress of the plantation now. What you think the master would do to you, he learn you asking questions 'bout her?"

"Not from you, he won't learn." Leon suddenly looked menacing, sending a jolt of fear through Bess. He took a step toward her. "You just keep your mouth shut. You hear, old woman? You old, wouldn't take much to . . ."

A scream came from the main house, interrupting him. Bess recognized it as coming from Hannah and started for the door to the covered walkway leading to the manor house. Leon had already slipped out, ghost-like, darting through the back door.

Hannah's voice came again. "Bess!"

She was already halfway to the cookhouse by the time Bess had maneuvered herself out the door.

"Gracious, honey, what ails you?"

"You have to come, Bess!" Hannah gasped out.

They had retired early that evening; at least Hannah had. She had taken a book from the library. Detouring by Malcolm's study before going upstairs, she had knocked on the door. "Malcolm, I'm going up to bed."

After a pause Verner had said, "I'll be along shortly, my dear."

Upstairs, Hannah had hesitated at the door to the master bedroom. Over the past month she had taken to sleeping most nights in her old room. It was at Malcolm's suggestion.

"You'll no doubt sleep better, Hannah. I often stay up late going over the books, and I only waken you when I come in."

Hannah knew this wasn't the whole truth. Malcolm was drinking again—not as heavily as when she'd first come to Malvern, but he almost always reeked of brandy when he finally retired. He would visit her room once, sometimes twice, a week, but usually the visits ended as an embarrassment for both, and, Hannah was sure, a humiliation for Malcolm.

Tonight Hannah had sighed heavily and gone on down the hall to her room.

She'd prepared for bed, leaving a candle burning in a holder on the bed post. Then she'd propped herself up against the headboard with pillows behind her back and settled down to read. This had grown to be a nightly habit now.

Along with the other things André was teaching her, he had introduced her to books, of which there were plenty in the downstairs library. He selected the books for her; some were novels, but most were concerned with the social graces necessary to produce a fine lady of the gentry. Hannah was even able to read a few phrases in French, the language many of the novels were printed in. The words and phrases she did not understand Hannah would underline and take to André the next day for interpretation.

To a certain extent, many of the novels were frustrating to Hannah. The milieu was often high society, telling of deathless romances between dashing heroes and beautiful young ladies. Reading them,

Hannah would sigh. No matter how much she learned, no matter how good André was as a teacher, she would *never* come to resemble the ladies she read about. . . .

After an hour's reading she grew drowsy. She slid down underneath the covers, blowing out the candle, and drifted into sleep, staring dreamily at the flickering flames in the hearth. With the cold weather, she knew that several times during the night a house servant would steal into the room and stoke up the fire so it would be warm when Hannah got up in the morning.

She awoke with a start at a movement on the bed. The first thing she noticed was the stench of brandy fumes. "Malcolm?"

"Yesh, dearest Hannah. Your devoted hush—husband."

He was drunk, quite drunk. For a moment Hannah felt disgust and was tempted to refuse him her bed. Did he find her so revolting he had to befuddle himself with drink before coming to her? But she desisted and lay quiescent. She knew that was not the reason, and she felt moved by pity.

His aged body was naked, and Hannah had to hold herself from flinching away from his fumbling touch. His caresses tonight were few, awkward, and hurting. There was a drunken urgency about him.

Thinking to hurry things along, she reached down for his member and found it only half erect.

"Sir, do you think you should? You have drunk overmuch. . . ."

"You are my wife." Already he was climbing on top of her. "Bound by the laws of God and man to obey my every demand."

Images of the drunken pirate paraded through her mind, and disgust again washed over her.

Malcolm was trying to penetrate her, and failing. But his lower body was moving, hunching at her, as though in the motions of coupling.

Suddenly a hoarse groan came from him, and he stiffened, his fingers on her shoulders biting cruelly into her flesh. Then he collapsed atop her.

Thinking that he had somehow managed his moment of pleasure, Hannah lay still for a little, waiting for him to move. But he did not. Had he fallen asleep? Often he did that of late. But on those occasions he began to snore almost at once.

Faintly alarmed, she said, "Malcolm?"

He made no reply, and did not move so much as a muscle. She began to push at him. Ordinarily she thought him frail, but now he was very heavy. Panic struck at her. Gathering all her strength, she gave a great shove and toppled him off.

Hannah scrambled out of bed and took the candle from the bedpost holder. With trembling fingers she lit it in the fireplace. She fitted it back into the holder and turned for her first good look at Malcolm. He had flopped over onto his back, arms flung wide, eyes open and staring.

Hannah came down on her knees on the bed, seizing him by the shoulders. "Malcolm, wake up!"

When he made no movement, no sound, she backed away from him in horror. She backed until she fell off the bed. Bouncing up from the floor, she snatched up her dressing gown to throw around her and fled the room in her bare feet, screaming.

She ran down the stairs and through the pantry. Vaguely she was aware of house servants gaping at

her. But she had only one thought in her mind—
Bess. She was halfway along the walkway when
she saw Bess emerge from the cookhouse.

"Gracious, honey, what ails you?"

"You have to come, Bess! Something's happened
to Malcolm!"

"Calm yourself, child." Bess patted her shoulder.
"We go see."

Hannah hurried along, stopping every few feet
to wait as Bess puffed up to her. She had to stop
several times on the stairs, urging the large woman
along.

When Bess finally stood beside the bed, she took
one look at Malcolm's naked body and said, "Lawd
God!" She swung at Hannah. "Fetch me a mirror,
child. Quick!"

Hannah hurried to get a hand mirror from her
dressing table and give it to Bess. Bess held it before Malcolm's open mouth for a full minute, then
gazed into it.

She heaved a great sigh. "A fit of apoplexy, most
likely."

"Shouldn't we send the coach into Williamsburg
for someone?" Hannah asked frantically. "Can't
you do something, Bess?"

"Nothing to do, honey," Bess said gently. "He
gone to glory."

For a moment Hannah couldn't accept it. She
stood frozen, staring at the still body on the bed.
And then, when Bess tenderly pulled the quilt up
over Malcolm's body and face, the full realization
crashed in on her. She began to cry, harsh sobs
shaking her body.

Bess folded Hannah into her arms, stroking her

hair. "You go on and cry, child. Cry to your heart's content."

Malcolm Verner was buried on Malvern, a hundred yards from the manor house, alongside the grave of Martha Verner. The gravesites were on a gentle rise of land overlooking the James River.

Hannah had refused to notify the neighbors. She knew that often, in Virginia, a funeral turned into almost as festive an occasion as a wedding. The same principle held; when people came from many miles around, it was expected that they would stay the night, and that food and liquor would be provided for them.

André scolded her. "Dear Hannah, defying convention is all right in its place, but you will be bringing down the wrath of your neighbors on your head if you do not invite them to the funeral of a man of Malcolm Verner's stature. I know that I regard funerals as barbarous affairs—still . . ."

"And have it turn into a fair?" she said fiercely. "No! I know Malcolm would have wanted it this way."

André regarded her shrewdly. "That is not the real reason, is it?"

Hannah looked away. "Not the only reason, no. Don't you think I *know* what they will be saying, what they're already saying? A man of Malcolm's age taking to wife a girl of seventeen, and that bedding her was the death of him?" She looked at him now, head thrown back proudly. "You think I want them here, the men smirking, the women whispering and laughing behind their fans?"

André shrugged, spreading his hands in surrender, and it was as Hannah wished.

A simple pine coffin was constructed in the carpentry shop, and a small marble tombstone made, with just Malcolm's name and the dates of his birth and death chiseled on it.

Hannah even refused to have a clergyman out from the village. "You say a few words, André. You're an educated man."

"Me? *Mon Dieu!*" he said in horror. "Dear lady, I have never even been churched. I know nothing of such things!"

"You can think of a fitting word or two to say."

All work was stopped on the plantation, and all the slaves gathered at the gravesite. Flanked by Bess and André, Hannah looked long at the closed pine coffin beside the freshly dug grave. Then she glanced at André and motioned. André took two steps forward and cleared his throat.

Under any other circumstances, Hannah would have been amused. It was the first time she had ever seen him hesitant, at a loss for words.

Finally he began, speaking haltingly, in hushed tones. "The Bard wrote, 'All that live must die, passing through nature to eternity.' And from the pen of the poet, John Donne: 'One short sleep past, we wake eternally; and death shall be no more; death thou shalt die.'" André coughed behind his hand. "I know not about such things, know not if we shall 'wake eternally.' But in the short space of time that I knew Malcolm Verner, I came to know him as a kind man, a man who did much good within the limitations imposed on him. His death was untimely, and sorely grieves those who knew him, but if eternal life shall be, there he shall dwell. We bid thee *adieu,* Monsieur Malcolm Verner." André hesitated, coughed again, and finally said awkwardly, "Amen."

He stepped back beside Hannah. She took his hand and whispered, "That was lovely, André. Thank you."

She motioned, and several slaves came forward to lower the coffin into the pit. But before the first shovel of dirt was thrown in, a sound began beside Hannah. She glanced at Bess in astonishment. Bess was humming. Then she burst into song, a hymn, singing in a rich, powerful voice. One by one, the other slaves joined in. In a moment all were singing, their joined voices rolling across the sloping land down to the river.

Hannah felt tears burn in her eyes, and she wept unashamedly, tears flowing for the first time since she had let herself go in Bess's arms beside Malcolm's deathbed.

When the hymn was finished, the slaves began shoveling dirt into the grave. Hannah turned away and walked back to the manor house on André's arm. She had no inclination to talk, and André for once was silent.

Hannah was trying to sort out her emotions. Although she hadn't loved Malcolm, she had been deeply fond of him, and his death grieved her. At the same time there was that other thought that had been trying to push to the forefront of her mind since it had happened.

She no longer tried to suppress it. She was now truly the mistress of Malvern! Everything here belonged to her. Within a space of less than half a year, she had come from an indentured tavern wench to being the mistress of the finest plantation in all of Virginia.

It was an exhilarating thought, and she was hard put not to express her joy. It was with an effort that she maintained a grave countenance.

Hannah was busy in Malcolm's study, trying to sort out his papers and account books. It was a struggle, and she knew it would take her some time to master them. Consequently she was a little annoyed when there was a discreet knock on the door.

"Come in!"

The door opened, and Henry, the overseer, came in, broad-brimmed hat in hand. "Mistress . . ."

"Yes, Henry, what is it? I'm occupied, as you can see."

"Mistress, it be about . . ." He twisted the hat in his hands, broad face agonized over the words he wanted to get out. "I was wondering, now that the master dead, do I be staying on as overseer?"

Hannah gave him a look of surprise. "Why, I can think of no reason why you shouldn't. You *are* happy in the task?"

"Oh, yes, mistress, I be very happy."

"I understand that Malcolm freed you?"

"Yes, mistress," Henry said eagerly. "He give me my freedom when he make me overseer." He added proudly, "I be paid wages."

Hannah nodded decisively. "Then there will be no change made. Malcolm himself told me that he trusted you completely, and that there were no white overseers he'd ever seen as good as you."

"Thank you, Mistress Verner," Henry said gratefully. He ducked his head and started to back out.

"Wait, Henry! There is one thing. You may not care overmuch for what I am about to say. But since I *am* now mistress of Malvern, I will expect you to teach me all you know about growing tobacco."

Henry's mouth had fallen open. Now he closed it with a snap, but still remained speechless.

"Do you agree to that?" Hannah demanded.

"Yes, mistress, if that be your wish," he mumbled. "Though I don't know what white folks gon' think...."

"As long as you agree." Hannah nodded firmly and dismissed him with a wave of her hand.

She turned back to the papers and books strewn across Malcolm's desk. Soon she began to make some sense out of it, and she was amazed. She had known that Malcolm Verner was a wealthy man, but the extent of his riches was beyond her expectations. In addition to the plantation, he also owned much property in Williamsburg, all business property....

Again she was interrupted by a knock on the door. "Damnation!" She slammed her hand down on the desk. "Come in!"

This time it was André Leclaire. He seemed oddly diffident, at least for him. "Mistress Verner..."

"*Mistress?*" She stared. "Why this sudden formality?"

"Well, it ... it came into my mind ..." His gaze wandered away. Then he straightened up and almost glared at her. "Do you wish me to stay on at Malvern now that your husband is dead?"

"You, too?" she muttered. At his look, she waved a hand. "André, are *you* happy here?"

"Dear lady, as long as I am forced to remain in exile in this uncivilized country, I can think of no place I would be more content!"

"Then why in God's name do you come in here asking such a question when you already know that I want you to stay?"

"Your neighbors, dear Hannah. Gossip will grow apace. A man living here with you . . ." That half-wicked, half-sad smile was back. "Since they have little knowledge of what I am."

"Pooh!" Hannah said impatiently. "You know what I think of their opinions. Now, stop playing the fool, and busy yourself elsewhere."

"Gladly, dear lady, gladly."

A few minutes later, she heard him playing the virginal in the music room. Listening for a moment, she smiled. It was the verse her father used to sing to her.

She returned her attention to the desk. Soon, among the papers, she found one that she read avidly. It was Malcolm's will, dated a little over a month ago. It was a short, simple document.

"I, Malcolm Verner, being sound in mind and body, do hereby bequeath all my worldly goods and properties to my dear wife, Hannah Verner. In the event there shall be male issue before or after my death, said male issue will, on reaching his majority, receive two-thirds of my estate, and my dear wife will be bequeathed the remaining third. Dated and signed this day of our Lord, 12 November, 1717, Williamsburg, Virginia."

At the bottom was Malcolm's scrawled signature, along with the signature of two witnesses.

So now it was *completely* legal, Hannah thought. She wondered briefly why Malcolm hadn't informed her of his making a will. The tone of the legal document seemed to hint that he had almost sensed his impending death. Tears stood in her eyes. How much she wished she *was* carrying his child, his son. But it was not to be.

Angrily she dashed the tears from her eyes and went on with the task of sorting out the papers.

An hour later, she made another, even more breathtaking discovery. In the last, bottom drawer of the desk was a large metal chest, nothing else. It took an effort to lift it out, for it was quite heavy. The chest was locked.

Hannah stared at it for a moment in frustration. Then she remembered something. Yesterday, Jenny had come to her with the clothes Malcolm had taken off in his room the night of his death, before coming to her. Hannah had gone through the pockets and among the items she had found were a number of keys.

She hurried to fetch them. Back in the study, she tried the keys. The third one opened the chest. Lifting the lid back, she gasped in wonder. The chest was filled to the brim with money, all British currency of various denominations, along with a great many gold coins and several documents she discovered to be letters of credit issued in England. After a few minutes of trying to total it all up, she dropped back into a chair, her knees weak. The value of the money and the letters of credit amounted to several thousand pounds!

With the plantation, the properties in Williamsburg, and now this, this ready money, she was indeed a wealthy woman!

Suddenly an idea sprouted in her mind.

Without further ado, she left the study. She

found Bess in the cookhouse overseeing supper preparations. She drew her outside, barely able to contain her excitement.

"Bess, do you know if Amos Stritch owns the Cup and Horn?"

"I ain't right sure, honey." Bess looked at her with undisguised curiosity. "But it likely he don't. He allus talking about being fearful of fire. Says he wouldn't own property, not since Jamestown burned to the ground. Many folks feel the same way."

"Do you know who *does* own the property?"

Bess shrugged her wide shoulders. "No, Miss Hannah, I don't. Old Stritch would hardly be confiding in me about business matters, now would he?" she asked drily.

"Thanks, Bess." Hannah impulsively hugged her.

"Thanks for what? I ain't told you nothing." She stood back and eyed Hannah with open suspicion. "What you got in that mischief-making head of yours, honey?"

"I'm not sure yet, Bess. I have to think on it some more. But if what I'm thinking comes true, we'll both be happy. We'll be getting back at old devil Stritch! You'd like that, wouldn't you?"

Bess laughed. "I would, child. I purely would!"

Hannah thought about it hard for the rest of the day and evening, so excited and yet apprehensive that she scarcely slept.

She was so busy with her thoughts at the supper table, responding not at all to André's flashes of wit, that he was finally driven to remark, "Dear Hannah, I know all this has been difficult for you, but . . ." He made that clicking sound with his tongue. "You did *not* love the man that much. We

229

have never had the need between us to enact a false role. So why the despondency, the gloom?"

Hannah came to with a start. "What? Oh, I *am* sorry, André." She reached across the table to pat his hand. "It's not that at all, believe me. I will tell you on the morrow what is in my thoughts."

"That devious mind of yours is scheming again." He twirled his wineglass between his fingers, scowling at her. "Am I not correct?"

Her laughter tinkled. "André, you know me so well!" To herself, she added, *Or think you do.*

The next morning, when Hannah outlined what she had in mind, André was horrified. "Dear lady, I would do anything for you ... well, almost anything. But this is beyond my talents. I am deplorable at business matters!"

"André, you *must* do this for me. I cannot. I would be laughed at and ignored should I undertake such a task. And you don't have to be a businessman to do what I ask. In fact . . ." She laughed. "The worse businessman you are, perhaps the better. I don't expect a profit from the transaction. All you have to do is find out who owns the Cup and Horn, land and building, and offer so much money the owner cannot resist. The money I have, André—do not worry."

André sighed. His features took on a worried look. "Dear lady, I can understand your need to avenge yourself on this blackguard. From what you have told me, the man is the blackest of villains. But, *mon dieu*—to go to such extremes!"

"I will go to any extremes to ruin him!" Hannah said vehemently. "I hate Amos Stritch so

230

much it turns my heart to bitter gall whenever I chance to think of the man!"

"Well, if you are so determined, I will play my part." He sighed and arose. "I understand your need to scourge your soul. But I beg of you, dear lady, do not let such hatred consume you until you hate all men equally. There are good men, even in this country. Cynic that I am, I know this to be true. You are young, you are beautiful. It would indeed be a waste to devote your life to hate, instead of love, for which you were intended."

Hannah's head went back. In a freezing voice, she said, "You go too far, sir! My private life is my concern!"

A month later came the day Hannah had been waiting for with much anticipation. Amos Stritch was summoned to Malvern to talk to her.

The Christmas season was past, and it was a very cold day. Christmas, coming so soon after Malcolm's death, had not been joyful on the plantation. Hannah thought it fitting that this day the weather was as cold as her heart.

She stood at a front window and watched the coach stop before the house. She watched Stritch climb clumsily out of the coach, the driver helping him. Leaning heavily on his stick, the corpulent figure hobbled slowly toward the house.

Hannah smiled grimly. His gout was bothering him. Good! She had heard that his gout always flamed up when he had an emotional upset.

She called Jenny to her. "Let Squire Stritch in, Jenny. I will be in the study."

"Do I serve anything, mistress?"

"No, nothing!" Hannah said sharply. "This is business, not a social visit."

She marched into the study. She had taken particular pains to dress for the occasion of Stritch's visit, getting herself up as carefully as she would for a ball. She wore a daring gown, revealing her shoulders and the swell of her bosom, and much jewelry. She wanted to dazzle Amos Stritch in every way possible.

She occupied the easy chair Malcolm had always used, leaving the room's hardback chair for Stritch. In her lap she had a single document—the deed to the Cup and Horn. In a little while she heard the thump-thump of Stritch's cane in the hallway.

At Jenny's timid knock, she said, "Let him in, Jenny."

Amos Stritch limped in, his gross face wearing a servile smile. He made an awkward bow. "Mistress Verner. 'Tis indeed a pleasure."

"Is it? I would not be so confident of that, Squire Stritch, until you have learned the reason I have summoned you to Malvern. The circumstances are quite different from when last you set eyes on me, are they not?"

Stritch said hastily, "When Master Verner came to me asking for your articles of indenture, I was most happy to accede to his wishes."

"Were you indeed?" she said drily. "I happen to know otherwise."

"Whatever Master Verner told you, gentleman that he was . . ."

Hannah cut him off with a sharp gesture. "I did not summon you here to talk of my husband. I think it would be better if you were seated while I explain."

A look of alarm crossed his features. He sat down with an effort, eyeing her warily all the while.

Hannah picked up the document from her lap. "Do you know what this is?"

His small eyes fastened on the document fearfully. "No, madam, I do not. ..."

"It is a land deed. The Cup and Horn and the land it sits on are now my property, sir."

Stritch flinched visibly, and slumped a little, and his normally red complexion took on a grayish hue.

Hannah continued relentlessly, "And as of the end of the month, I intend to increase the amount of your rent."

"But I am hard put to meet it now!" He swallowed. Self-pity made his voice a whine. He asked cautiously, "What is the sum to be?"

Hannah named a figure.

"That is three times what I now pay!"

"I am not an uneducated serving wench now, sir. I know well how to figure. And not only will the sum be increased, it will be due the first of every month."

"But that is against custom! It is due yearly, after harvest time, when my customers pay their creditors!"

"There is no law, sir, that says that I must follow custom. Those are my terms, Mr. Stritch."

"I have just paid my yearly rent money to the landlord, not three months past. I will have nothing with which to buy liquor and food." He moaned. "It will drive me out of business. I will have to close my doors!"

Hannah gave an indifferent shrug.

He squinted at her, his color flooding back. "That is your intent, ain't it? You ungrateful wench! I took you in in rags, gave you honest work, and . . ."

Hannah leaned forward. "And took me into your bed, caning me until I had no resistance while you had me. And even worse, turned me into a tavern whore!"

Stritch was struggling to keep his temper under control. "I am sorry, Mistress Verner, if I dishonored you. Your beauty was such that lust drove me clear out of my senses. . . ."

Even as he was speaking, his eyes were devouring the rosy-white flesh of her shoulders and upper breasts. Hannah shivered, as though he were actually touching her. "Spare me your grovelings, sir. You think me stupid enough to believe you sincere? You are a vile man, Amos Stritch, and I am now in a position to repay you for your villainy." She got to her feet. "I believe our business is concluded."

He lurched to his feet, cursing. "You damnable bitch! You think just because you whored your way into a rich gentleman's bed and got him to wed you that it makes you any more than what you are?" He sneered. "Playing at the fine lady when you're nothing but a gutter strumpet!"

He raised his stick and limped toward her, his face contorted and evil. The stick whistled through the air as Hannah stepped nimbly aside. Stritch staggered on, almost falling. Hannah snatched up a bell from the desk and rang it.

Almost at once the study door opened and John stepped in. "Yes, Mistress Verner?"

Hannah gestured. "Throw this scum out and see that he leaves Malvern at once!"

John advanced on Stritch, who drew himself up.

"Keep your black hands off me! I'm a-going." He glared at Hannah. "You ain't heard the last of me, missy! My word on it!"

In the rented coach Amos Stritch fell back onto the seat with a groan.

He was a ruined man!

He could foresee no way that he could pay the increased rent to Hannah Verner and continue to operate the Cup and Horn. What money he had squirreled away would be gone within a month, two at the very most, to pay for liquor.

Much of the liquor he bought at bargain prices from the pirate ships. The buccaneers preyed on merchant ships from England, France, and the West Indies, and many of those ships carried cargoes of wine, brandy, rum, and other liquors. What drink the pirates could not consume themselves they sold to tavern owners at bargain prices. Many innkeepers would not deal with them, but Stritch had no such scruples. The trouble was, the pirates extended no credit, demanding payment on delivery, preferably in Spanish gold.

Stritch knew he had to close the tavern at once. What good would it do him to hold onto it until all his money was gone? He would need what little he had to live on until he found some way to earn a living.

He groaned again, a groan that came close to tears. He had known little but tavern life, working at the bar in various inns. It was only by happenstance that he had learned of the pirates having stolen liquor for sale. Stritch had wormed himself into the good graces of Blackbeard and other pirates, and had offered to act as an agent for them. He had been able to cheat both the pirates, who knew little of the value of the liquors they had for sale, and the tavern owners. In this manner, he had garnered enough money to open the Cup and Horn.

Stritch sighed. He supposed he would have to return to that risky trade—risky because a pirate was never to be trusted, was likely to slit a man's throat on a drunken whim; and risky because traffic with pirates was daily growing more unpopular in Virginia. But a man had to make his way. And if he had to give up the Cup and Horn, Stritch certainly couldn't return to working behind the bar, not in his poor state of health.

He brooded on the injustice of it, his gouty foot twinging as he seethed with hatred for that copper-haired bitch. He vowed that some way, some day, he would be in a position to strike back at her, to make her rue the day she had ruined Amos Stritch!

He sat bolt upright as an idea came to him. If he joined forces with the pirates again, mayhap he could cajole them into a raid on Malvern. There had to be much of value there. That bitch had been wearing a fortune today in jewels alone. And Stritch had a strong feeling there was also a great lot of money there.

Teach, when roaring drunk, was foolhardy enough to attempt almost anything if there were profit and women involved. He was a great one for the wenches, was Blackbeard. Stritch was sure that he had only to convince him that Malvern had riches worth the risk, plus a toothsome wench!

They could probably sail right up the James River, almost to the back door of the plantation house. And who would be there to defy them? A lone woman and some slaves, who were frightened of their own shadows. Everybody knew that niggers wouldn't fight.

Much cheered now, Stritch leaned back. Closing his eyes, he could visualize that bitch being taken again and again by Teach and his men. And he, Stritch, would be there, watching and gloating. And she would beg him for help, promising to do anything for him if he would only make them stop.

Stritch dreamed on, dreaming of that fine day when he would have his revenge on the high and mighty Hannah Verner!

Chapter Thirteen

"It would be a mistake, dear Hannah," André Leclaire said.

"But why?" Hannah asked fiercely. "There has been little but gloom and hard work at Malvern since Malcolm's death. . . ."

"That is the reason. A year has not passed since Monsieur Verner's demise. It is the custom for a widow to grieve for a period of one year."

"Custom! Pooh! Always I'm being prattled to about custom! I have worked hard, overseeing the planting and the harvesting just finished. I have driven myself day and night." Her head was held proudly. "And it is my thought that I have done a good job. Even Henry grudgingly admits as much."

"Work!" André grimaced. "Sweaty field work, befitting a man, not the lady you have become.

You have scandalized your neighbors all the more—a woman managing a vast plantation!"

"Somebody had to do it. Would you have had me let the plantation work go? We have had a good harvest, and I handled the sale of the tobacco as well as any man."

"You should have hired a man to manage the plantation. That would have been the proper thing to do."

"Proper?" She grinned at him mischievously. "Since when has André Leclaire considered the propriety of *anything*?"

"This is different," he said defensively. "There are certain things a lady simply does not do."

"I intend to run my plantation, and that is the end of it. Do you think I would trust some hired man to do it?"

"That is what concerns me, dear lady. You seem not to trust *any* man, and you not yet of legal age. You have hardened your heart against the male gender. . . ."

"That is not true! Only those men . . ." She broke off, turning her face away. "Anyway, the condition of my heart is no affair of yours."

"But it is. It grieves me to see it. You *must* know how very fond of you I have become, Hannah."

Instantly her pique was gone. She could never stay angry with André for long. "Dear friend. I know." She reached out to take his hand. "Then you will help me make preparations for the ball?"

"*Mon Dieu!* As your late husband once remarked to me, you *are* a willful wench!" He sighed, gave the Gallic shrug, and fluttered his hands. "Do I not always give in to you? But you will regret it, I am sure," he added darkly.

240

"Why? Because a few pious hypocrites refuse to attend? We'll do without them. I want young people, people who are gay and charming. Besides, the others will come, I know they will. Dear Malcolm himself once told me that Virginians love nothing more than an excuse for a ball, for merry-making. You yourself said I now have all the graces of a lady, André."

"Sometimes . . ." André heaved a sigh. "Sometimes, dear Hannah, that is not enough."

And even Bess was against it.

"Bess, I know it'll mean more work for you, but . . ."

"It ain't the work, honey. Lawd, I enjoys a grand ball much as you. But it's you, child, who going to be hurt. These fine white folks won't take kindly to you giving a ball so soon after Master Verner's death."

"But Bess, it's been nearly a year!" Hannah wailed. "You're talking just like André."

"You pay attention to that André. A fine gentleman like him, he knows 'bout such things. I didn't cotton much to that man first off, but he smart. And he got your best interests at heart. You listen to him, if not to old Bess."

But Hannah was not to be dissuaded. "I'm sending out invitations this week, Bess, and that's the end of it!"

Bess was shaking her head. "Lawd, Lawd, honey, there just seems to be some devil in you makes you want to all the time stick your tongue out at people!"

241

Bess and André were right. The ball was a dismal failure.

Hannah made elaborate preparations, with much food and drink, and she employed a group of musicians from Williamsburg. She had André design and make a new gown for her, white silk this time. And she was glittering with jewelry, her exposed shoulders and arms draped with it. André told her that she was beautiful, more beautiul than ever, and she knew this to be true.

But the number of guests was sorely disappointing. Few women appeared, and those who did, Hannah realized, came only to stare at and whisper about her, refusing to let their bedazzled husbands dance with Hannah. The men far outnumbered the women, and they were, for the most part, unmarried.

"I cannot see why you are so surprised, dear lady," André murmured. "You are a prime catch, a prize indeed for the young bloods."

"Why is that?"

"Because you are a beauty, and because you are a widow. Most of all, because you are a *wealthy* widow."

"You mean they want to wed me?" Hannah asked in dismay.

"Naturellement." He flashed that wicked grin. "They will be in full pursuit now, now that you have given this ball to let them know that you are available."

"But that's not the reason for the ball!"

"They will believe so. Oh, you may be sure, dear Hannah, that they will be baying at your heels from this evening forward."

"I don't believe you!"

242

"My dear Hannah, whatever you may be, you are not stupid." André gave an elaborate sigh. "You will soon see that I am correct."

As the evening progressed, some of Hannah's depression dropped away, for there was one advantage to being the only unmarried woman present. She never lacked for dancing partners. Always there was some young man in constant attendance. She danced and danced, sometimes having the floor all to herself and her partner. Often André was also dancing, paying gallant attention to the married ladies. But rarely did a man and wife venture onto the ballroom floor.

Yet Hannah noticed they were all partaking of the food and drink available. This ignited her temper, and she began to flirt outrageously with all the men, single and married alike. This made her the target of murderous glances from the ladies, but she tossed her head and went on her merry way, frequently directing her current partner to fetch her a glass of wine.

André, watching her closely, felt a throb of pity. But it wasn't long before he realized how wrong he was. Hannah might think that the ball was a failure—hence her outrageous behavior—yet it was evident that she was having the time of her young life. The young gallants were in blatant pursuit, vying with each other for her favors. Watching Hannah as she whirled across the floor, hair glinting like gold in the candle shine, lips as red as a new rose, eyes bright as the gems she wore, her full breasts threatening to burst free of the tight confinement of the low bodice at any moment, André wondered how many of the young men had had to turn away and hastily retreat outside until the bulge in their tight breeches softened.

Pity, indeed! He threw back his head and laughed.

Pouting, the clumsy, buxom woman in his arms said, "Am I such a poor dancer that you find me humorous, Monsieur Leclaire?"

The atrocious accent she placed on "Monsieur" made André wince. To conceal his reaction, he said quickly, *"Non, non,* madam. It is not you I laugh at. It is a private joke in my own head." He freed an arm to tap the side of his head with a forefinger. "As I once said to someone else, perhaps I am a little mad."

Between the dancing and the wine, Hannah's head was muddled. To her dancing partner, she said, "I feel in need of air. Would you escort me outside, Jamie?"

"With pleasure, milady," said Jamie Falkirk. He stepped back, made a knee, and extended his arm.

Of all the young men present, Jamie was the one Hannah liked most. He was tall and rawboned, with grave green eyes and flaming red hair—his own, not a wig. Although he was twenty-three, he still struck her as somewhat callow. Hannah felt years older than he. Yet there was a sincerity about him. He spoke little, whereas the others flocking around her tonight had been profuse with flattery; but when Jamie did speak, his words had that ring of sincerity. And while he dressed well, he wasn't foppish, as so many of the others were. The Falkirk plantation was the adjoining one north, only an hour's ride distant.

Outside, the air was cool, faintly chill. Hannah drew two deep breaths before she noticed that others were also outside. They had been talking animatedly, but now all fell silent at the sight of Hannah.

Hannah touched Jamie's arm lightly. "Do you like horses?"

He glanced at her in surprise. "Of course, madam. I am a-horse much of a working day."

"Then let's stroll down to the stable. There is something I wish to show you."

Murmurs of low conversation started up behind them, and Hannah smiled as she imagined what they were saying.

One dim candle lantern burned in the stable. Hannah led Jamie halfway down to Black Star's stall. Black Star whinnied at the sight of her, neck arching out. He shied away when he saw Jamie.

"It's all right, beauty," she crooned. "Jamie's a friend." She reached in to caress his neck, which was trembling. The trembling gradually subsided, and the animal crowded close again.

"What a beautiful horse!" Jamie exclaimed.

"Yes, isn't he? Of late, I've been so busy with the harvesting that I haven't had much opportunity to ride him just for pleasure." On impulse, she looked around at Jamie. "Would you care to come over some afternoon and ride with me?"

"I would love to," he said eagerly.

"What about your parents? Would they approve?"

"They have nothing to say. I am beyond the age of consent." He drew himself up stiffly. "They did not wish me to come...." He broke off, looking away from her.

"They didn't wish you to come here tonight?" Hannah said softly. "Attend a ball given by a wanton woman who was once a tavern serving wench? They said that you would shame them by coming?"

"You are not all those things they say. I know you're not," he said intensely. "You are a lady, the most beautiful lady I have ever seen!"

"Thank you. You're sweet." She touched his face with her fingertips, a gentle caress.

With a muttered groan, he swept her into his arms, his mouth seeking hers. For a moment Hannah let him have his way. In spite of herself, she felt a pulsing of response. Despite Jamie's callowness, there was an air of great vitality, of virility, about him. Hannah fancied she could smell it on him. He would make a strong lover.

Finally she gently disengaged herself. She murmured, "I think perhaps we should return to the house."

"I'm sorry, madam," he said in an agony of embarrassment. "I don't know what came over me."

"It's all right, Jamie. Really it is." She took two steps away, then turned back. "I will ride tomorrow. At two. If you would like to ride with me, it would please me greatly."

Although it was mid-November, a warm spell had moved into Virginia, a delayed Indian summer, and Hannah and Jamie Falkirk were sharing a picnic basket under a shady oak on the banks of the James River.

Two weeks had passed since the ball, and Jamie Falkirk had come over at least twice a week to ride with her. And today, since the weather was nice, Hannah had cajoled Bess into preparing them a picnic basket, along with a bottle of wine.

Jamie was a good horseman, better than she was,

except that his mount, a big chestnut, could not come close to competing with Black Star for speed, endurance, and jumping ability.

Realizing this, and careful of Jamie's male pride, Hannah had kept a tight rein on Black Star after their first ride together, allowing Jamie to take the lead. Black Star hadn't been too happy about giving way to an inferior animal, yet he had heeded Hannah's touch on the reins.

At the moment both Black Star and Jamie's horse were grazing a few yards away from where they lazed under the oak.

Jamie seemed unusually pensive this day. Hannah, chewing hungrily on a chicken leg, waved it before his face. "Care to tell me what's in your thoughts?"

Jamie started, pulling his gaze from the river, and looked over at her. "I beg your pardon, madam. I was unforgivably rude."

"It's not that important. You just seemed so sunk in thought, I feared something dire might be troubling you."

"You are, Hannah. You have been troubling me' sorely."

Hannah said archly, "In what way, sir?"

"You are in my thoughts constantly. And you are in my dreams at night."

"Pleasant dreams, I hope?"

"Pleasant and yet not pleasant. I dream that I hold you in my arms, in love. And then I awake and you are not there."

Hannah was both surprised and moved by his eloquence. And then, before she fully realized it, he had moved around the picnic spread and was beside her on the blanket.

"Hannah, dearest Hannah!" he said passionately. "You are so beautiful. The very thought of you inflames me until I think I will go mad!"

His arms went around her, and he was kissing her. His shirt was open, and his broad chest heaved against her bosom with the agitation of his breathing.

For just a moment Hannah felt anger, and she placed her hands on his bared chest to push him away. She felt the muscles rippling there as he strained against her. Suddenly his urgent hunger awoke an answering hunger in her own body, and she thought, *Why not?* They were alone here, there was no one to see. Mouth still pressing on hers, he had pushed her skirts and petticoats up, and his hands caressed her inner thighs. A sweet languor stole over Hannah. With a breathy sigh, she lay back on the blanket.

Jamie stretched out beside her. The wine she had consumed with the food and the stroking of his hands on her thighs and the rough yet sweet feel of his mouth on hers made Hannah feel faintly dizzy. And above all else, she was curious. This was the first time she had lain with a man close to her own age, a man virile, in his prime, a man enamored of her charms. What would it be like? Would love with Jamie help ease the feeling of discontent within her?

Jamie was not the accomplished lover that Malcolm had been, yet he more than made up for it by his youth and the hard strength of his body. And he was not crude and brutal as Stritch and the drunken pirate had been.

Somehow he had unlaced her bodice and freed her breasts. She stroked his hair as he kissed the tumescent nipples. Her nerve ends tingled; she was alive, vibrant with sensation. And when finally, with a groan, Jamie moved back from her to lower his breeches and then entered her, Hannah murmured with pleasure and arched her hips to meet him.

Still he was gentle with her, moving slowly while her passion built, until she was aware of nothing else. It was only toward the end that he became rough, driving against her hard. He called out her name in a guttural voice. As his body began to shudder, Hannah clasped him to her breast. At the last instant she experienced a warm flood of pleasure, and she quivered, crying out, before she was still.

Yet even as she lay quiet beneath him, still savoring her first moment of real pleasure from love, there was a small, nagging doubt squirming through her mind. She still felt somehow deprived. It was not the overwhelming ecstasy she had been expecting.

Hannah sighed. Perhaps she had been expecting too much. Bess had told her how pleasurable love could be between a man and a woman who loved each other. Mayhap the fault lay within herself. Although she felt some fondness for Jamie, certainly she didn't love him. Into her mind crept André's warning: "It would indeed be a waste to devote your life to hate, instead of love, for which you were intended."

Had she allowed her hate for Amos Stritch and Silas Quint to warp her, burn all the love out of her heart? Could it be that she could never love *any* man?

Her speculations were interrupted as Jamie said,

"Are you unhappy, Hannah? You seem so.... Did I displease you?"

"No, Jamie dear." She reached out to stroke his cheek. "You pleased me greatly."

"I've wanted you *so* much, Hannah. But I didn't intend to force myself on you like this."

"It's all right, Jamie, don't fret so," she said, slightly annoyed. Then she smiled and said lightly, "After all, Jamie, it's not as if you've deflowered a virgin. I have been married, you know."

A faint blush stained his cheeks, and Hannah had to stifle her amusement. She became brisk. "It grows late. I must get back to the house."

Jamie accepted the suggestion eagerly—almost, it seemed to Hannah, with relief.

They gathered up the blanket and picnic things and rode back to Malvern. Jamie got down to open the pasture gate, then closed it behind the horses. He stood a moment at her stirrup, staring up at her.

"I cannot put into words what today meant to me, Hannah."

"Then don't try," she said, suddenly very cross with him.

"Shall we ride together later in the week?"

Hannah shrugged. "If you wish. I ride at the same time every afternoon, with or without you." With her knees she urged Black Star toward the stable. Just before they went through the stable door, Hannah glanced back. Jamie was still standing where she had left him, staring after her.

Inside the stable, John and Dickie were standing together. Dickie was talking excitedly. John came to help her off Black Star, then led the horse away to unsaddle him.

Dickie said, "John just returned from Williamsburg, m'lady. The village is agog with the news!"

"What news is that, Dickie?" Hannah asked absently.

"Teach the pirate and his crew have all been captured or killed, Blackbeard himself killed! Happened this week past. Troops under the governor's orders boarded Blackbeard's ship, the *Adventure*. When Blackbeard was killed, his head was severed from his body and hung beneath the bowsprit of the troop ship!"

"How awful!" Hannah shivered delicately.

From Black Star's stall, John said soberly, " 'Tis a goodly thing that pirate is finally finished. He was the devil's spawn!"

Hannah was not really interested in the news of Blackbeard's death, and she left the stable. Halfway to the house, her step slowed as she recalled that last night at the Cup and Horn and the great drunken hulk of a pirate who had taken her by force. She vaguely remembered that he had been one of Blackbeard's men. She devoutly hoped that he had been one of those killed. But since she didn't know his name, she supposed she would never know. Certainly she could not bring herself to view the corpses of all the dead pirates in an endeavor to identify that particular one, even though she did hate him with all her being.

She shivered again, and continued on toward the house.

"I love you, Hannah dearest!" Jamie said as he shuddered out his passion.

Hannah murmured inaudibly in response.

A few minutes later he sat beside her on the

blanket, decorously clothed again. Hannah leaned back against the tree trunk, staring dreamily at the flowing river.

"Hannah?"

"Yes, Jamie?"

"I want you for my wife."

Hannah swung her face toward him, not sure she had heard aright. "What did you say?"

"I want you to be my wife!" His face was intense. "I love you."

"That's sweet, dear." She didn't know whether to laugh or to be angry. "And I'm sure you think you love me. . . ."

"Not think—I know!"

"It wouldn't be Malvern you're in love with?" she said in a teasing voice.

His face took on a wounded look. "That's unkind, Hannah. You know that is not true!"

"Do I?" She sat up. "Jamie, I'm flattered by your proposal, but you see, I can't wed you."

"Why not?" He was almost belligerent.

She sighed. "Because I don't love you."

"You will learn to love me!"

Hannah shook her head. "No, Jamie. I won't wed you. If what has happened between us has given you to think that, I am sorry."

"You didn't love Malcolm Verner, yet you became his wife!"

"What gives you cause to think I didn't love him?"

"How could you have loved him?" He gestured contemptuously. "A man old enough to be your grandfather!"

Without thought Hannah's hand lashed out,

slapping him across the cheek. "How dare you, sir! You will not say such things about a dead man!"

His face turned a dark red. "Then you've been dallying with me, tumbling with me out here like ... like a strumpet! What they say about you is true!"

"Perhaps it is." She got to her feet, icy in her fury. "And if such be the case, you wouldn't want such a wench for your wife, now would you?"

Jamie sprang up, seizing her hand. "I'm sorry, Hannah," he said wretchedly. "I don't know what made me say that. I know the things they say about you aren't true."

"But they are true, you see." She pulled her hand from his grip. "I do not wish to see you on Malvern again, sir."

She strode toward Black Star.

"Hannah, wait! Listen to me! I love you. I swear I do!"

Unheeding, Hannah mounted the stallion. In her raging fury, she used for the first time the riding quirt she carried, striking the horse across the flank. Startled, Black Star bolted. He was racing at a full gallop within a few yards.

She rode him hard all the way back to Malvern. Not wanting to bother with the gate, she urged the horse on, and he cleared the fence in a mighty leap. Her anger cooling now, Hannah gradually slowed him down as they approached the stable.

It wasn't until she was almost to the stable door that she noticed the stranger lounging against the wall, watching her through eyes squinted against the smoke drifting up from the cigar in his mouth. He was young, tall, with dark eyes and hair, and was well-dressed.

She drew the lathered horse to a stop short of the stable door and slipped off.

The man's face was clouded by a scowl of disapproval. "Riding him a little hard, weren't you, madam?"

"What business is that of yours, sir? The animal belongs to me!"

At the sound of the stranger's voice, Black Star whinnied and moved toward him, jerking the reins out of Hannah's hands. The stranger stepped away from the stable wall and caressed Black Star's mane.

There was something hauntingly familiar about this man, yet Hannah was certain that she'd never seen him before. She said, "Who are you, sir?"

He studied her through hooded eyes. "Why, I am Michael Verner."

Hannah gasped. "That's impossible! Michael Verner is dead!"

"Obviously that is not true, madam, since here I stand." His smile was mocking. "And I am not a ghost, I assure you."

PART THREE

Michael Verner

Chapter Fourteen

On that afternoon in Williamsburg when Michael Verner had exchanged bitter words with his father, most of the quarrel had been a sham on his part. It had been a show, a role he played so that the bystanders would believe that he was parting forever from his father and forsaking the Verner name, and so that word of it would eventually reach the ears of Edward Teach.

And yet, part of the feelings he expressed were true; Michael knew he would have to live with this. He did have a distaste for the dull life of a planter. He yearned for some great adventure, for something he couldn't put a name to.

But in his heart, he loved his father.

In those few minutes in the stable the night Malcolm Verner had given him Black Star as a birthday gift, Michael's love for his father had filled his heart, and he had come close to revealing his secret.

At the last moment Governor Spotswood's warning had stayed him: "Tell no one of this, Michael. Certainly not your father. If he knows that your bitter parting, when it comes, is not all it sounds, he may inadvertently give you away. We know not who to trust. You could place your life in grave peril, perhaps even your father's own life. Blackbeard is a shrewd devil and mightily suspicious. He has to be utterly convinced that you have chosen a life of piracy. So tell no one, absolutely no one. Only we two shall know. Do not worry, lad—when it is all over and you have accomplished your mission, your father will forgive you and be proud."

Michael had been astonished when Colonel Alexander Spotswood, the royal governor of Virginia, had summoned him to a secret audience in the Governor's Palace late one evening. He had also hidden a smile behind his hand as he recalled the story behind the name "Governor's Palace." Work on the original structure had begun in 1706, during Governor Nott's term of office. Three thousand pounds had been appropriated to build a suitable estate for the royal governor, but the costs had soon exceeded that. The burgesses had complained mightily about the high-handed manner in which Governor Nott was lavishing the public's funds on the building. Townspeople were soon referring to it sarcastically as "the palace," a term that had unfortunately gained wide acceptance. . . .

That evening, with little more than a hasty

greeting passing between them, Governor Spotswood said abruptly, "Something needs to be done about that devil, Blackbeard, and by the Lord above I intend to do it! Prominent citizens from all over Virginia, and even from North Carolina, have come to me clamoring for something to be done. And all the while he has sanctuary down there in North Carolina, practically an honored guest of Governor Eden!"

In his agitation Governor Spotswood began to pace. "And all the while this damned cutthroat sails out and waylays and loots merchant ships, and Spanish galleons carrying gold, often setting the torch to the vessels and murdering their crews. Then he flees back to safety in North Carolina." He wheeled on Michael. "Did you know that there have even been ugly rumors that I, the royal governor of Virginia, am his cohort—that I allow him to plunder and murder off the coasts of Virginia for a share of his plunder?"

Cautiously, Michael said, "I have heard such tales, sir, but they are rumor only—no one believes them."

"But they will, they will!" Governor Spotswood waved his hands. "That is why I must take action!"

"Governor, I must confess to puzzlement. Why have you summoned *me* here?"

"You, young Verner, are about to become a pirate, a member of Teach's unholy crew!"

Stunned, Michael said, "I'm afraid I don't understand, sir."

"You will, you will." The governor waved a hand. "Oh . . . forgive my poor hospitality, sir,

Would you care for a drink, Michael? A spot of brandy?"

Michael, beginning to relax now and intrigued by this voluble man, leaned back and crossed his legs. "A brandy would be fine, sir."

At the sideboard Governor Spotswood splashed brandy into two glasses, then strode over to give Michael one. The governor, an elegantly attired gentleman with a florid face dominated by a large nose, wore a full, shoulder-length wig. He sipped at his brandy and then took up a stance before the fireplace, one hand on the carved marble mantlepiece.

"What do you know of Blackbeard the pirate?"

"Not a great deal, I'm afraid, sir."

"He *is* a man of great mystery, true. But I have made it my business to learn all I could about the blackguard," the governor said grimly. "His origins are obscure. No one is even sure of his name, there being much doubt that his right name is Edward Teach. He is known by many names, and is called by most who have known him, even by his own men, a swaggering, merciless, godless brute. Evidently he began life in Bristol, in the mother country. He became a pirate, according to most accounts, aboard a privateer sailing out of Jamaica during the last years of Queen Anne's War. He started out with another blackguard, Stede Bonnet, a devil's spawn we often had to contend with here in Virginia. But he was too shrewd for Bonnet, and was soon lording it over him. 'Tis said that Teach now has many men at his command." Governor Spotswood stepped forward to wave his arms. "The man must be stopped at all costs, Michael!"

"This Governor Eden of North Carolina you

spoke of . . . why does he not do something?"

"Because the man is in league with Teach!" the governor said with a scowl. "It is my understanding that Eden shares in the plunder! He permits the pirate to rendezvous on the coast of North Carolina. He goes and comes freely at Bath. Blackbeard's favorite refuge, as I understand it, is Ocracoke Inlet." The governor's lip curled. "'Tis even said that Teach has a house there, known as Blackbeard's Castle, where he retires to wench and drink. Blackbeard is a notorious wencher. 'Tis said he has been wed fourteen times. Marriages mostly farces, of course, since the women he takes to wife often are those he has captured from the merchants' ships."

"The man does have a fearsome reputation, from the tales I have heard," Michael said.

"And well deserved, you may be sure. He is a huge hulk of a man, with a powerful physique, well schooled in the use of pistol and cutlass. He allows his black beard to grow untrimmed, rising on his face almost to the level of his eyes, plaited with little tails, the ends tied with fanciful colored ribbons. Yes, Michael, he is a fearsome sight, but also absolutely fearless, 'tis my understanding, and proficient in the handling of all weaponry."

"It seems to me, Governor," Michael said with an amused smile, "that you are attempting to frighten the wits out of me about this man before I even know the nature of the task you wish me to perform."

"I am, Michael, I am," the governor said vehemently. "I wish you to have full knowledge of the villainy this scoundrel is capable of."

"All right, now that I am sufficiently frightened

259

and impressed, mayhap you would be so kind as to tell me what part I am to play in your plans?"

Governor Spotswood drained his brandy glass and set it down, straightening up to his full height. It seemed to Michael that it was his intention now to assume the mantle of authority, to place some distance between them.

"The task I wish you to undertake, Michael Verner, is to become a member of Blackbeard's crew of pirates!"

"I understand that, sir, but to what purpose?"

"I need someone I can trust—I need a spy in the enemy camp."

Michael stirred uneasily. "If I may be so bold, Governor, it strikes me that there are many men more fitted for this task than I."

"More fitted, perhaps, but I know not whom to trust. I have sent others in, and they come back telling me they can learn nothing, can get no evidence. I dare not use my authority to go into another colony and take this villain. It has even been whispered to me that Richard Fitzwilliam, collector of customs for the lower James River, is in league with Blackbeard, is his agent and solicitor in these parts. You comprehend the problem confronting me?"

"Well, yes, I see, sir. But, again—why me?"

"You, because of the Verner name, are a man I can trust. And if I may be frank, because you are heir to a wealthy estate. For that reason alone, you would not be so apt to be corrupted by this man. And . . ." The governor smiled grimly. "There is another reason that makes you ideal for the task. Teach has a quirk. He delights in recruiting members of the gentry into his band of cutthroats. Coming from peasant stock himself, he takes great delight in making gentlemen subservient to his cruel whims, in making them his lieutenants. Since Blackbeard has little learning and his men are without any at all—they are mostly drunken louts, the very scum of mankind—he has need of a few men like you, Michael."

Despite his initial astonishment, Michael was becoming more and more intrigued by what Governor Spotswood proposed. And from the governor's smile and his next words, Michael realized that he had revealed himself.

"It appeals to you, does it not? I thought it would. Oh, do not bother to deny it." Governor Spotswood's voice took on a wistful note. "I well remember how I was at your age, blood flowing hot, chafing sorely at restraints and conventions, yearning for a spot of adventure. I have well noted your restless—nay, even reckless—nature this year past. It is your twenty-first year within a few days, is it not?"

Michael nodded.

"And I have heard of your ability with sword and pistol, and of your horsemanship. . . ."

"Merely at play, at harmless sport, sir, never once in serious combat." Michael shrugged. "And, unfortunately, the last will do me little good aboard a sailing vessel." Michael abruptly realized that they were proceeding as though he had already agreed. And he supposed he had, without putting it into words.

Governor Spotswood was saying, "Seamanship is easily learned. And whatever else may be said of Edward Teach, he's an excellent ship's master, an exceptional seaman. You understand, Michael, that

261

I cannot provide you with any funds to finance your mission. You must come into Blackbeard's presence in dire need of funds, else he will not believe you. There will, however, be a substantial reward if your mission is successful. You must needs, as they say, live by your wits until you have joined Teach's crew."

Michael leaned forward. "This mission, sir, you have not exactly defined it. Precisely what am I to do?"

"Gather evidence for me that Blackbeard is indeed a pirate and a cutthroat, so if necessary I will have sufficient cause to send troops into Governor Eden's colony of North Carolina and apprehend this prince of villains. Or better still, get to me information that he is conducting forays on Virginia's soil or in the waters off Virginia's coast, so that I may send out troop ships to capture him. The Crown will not provide funds to outfit a fighting sloop or two for this task, but I will use my own funds for such a purpose, and gladly! Also, I want all the evidence you can garner concerning his cohorts. He must have the cöoperation of more than just Governor Eden. I have a man in Bath, a blacksmith by the name of Will Darcy, who will relay messages to me."

"This could take an extended length of time."

"It could, Michael, and probably will." Governor Spotswood nodded. "Which quite naturally will not be pleasant. I can well imagine that a short span of time spent among these pirates might strike a young man as romantic, adventurous—but over a period of time ... prepare yourself for at least a year, perhaps more. And gird yourself for an even more bitter chore. You must, in the presence of witnesses, provoke a severe quarrel with your father. Edward Teach must have knowledge of this to convince him. I know this will be as bitter as gall to you, but it must needs be done."

It was then that the governor swore Michael to absolute secrecy.

So it was done, and it left a much more bitter taste in Michael's mouth than he had anticipated. Following those acrimonious few minutes with his father on the street in Williamsburg, it took a powerful effort of will for Michael to turn his back and walk into the tavern after Malcolm Verner had slapped him. He wanted nothing more than to throw his arms around his father and beg his forgiveness.

He lingered on for a time in Williamsburg, until he had won enough at cards to buy a cheap horse, a brace of pistols and a sword, and rough clothes befitting the man he intended to be for the next year, or however long it took.

Riding out of Williamsburg, he experienced a feeling of freedom and release. He was embarking on an adventure!

He rode in the general direction of the North Carolina coast, the village of Bath his immediate destination.

He found Bath to be primitive, even by the measure of the time, and inhabited by a rougher element than he was accustomed to. Many ships rode at anchor in the port of Bath. While none flew the pirate flag, the skull and crossbones, Michael soon learned that many were engaged in piracy.

Most of the men in Bath were seafaring men,

263

and many of them made no secret of the fact that piracy was their way of life. Cultivating a rougher manner of comporting himself, Michael drank with them and played at cards. Fortunately he had a strong capacity for liquor, so he could match the men he met drink for drink and still be reasonably clear-headed while they were well into their cups and careless of tongue. Still, it was nigh onto four months before he heard anything more substantial than rumor about Blackbeard. Then he heard that Edward Teach had recently taken two prizes at sea and had sailed into Charleston, South Carolina, to dispose of his plunder.

"He'll be stopping off in Bath ere long," said Michael's source of rumor. He waited for Michael to provide another mug of rum. "Blackbeard allus stops off here on his way home to buy his old mates a tot or two."

And so, a few days later, late in the afternoon, Michael stood on the wharf and watched Blackbeard's ship, *Queen Anne's Revenge,* sail into Pamlico Sound. The anchor was dropped out a distance, the sails lowered and furled, and soon two boats were rowing toward the shore.

Michael stood well back in the crowd, smoking a cigar and observing. There was no doubt in his mind as to the identity of Edward Teach, Blackbeard the pirate, Governor Spotswood's prince of villains.

In the bow of the first boat stood a tall, black-bearded man, the beard plaited and tied off with colorful little ribbons. A foot in a seaboot was propped upon the prow of the boat. Although the water was calm here, there was a slight pitch to it, and Blackbeard rolled with the motion of the boat as though it came as naturally to him as breathing. In one hand he carried a cutlass, the westering sun glinting off the steel blade. As a roar went up from the men on the shore, he raised the cutlass and brought it down in a chopping motion, as though slicing off a head. Another roar went up. Then Blackbeard raised his other hand, this one holding a rum bottle. He drank lustily from it, head thrown back.

As soon as the men in the boats were ashore, it was readily apparent that they were all drunk. Blackbeard loomed tall above the heads of the men around him, swaggering, roaring out the tale of his latest villainy as they headed toward the center of the village in a group.

"Where are the wenches, Captain Teach?"

"No wenches on board these last two double-damned ships," Blackbeard bellowed.

With Blackbeard in the lead, they went into the nearest tavern. The pirate strode forward and scattered a handful of gold pieces on the bar. "Rum for all. Teach is paying!"

Michael made himself as inconspicuous as possible in the background. He wasn't ready to contact Blackbeard as yet, although a vague notion of how he would go about it had formed in his mind.

He watched Blackbeard and his men, including the hangers-on, guzzle rum until far into the night. They were still there when Michael finally retired to the miserable room he had gotten for himself in an inn up the street. The next day, late in the morning, when he finally returned to the tavern, Blackbeard was still there, at a table regaling those still able to listen with tales of his bloody deeds. Men were sprawled on the tables and on the floor in drunken slumber, but Teach seemed little affected by the rum he had consumed. The tavern stank of spilled rum, vomit, and excrement.

After a moment Michael slipped out. He spent the afternoon scouring the village for two men to help him carry out his plan. Most men he accosted turned pale with terror at his proposal and scuttled away. Finally, late in the afternoon, he found two evil-looking men who had once served under Teach and had been thrown out of his crew. They were big men, heavily armed. One had a zig-zag scar down one cheek. But even they would not perform the chore he asked until Michael had nearly emptied his pockets of all the money he had.

"For that sum, I'll *kill* the bloody bastard, do ye wish me to, matey," said the one with the scar, jabbing a dirty finger at the blood-red mark. "Ye see this? 'Twas Teach, the bloody sonofabitch, what gave me this!"

"No, no!" Michael said sharply. "Dead, he'll do me no good. Just think of it as a bit of play-acting, but make it look real. When I come upon the scene, pretend to attack him. Ere long, flee as though for your lives. And remember, wait for my signal!"

Michael hurried back to the tavern, half fearful that Teach had wandered off to find a place to sleep. His fears were groundless. The pirate was still there, fresh faces around him now, all listening avidly to his self-glorifying tales.

Michael sat on a bench against one wall, slowly sipping ale. He drank very little, and none of the strong stuff, wishing to keep his wits about him.

Edward Teach didn't leave the tavern until

nearly midnight. And Michael decided then that he only left because most of his listeners were long since too far gone in drink to give him their full attention.

Finally the pirate stood, swaying a little, catching himself against the wall. "Well, it's back to me ship, mates. Aye, it's time Teach had a little slumber."

As Michael had hoped, the pirate's shipmates were all too drunk to accompany him. Blackbeard walked out alone, his big frame still retaining a remarkable equilibrium, considering the amount of rum he had consumed.

Michael waited for a moment, then followed him out. The night was black; only a few torches burned at street corners. Michael kept a few yards behind as Blackbeard strode unevenly down the street, singing a bawdy ditty at the top of his powerful lungs. Michael kept a sharp lookout ahead. Finally he glimpsed two figures lurking in the mouth of an alleyway. Michael drew his sword and waved it over his head in the agreed-upon signal.

The pair came charging out of the alley, curved cutlasses swinging, with blood-curdling yells. For a man so rum-sotted, Blackbeard reacted amazingly fast. He ducked and weaved, avoiding vicious cutlass swipes from both his attackers, and whirled about to place his back against the wall. His own cutlass appeared as if by magic in his hand, and he engaged them, roaring great oaths.

Even though Michael came running, Blackbeard was more than holding his own. Michael ranged alongside the pirate, joining in the fray.

Blackbeard gave him a piercing glance, no doubt to see if he had yet another adversary to deal with.

Then, elbow to elbow, they formed ranks and pressed the fight. Steel rang against steel, sparks flying in the night. All the while Blackbeard was roaring, swinging his cutlass with mighty strokes. There was enough power in those strokes, Michael realized, to slice a man's torso in half should one connect. And a corner of Michael's mind was wondering at the sagacity of his planning. This man, drunk or not, needed about as much assistance as a bear being attacked by gnats.

Under heavy attack from Michael and Blackbeard, the others began to give ground. Suddenly pinked on the arm by Blackbeard's cutlass, one of the men dropped his own weapon, clutching at his bleeding arm. With a cry he turned on his heels and fled down the street. The other fought for a moment longer, then also turned and ran down the dark street.

Blackbeard took two steps after them. "Stand and fight, ye chicken-livered sculpins!"

Then he calmly wiped the blood from his cutlass on his breeches, sheathed it in the scabbard, and turned a fierce scowl on Michael.

"And who might ye be, bucko?"

"Why, I . . ." Michael hesitated. "Michael Verner is my name."

For a long moment Teach studied him, still scowling, and Michael held himself tense, sword still in his hand.

"Michael Verner? Of Williamsburg? Rumors have reached me about ye. Ye do speak as a man of the gentry. How does it happen that a fine young gentleman like yourself is wandering the streets at this hour? Have it in mind to become a pirate, do ye?"

"It has been in my thoughts, yes."

"Be ye looking for plunder and adventure?"

Michael nodded. "Something like that."

Teach combed his beard. "Ye fight well, a little clumsy mayhap, but light on the feet, like a dancer." He gestured. "That sword ye tote around is too light for my liking." He studied Michael with furrowed brows. "Have it in mind to join up with old Teach?"

"If you'll have me."

"Fine and dandy, bucko!" Suddenly Blackbeard bellowed laughter and threw a huge arm around Michael's shoulders. "Welcome aboard, bucko! And thankee for pitching in. Not that I needed ye, understand!" He drew back, again with that fierce scowl. "The day comes when Teach cannot handle scum like that with me hands lashed behind me back . . ."

One thing the governor had said about this man was true, Michael was thinking. Blackbeard was utterly without fear.

Blackbeard was laughing again. "Sheath the weapon, bucko, and let's go aboard me ship." He gave a huge yawn. "I be in need of slumber. Aye, that I do."

They made their way to the wharf. On the way Teach roared again his lusty ditty. The wharf was deserted, Blackbeard's boats bobbing against the ropes.

Teach threw back his head and bellowed. The shout echoed along the shore. There was no answer.

"Damned louts," Blackbeard muttered. "One thing I cannot stomach is a man cannot hold his rum. All drunk and asleep, no doubt." He stooped down to untie one of the boats and motioned Michael in. "Let them that cannot get in one boat swim back to me ship."

Teach sat in the stern of the boat and picked up the oars. Without any apparent effort he rowed the heavy boat out to his vessel, singing all the way. At the sounds of his approach there was a scurry on deck as the skeleton crew left on board hurried to lower a Jacob's ladder. Blackbeard tied the boat up and went up the ladder, agile as a great monkey. Michael followed more slowly, his stomach queasy. The only boats he was familiar with were the small craft sailing on the James.

On board, Teach waved away the pirates and led Michael to his cabin. The cabin was rather larger than Michael had expected, and furnished with a hodgepodge of fancy furnishings he felt sure had been scrounged off captured merchant ships. Teach motioned to a rope hammock strung across one end of the cabin. "Ye can bunk there for the night, bucko. 'Tis where I bed down me special guests."

He laughed his great laugh and stumbled toward a bunk bed against the far wall. Now that he was in his own private domain, Teach seemed quite drunk. He sprawled across the bunk bed, removing only his weapons, and was snoring almost at once.

Michael was also tired, and the past hours had been a strain. He removed his shoes, stockings, and shirtwaist, and stretched out in the hammock. His thoughts ranged ahead with some trepidation. Heretofore, he hadn't given a great deal of thought to what lay ahead of him. Now he wondered how he would take to a life of piracy. Certainly, to remain a member of Teach's band, he had to gain the pirate's confidence; he would *have* to be a pirate until his mission was completed.

Soon his thoughts slowed, and the slight sway of the ship lulled him into slumber.

Some time later he woke to the motion of the ship. They were under way. He shot a glance toward Blackbeard's bunk. It was empty. He started to get up, then sank back with a shrug. He would soon enough find out their destination. He went to sleep again.

The second time he was awakened by the toe of a boot prodding his buttocks through the hammock netting. Michael opened his eyes and saw Blackbeard towering over him.

"Up, bucko! Into your clothing and on deck, young Dancer!"

Michael sat up, blinking. Then the import of what Blackbeard had said sank into his sleep-drugged senses. "What did you call me?"

"Why, Dancer, mate!" Blackbeard laughed heartily. "Michael Verner is no more. No man in Teach's crew goes by his birth name. Michael Verner, should some'un be curious, is dead and buried at sea. And since ye move like a dancer, that be your name henceforth. So on deck with ye, Dancer!"

Blackbeard strode from the cabin. Bemused, Michael put on his clothes. He noticed that the ship's motion had stopped. On deck, he found Teach at the railing staring toward shore. They were anchored in a small cove somewhere off the Carolina coast, Michael assumed. He noted that he had slept the night away. The sun was just coming up behind them, which meant that they couldn't be too far from Bath.

Blackbeard gestured grandly. "Heard of Blackbeard's Castle, bucko? There 'tis!"

A hundred yards away was a spit of land. It seemed little more than a sand bar, with a few wind-stunted trees and shrubs stubbornly growing on it. Blackbeard's Castle was one of the oddest structures Michael had ever seen. It looked as if it had been constructed from two, or perhaps even three, ships joined together, with the masts removed.

Blackbeard roared with laughter. "Ye were expecting something grand, mayhap? Aye, it's just what it looks like, three ships Teach captured, sailed onto the beach, and nailed together. I had the insides gutted and made meself a place to abide. Few people are privy to where Blackbeard's Castle be. Not even all me men know. And it's grand enough for Teach, grand enough indeed!"

Teach turned to bellow for a boat to be lowered over the side. As the pirates scurried to do his bidding, Michael noticed there was still only a skeleton crew aboard. When the boat was in the water, Teach motioned and Michael followed him down the Jacob's ladder. Teach himself rowed the boat to shore, leaving the others on the ship. He beached the boat on the sand. There was no sign of activity from the "castle," and Michael wondered if it was deserted. He felt a twinge of apprehension. Had Teach brought him here to kill him?

He shrugged and followed the pirate into a door cut into the side of what was actually the middle ship. Inside, Teach bellowed, "Sally, Nell, where be ye? Move your backsides!"

Michael looked around with undisguised curiosity. All that remained of the ships were the sides, and the decks, which served as a roof. The rest had been scooped out and was filled with bits and pieces of furniture, all a bewildering mismatch, and he knew that everything here had also been taken from plundered merchant ships. The floors were covered with richly colored rugs, and the walls were draped with every kind of material, all colors of the rainbow. A huge fireplace had been made of rough stones in the far wall. Two canopied beds stood against the wall, one on either side of the hearth.

His study of the room was broken off as two women came running in through a door set in the south end of the room. They ran squealing toward Teach, throwing themselves into his arms. Roaring with laughter, he lifted them high and swung around with them. They were wearing nothing but sleeping garments, and Michael caught flashes of white limbs as they were whirled about.

Finally Blackbeard stopped spinning and stood with a woman tucked under each arm. "Me wives, Dancer. Sally, Nell, meet Dancer. You're going to be seeing a lot of this bucko."

Nell was young, not far past sixteen, with a buxom figure, merry blue eyes, and long brown hair. Sally was a few years older, taller, graver, dusky in complexion, with dark hair and eyes. Michael suspected that she was an octoroon.

"Which one do ye prefer, bucko?"

Michael was startled. "What?"

"Which wench do ye want? Damnation, cannot ye understand the king's English?" When Michael still made no response, Teach shoved Sally at him. "Ye take Sally to bed. If memory serves, I bedded her the last. Or was it both together?" His laughter rolled. "No matter. Both wenches are firebrands in bed. Aye, that they are. You may sample Nell later."

Propelled by Teach's hard shove, Sally had staggered against Michael. He caught her to him, one arm going around her waist. He could feel the contours of her body, both hard and soft, through the thin garment she wore. Despite himself Michael felt a spark of arousal. He stared over her head at Blackbeard. The pirate stared back, eyes unreadable.

Then Teach laughed and swept Nell toward one of the beds. He gestured. "I'll tumble mine on this bed. Ye use t'other one."

Slightly shocked, Michael said, "You mean, in the same room?"

Blackbeard paused, looking back, his gaze artless. "That's what I mean, bucko. Or do the gentry ye sprang from look with disfavor on tumbling a wench with another man present? I have no such feelings, and if ye have, 'tis time ye shed them."

It came to Michael that this was a test of sorts. He managed a careless shrug. "I have no objections, if you don't."

"Then on with it!" Teach shouted.

As if this were a signal, Sally broke free of Michael's grasp, quickly shucked her single garment, and stood for a moment, unsmiling, for his inspection.

She was a comely wench, no doubt at all of that—high, firm breasts, flat belly, and long, slender legs, all a dusky rose in color.

Michael's heartbeat quickened, and he felt himself hardening. If this was the worst thing Blackbeard ever asked of him . . .

He forced from his mind all thought that the pirate had had her before, undoubtedly many times. He gave a mental shrug. Why should he be so fastidious? He had lain with whores before.

Sally was on her back on the bed, a faint smile on her face now. Teach and Nell were naked on the other bed, Teach roaring and Nell laughing.

Michael stepped out of his breeches, removed his clothing, and joined Sally on the bed. She turned into a laughing wanton, alternately teasing and doing things to further arouse him. They rolled and tumbled back and forth across the bed. Michael glanced once across the way. The small body of Nell was buried almost out of sight beneath the great hulk of Edward Teach.

Michael turned back to Sally and took her, rough and demanding now. She screeched, wrapping her arms and legs around him, and met his every demand.

Coupled, they moved together. But even as Michael's body blazed with pleasure, he voiced a small prayer in his mind: *Dear Lord above, do not let the wench be diseased!*

Chapter Fifteen

As *Queen Anne's Revenge* drew within easy firing range of the French merchant vessel, Blackbeard gave the order to run up his flag, the flag he called his "black ensign with the death's head."

Michael at his side, Teach stood on the foredeck. Fast approaching the heavily laden French ship, Blackbeard shouted an order to the helmsman, and the ship swung about, broadside to the other ship.

Blackbeard roared, "Fire, damn you, and aim true!"

The guns on the port side were primed with swan, partridge, and other small shot. Teach seldom used larger shot, not wishing to damage his prize too severely before he boarded her.

The broadside swept the decks of the French ship. The merchant vessel carried only a few guns, and would soon be listing in the water, at their mercy. Sailing in close as the pirates manning the cannon reloaded, Blackbeard ordered another barrage. This time, when the smoke cleared, Michael could see no one on his feet on the decks across the short stretch of water. The French ship yawed wildly, out of control. In close now, the pirate tossed handmade grenades—bottles filled with powder, small shot, and scrap iron, with smoking fuses—onto the decks of the crippled ship. Blackbeard brought his vessel in close, preparing to board.

When preparing for combat, Blackbeard was a fearsome sight. He had a bandolier over his shoulders containing three braces of pistols, loaded, primed, and cocked for instant firing. In a belt around his waist, he carried additional pistols, daggers, and his cutlass. But perhaps, Michael thought, what made him an even more fearful figure were the lighted wooden tapers he had tucked under his hat, wreathing his features in wispy curls of smoke, as if he were the devil himself, fresh from the inner reaches of hell.

As the two ships bumped together gently, Blackbeard swung his cutlass high in a boarding command. He himself was first aboard the French ship, rope in hand to lash the two ships together. Michael followed right on his heels. Behind them, the other pirates scrambled over the gunwales like ants over a dung heap.

There were still men alive on board the other ship. They came swarming up from belowdecks, armed with cutlasses and pistols. The decks rang with angry shouts, crackling pistols, and the clang of swinging cutlasses. Over it all sounded the roar of Blackbeard's thunderous voice.

Michael and he advanced side by side. Teach had a cutlass in one hand, a pistol in the other. Michael had only his sword. They had taken a great many ships since Michael had joined Teach five months ago. Michael always tried to avoid killing anyone, without being obvious about it. However, he had killed a few men, forced into it in self-defense.

They engaged three men. One fired a pistol, the ball whistling past Michael's ear. Michael charged him with his sword before he could reload and fire again. The man dropped his pistol and fled below. Michael turned to see if he could assist Teach with the other two Frenchmen. The pirate chieftain, as usual, needed no assistance. He fired the pistol in his left hand point blank into the face of one man, blowing him backward. Then he charged the second, cutlass swishing through the air, bellowing vile oaths. The man dropped his cutlass and backed against the railing, eyes wild with terror. Blackbeard calmly ran him through, the point of his cutlass piercing the man's heart, blood gouting like a fountain.

Michael quickly glanced away from the carnage. He looked around the decks. It was all over; the pirates were in command of the French ship. Dead bodies littered the blood-slippery deck. Michael almost gagged. The odor of gunpowder and blood together was one he doubted he would ever become accustomed to.

Later, he learned that ten of the French crew had been killed. Teach had lost not a man, though a few had suffered minor wounds.

The French ship's master was still alive. Through Michael, who had command of enough French to make himself understood, Blackbeard explained that the French ship could continue on its way—no one else would be killed—if they offered no further resistance. They could sail as soon as they were relieved of their cargo. The Frenchman, having little choice, nodded in sullen agreement.

Edward Teach rubbed his hands together gleefully. "Leave us hurry below, bucko, and see what we have earned from this day's work."

He threw an arm around Michael's shoulders and led him below. The ship carried perfumes and some silken dress goods, but most of the cargo was French brandy, wines, and other liquors.

"Aye, a good day's work!" Blackbeard crowed. "I have ready customers for much of Frenchie's brandy!"

Michael stood at the railing of the pirate ship, smoking a cigar. The ship, wallowing heavily now with their prize cargo, was sailing north, up the coast of Virginia, their eventual destination Williamsburg. His thoughts were bitter. This was the chance he had been waiting for—Blackbeard was sailing into Virginia. But there had been no chance for him to send word to Governor Spotswood. Instead of putting into port, Teach had chosen to sail directly up the coast after sending the French ship on its way.

The last few months had been strange ones for Michael. The pirate way of life was one he would never have dreamed he would experience. There had been some excitement and a spirit of adventure in the beginning, in the newness of it. But now he was sick of the plundering and the killing.

Outwardly he had changed a great deal. It had been Teach's idea. For one thing, he had grown a full black beard.

"Ye're me right hand, bucko," Teach said. "A beard on ye like mine will let these scum sailing under me ensign know ye be the man to listen to when Teach's not around."

And Michael had become almost a fop, again at Teach's urging. He wore the finest of clothing, and an earring set with a pearl dangled from one ear. The clothing wasn't hard to find. Nearly every ship they plundered carried many fine clothes befitting a gentleman. Michael suspected that Blackbeard looked upon it all as a huge joke, yet he never jollied him about it.

Brooding, Michael had to wonder if he had changed inside as well. Could a man live the brutal life of a pirate for long and not be changed internally?

He brooded on Edward Teach, too. A strange man, a paradox, contradictory. Murderous, yes; he killed without compunction in a battle. But when the heat of battle was over, he showed a compassion that Michael knew had to be lacking in most pirates. He never tortured his captives, usually letting them go free after he had plundered their vessels. And the tales about his taking any woman he found aboard captured vessels weren't true. At least, it hadn't happened since Michael had been with him. The few women they had encountered had been let go, often over the mutinous mutterings of Teach's men. True, Teach kept women, often several at a time, at Blackbeard's Castle, and changed them about as often as God changed the tides. But most of them seemed more than willing to consort with Blackbeard.

But most of all, Michael found his attitude toward Negroes puzzling. He had been astounded to find that at least a third of Teach's crew were black men, the majority runaway slaves. And Teach saw to it that they received their equal share of the loot.

Intrigued, Michael had once questioned him about it. Teach had growled, "Ever' man should be free to do as he wishes, bucko. Color and race, they don't matter. Aye, a black man to Teach is just another man, be he able to do what I ask of him. What do ye think a life of piracy is? A free life, a life where ever' man be equal, taking from others whatever he be capable of. Aye, the gentry think old Teach a villain and a blackguard. Mayhap I am. But in war they be no different. And Teach is always at war!" He turned a sneer on Michael, making a rare personal remark. "I know that ye, or at least Malcolm Verner, keeps slaves on your fine plantation. Ye think that makes ye better than old Teach?"

Michael had been able to think of no response to that.

Yet for all this, Blackbeard had a perverse, almost sadistic, sense of the humorous. Michael had witnessed numerous incidents illustrating this side of the man. One in particular remained in his mind. . . .

One night Michael and other members of the crew were drinking in Teach's cabin. Suddenly Teach drew two pistols from his belt, cocked them, and held them under the table.

"Which one of ye shall I shoot first?" he roared.

All fled the cabin but for Michael and one other. Later, Michael suspected that the other pirate had been too terrified to move. Michael himself was frightened, yet he forced himself to remain still.

Blackbeard threw back his head and roared out his laughter. Then abruptly he became grim. Crossing his hands beneath the table, he fired both pistols. The other pirate received the full charge of one pistol in his left knee. The injury was to leave him lame for the remainder of his life.

Teach bellowed to the pirates cowering outside the cabin to come and fetch the wounded man to the ship's surgeon. Teach swigged rum, laughing, as the injured pirate was taken out.

Michael asked, "Why, sir, would you deliberately injure a man you called friend only moments ago?"

Teach looked surprised. "Why, 'tis simple, bucko. Teach must have a little fun to make life more lively. Besides, if I did not now and then kill or injure one of the scum, they would forget who I be, forget that Teach is their captain!"

And for all the time Michael had spent at sea with the pirates, he had learned little of seamanship.

Blackbeard had refused to be bothered with teaching him. "Don't need ye for that, bucko. I want ye at my side, me good right arm. A man of the gentry, of education, I need. These sculpins aboard me ship can neither read, write, nor do their sums. Nor can I."

Michael had expected to gain access to documents pointing to a conspiracy between Governor Eden, Tobias Knight (who was secretary of the colony of North Carolina and collector of customs, and a man Michael was convinced was deeply involved), and Edward Teach. Michael had seen, and heard, enough to know that such a conspiracy certainly existed. But Teach had yet to take him that far into his confidence. Often, when at anchor at Bath, Teach would disappear for long periods, meeting with Governor Eden and Tobias Knight, Michael was sure.

As for not knowing his sums . . . Michael doubted this about Teach. True, it had become Michael's chore to divide up the plunder, an equal share to each man—except to Teach, of course, who took half of everything for himself. But Michael noted that Blackbeard kept a close watch. Twice, as a test, Michael had made an error, and Teach had called his attention to it.

All the while Teach was growing richer and more powerful. Over rum he had confided plans to Michael for the taking over of Stede Bonnet's ship, the *Adventure*—the only vessel sailing the sea lanes built especially for the pursuit of piracy—and Michael knew that he had the cunning and the ruthlessness to do it. Teach had plans for three ships and close to four hundred men under his command. If that came to pass, he would be close to invincible.

Michael pounded his fist on the railing in frustration. To make his own situation even worse, for some reason communication with Governor Spotswood had broken down. Several times Michael had sent messages through Will Darcy, the taciturn blacksmith, but he had yet to receive a single reply.

Possibly he would have an opportunity to contact Governor Spotswood on this quick trip to Williamsburg, if Teach would allow him off the ship. Michael was of a mind to tell Governor Spotswood that he was resigning from the mission. He had gotten nowhere, and he was ill of temper over the governor's failure to contact him.

Somewhat to Michael's surprise, Teach made no effort to keep him on board ship when they anchored near Williamsburg.

"Just remember, bucko, that ye now be Dancer, not Michael Verner. And be back aboard me ship at dawn. We sail at sunrise."

Teach gave no hint about whether he intended to leave the ship or not. He was standing at the railing when Michael left on the first boat bound for shore.

To allay the suspicions of anyone to whom Teach might have given orders to keep an eye on him, Michael visited several taverns, having a brandy in each. By the time he reached the Cup and Horn, he was convinced none of the pirates were following him. They were interested only in filling their bellies with drink and in searching for wenches to bed.

When the innkeeper at the Cup and Horn made his sly offer of a comely wench upstairs, Michael was motivated partly by lust and partly by an effort to make it appear certain that his actions were in no way suspicious.

And when he stormed out of the tavern shortly thereafter, seething at the brutality of the innkeeper, Michael's thoughts were still filled with images of the beautiful, copper-haired wench

naked on the bed. He cursed himself for a fool.
Why hadn't he taken advantage of the delightful
piece she would have made? Surely she had been
taken before, and would be again, so why should
he be so squeamish?

She had been beaten cruelly, and he didn't approve of that; still, it was no doing of his. But he
did make up his mind to one thing. If and when
he returned to Williamsburg as Michael Verner, he
fully intended to seek out that corpulent innkeeper
and lay the flat of his sword across the villain's
back.

He strode on toward the Governor's Palace to
keep his rendezvous. Of course, it could scarcely be
named a rendezvous, since the governor had no
inkling of his coming . . . Michael traveled by the
way of back streets, keeping a wary eye behind
him.

Governor Spotswood was already abed and finally came to meet Michael in his nightshirt. His
eyes widened, and he stared at Michael as if at an
apparition.

"Michael! It *is* you, is it not? With the beard
and all . . ."

"All Teach's idea."

"I must say you *do* look like a pirate." He
clasped Michael on the shoulder. "Lad, word
reached me that you were dead these many
months, lost at sea!"

"It seems I am not," Michael said drily. "That is
also Teach's doing. He told me he had in mind
to send rumors abroad of my death."

Governor Spotswood fell upon him in a fervent
embrace. After a moment Michael pulled back,

scowling. "Speaking of the dead ... you might well have been, sir, for all the messages I have received from you. Did you not receive mine?"

"Yes, but I . . ." Governor Spotswood hesitated, looking away. "I thought the rumor true, that you were dead, and the messages were false." He stopped short to stare at Michael. "But what are you doing *here*?"

When Michael had explained, the governor strode about, waving his arms. "Blackbeard here, in Williamsburg! And I have no troops at hand to take him! The opportunity of a lifetime, and I cannot take advantage of it. Ah, well." He sighed, then looked at Michael intently. "Tell me what you have learned."

The scene struck Michael as incongruous, his telling of his months with Blackbeard to this royal governor of Virginia wearing a nightshirt and a sleeping cap. Michael finished his report with his suspicions that Governor Eden, Tobias Knight, and Teach were working together.

Governor Spotswood sighed again. "But you have no proof, beyond what you have observed, no documents of proof?"

"No, but I'm sure they exist. And surely my testimony alone, of what I have observed, should be proof enough that Blackbeard is operating as a pirate!"

"It would have been, months back. But there has been a change." The governor got up to pace. "A new element has been added. This damnable Act of Grace!"

Michael leaned forward. "I have heard something of this. But being with little human contact

287

other than the pirates these past months, I am hazy as to the details."

"It's an act of the king, thought to be a means of putting an end to piracy. Yet it works otherwise with Governor Eden," Governor Spotswood said bitterly. "Under the Act of Grace, a pirate can turn himself over to a royal governor, forswearing his past life of piracy, and swearing an oath to God that he will never sail again as a pirate. In so doing, he will be granted a full pardon. Since many pirates began as privateers in time of war, it was the king's thought that they might welcome a chance to become honest, decent citizens again. With some it has succeeded. But Governor Eden, and Blackbeard, have perverted it! Blackbeard sails out, takes a prize, rids himself of the plunder, giving Governor Eden his share, and then receives a pardon from that self-same governor under the king's Act of Grace . . . until the next time!"

Michael leaned forward in dismay. "Then everything I've done is futile, or anything I do in the future?"

"Not so, lad, not so!" The governor waved his hands frantically. "Do not be discouraged. Find me evidence of this conspiracy, and I will send sloops to take Blackbeard, Governor Eden be damned! That way I can justify my actions to the king, do you not see? I already have the sloops ready and on notice, and at my own expense. If only they were here this night! If they were, this could be settled once and for all. We could capture this prince of villains in Virginia, and nobody, not even the king, could gainsay me. But you tell me the scoundrel sails at sunrise?"

Michael said wearily, "Then you wish me to continue?"

"Please, Michael, I beg of you. I beseech you!"

Michael stood up. "This rumor of my death ... my father has heard of it and believes it?"

Governor Spotswood said in a choked voice, "I fear so. But he is bearing up well. I beg of you not to inform him otherwise. Do so now and it would throw our plans into disarray, and all you have done would have been for naught! Bear with me a while longer. Think of the honor it will bring to the Verner name when your mission is finally accomplished and the word may be spread throughout Virginia!"

They said their farewells, Governor Spotswood once more embracing him, and Michael left the palace. He made his way back in the direction of the ship, using back streets. Despite Governor Spotswood's words of caution, Michael was of two minds about his father. He was strongly tempted to pen a short message to the effect that he was alive and well and dispatch it to Malvern.

In the end he decided against it.

The governor's assurances that it would all soon be over proved to be sadly in error.

In November, 1718, almost fourteen months since that clandestine visit to the Governor's Palace, Michael Verner was still aboard Teach's ship.

It was a different ship now. Most of Teach's grandiose plans had come to pass. He had taken over the *Adventure* for his flagship, with his old ship, *Queen Anne's Revenge,* and a second, the *Revenge,* giving him a fleet of three. At one time

289

he had had four hundred men under his command, and had ravaged the sea lanes between the West Indies and the mainland. With these forays he had become a wealthy and powerful man. He had disbanded to a certain extent late in the summer of 1718, ridding himself of most of his crew and sending the other two ships off on their own, leaving him with just the *Adventure* under his immediate command.

· But the end was now happily in sight. It was a pleased Michael Verner who leaned against the railing of the *Adventure* early in the evening of November 19, smoking a leisurely cigar.

His long service with Teach had finally borne fruit. Teach had taken him more and more into his confidence. Emboldened by his repeated successes, becoming more arrogant in his continued freedom, he had come to believe he was truly invincible. And so he had started to boast to Michael. By this time Michael had finally decided that was the real reason Teach had taken him into his crew—he wanted a man of the gentry near him to whom he could boast of his exploits.

But no matter. Michael now knew the whereabouts of the evidence Governor Spotswood desired. In a chest in Teach's cabin were a number of damning documents—several letters from prominent merchants in North Carolina and Virginia, even in faraway New York, telling of transactions with the pirate; and an account book recording the disposition of booty taken over the past two years, detailing the sharing of that plunder with both Tobias Knight and Governor Eden. Besides those, and even more damning, was a letter addressed to "My Friend, Edward Teach," and signed by Tobias Knight. It suggested that Governor Eden would welcome an early visit from Teach. Also, Michael had learned from Teach that there were many records lodged in the home of John Lovick, deputy-secretary of the colony of North Carolina, implicating both Knight and Governor Eden. And Michael knew that many of the pirates Teach had set loose when he had reduced his forces were disgruntled, and more than willing to testify against Blackbeard in return for leniency.

All of this information Michael had dispatched to Governor Spotswood through Will Darcy this week past, along with the suggestion that the governor's two armed sloops be sent posthaste to Ocracoke Inlet, where the *Adventure* lay at anchor and would for another week at least. If Teach had planned to sail, he would have mentioned it, Michael was sure. In the message to Governor Spotswood Michael had also recommended that an armed force be sent overland to Bath, there to arrest those of Teach's men roistering in the taverns, and to check the house of John Lovick for the records.

Michael sighed, blowing smoke. He was content. It would appear that his long sojourn as a pirate was about finished. The life had grown increasingly distasteful to him. He remembered his earlier desire for a life of adventure, and he laughed softly. He'd had his fill of the adventure of being a pirate!

Teach's bloody career was coming to a close. Governor Spotswood had Michael's message by now, and if he had acted promptly, his sloops should be sailing into Ocracoke Inlet almost any time. Sailing time down the coast was about three days, given good weather....

Michael's thoughts were interrupted by the sound of a loud voice. "Ahoy the boat! Who goes there?"

It was the deck hand on watch.

Michael moved around to a spot where he could see better. A small boat with the figure of one man in it was rowing erratically toward the *Adventure*. A voice from the boat answered the hail, the words not audible to Michael's ears. Some sixth sense warned him to remain out of sight. He drew back into the shadows and watched as the Jacob's ladder was lowered. He felt a slight shudder go through the ship as the boat bumped below. In a little while a large, corpulent figure, wheezing from the climb up the rope, clambered over the side and onto the deck. In the light of the torch held by the deck hand, Michael got a good glimpse of the visitor's face. There was something naggingly familiar about him. Then, as the man passed from his view, being ushered to Teach's cabin, Michael remembered where he'd seen the face before.

It was the innkeeper, the one from the Cup and Horn in Williamsburg. Damnation, what was *he* doing here?

Michael had long since learned that Teach sold the surplus liquor from plundered ships to tavern owners at reduced prices. But Teach had no liquor for sale now, had not had for some time. So why was this man here?

Michael knew that he had to find out. Teach had been over-generous with the rum portions tonight, and most of the crew, except for the watch, were drunk and snoring. Had Teach known of this visit in advance and wanted the decks cleared for that very reason?

Michael had to learn why the innkeeper was here, a long way from Williamsburg, a long way from any habitation. The need to know itched at him like an insect bite. At least, with the decks deserted, it was fairly easy to sneak unobserved up alongside Teach's cabin, where he crouched below the open porthole.

Even so, he could overhear only snatches of the conversation.

The innkeeper was complaining in a whining voice. ". . . ain't been any liquor to peddle for some time, Captain Teach . . ."

". . . bother with such these days."

". . . man has to make his way . . ."

Teach's voice rose. "Then make it! Do not depend on old Teach for ever' shilling!"

"A proposition, then . . ."

The voices dropped again, and Michael's attention wandered. Apparently it was a business transaction after all. Michael drew on his cigar, and then had to stifle a cough. He'd forgotten the cigar. He started to toss it overboard when the name Malvern, spoken in the whining voice of the innkeeper, froze him to the spot.

". . . take that risk just for a wench? Something's addled your wits, Stritch! Wenches I can get. . . ."

". . . fortune in jewels, too. Gold, much gold. My word on it!"

"Well now, that's more to me liking. S'pose ye tell me more. But softly—some'un might overhear. . . ."

Strain his ears as he might, Michael could hear little of the rest of the conversation—only enough

293

to gain the impression that the innkeeper was proposing that Teach raid Malvern!

Incredible!

A few minutes later Michael heard a stirring inside the cabin, and he melted back into the shadows. He couldn't see, but he could hear the sounds of the innkeeper climbing clumsily down the side of the ship. His mind in a turmoil, Michael leaned on the railing and listened to the splashing of the oars as the innkeeper rowed away.

He stiffened at the sound of a footfall behind him, and whirled. Blackbeard stood grinning at him, a pistol in his hand. The cocking of the weapon was loud in the still night.

"Overheard, did ye, bucko? Don't be giving me the lie now, I smelt the stink of that cigar of yours, and knew ye were lurking about."

Michael said incredulously, "Surely you're not thinking of raiding Malvern!"

"Haven't decided yet. Tickles me fancy, it does."

"But what can you hope to gain?"

"According to the man just here, there's plunder to be had, and. . ."

"He lies!"

". . . old Teach is getting weary of chasing after prize ships." He combed his beard with his fingers. "Sailing boldly in under the noses of Spotswood and his like tickles me."

"I tell you there's nothing there worth your time!"

Teach laughed. "Now bucko, ye be expecting me to believe ye, ye being a Verner? The richest plantation in Virginia? But I be yet thinking on it. Something else needs tending to first. Now . . ." His manner became brusque, and he motioned with the pistol. "It's below with ye, bucko, into the hold till I make up my mind. Or until I carry out the plan. Ain't the quarters a gentleman like ye be accustomed to, but 'twill have to do."

Michael, raging inside, took two steps toward the pirate. The pistol moved slightly, centering on his heart. "Don't try it, young Verner. Don't be thinking I won't blow ye off the decks. Ye have seen me do it!"

Michael knew that he would indeed. At least as long as he remained alive, there might be some action he could take later. And he realized it was futile to try and argue Teach out of it. Probably that would only harden the man's resolve.

The hold was foul and stinking, dark as pitch. The only way in was through a hatch in the deck; a narrow ladder led down. The hatch cover, of course, was locked from without.

Michael's head had barely cleared the hatchway opening when the heavy hatch slammed down to the rumble of Teach's laughter and the sound of the wooden latch being shoved into place.

All of Michael's earlier elation had dissipated. The thought that Teach was considering a raid on Malvern and he could do nothing about it was agony. There was little that those on Malvern could do to stop him, especially if they had no warning. His father had only the slaves, and they weren't fighting men, although most of them had been taught to handle weapons in order to hunt game.

His only hope was that Governor Spotswood's war sloops would arrive in time. But now there was no assurance that Blackbeard would still be here when they did arrive.

On Michael's second day in the hold, he was

awakened early from an uneasy slumber by shouts on deck and the sounds of cannon being rolled into position. It was daylight—enough light seeped through cracks in the deck above to allow him to see things in the hold. But there was no way he could get outside.

He got up and paced about to loosen his muscles. He'd had nothing to sleep on but the wooden decking, and it was all damp. Puddles of water stood where the bulkheads had leaked. He was stiff and sore.

There was a door set in one end of the hold. It opened into the powder magazine, Michael knew. It was locked, naturally. Because the extra powder was stored there, it was kept well caulked and dry. Out here in the hold, they didn't bother, unless a leak became too severe.

As he paced back and forth, wondering what was causing the excitement, praying that it was the arrival of the governor's troops, there was a sound from above, and the hatch cover was lifted.

A Negro Michael knew by the name of Caesar was climbing down the ladder. He carried a coil of rope. Behind him came Teach. Teach paused halfway down, pistol aimed at Michael.

His grin was merry. "A little fun coming up, bucko. Whilst it goes on, ye going to be lashed up. Me pardon for that, but 'tis necessary. Tie him up good, Caesar, hands and feet behind him.

As Caesar went about tying Michael's hands behind his back, Teach went on, "We be about to engage a couple of sloops. Likely we'll scuttle them with little trouble. But if by bad luck we don't old Caesar here is to lay a train of powder to the magazine yonder. He remains below, with a burning candle. Should things go badly for us, word will be passed to him and he will fire the powder train. Nobody, man or devil, is going to take me ship! He'll have time to get out before she blows. Ye, now . . ." Teach chuckled. "Better pray, Bucko, that old Teach comes out on top once again, or ye'll blow sky high with the *Adventure*!"

Michael was bound securely now. Caesar stood up and nodded to Teach, who saluted Michael with the pistol and rammed it, still cocked, into his belt. "I wish ye good fortune, young Verner, hoping we meet in the netherworld, should it come to pass. Caesar, keep a sharp eye out, now."

"Aye, Captain Teach."

Blackbeard climbed back up the ladder and disappeared from sight. Michael, thrown into a crumpled heap against the seeping bulkhead, tried to engage Caesar in conversation. Caesar ignored him completely. He had used a key to open the door to the powder magazine, and was now spilling a trail of powder along the floor. All the while he talked, Michael's bound hands were searching behind him for a piece of metal, anything sharp that might saw through the ropes binding his wrists. He could find nothing.

Michael had no way of knowing that Edward Teach had been warned of the approach of the war sloops dispatched by Governor Spotswood. Tobias Knight had sent him a message telling him that they were coming. Consequently, he had not been surprised to see two small sloops sail into Ocracoke Inlet late the afternoon before, shortly before dusk. The war sloops had dropped anchor for the night.

Teach had no thought of trying to flee from them. He had no fear, being supremely confident of his ability to defeat them. The *Adventure* was bigger and faster than either of the two sloops, and Teach was certain he had them outmanned and outgunned.

He made no unusual battle preparation, but spent most of the night drinking rum in his cabin, wondering if, when the coming battle was finished, he would act on the interesting proposition Amos Stritch had broached to him. It amused Teach immensely that the young man now locked below in the hold had once been heir to the Verner estate. For that reason alone, Teach thought that perhaps he would go through with the plan to plunder Malvern. It would be a feat that could add to the legend of Blackbeard.

The action began at nine the next morning. The two sloops moved in toward him, one maneuvering within shouting range of the *Adventure*. Neither of the sloops flew colors.

Teach, lounging on deck with a mug of rum, shouted across the water, "Damn ye for villains! Who be ye? And from whence came ye?"

Suddenly the British flag was sent aloft. A voice came across the distance between ships. "You can see by our colors that we are not pirates! I am Lieutenant Robert Maynard of Williamsburg. Who are you?"

"Come aboard me ship, and ye will learn who I am!"

"I cannot spare a boat, but I will come aboard you as soon as I can with my sloop."

Teach took a deep draught of rum and cried,

"Damnation seize my soul if I give you quarter or take any from you!"

"Then I expect no quarter from you, Blackbeard, nor shall I give you any!"

Teach ordered his death's-head ensign run up. Men already stationed there cut the anchor chains, and the sails were unfurled. The *Adventure* made for the channel through which Lieutenant Maynard had brought his two sloops. The second sloop, its commander thinking Teach was heading for the open sea, maneuvered his ship to block the pirate's passage. When the distance between them narrowed to within half a pistol's shot, Teach swung his ship around and delivered a broadside. Half the sloops' crew, including her commander, were killed, and her jib and foremast were shot away. All but out of the battle, the sloop began to drift helplessly.

Meanwhile, Lieutenant Maynard was fast closing in on the *Adventure*. Teach, noting that Maynard's crew seemed all crowded on deck, ordered another broadside. The deck of Maynard's sloop was swept clean, twenty-one men falling wounded.

Fearing a slaughter, Maynard ordered all of his men below, and he fled to his cabin.

Teach, seeing the empty deck of his foe's ship, was certain there were no longer enough men left of offer any stiff resistance. He brought his ship alongside. As usual, he was the first man to board the other ship, his crew scrambling after him.

Maynard at once ordered his men back on deck, and a furious battle ensued. In a moment Teach and Maynard were face to face. Both fired pistols. Teach's shot missed, but Maynard's ball plowed into the great figure of the pirate. He scarcely staggered. He drove forward, and the two adversaries had at it with their cutlasses. Then one powerful blow from Teach's cutlass snapped Maynard's like a twig. Teach prepared to deliver the killing strike. In desperation, one of Maynard's men lunged at the pirate, his dagger slicing into Teach's throat. This threw him off balance enough so that his cutlass slash merely glanced off Maynard's upheld arm.

Now Teach was surrounded by Maynard's men. The pirates were badly outnumbered; their leader had made a fatal miscalculation. Pistol balls thudded into Teach's massive body. Cutlass slashes opened bleeding wounds in him. Still he fought on. Jerking still another pistol from his belt, he started to cock it—and toppled over dead.

Edward Teach died as he had lived, asking no quarter and giving none. It was later found that he had twenty-five separate wounds in his body, most of them severe enough to have killed an average man.

The battle was over; it had lasted scarcely ten minutes. Nine of Teach's pirates were dead. Others jumped overboard and were dispatched in the water. Those remaining alive threw down their arms and surrendered.

Standing over the body of the dead Teach, Lieutenant Maynard said, "Sever the villain's head and swing it beneath the bowsprit of our ship. Let the world know that the prince of villains is no more!"

With that order, Maynard swung himself aboard the *Adventure*, remembering Governor Spotswood's instructions to make an immediate search of the ship for incriminating documents.

In the hold of the *Adventure*, Michael's own search had finally borne results. In a puddle of sea water his groping hands had discovered a dagger. His fingers told him that it was rusted and corroded; he could only hope that it would not break before he could saw through the ropes.

It wasn't an easy task. His fingers were numb from poor circulation brought on by the tight ropes around his wrists. And it was very awkward holding the dagger and sawing at the ropes behind his back. A number of times he felt the metal slice into his flesh.

He was fortunate in one respect. Once the battle started, Caesar's attention was elsewhere, and he paid no heed to the rocking motion Michael made with his body in his attempt to saw through the bonds. He dropped the dagger repeatedly and had to fumble in the water to find it again. The sea water stung like fire in the cuts on his hands.

Finally the last strand of rope was free. Michael rubbed his hands together behind his back to restore feeling to them.

The firing without ceased abruptly. Caesar's head came up alertly, and he crouched at the end of the powder train, the burning candle stub set in its own wax within arm's reach.

The overhead watch was flung back, and a pirate stuck his head into the opening. "Captain Teach is dead, Caesar. They have killed him! Fire your powder and scramble your butt out of there! I'm a-telling ever'body left on board to abandon ship!"

The face disappeared; the hatch cover was left open. Caesar reached for the burning candle.

Michael knew he had little time. He groped in

the water for the dagger and couldn't find it. Caesar was about six feet distant from him. Michael gathered himself and sprang, by sheer force of will making his bound legs work for him.

He generated enough power in his numbed legs to hurl himself across the space between them, landing on Caesar's back. His weight knocked the man sprawling, the candle flying out of his hand. The impact apparently stunned the other man, for he lay still for a moment under Michael. But he began to stir almost at once, groaning. Then a roar of rage erupted from him as he realized what had happened.

Michael squirmed frantically until he could get one arm around the man's neck from behind. He locked his wrists together and held Caesar's neck in a viselike grip.

Caesar was a small man, but wiry and strong. He thrashed and kicked like a gaffed fish. It was like trying to remain on the back of a wildly bucking horse. Michael tightened his grip with all his waning strength. Caesar began to gasp for breath. He clawed at the arm around his neck. Long nails dug into Michael's flesh. Michael held on grimly.

Gradually Caesar's struggles weakened. Michael couldn't last much longer. His arms had little feeling left in them, and his fingers were close to losing their locked grip on his wrist.

Then Caesar arched up once more in an effort to throw Michael off. Failing, he collapsed and lay still. Not wishing to kill the man, Michael held his pressure on the neck for only a moment more before releasing it. He was wary, fearful that Caesar was feigning unconsciousness. But the man under him didn't move.

Michael rolled off, gasping for breath, his strength gone. He checked to see if the candle was still burning. It had landed in a pool of water and gone out. He fumbled with the bonds around his ankles, but his fingers had no strength left in them. He gave up for a moment, head hanging.

Then his head came up at a sound from above, and a feeling of weary despair swept over him as he saw that a man was already halfway down the ladder, a cocked pistol in his hand. It had all been for naught. Now they would kill him, and fire the powder train after all. He blinked tired eyes, and relief surged through him as he saw that the man wore the king's uniform.

The man asked in a harsh voice, "What's happened here?"

"Blackbeard left orders to fire this train of powder and blow up his ship if he was killed. I . . ." Michael gestured. "I was fortunate enough to stop his man in time." He blinked up at the man on the ladder. "And who are you, sir?"

"I am Lieutenant Robert Maynard, of the king's command, commissioned by the royal governor of Virginia to capture Blackbeard."

"It's true, then? Edward Teach is dead?"

"The villain lives no more," Maynard said grimly. "His head hangs on my ship, and those of his men left alive will be taken to Williamsburg forthwith, and there they will hang. And may I inquire *your* name, sir?"

"I am called . . ." Michael broke off, laughing shortly. He had been about to identify himself as Dancer. "I am Michael Verner."

Chapter Sixteen

"Michael, lad!" Governor Spotswood exclaimed. "You look more like your natural self! The last time we talked, you looked like a proper villain."

On his return to Williamsburg, and before seeking an audience with the governor, Michael had shaved off the beard and bought more sober clothing for himself. Now he smiled wryly. "It is a relief, sir, to be myself again. Anything smacking of piracy sickens me, the things I have seen and done these two years past...."

"I am sure, Michael, I am sure," the governor said gravely. "But I am indeed grateful, as all of Virginia will be. You have rendered splendid services, my boy, splendid! I was able to persuade the Assembly to post an award of two hundred pounds to the man who saw to it that the prince of villains was brought to his just end! I will see to it that this sum is yours."

Michael gestured wearily. "That is unimportant, and not the reason I undertook your mission." He found the governor puzzling in his behavior, evasive in manner. "Does my father yet know of my return to life?"

Governor Spotswood glanced away. "No, Michael."

Michael rose. "Then I will ride immediately to Malvern and so let him know. By your leave, sir."

"Michael ..." A stricken note in the governor's voice stopped Michael in his tracks. He looked back with a growing feeling of dread.

"Michael ... lad, your father is no more. He died. Last year, not long before Christmas."

"Dead! Father is dead?" Stunned, Michael sank into the nearest chair. Then he looked up in anger. "A year ago, you say? Why was I not informed?"

"I thought hard on it, but then I thought, 'What good?' As God is my judge, I thought it the best course." Governor Spotswood finally looked at him. "To have to give you this news grieves me sorely. But he was dead and buried two weeks before I had news of it myself!"

"And he died still thinking I had been lost at sea," Michael said in a dead voice.

"I fear so."

Anger rose in Michael until he thought he would choke on it—anger at this vain man so obsessed with bringing about Teach's end that he had kept the news of Malcolm Verner's death a secret from him! Michael knew intuitively that that was the reason. The governor had been fearful that he

306

would come home if he learned the news. It was a contemptible act, Michael felt, and he knew he would always despise Spotswood for it.

"Then I'd better ride to Malvern and see to matters there," he now said evenly, getting to his feet again.

"There's more, Michael. Malcolm Verner was wed some three months before his death. There are some who say that was the cause of ..." The governor stopped, clearing his throat.

"Wed?" Michael said, trying to absorb this second stunning blow.

"That was one reason I didn't send you word of his death. It was my thought ..."

"Who? Who is the woman?"

"Some young wen ... some girl. I have never met her." The governor shrugged. "Her name is Hannah, I believe. I never knew her unwed name."

"Hannah?" Michael said slowly. "I know of no woman of my father's acquaintance named Hannah."

"I believe he, uh, met her after your departure."

Michael's short laugh was bitter. "Then I suppose I must go at once to Malvern and pay my belated respects to my stepmother!"

"There's a will, I understand. Thinking you dead, your father left Malvern to his new wife."

Michael shrugged, turning away.

Once more the governor stopped him. "Michael?"

Impatient to be away, Michael turned back.

"Under English law, as I'm sure you know, you are entitled to two-thirds of your father's estate as his male heir, no matter if his last will and testament decrees otherwise."

So now he was confronting his late father's wife. *His stepmother,* he thought, with mingled amusement and disgust.

He recognized her as she slid off Black Star and came toward him.

Still with that dazed look, she said, "But Michael Verner is dead, it is a known fact!"

"I assure you that I am not, madam. I am alive and well."

"But what happened?"

"The story is long and tedious. I'm sure it would only bore you." He gestured indifferently. Then he looked at her, his brilliant black eyes alive with amusement. "The circumstances are quite different from when we last met, are they not?"

Hannah, recovering from her initial shock, stared at him, baffled. "We have not met before, sir!"

"Oh, but we have. A brief meeting, to be sure, but a memorable one. On that occasion you were naked. A fetching sight—I can still recall it vividly."

She came closer to him and looked up into his face. The eyes, those black eyes. But the face, she recalled, had been bearded, and he had been dressed differently. She said hesitantly, "You're the man called Dancer?"

He made a mocking half bow. "At your service, milady."

Remembering the occasion of their meeting, Hannah felt her face suffuse with blood.

His smile broadened, then suddenly died. "Is

308

that the way my father first saw you? Naked on that bed? Was it in such a manner as that that you dazed him into taking you to wife?"

Involuntarily her hand flashed out toward his face. But before she could slap him, he caught her arm and pulled her against him. She could smell the tobacco on his breath and feel the hard, muscular length of his young body against hers. His eyes bored into her own, and his parted lips were close, very close. Hannah's senses whirled. She was certain he was going to kiss her. She yearned toward it, her eyes fluttering closed.

Then he released her and stepped back. Hannah swayed, as if about to fall, still feeling dazed and witless. When she opened her eyes, his handsome face wore again that mocking smile, as if he had read her every thought.

She shook her head to clear it. For the first time she thought about what the implications of his return from the dead might mean to her personally. She said hesitantly, "If you have come about the . . . the plantation is doing well."

"So I understand. I made inquiries. I was told that you have taken well to the task of growing tobacco." He laughed, a short bark of sound. "Yes, I was told that about you . . . among other things. Do not worry, madam." He motioned negligently. "I am not here to claim my inheritance. I have little taste for plantation life. You may continue . . . at least until I decide otherwise. If by chance I do return to Malvern, I will see that you are amply compensated. An overseer's salary at least. But there is one thing I do lay claim to. . . ." He nodded his head. "Black Star."

"No!" she cried in dismay. "Black Star is mine!"

309

"Not so, madam," he said coldly. "Surely you have been told that Black Star was my father's birthday gift to me?"

Hannah was silent, knowing there was nothing she could do to prevent him from taking the horse.

"I will be in Williamsburg, for a time at least. So, I bid you good day, madam." He made a knee, a gesture obvious in its contempt.

He mounted Black Star, gathered up the reins, then halted to look down at her. "One question, if I may, madam. Did my father speak much of me?"

Hannah's head went back. "Not once in my presence did your name pass Malcolm's lips, sir!"

"I see." His face went pale, those black eyes filling with pain, and for just a moment Hannah wished that she had lied to him.

Then he lightly touched Black Star's flanks with his heels, and man and horse started off.

Hannah watched as Black Star broke into a smooth trot, watched until man and horse disappeared from view on the main road into Williamsburg. There was an ache in her throat. She had come to love the animal so much. . . .

But the moment he was gone from sight she gave a start, as if shaking herself loose from a spell, and the full dimensions of her predicament crashed in on her. In a few minutes' time, with the return of Michael Verner from the dead, everything she had become, had gained, over the past year was in jeopardy of being swept away in an instant. She had no illusions about what would happen should Michael decide to return to Malvern for good. Even if the law did give her a one-third interest, Hannah knew she would never be able to live here with Michael the master—not after having been mistress of Malvern for a year. Her pride would not allow that.

Feeling the hot sting of tears in her eyes, Hannah hurried into the main house before she broke down completely. Hearing the virginal in the music room, she rushed in, slamming the door behind her.

André whirled around. One look at her stricken face, and he jumped to his feet. *"Mon Dieu,* Hannah! What has happened?"

She flung herself into his arms, crying brokenly for the first time since Malcolm's death. Between sobs, she gasped out the story.

"Dear lady, I am truly sorry. I can readily see why you are so distraught." He sighed, helped her dry the tears, and then made her sit down. He went to fetch a glass of brandy. She drank from the goblet, and sat back as warmth and renewed strength flowed back into her from the brandy.

André regarded her with concern. "The return of the prodigal son has placed you in a dire situation, has it not, dear lady?"

She sat up. "I'll fight him! He can't just come back and . . ."

He cut her off with a wave of his hand. "But he can, dear Hannah. I warned you about the property rights of women under your British law. If he chooses to come back and take his rightful place here, there is nothing you can do. The law might even be on his side, should he decide to force you to leave here. However, I cannot conceive of any man being so cruel. Especially not the son of Malcolm Verner . . ."

"If he comes back here to live, I will not stay. I refuse to live in the same house with that man!"

"Oh?" His eyebrows rose. "Your animosity seems rather severe toward a man you have just met, and only for a few minutes." His eyes got that shrewd look. "Or is there more to it than that?"

Hannah was silent. She had told André most but not all of what had occurred at the Cup and Horn. She had not told him about the drunken pirate or the man who had called himself Dancer. André was an understanding person, but he *was* a man, whatever else he might be, and she refused to humiliate herself by going into more detail.

André began to pace. "Perhaps we are concerned for nothing. This young man wandered afar in search of adventure. You say he told you he cares little for the life of a planter. We can hope that he may wish to resume his travels. It is my understanding that once a man becomes fiddle-footed he may then never be satisfied with a settled life." His face became bitter. "That is not my feeling, however. I would dearly love to return ... but no matter." He turned a frowning face on Hannah. "We must needs think of something to cheer you up. I have it! A ball, a grand ball!" His face became animated, and he clapped his hands together in delight. "A capital idea!"

"A ball!" She stared at him as if he'd gone mad. "That idea from you, André? You know how against the other one you were, and what a failure it was!"

"Circumstances are different now, madam. The most important fact of all is that your husband has been dead more than a year—the proper period of mourning has passed. Now, if we can dream up an idea, a motif ..." He began to pace.

She watched him in fascination, her thoughts a jumble.

"I have it!" He clapped his hands again. "It shall be a charity ball. A charity ball is always a marvelous attraction. *Mon Dieu*, yes! The gentry dearly love to feel that they are contributing some of their wealth to something, or someone, less fortunate than they."

"A charity ball? Charity for whom?"

His brow knitted. "Mmmm-m. For the orphans. *Naturellement!*"

"What orphans? I don't even know any orphans!"

"There are always orphans, dear lady. We will find some, never fear." That wicked grin was in evidence again. "People will come, you may be sure. They will come to see how the mistress of Malvern is bearing up. True, some may come out of vulgar curiosity, in search of food for gossip. And now that young Verner is resurrected, they will be even more curious. It might even be a splendid idea to invite . . ." He broke off, eyeing her warily.

"No! I will not have that man at Malvern at my own inviting!" Hannah jumped to her feet. "And that's the end of it!"

André, noting her heightened color and undue agitation, had to wonder if there was more to it than she was willing to admit. Could it be that this young man had somehow managed to reach her hardened heart? *Non, non*, not possible. He shrugged, spreading his hands. "It shall be as you wish, dear lady."

Since Christmas was only a little more than a month hence and Hannah wanted the ball to take

313

place before then, she was very busy over the next few days. She wrote all the invitations in her own hand, taking the names from the list Malcolm had used for their wedding ball. Each day she sent John and Dickie out in the coach to deliver the invitations. Nearly sixteen years old now, Dickie had grown into almost full manhood since coming to Malvern.

One day after the coach had been into Williamsburg Dickie came home bursting with news. The lad told Hannah and André where Michael Verner had been during the two years past and what he had done to bring about the end of Blackbeard's reign of terror. Michael was a hero to all of Williamsburg.

"Hero, is he? It would indeed seem so," André murmured. He looked at Hannah with arched eyebrows. "Perhaps, dear lady, you should ..."

"No! I know what you're thinking, André," she said sharply. "I will not invite him, hero or not!"

"He will not be at the ball, m'lady?" Dickie said, visibly disappointed. "But think of the tales he would have to tell!"

"He will *not* be here. And who wants to hear tales of bloody pirates?" She made a face. "Probably his own hands are bloody, did he sail with them all that time. Now, I'll hear no more of it."

This time Hannah knew beforehand that the ball would be a success. She received a number of notes in response to her invitations, each expressing pleasure at being invited. Several ladies and gentlemen even came to call—the first time such a thing had happened.

Hannah received them as a proper mistress of

314

Malvern should, offering tea and sweets, something stronger for the gentlemen if they desired. She exchanged gossip and small talk with them, handling herself with confidence and ease. Hannah was delighted at these visitations, even though she knew that many came in the hope of espying Michael, or at least receiving news of him.

The plantation buzzed with activity and anticipation. Bess put everyone to work to assure that it would be the grandest ball of this, or any, year. Upstairs in the sewing room, André hummed happily to himself as he went about designing and making Hannah a new gown.

"It will be the grandest ball gown ever designed, dear lady. It will be the talk of all Virginia, because it will both enhance your great beauty and scandalize all!"

And on the night of the ball Hannah was more than gratified at the reaction to her appearance. She came in alone, as André had strictly forbidden her to make an entrance until all, or most, of the guests had arrived. He had arranged for one of the male house servants, dressed in splendid livery, to announce the guests. As each guest arrived, he would ring a silver bell and announce to the assemblage at large the names of the arrivals.

When Hannah finally appeared at the top of the stairs, the servant rang the bell with more than usual force, and announced in a voice loud enough to be heard over the chatter of the guests: "Mistress Hannah Verner!"

There was a concerted gasp from the throng waiting below as Hannah began to gracefully descend the wide stairway. Her heavy red-gold hair was unpowdered, and it had been artfully teased and

315

piled flatteringly above her lovely face. Several long ringlets fell to her back and shoulders, accenting the whiteness of her skin against the luxurious green of her gown.

For this occasion, Hannah had condescended to wear the required stays and hoops. The stays, however, were of André's own design, and were much more comfortable than the normal rib-crushing cage. They were unusually constructed in front, so that her bosom, while being pushed up, was not covered—an important fact, considering the design of her gown.

The gown, fashioned in yards and yards of emerald green silk, had long, full sleeves that belled out to just above her elbows. The back, which her audience could not yet see, swooped daringly low, and the skirt, buoyed by the hoops, accentuated her small waist.

However, it was the bodice, André's masterpiece, from which no man present could divert his eyes. The startlingly rich green silk had been cut around the outside of Hannah's plump white breasts almost down to the waist in front. The space thus created was filled with a panel of sheer, flesh-colored lace, behind which the flesh of her bare breasts could be seen, if one looked carefully, and every man there, and most of the women, looked very carefully indeed.

André had convinced her to purchase new jewelry to go with the gown. "You are entitled, dear lady. You have made the plantation profitable, so you are deserving. The jewels dear Malcolm gave to you are fine, but those jewels are not what this gown cries out for."

So around her throat she wore an emerald necklace. In her ears, brilliant against her coppery hair, were matching emerald studs.

There were a few shocked whispers, and many gasps of indrawn breath—whether of outrage or admiration, it was difficult to tell.

André stepped smoothly to the base of the stairs and took her hand. In a carrying voice, he announced, "The latest thing from Paris, ladies and gentlemen. I understand that the court ladies are much taken with this new style."

Then he offered Hannah his arm. Into her ear he whispered, "You see? The queen of the ball, dear lady."

Hannah held her head high and proud against the stares, and ignored the whispers. The instant they entered the ballroom, the musicians, apparently on prior instructions from André, struck up a tune. It was the melody her father used to sing to Hannah.

Hannah bestowed a smile of gratitude on André, stepped toward him, and they began to dance. At first they were alone, but one couple after another joined them, and soon the ballroom floor was crowded with dancing couples.

Just before the piece ended, André said softly, "This will undoubtedly be my last dance with you this night. You will be much in demand."

His words were true. As the music ended and André stepped back, bowing from the waist, the young men moved in, clamoring for the next dance with Hannah.

After that, the evening was a blur of music and glittering candles and dancing until her head was dizzy. All the gallants were paying court to her. Hannah flirted, fending off their not-so-subtle advances, laughing at their flattery—few of their words actually penetrating her consciousness.

This was the ball she had always dreamed of. It was a great success; there was no longer any doubt of that. Hannah was giddy from the dancing and the attention, but remembering what had happened at the other two balls, she took very little wine—only a sip or two from the glasses her partners plied her with.

Hannah watched all evening for Jamie Falkirk, and did not see him. She had not sent him an invitation, and apparently he had accepted the fact that she didn't wish to see him again....

It was nearly midnight when the musicians stopped suddenly, in the middle of a piece, and a strange hush fell over the ballroom. Puzzled as to the cause, Hannah stepped back and looked around. Then she saw him.

Michael Verner stood in the doorway of the ballroom, the focus of all eyes. He was elegantly attired in a camlet coat with the sleeves ending in lace ruffles, breeches of expensive plush, olive in color, black hose, and black shoes with silver buckles. Across the ballroom his brilliant black eyes met hers, and he came directly toward her, the dancers clearing a path for him. He ignored the startled looks and the whispers rustling like autumn leaves, and strode on. He wasn't wearing a wig, but he didn't need one—his hair was long and black and lustrous. A lock of it hung over his brow.

Reaching her, he made a mocking knee, one hand across his waist as though he were doffing a nonexistent hat. Straightening, he staggered slightly, and Hannah caught the distinct odor of brandy fumes.

"Madam, may I claim this dance?"

Before Hannah could speak or even move, Michael motioned to the orchestra, and the music started up again.

As he swept her around the floor, she said in a furious voice, "How dare you come here, sir! You weren't invited!"

"Why should I need an invitation?" he said with studied insolence. "Malvern is my home, mine to claim any time I wish."

"And you're drunk! You reek of brandy!"

"Why should that bother you, madam? As a tavern wench, you must have served drink to many far gone in their cups."

"You go too far, sir!"

"I tell the truth, do I not?" he said in an innocent tone. "Or mayhap I have been lied to. Is it the case that you have *not* been a serving wench? Could I be mistaken? Was it some other naked wench I saw that night abovestairs in the Cup and Horn?"

Hannah tried to pull away from him, but he held her in a grip of iron. Then she remembered where she was. Glancing around, she saw people staring at them. She subsided, but determined to respond to no more of his gibes.

When the music ended, he bowed from the waist. "It was indeed my pleasure, milady."

He turned his back and strode away. Hannah seethed with rage. How she longed to order him thrown out! But she knew she dared not. Not only would that serve to inflame the gossip, it might so

319

anger Michael that he would reclaim possession of Malvern.

Hannah made up her mind firmly that she would not dance with him again, even if she had to flee the ballroom. He didn't approach her. During the next two hours, she saw him dancing with someone every dance, always with a different woman. She found herself inexplicably piqued by this.

Busy with her own dancing partners, she now began to drink the wine they fetched for her.

It was some little time before she realized that Michael's presence had cast a strange pall over the ball. As soon as their curiosity was sated, people began to leave. Very soon there were only a few left.

And then, finally, Michael did approach her—in the middle of a dance. Rudely he elbowed her partner aside and seized her by the waist. Without a word, he started pulling her across the ballroom floor.

"What are you about, sir?"

Michael didn't reply, but forged ahead, the dancers moving aside to let him pass.

Hannah, acutely aware of the startled faces of those still present, tried to pull her arm free, but his fingers were as unyielding as an oaken band encircling her wrist. In an attempt to stop their forward progress, Hannah pulled back with all her strength, slipped on the polished floor, and fell to her knees.

Still without speaking, Michael turned about, pulled her up, grasped her wrist again, and continued on his way.

Hannah, both angered and frightened now,

screamed, but the guests, seemingly mesmerized by the scene, made no move to help her.

Across the ballroom, hearing Hannah's scream, André Leclaire began to hasten to her rescue. Then, as he saw who it was towing her, his step slowed, and stopped altogether. It was not from fear that he stopped. André feared no man. He had killed before and would kill again if given cause. That was the reason he was presently exiled in this uncivilized country, instead of being in his beloved Paris.

André's wicked grin flickered. Perhaps this country was not so uncivilized, after all. Or perhaps something could be said for a raw, elemental display of passion.

Dear lady, he said silently, *open your heart for once. If pleasure comes to you, accept it gratefully!*

In the entryway Michael headed for the staircase. Hannah reached in a desperate grab for the stair post and clung fiercely. Michael, striding on, lost his hold on her wrist.

"Madam," he said through clenched teeth, "we are going upstairs . . ."

"No!"

". . . even if I have to carry you!"

Without another word he bent down and scooped her up in his arms. Hannah, surprised and outraged, let go her grip on the stair post. Michael mounted the stairs, carrying her easily. Hannah struggled, hitting him in the face with all the strength of her anger, screaming at him to release her. Then, over his shoulder, she saw the guests, collected at the bottom of the stairs, looking up. She fell silent, determined that they should not be treated to a further spectacle.

Upstairs, Michael strode past the master bedroom and into Hannah's own room. Crossing to the bed, he dropped Hannah onto her back, then returned to lock the door.

He came back to stand looking down at her, that lock of hair falling over his forehead, his eyes glittering like black jewels.

Hannah was conscious of the blood rushing through her body. The mixture of anger and fear he inspired in her was exciting. Distressed as she was, Hannah realized that she had not felt so alive in months.

She said defiantly, "What are you going to do?"

"Why, madam, I am going to claim my seignorial rights, as lord of the manor."

"You said you weren't interested in claiming the plantation."

His cold smile did not reach his eyes. "A mere quibble, madam. Under the law, I am lord of the manor, and legally permitted to take anything on my property. But let's dispense with this idle talk. After all, this will not be the first time you've lain with a man. Surely I am not so distasteful as the innkeeper, and I am much younger than my father. Also, I would like to learn what it is about you that enticed a man of my father's age and habits to the extent that he would wed you."

He leaned down, placing one hand on each side of her on the bed. She could see the feverish glitter of his eyes, and smell the brandy on his breath, mixed with the not unpleasant masculine scent of him.

"You need not fear, madam. You may keep the plantation, at least for now. I only wish to amuse myself with you, as did my father."

"Your father did not *amuse* himself with me!"

"Did he not?" His full lips formed a cynical smile. "Could he not bed you, then?"

"I didn't say that!" Hannah felt herself flushing. She sat up, pushing his arms aside, and arranged her clothing.

"Perhaps you won't believe this, but your father loved me. He never treated me with anything less than kindness and respect."

"Respect?" He laughed. "Respect has no place in the bedchamber, milady—but perhaps at his age, that was all that he could bring you!"

Hannah glared at him. "Since you are so interested, sir, that was not the case. Your father was still a man in every respect."

Michael's face grew dark with blood. "So he loved and respected you. You, a tavern wench, who bedded men for money!"

Hannah lifted her chin and looked directly into his eyes. "A tavern wench, yes. But I've bedded no man for money, not of my own doing. Another thing I know you'll not believe, but 'tis true. 'Twas all Amos Stritch's doing. And what right have you to talk of your father? You ran off. You left Malvern and your father to become a pirate. You broke his heart, and he never recovered from it. If he found friendship and pleasure with me, why should your begrudge him that small comfort?"

Hannah experienced a small thrill of triumph, seeing by the expression on his face that her words had wounded him. He grew pale with anger, and he drew his hand back as though to strike her. Instead, he fastened his fingers like claws in the low bodice of her gown, and ripped it all the way down, petticoats and all, exposing the naked front of her body to his gaze.

Hannah's first instinct was to try and cover her body with her hands, but she forced herself to lie still under his gaze. Instinctively she felt that in this confrontation she must retain what dignity she could. She must remain strong. If she showed weakness before this man, she would be lost to him.

The brilliance in his black eyes glazed over as he stared down upon the lush mounds and valleys of her body.

She felt her flesh grow hot under his gaze, but she made no move to cover herself.

"You would take me by force, then?" she asked.

His voice was thick. "I will take you, madam, in whatever way necessary!"

He began to hurriedly disrobe, pulling off his clothes carelessly.

In spite of herself, Hannah could not keep her gaze from straying to his body. She had never seen a man with such a beautiful physique. Broad shoulders tapered down to a narrow waist and flanks. His legs were long, columnar, and well muscled, and between his legs ...

Her face flushing, Hannah turned her face away. Although the sight of his naked limbs had kindled a strange feeling in her own body, she was determined to be unyielding and cold in his arms. She could not stop him from taking her as he would, but she would show him the insult of her coldness and disinterest.

Then he blew out the candle and joined her on the bed. His hands ripped in heedless impatience at the remaining shreds of her clothing. He gripped her shoulders with hurting hands and kissed her with demanding passion, bruising her mouth.

Despite her resolve, Hannah's body responded. Fighting it, she wanted to struggle, struggle against her own feelings as well as his.

Michael's mouth moved down to the hollow at the base of her throat. Oh, traitorous body! Lying still and cold was beginning to be a torment. Hannah moaned, deep in her throat.

Michael laughed and moved his lips down to her breasts. His tongue teased her nipples until they were hard and pulsing.

Half sobbing from outrage and anger, Hannah found herself kissing him back. The heat of his body had spread to hers, and, in the secret places of her lower body, a feeling grew, a hunger that demanded to be appeased. And all the while she was aware of his long, hard-muscled legs on hers, the feel of his smooth skin and supple body. A young man's body.

His hands, exploring her body, were rough, hurting, yet wherever he touched, Hannah felt almost painful pleasure. The strange pleasure-pain rose, wavelike, each wave reaching a greater peak of wanting, until she cried aloud his name and grasped his shoulders.

"Yes! Now, madam!"

He spread her thighs apart and mounted her, penetrating her with one brutal lunge. She cried out again, beating against his chest with her fists. But already he was thrusting. The sensations in her body mounted, and she began to respond to his thrusts.

She moaned and arched against him as the speed of his thrusting body quickened. She was caught up in a maelstrom of hot pleasure.

Then he groaned loudly, and drove into her with one last thrust. Something very like an explosion burst in her, and she was caught up in a sweet ecstasy almost unbearable in its intensity. Hannah clung to his now still body, shuddering, crying out, as she finally knew the unbelievable pleasure of fulfillment.

She went limp. She felt weightless, boneless; her limbs were heavy with languor. Her senses still spinning giddily, Hannah made a small sound of protest as she felt him leave her. For a moment she thought he was getting up from the bed, and she wanted to beg him not to go away. With an effort of will she remained silent. But Michael did not leave. Instead, he stretched out beside her on his back.

Hannah waited with bated breath for him to speak. He remained silent, only his panting breath loud in the room.

She felt a pang of disappointment. But she was still in the grip of a contentment such as she had never known, and her disappointment was fleeting. Heavy with the languorous aftermath of love, she drifted into sleep.

Hannah woke with a start, blinking up into darkness. Had she been dreaming again of Black Star? It seemed so, but the substance of the dream, if she *had* dreamed, was too elusive to grasp.

Full memory returned to her, and she held her breath, listening. Was she alone?

She reached out a tentative hand, touched warm flesh, and recoiled.

"Yes, love? What is it?" Michael's voice seemed slow, drugged.

Still trying to reconstruct her dream, she said timidly, "Black Star, is he all right . . . ?" She hesitated before speaking his name for the first time. "Michael?"

"The horse is fine, madam." A drowsy chuckle sounded. "I have raced him several times, and won in the bargain. My apologies for charging you with abusing the animal. You have trained him well. . . ."

He broke off, his voice taking on a puzzled note. "Hannah?"

A hand found her in the dark, found her face, the fingers tracing the outlines of her mouth, then moving down to her breasts, and on down. Hannah gasped, arching against his stroking hand.

Michael groaned. "Hannah, my dearest Hannah! You have haunted my dreams these days past! I have been in a fever, love!"

Boldly, remembering the pleasure he had given her once this night, Hannah explored a man's body for the first time in her life. She let her hands mold the hard muscular ridges of his chest. His nipples felt like poking thumbs against her caressing palms. She moved her hands on, down across the washboard hardness of his belly, and on down.

Michael sucked in his breath and shifted on the bed, taking her into his arms. His mouth found hers, and they kissed lingeringly.

Hannah lost herself in renewed sensation. It didn't seem strange to her that she had thought

327

she had hated this man on sight, that she had been sure she despised him earlier tonight.

All she wanted to think about was that he desired her. He had made it wonderful for her—not shameful and hurting as it had been with Amos Stritch and the drunken pirate, not pitiful, as it had been toward the end with Malcolm. Love with Michael was exalting, marvelous, sweeping her to great heights of pleasure. Everything they did seemed natural and right.

He must love her, he *must*! If he didn't, would he hold her in his arms this way, would he call her "love?"

His lips burned a trail down to her breasts. He kissed the nipples tenderly, teasingly, and Hannah was proud that she had well-formed breasts for him. As his lips and fingers played over her body, Hannah's hands traveled up and down his back, marveling at the tensing and untensing of the slabs of muscles there. She ran her fingers deep into his long hair and forced his face harder against her. Her body leaped with need now, and she wanted to feel the sweet hurt of his wanting her.

And quite before she realized it, he was within her again, filling her, moving slowly. This time, perhaps because neither was fully awake, their loving was slow, tender, languorous. It made Hannah think of moving under water, of the slow-motion movements in a dream.

Now the rate of his breathing increased, as did the pace of his thrusts. With the knowledge born of the ageless instincts of womankind, Hannah knew how to match her movements to his.

Once again she experienced the beginning of the now familiar ecstasy. Her body arched and twisted and drove toward his as his thrustings speeded up, sweeping her into forgetfulness and pleasure.

"Yes," Michael muttered. "Now, love!"

Her fists pummeled his back, her head arched back against the pillow, and a shrill cry escaped her lips as sweet-hot pleasure flooded her, almost savage in its fury. . . .

Hannah was mindless for a few seconds, reveling in it, her body awash with wondrous sensation.

When she was aware again, Michael had withdrawn, his weight leaving her. With gentle fingers he brushed the damp hair from her eyes and kissed her brow. Then he turned away, his back to her, settling down with a sigh.

For a moment Hannah felt disappointment. She wished for him to hold her again. In his arms, she felt secure, safe from all harm.

But then he was weary, she knew. Her own limbs were heavy; it took an effort to move them. She dreamed along for a little, almost asleep.

She stirred, turning toward him. "Michael?" she said softly. "I love you. I think I have loved you from the first time I ever saw you, when I thought you were a pirate named Dancer. . . . Michael?"

He made no response, his breathing deep and even. He was asleep.

It was all right, Hannah thought. There was plenty of time now in which to talk. An entire lifetime was before them!

She snuggled close against the warmth of his back and went to sleep—a deep sleep of contentment.

Chapter Seventeen

When Hannah awoke, the sun was streaming into her window. She sat up with a cry. "Michael?"

He wasn't there! A sudden feeling of panic set her heart to pounding. Where had he gone?

Then, remembering the past night, she lay back, beginning to smile. He had been thoughtful, and had crept out without waking her. He had probably gone downstairs for breakfast.

From the angle of the sun she knew that it was quite late, and now that she thought of it, Hannah realized she was hungry herself. Yet she lay quiet for a moment, letting her thoughts roam back over the night before, reliving and savoring the glory of every moment. Her heart ached with love. How marvelous the future seemed! Living here with

Michael, still mistress of Malvern, but now having someone to really share it with.

Finally she got up. She had never felt so complete and happy. Humming to herself, she went about getting dressed, putting on a garment almost prim in its modesty, hoping to lessen the shock experienced by the house servants and the remaining guests the night before. Hannah stopped what she was doing, laughing aloud. They *had* been shocked, of that she was sure. The shock wave would spread throughout the Williamsburg area before many days passed. But let them have their gossip; she didn't care! Last night she had found what she had unknowingly been waiting for. She felt impregnable in her new-found happiness.

She laid her hands on the soft curve of her lower stomach. Had Michael gotten her with child last night? Oh, she did indeed hope so!

Her thoughts swung to Malcolm. Would he have approved? Being the kind of man he had been, Hannah felt sure that he would not only have approved, but applauded.

"You wanted a son, dear Malcolm," she said. "You have a son. Michael is alive and back! You have a son to carry on the Verner name. But what if you had a grandson? Wouldn't that be even better?"

Not realizing at first that she had been speaking aloud, the sound of her voice startled her. She glanced around furtively, hoping no one had overheard.

A few minutes later, she left the room and went downstairs, hands folded decorously, wearing a sober face—as a proper lady should.

But she was singing inside.

The house was strangely quiet. At least there were no guests still about. All must have departed in haste, and shock, after Michael had carried her upstairs.

Well, damn them, she thought recklessly; *I have managed without their approval all this time. And Michael and I together can still manage without it!*

The dining room was empty. She passed on into the serving pantry, pausing just inside to sweep the room with a glance. The only person in the pantry was Jenny, who gave her a quick, furtive look.

"Have you seen Michael, Jenny?"

"He left the house more'n an hour ago, Mistress Hannah."

"Where did he go?"

"He go toward the stable, mistress," Jenny said with downcast eyes.

Hannah left the house, hurrying toward the stable. She found John inside, mending a set of harness.

"John ... did Michael ride out?"

"Yes, mistress."

"To inspect the plantation? I suppose he's eager to see it again, after such a long absence. . . ."

"No, Mistress Hannah." John's gaze was level. "He rode toward Williamsburg."

Hannah's heart sank. Why had he left, left without a word to her? She turned away to hide her distress, and stood in the stable door, staring up the road toward Williamsburg. It was possible he had ridden into the village for some personal things. But in that event, wouldn't it be more likely he would have had John take him in the coach?

Pushing back her rising fears, she turned again to John. She must do something to busy her thoughts. She said, "John, will you saddle my horse for me? I'm going into the house to change clothes. Then I wish to ride."

Since Michael had taken Black Star, Hannah had been riding Malcolm's horse, a big bay. A good enough animal, but not in a class with Black Star.

John said, "Right away, Mistress Hannah."

Hannah strode toward the house, her joyous mood of a moment before replaced by a feeling of foreboding. She couldn't understand why Michael should ride off without so much as a word to her. But he would return. After last night, she was sure he would return.

Having fallen again on hard times, Amos Stritch had lost some few pounds. But the gout still troubled him, and he had to use the cane to get around.

He was in a foul mood as he hobbled along the streets of Williamsburg. He had been doing grandly with Blackbeard, selling the pirate's plundered liquor, acting as an agent for other pirates too. Now Blackbeard was dead, and because of his death the remaining pirates along the coast were giving Virginia a wide berth, fearful of coming near with liquor to sell.

Stritch knew he had to find another means to make his way, or what money he had saved up would soon be gone. Perhaps it would be best to leave Williamsburg.

Turning onto Duke of Gloucester Street, he saw a tall young man striding along, head down.

Stritch recognized him. It was young Michael Verner. Fury burned in Stritch. This man, from the stories abroad in Williamsburg, was more responsible than anyone else for Blackbeard's death. And then an idea sprouted in Stritch's mind.

He crossed the street to intercept Michael Verner.

"Master Verner . . ."

Michael stopped, glancing up, his eyes narrowing at the sight of Stritch.

Stritch doffed his hat. "Good day to you, young sir. Mayhap you are not aware of this," Stritch said boldly. "But your father, may his soul rest in peace, made a bargain with me afore his death. He purchased the indenture papers on Hannah McCambridge, now Mistress Verner. He agreed to pay me fifty pounds when last year's tobacco crop was sold. The poor man died before he could pay. Now you, sir, being the gentleman that you are, surely would like to see a debt of your father's honored, would you not, sir?" Stritch told his lie with a straight face, staring directly into Michael's eyes. "I did ask Mistress Verner to pay me my due. She refused, and . . ."

Michael's eyes blazed. "How dare you, sir! How dare you accost me in such a manner? You think I do not know what you are? You think I do not know of your dealings with Edward Teach? And that you were trying to persuade him to raid Malvern?"

Michael raised his hand as though to strike out, and Stritch cringed, stumbling back. "Not true, young sir! Some'un has told you false."

"I was there, you despicable creature! I heard, and I know. What do you think would happen to

335

you should I report this to Governor Spotswood? He would have you hanged for a pirate!"

Truly frightened now, Stritch cried, "Please, young sir. I beg of you, do not do this! We will forget the debt your father owed. . . ."

"There is no debt, and even if there were, I would not honor it. If I had my sword buckled on, I would run you through!"

Stritch held up his hands in fright. "I am not a man for battle. I carry no weapon, I am sick and lame. . . ."

"You will leave Williamsburg at once, Amos Stritch," Michael said harshly. "If ever I see you on the street here again, I will kill you! If ever I see you again *anywhere,* you are a dead man! You have my promise on that. You will leave Williamsburg this very day!"

Michael turned and strode away, his back held rigid. Amos Stritch stared after him in dejection. He was too concerned about his own immediate welfare to longer indulge himself in anger. He knew very well that the young firebrand meant every word of his threat.

It had been a rash, foolish action on his part, Stritch realized in a rare moment of self-truth, and now he was in danger of his life because of it.

He had to leave Williamsburg this very day!

But where would he go?

He would have to leave Virginia, no question of that. Perhaps he should leave the South altogether, go north to some village where he could get into some phase of the liquor trade. Perhaps, if fortune smiled on him, he might someday have his own tavern again.

But as he gimped along the street toward his

336

quarters, he cursed the day he had ever set eyes on Hannah McCambridge. That bitch out of hell had been his downfall, and it would seem now that he would never have the chance to even accounts with her.

Michael Verner was a tormented man. It had been over a week now since the night that too much drink and his own cursed passions had driven him to attend the ball at Malvern, and then to take Hannah to bed.

He groaned aloud. Damnation, how that woman haunted him, haunted him day and night. She raged through his blood like a fatal fever.

On the morning he had ridden away from Malvern, he had talked at length with John, who had been closer to him while growing up than anyone else at Malvern. John had corrected a number of misconceptions Michael had been harboring about Hannah.

At the end, John had said, "She a fine woman, is Mistress Hannah. She's made Malvern a happy place, and has taken to plantation life well." John had smiled with pride in her. "Mistress Hannah runs Malvern almost as well as your father, Master Michael."

Still, she *had* been a tavern wench, no matter how it had come about. But what tormented Michael the most was the fact that he had made love to a woman his own father had bedded. His own stepmother! It was incest—not of the blood, of course, but it was incest in his own mind.

And the thought that the villainous Amos Stritch had once bedded her was almost too much to bear; the thought of that gross body violating

Hannah! During his encounter with the scoundrel a few minutes ago, a red curtain of pure rage had descended over Michael's eyes. He was sure he would have killed the man then and there had he been carrying a weapon.

Yet none of this could erase from his mind the images of the night he had spent with Hannah. Never had he taken more pleasure from a woman. He knew she was waiting for him to return, and every day of the week since his abrupt departure Michael had to fight the powerful temptation to go again to Malvern. He had spent the week drinking, gambling, racing Black Star—anything to take his thoughts away from Hannah. He had even taken to bed a tavern whore, but then had risen from her bed in disgust at himself. Nothing worked; nothing washed thoughts of Hannah from his mind.

Michael entered the Raleigh Tavern and went up the narrow stairs to the quarters he shared with numerous other gentlemen. Only a few taverns in Williamsburg provided private quarters, it being the custom to sleep in a room crowded with other wayfarers. But the Raleigh was the best tavern in the village, and Michael thought that his new prestige as the village hero required his residence at only the best. He always smiled grimly when he thought of being made the hero of Williamsburg. If people knew the things he'd done while he'd been with Blackbeard, they would probably turn from him in horror.

Michael was wise enough to know that hero worship was short in duration, and that soon he would be replaced by someone else. He hoped it would happen soon. His elevation to village hero, his miraculous return from the dead, the whispers of gossip generated by his residing in the tavern instead of taking his rightful place as master of Malvern—it all added up to more notoriety than he desired.

At least he had a corner to himself in the large bedroom upstairs, a corner for his clothes and personal things. There was even a writing table for his own use.

He changed into riding clothes. The five times he had raced Black Star, the horse had come in the winner, and the challenges were coming at Michael thick and fast. Now he had been challenged to a match race by Jamie Falkirk on his big chestnut, Smoker. Michael recalled that the challenge to race had been flung in his face with grim purpose, almost as if Jamie were challenging him to a duel. That was strange in itself. Living on neighboring plantations, they had been fairly close friends as boys. Now Jamie seemed to harbor some inexplicable animosity toward him. Michael shrugged. Perhaps his old friend was envious of his being hailed as a hero. If Jamie only knew how he hated it!

The size of the wager had surprised Michael. Jamie had bet fifty pounds on his horse against Black Star. It was a large wager, several times larger than was usual. Jamie must be almighty confident.

However, the amount of money was welcome. At first Michael had been reluctant to accept the governor's award money—it had seemed too much like blood money. But after Michael had realized that he could not, under any circumstances, remain at Malvern with Hannah there—and he couldn't bring himself to turn her out—he had found he needed money. So he had swallowed his pride and accepted the two hundred pounds. It had been most welcome. He had used it for gambling at cards and to wager on Black Star.

Leaving the Raleigh, he walked to the stables at the edge of the village where he kept Black Star. From his stall the horse nickered, head tossing. Michael had a lump of sugar for him. He let the horse take it from his hand. He waved away the stable hand and saddled Black Star himself.

He led the animal outside and mounted up, then rode the mile beyond the village to the crude race track. Many villages in Virginia had better race tracks, some even with accommodations for spectators, but Williamsburg had yet to build such. The race course was a circular track in what had once been a pasture; the course was roughly half a mile in circumference. Two posts with flags signaled the end of the course. Since it was a week day, there were only a few spectators. Jamie was already there, with several of his friends.

Michael had walked his mount out from town, keeping a tight rein to hold back Black Star's natural inclination to break into a canter. He pulled up where Jamie stood with his friends.

Jamie brushed back his flaming red hair and looked at him, rawboned face caught in a scowl of displeasure. "You are late, sir." He tried a sneer, which only succeeded in making him look peevish. "We were thinking you were afraid to match your horse against mine."

"Why should I be afraid, Jamie?" Michael said easily. "And it is you who are early. The time we agreed on was ..."

"To be fair, I believe I should tell you," Jamie

340

broke in, his voice loud, his manner belligerent. "I have raced Smoker against Black Star, sir, with Hannah Verner astride him, many times. And I have won every time."

Michael felt himself tightening up inside, but he managed to keep his voice even. "I do appreciate your concern, Jamie. You are indeed being more than fair. The wager still stands. And since you seem unduly impatient, shall we proceed?"

Jamie drew himself up. "So be it! You cannot say you were not forewarned."

"No, Jamie," Michael said drily. "I cannot say that."

Quickly they selected two men to station themselves as judges at the flagposts at the end of the course, a man to remain here to give the starting signal, and another as stakeholder. Jamie vaulted into the saddle, carrying a quirt in his hand, and the two men lined their horses up side by side. They waited until the judges had reached their posts.

Then the starter said, "Ready, gentlemen?"

They were ready.

"Then good fortune to you both. Go!"

The horses sprang forward as if unleashed from a bow. Michael let Smoker take an early lead. Michael had learned an important fact from the earlier races. Black Star *hated* it when another horse was leading him. If he took the lead at once, he tended to slacken off. But if another horse was in front of him, he went all out when Michael finally loosened the reins, belly almost flat to the ground, skimming over the earth like a speeding bullet. Today, Michael held him a half length behind Smoker until midway in the course. Once

Jamie looked back, teeth flashing in a triumphant grin.

Michael could feel Black Star's displeasure—the animal was pulling on the bit. Finally Michael loosened the reins and leaned forward to shout, "All right, beauty! Go, Black Star! Take him now!"

In a great burst of speed, Black Star drew abreast of Smoker. Jamie glanced over, startled and disbelieving. Then Black Star was drawing ahead. They were only yards from the flagposts now. Out of the corner of his eye Michael saw Jamie applying the quirt to Smoker's straining hindquarters.

With a touch of his heels to Black Star's flanks, Michael urged a little more speed out of the animal, and they flashed by the flagposts a length and a half in front of Jamie's mount.

Michael let Black Star take his own time to slow to a stop. Then he rode back to the flagposts and slid off. Jamie came wheeling back on Smoker and jumped down as the stakeholder was giving Michael his winnings.

"You rode well, sir."

Michael merely nodded in acknowledgement, watching the money being counted into his hand.

"Did you ride Hannah Verner as well?"

Michael's head came up. He wasn't sure he'd heard aright.

Jamie was sneering openly. " 'Tis common knowledge hereabouts that you spent the night of the ball in her bed. . . ."

"You dishonor a lady's name, sir!"

"A lady? A tavern whore, had by anyone with . . ."

Fury boiled up in Michael, a fury such as he had never known, and he lashed out, striking Jamie across the face with the back of his hand.

Jamie reeled back. His face went pale under the mop of red hair. His hand came up to caress the marks Michael's hand had left. In a cold voice he said, "I must demand satisfaction, sir!"

Just as coldly, Michael said, "And it shall be my pleasure to *give* you satisfaction, sir!"

"And what shall the weapons be? I prefer swords. I understand you made much use of yours as a pirate, and I would not wish to take advantage."

"It is your choice, Jamie Falkirk. Swords it shall be."

"My second will call for you at dawn. We shall meet at sunrise."

"We meet next at sunrise, then, sir." Michael made a half bow. "By your leave, gentlemen."

Without another word, not trusting himself in his state of anger to speak further, he mounted Black Star and rode away at a gallop.

His anger began to cool before he'd ridden halfway back to Williamsburg, and he slowed Black Star to a walk.

Michael was appalled at what had just happened. Was he doomed to having to call out every man in Virginia? His short laugh was bitter. He had been convinced that once his time with Edward Teach was finished the killing would be over. It seemed he had been mistaken.

And Jamie . . . he remembered when they had played together as boys, fighting mock duels with crude wooden swords. Jamie had been as awkward as a boy on stilts, falling all over himself. He was not much more graceful now, that was obvious, while Michael had honed his skills with a sword until he doubted few men could get the better of him. It would be nothing but murder, sheer murder!

Suddenly he knew that he couldn't go through with it. If he was forced to kill Jamie, no matter what the reason, he would never be able to live with himself.

He almost turned Black Star back to the race course. But he knew that would accomplish nothing. For some reason Michael couldn't fathom, Jamie Falkirk was spoiling to do battle with him. Thinking back on it, he knew that to be true. If he rode back there and tried to refuse Jamie's challenge, the duel would probably be forced on him then and there.

Michael rode on, despondent, deep in gloom. In Williamsburg, he said to the stable hand, "Unsaddle the animal, rub him down good, then feed and water him. I will be needing him again ere long."

He strode up the street to the Raleigh, and went on upstairs. At the writing table, he dipped a quill into the inkpot and penned a note:

Madam: I am leaving Virginia this day. I am sure I leave Malvern in capable hands. My behavior the night of your ball was inexcusable. I can only plead excess of drink. I do not presume to beg your forgiveness, since I know it would probably be in vain. But perhaps you might find it in your heart to think more kindly of me with the passage of time. I do not, at this present time, know how long I shall be away. Meanwhile, may God in his wisdom be kind to you, madam.

Michael signed his name to the letter, and then sat long brooding over it. There was so much more he desperately wanted to say, but he knew he dare not let himself do so.

Finally he muttered an oath, folded the paper over, sealed it with a drop of hot candle wax, and scratched "Mistress Hannah Verner" on it. Carrying the letter in his hand, he strode to the top of the stairs and bellowed for a boy to be sent up. In a moment a young lad of fourteen, one of the several indentured youths at the Raleigh, came flying up the stairs.

"Yes, Master Verner?"

"You know where Malvern plantation lies?"

The lad bobbed his head.

"Hire a horse at the stables," Michael said. He took several coins from his pocket. "What is left over is yours, lad. Deliver this message to Mistress Hannah Verner at Malvern. To no one else, do you understand?"

The lad nodded vigorously. Michael gave him the coins and the message, and then went back to his room with a heavy step. He began to collect those of his personal belongings he could without loading Black Star down too heavily.

No gentlemen ever fled into the night, not on the eve before a duel, without facing disgrace, without being branded a coward.

Well, so be it, for that was exactly what he was going to do.

An hour later he was astride Black Star, riding out of Williamsburg, heading in a generally westerly direction, not sure of his eventual destination. He rode away without once looking back.

Even after she received Michael's letter, Hannah couldn't bring herself to accept the fact that he was gone. She read the brief note again and again, trying to read hidden meanings into it, but the stark fact remained—he was riding out of her life.

She was faintly surprised that his pride would allow him to apologize for his behavior. But she didn't want an apology from him; she wanted Michael himself! His leaving her like this, if it were true, was what she found unforgivable.

She showed the letter to André.

He frowned over it for a long time. Finally he looked up, and tried to make light of it. "There is one thing to consider, dear lady. If young Verner is truly gone, you need have nothing more to fear as regards Malvern. He instructs you to remain as mistress of the plantation. . . ."

"But I thought he loved me!" she wailed.

"Ah . . . I see!" He studied her quizzically. "Did he give you cause to think so?"

"Yes. At least I thought so."

"Perhaps the more important question is: Do you have love in your heart for him?"

"Yes. I . . ." Her head went back. "Ah, André, I don't know! I thought that I . . . how can I love a man who runs away and leaves me like this?"

"Hannah, dear Hannah! We don't know that he is fleeing from *you*. There could be many reasons why he has decided to leave Williamsburg."

"He never even said good-bye, not even the morning he left Malvern!"

André waved the letter. He said in a dry voice,

"This, I would think, is his manner of saying good-bye."

"'Tis a poor means of saying it, and cruel as well! I will never forgive him for this!" She snatched the letter from his hand and marched from the room.

Jamie Falkirk came riding up to Malvern late that afternoon. Warned of his approach, Hannah met him outside. She didn't invite him in, just stood outside the door looking up at him. It was a chill day, and Hannah had to hug herself to keep from shivering.

Before she could speak, Jamie said, "Your lover is a coward, madam!"

She didn't flinch at his use of the word "lover," but stared back at him coldy. "What is your meaning, sir?"

"I had challenged Michael Verner to a duel at sunrise this morn. He accepted my challenge before witnesses, but then was too cowardly to appear. In Williamsburg, I learned that he rode out of the village at dusk yesterday afternoon." His smile was taunting. "Michael Verner has revealed his true colors at last. No gentleman refuses to appear when he is challenged. The name of Michael Verner will be despised from this day forward in Williamsburg!"

"For what reason was this duel to be fought?" Hannah asked. Then she knew, knew without asking further. She said it anyway, "It was over me, wasn't it, Jamie? Something you said about me!"

Jamie flushed. "A true lady does not inquire into the affairs of gentlemen, madam." He threw back his head and laughed harshly. Then, without

347

asking her leave, he reined his chestnut about and rode away.

Hannah stood looking after him, shivering now in the cold. But she didn't turn back into the house right away. She felt lorn, betrayed; despair shrouded her. For now she could, finally, accept the fact that Michael had left Virginia. And she knew the reason why.

Michael Verner was not a coward; she knew that in her heart. There could be only one explanation. He had not considered the honor of her good name worth risking his life in a duel for.

Were *all* men vile betrayers of women?

Chapter Eighteen

The children were again demanding a tale about High John the Conqueror.

"Well now," Bess said, and she looked out at the eager dark faces collected around the blazing hearth in her cookhouse. It was late February, and it was a colder February than normal. There were patches of snow on the ground, and a cold wind nosed around corners, whistling through cracks. In here it was snug and warm, fragrant with cooking odors.

Bess looked past the children's faces at Hannah, sitting in the back, her face pinched as if from the cold, huddled within herself, arms wrapped around her knees. Poor child, it seemed there was no end to her trials and heartbreaks. . . .

"Please, Bess!" said the children in unison.

349

"Seems to me I said last time I'd told you'uns all the tales I knows of High John. . . ."

The children groaned.

" 'Course, now, High John didn't allus win against ole massa. Once in a while High John git too high and mighty for his own good, and stub his toe. . . ."

Suddenly Bess remembered the last time she'd told a tale of High John with the new slave, Leon, listening, and the things he had said to her afterward, accusing her of stirring up rebellion and such like. Was that the reason she was thinking of another kind of High John story tonight?

She shoved such thoughts out of her mind and began: "Many days High John had to tote water from the river up to the manor house on that bad plantation where he a slave. Ever' time he had to do that, he'd fuss, 'I'se tired toting water ever' day.' Now one day it happened a turtle was a-squatting on a log when John came down to tote water. When John started fussing, turtle raised up and looked at him, saying, 'High John, you talk too much.'

" 'Course High John didn't want to believe that a turtle was a-talking to him, so he just pretended he didn't hear. But the very next time he went to the river for buckets of water, there was turtle a-squatting on his log. John says, 'I's tired toting water ever' day.' And ole turtle says, 'High John, you talk too much.'

"High John dropped his buckets and scampered up to the manor house and told massa that there was a turtle down at the river talking to him. Massa laughed and laughed, saying John must be teched in the head. But John kept saying the turtle was talking to him. He wanted massa to come see for hisself.

"Massa finally said he'd go. But he tol' John that if that turtle didn't talk, he'd give John a good caning. Together, they went down to the river. Sure nuff, turtle was on his log, his head drawn back into his shell, only little beady eyes peeking out.

"John said to turtle, 'Tell massa what you been telling me.' Turtle, he don't say nothing. John begged and begged that ole turtle to speak. Turtle, he still don't say nothing. So massa taken John back to the barn and hides him good. He tells him he gon' have to tote water *ever'* day now for lying to him.

"The next day John, he goes down to the river with his buckets. Turtle was on his log, head sticking up. John don't pay no 'tention to him, just mutters, 'Guess I must be hearing things. Any fool knows turtles don't talk. Now I got me a bloody back 'cause of it!'

"Ole turtle raises up his head and says, 'High John, didn't I tell you you talk too much?' "

Bess's laughter rumbled, and the children laughed and clapped their hands. Bess got to her feet. "High time you chilluns all on your pallets. Now scat!"

She waited until the children were all gone, and then approached Hannah, who still sat in a huddle. She had merely smiled wanly at the end of Bess's tale.

Miss Hannah was with child.

Hannah had told Bess about it shortly before Christmas. There had been a glow about her as she hugged Bess and kissed her cheek.

351

"It's Michael's child, Bess! It will be a Verner, and it will be a child of love!"

Bess had felt she should add a cautioning note. "Are you sure Master Michael will be coming back, honey? If'n he don't come back and marry you, 'twill be a bastard child. White folks don't look with favor on that."

Hannah had spoken with intensity. "Michael will be back. I know he will! He loves me, I'm sure he does! I'm carrying proof of it inside me!"

Bess had thought of telling her that carrying a man's child didn't always mean that he loved the mother, but she'd kept quiet.

Hannah had hugged her again. "This is going to be a grand Christmas at Malvern, Bess, a happy Christmas! Not like last Christmas, so close on Malcolm's death."

And it had indeed been a happy Christmas. Still retaining that glow, Hannah had been extravagant with gifts to every man, woman, and child on the plantation, and the Christmas feast for all had been something to treasure. Hannah had even thought of giving a Christmas ball; finally Bess and André had talked her out of that idea.

But as the weeks passed and there was still no word from Michael Verner, not even any indication as to his whereabouts, gloom slowly overtook Hannah, and she became despondent.

Once, Bess came upon her weeping softly. "I was wrong, Bess! He doesn't love me. I was only a bit of pleasure for a night! I wish, God help me, that I wasn't carrying his child!"

She began to beat on her belly with her fists, and Bess folded her into her arms, crooning softly. "Hush, child, hush. You liable to hurt yourself, or the child. You'd be sorry, you do that, take old Bess's word. It will be fine—don't fret so."

But it hadn't been fine. Hannah had grown steadily more despondent, and nothing Bess could say or do would cheer her up for long.

Now Bess said gently, "It's time you were abed, honey. Lady in your condition, out on a cold night like this."

Hannah glanced up with a start. "What? Oh, yes . . . an amusing story, Bess." Her smile was unconvincing.

Bess helped her up, and Hannah leaned on her arm all the way along the walkway to the main house and as they went upstairs to her bedroom, where Bess put her to bed.

She's like an old woman, Bess thought gloomily; *she's not yet twenty and she's acting like a woman old before her time.* The feisty spirit had been drained right out of her. Even during those terrible days at the Cup and Horn Hannah had shown more spirit.

Bess hoped something would happen soon to bring back the Hannah she had once known.

Hannah was already asleep by the time Bess had tucked the quilts around her chin. She shook up the fire, adding more fuel. With a sigh, she leaned down to brush her lips across Hannah's brow.

"Sleep well, honey, and may the morrow be better for you."

Bess made her way out of the room, and she was halfway down the stairs when there was a heavy pounding on the front door and a loud voice shouting incoherently. A wide-eyed Jenny darted out of the dining room.

Bess gestured her back. "Never mind, girl. I'll

answer the door. Can't figure who'd be coming to Malvern this late, anyways."

Still grumbling under her breath, she waddled to the door and opened it wide.

Silas Quint stood there, swaying, face red and chapped from the cold. His nose was rose-red, and fumes of rum came from him in waves.

"You!" Bess made a face. "What you want here? Miss Hannah done give orders if'n you come around to have you run off."

"Hannah, that bitch," he mumbled. "Want to see her."

"Don't be calling that child names!" Bess rumbled. "Now you git, afore I rouse John to run you off!"

She slammed the door in his face.

Silas Quint uttered an oath. He stood a moment, still swaying, undecided if he should knock again.

Finally he shambled away. Turned away again, while that sorry wench slept in a fine soft bed, ate the finest of food—and *he* had to scrounge for food and drink, stealing it when he could find no other way to get it.

Time and time again he had returned to Malvern, lurking out of sight, watching and waiting for his chance to confront her, to demand his due. It had become an obsession with him. But nowadays she didn't even ride out every afternoon. She was always indoors, where he couldn't get at her.

Quint staggered down the driveway to an oak he had tied his horse to. So obsessed had he become with coming here again and again that he had bought a horse, promising to pay for it when he got his due. It was a sorry nag, and he suspected that the stable owner in Williamsburg had been only too glad to be rid of the animal, so he wouldn't have to feed it. But it did provide Quint with a means of getting to and from Malvern.

He made a try at mounting the horse, missed, and fell sprawling. He sat up, cursing. He shook his fist at the manor house, almost weeping. "Damn your soul to hell, Hannah McCambridge!"

"McCambridge? Hannah McCambridge?" said a low, harsh voice behind him. A hand gripped his shoulder, strong fingers digging in.

"Wha ... ?" Quint peered around. It was so dark that all he could see was the figure of a man behind him. "Who you be?"

"The mistress of Malvern, she once Hannah McCambridge?" The pressure of the fingers increased.

"Yes, damn her! McCambridge was her mother's name when the damnable woman wed me!" Quint tried to knock the hand away from his shoulder. "Who be ye, and why ye want to know about Hannah?"

The figure gave a start, and the fingers loosened. "I'se sorry, massa. Didn't mean no harm. I just went witless when I heard the name McCambridge."

The man gave Quint a hand up. Swaying, Quint peered closely. "Why, you a nigger! What do ye mean, laying hands on me?"

The Negro almost groveled. "I sorry, massa. You gon' tell the mistress?"

Quint's rum-fuddled mind cleared somewhat. He was still indignant at being handled by a black man, but there was something odd here. Quick to

sniff an advantage, he said in the most command-
ing tone he could muster, "What's your name,
boy?"

"Leon. I be Leon, massa. I'se a slave on this here
plantation."

"Leon, heh? I'm Silas Quint, Leon. Now I want
ye to tell me somethun. . . ." Quint threw an arm
around the slave's shoulders in a companionable
manner. It wasn't true to his nature to come this
close to a black man, but his cunning brain had
fastened onto something here, and he intended to
explore it. Besides, there was no one around to see
him. And there had been many a time he'd lain
with a slave girl in his younger days and taken his
enjoyment of her. He felt Leon cringe away from
his touch. He *was* frightened witless, and not from
just his touch, Quint was sure. He could almost
smell the fear in the slave.

He tightened his grip. "Why did ye say ye were
made witless by the name McCambridge?"

"I be mistaken, must be. Once I knows a man
named McCambridge. Had a girl chile with red
hair. But she couldn't now be mistress here."

"McCambridge ain't a common name. What was
his given name, this McCambridge ye knew?"

"Robert, Robert McCambridge."

A dim memory stirred in Quint's brain. He
groped for it, but it escaped him. "Where'd ye
know this Robert McCambridge?"

"Why, we was together on 'nother plantation."

"He was a slave? A *black* man?"

Leon looked down. "Well, he *part* black, anyways. He was the massa's son and treated special."

Now the memory became clearer. Mary had told
Quint one time that Hannah's father had been a

356

man named Robert McCambridge. Excitement heated Quint's blood and cleared the last of the rum from his brain. "Was this down in North Carolina ye knew him?"

"Yes, massa. That be the truth, I swear!"

"And he sired Hannah?"

"Yassuh. He living with this white woman. He a freed man then. But Mistress Hannah must not be the same ..."

"Ye let *me* be the judge of that," Quint said sharply.

By the Lord above, he saw the way clear to get his proper due now! Had nigger blood, did she? Oh, what great news! With that knowledge as a club, he would get her to pay and pay!

With a crowing sound, Quint did a little jig on the frozen ground. He almost broke into a run toward the manor house. Then a wind of caution dampened his excitement a little. He had to know more, know everything there was to know, before he faced her with it. That way, she couldn't give the lie to him.

He remembered the slave and looked at him. He also remembered the smell of fear, and another thing Mary had told him came back. Her former husband had been killed by a runaway slave, and this slave, this Leon, had to be that runaway slave! That must be the cause of his fear.

Craftily, Quint calculated how he could also use this to his advantage. Again, he realized that this wasn't the time. It was another club he could use, but only at the proper time.

"Leon ..." He lowered his voice to a confidential tone. "How'd ye like a way to get enough money to get away from here, enough to run far away where ye could stop being a slave? Ye'd like that, heh?"

"I happy here, massa," Leon said worriedly. "This a good plantation. I got no wish to run away, massa."

"But you've run away before? 'Course ye have. But with plenty of money in your pockets, ye could run so far they'd never catch ye again."

"What Leon have to do to get this money?" the slave asked warily.

Knowing that he had him now, Quint chuckled, and clapped the man on the shoulder. "Ye let old Quint worry about that. We'll be talking again soon, make our plans. I need to know more. We meet one week from today, around the same time, but farther out toward the main road, in that grove of trees. Don't want some'un snooping around, hearing us. Heh, Leon?"

Leon nodded silently.

Quint turned away, this time mounting the nag without too much trouble. He was sober as he rode away, the horse clip-clopping along at a snail's pace.

He knew he had to think the whole thing out carefully, take his time. He had to know it all, and he had to figure out how to lay it out to the wench, so she'd know he had her in a bear trap.

So Hannah Verner, the fine lady of Malvern, had black blood in her veins, did she? Quint laughed aloud and dug his heels into the horse's flanks, cursing at the animal, all to little effect.

With the begining of March, the cold weather broke, and an early spring came to Malvern. It grew so warm that some of trees even began to bud.

And with the arrival of spring, Hannah's spirits revived somewhat. She had reconciled herself to the fact that Michael might be gone for good. And the longer he was gone, the more time that passed without word from him, the more she hardened her heart against him. She had been wrong about his loving her; she had been nothing more to him than a comely wench to bed—and he had had the opportunity to humiliate her in the bargain. It was a fact she had to face.

She turned her thoughts more and more to the life growing in her belly, and began to take joy from it again. If she could not have Michael to love, she would at least have a child she could clasp to her bosom.

On a warm, sunny day, she decided to go riding. She hadn't ridden since before Christmas.

Bess put her foot down. "You must be addled, honey! Thinking of riding a horse in your condition! If you ain't worrying about yo'self, worry about the baby you're carrying."

"Oh, Bess!" Hannah laughed. "I'm not that far along yet. The baby would receive no harm from my riding a horse, for heaven's sake!"

"And what if you be throwed? You think I don' know how fast you ride? That animal could be spooked by a snake and throw you ass-end over tea-kettle. Over my dead body, you be getting on any old horse!"

In the end Hannah desisted. As an alternative, she started the house servants on a flurry of house cleaning, supervising every moment, keeping herself busy, and in the process driving the girls out of their wits.

Consequently she was wearing an old house dress, with her hair bound up in a dustrag and smudges of dirt on her face, when one afternoon there was a loud knock on the door. Since she happened to be in the entryway at the time, she answered the door herself.

When the door opened, Silas Quint stood there grinning at her. For a moment Hannah wasn't sure she recognized him. His clothes were cleaner than she had ever seen them. Even his face was without stubble, and for the first time since she could remember he didn't stink of drink.

Then he spoke, and there was no longer any doubt in her mind. "A good day to ye, *Mistress* Verner."

"What are you doing here? Didn't I tell you to never . . ." She started to swing the door shut.

He stepped forward, and with his shoulder knocked the door out of her hand, slamming it back against the wall. "I'll be having a word with ye, your ladyship."

"If you don't leave at once, I'll call someone. . . ."

Quint was no longer listening. His gaze had fastened onto her belly, onto the rounding swell there, and he chortled aloud. She was with child! And it had to be young Verner's brat, no other. Now Quint knew he had her, had her for sure! He broke into her tirade. "You'll stop the blathering, wench, and lend an ear to what I have to say. If'n ye know what's good for ye, ye will. My word on it!"

Something in his voice stopped Hannah. And

there was an air of arrogant confidence about Silas Quint she had never seen before or ever expected to see. A quiver of fear passed over her like a chill. Crossing her arms over her breasts, she said, "Then say what you have to say and have done with it!"

"Here? With m'lady's serving girls listening?" Quint grinned mockingly. "It matters not to me, but methinks ye will be sorry. What I have to say is for your ears alone."

Hannah hesitated, again tempted to have him thrown off Malvern, but this new Silas Quint made her uneasy, and from his knowing grin, Hannah knew that she had hesitated overlong.

She tossed her head. "All right, Silas Quint, I'll talk with you. But it had better be something of substance. Come along."

Quint trailed in her wake as she went down the hall. He took his time, his greedy gaze taking in everything he saw. Some of the pieces of furniture in sight would keep him in food and drink for weeks! *Oh, Hannah, me fine lady, are ye going to pay for all the harsh words ye have spoken to your poor old stepfather!*

"Quint!"

He came to with a start. She was standing in the doorway to a room off the hall.

"Are you coming in, or would you rather stand out there and gawk?"

"Coming, Mistress Verner, coming!"

Quint hastened inside, and Hannah immediately slammed the door and whirled to face him. "Now, shall we get to the point? What is it you have to say to me?"

"The point, me dear stepdaughter, is that man who sired ye . . ."

361

Hannah stiffened. "My father? What do *you* know of my father?"

"I know that he had black blood! And ye know what that makes ye?" He sneered. "That makes ye part nigger!"

Hannah recoiled, stunned. "You're lying, Silas Quint! As always, you're lying! You've never told the truth in your life!"

"'Tis the truth I'm telling. I have the proof."

She made her voice scornful. "What proof could you possibly offer?"

"There's a man here, right here on this plantation, who knew the man who sired ye, knew Robert McCambridge."

"What man is that?"

"Oh, no, ye don't," Quint said slyly. "You won't catch me speaking his name. But there is such a man, me word on it!"

Hannah was silent, thinking hard. She knew Silas Quint well, and she was convinced, somehow, that he was telling the truth for once. Then her head went back. "What does it matter if you *are* telling the truth?"

Quint grinned. "The fine neighbors ye have, wouldn't black blood in your veins be a juicy bone for them to gnaw on, now?"

"I care nothing for the good opinion of my neighbors. They think little enough of me now. Why should their knowing of my parentage bother me?"

Quint was taken aback. He had hardly expected this reaction from her. For just a moment his confidence was shaken. Then he remembered. "That brat in your belly . . ." He gestured. "'Twouldn't be Michael Verner's, now, would it? What do ye think he'd be feeling, should he learn a child of his siring is part nigger?"

This hadn't occurred to Hannah, and it shook her to the core. If Michael returned and learned . . .

She was thinking back now, trying to probe the mists of memory. She dimly remembered her father—tall, broad of shoulder, with powerful hands; a gentle man, yet he had also been very dark in color. And if he had been partly black, perhaps a runaway slave, it could explain why her mother had always been evasive, quite vague, whenever Hannah had questioned her about Robert McCambridge.

Quint, knowing he had the upper hand again, said gloatingly, "Well, your ladyship?"

"Well what?" Hannah asked, still trying to absorb the shock. "I demand to see and talk to this man you speak of. If he is telling the truth, and has told you of this, will he not tell others?"

"Ye leave that to old Quint. He'll keep his clapper quiet, ye can be sure. And I'll not be telling ye who he is, so stop blathering about it!"

"You didn't come here just to tell me this. What do you want?"

"I need some money for food and drink. I am in poor straits." His voice took on the familiar whine. "I'll not be asking overmuch to keep your secret safe, just enough to get along. Ye owe that much to your old stepfather, anyways."

Hannah knew his greedy nature; he would demand all he could get. Yet she needed time to think it out. It was probably a mistake to give him money at all, but at least it would serve to rid herself of him for now. "I don't have much money at hand. I never keep much here at Malvern, fearing thievery," she lied as convincingly as she could. "I'll give you what I have—twenty pounds."

Quint smirked. "That'll do me fine . . . for now."

Hannah turned away to Malcolm's desk. She stationed herself so as to partially block off Quint's view of the desk. But she had to pull out the bottom drawer and unlock the strongbox, so he was sure to catch at least a glimpse of it. She took the money from the strongbox and gave it to him.

Quint's small eyes lit up at the sight of the notes, and he actually licked his lips. He took the money and rubbed it between his fingers, as if assuring himself that it was real. He put it into his pocket and bobbed his head. "I thankee, Mistress Verner," he said, grinning. " 'Tis good ye are to old Quint. I'll take me leave now. But I'll be looking forward with pleasure to when next we meet."

"I'm sure you will," Hannah said dully.

She watched him leave, then shut the door after him. She dropped down into Malcolm's old chair and tried to assess what all this meant to her. But instead of thinking of the more immediate problem—what to do about Silas Quint—she found her thoughts returning to that cabin where they had lived before her mother had packed them up hurriedly and fled in the cart. There was some memory that nagged at her, something tinged with horror, that she realized now she had blocked out of her mind since that fateful day.

Perhaps if she thought long and hard, it would come back to her.

Chapter Nineteen

Isaiah, known as Leon, was a very worried man. Already regretting what he had told Silas Quint, he had watched the man ride up to the manor house, and had lurked out of sight, observing, until Quint had ridden away.

He had been a fool to tell the white man as much as he had. But he had been so shaken to learn that the mistress of Malvern might be the daughter of the Robert McCambridge he had killed on that long-ago day that he had spoken without thinking.

They had met twice more the past three weeks, and Quint had promised him much money. Isaiah was sorely tempted to play the game out. He had never had more than a few coins at a time in his life, and most of those had been stolen. Yet Isaiah knew that he couldn't trust the man. He recognized Quint for what he was—white trash and a sot.

They had a rendezvous for tomorrow night, when Quint was supposed to give him his share of the money he had gotten from her today, and they were to plan further what to do.

All of Isaiah's instincts for self-preservation cried out for him to flee *now*. He had no heart to conspire with Silas Quint, he realized that now. He suspected that the man intended to stick a dagger into his back once he had all the information he wanted. Isaiah was sure he would share little of the money with him. Maybe some in the beginning—small nibbles to lure a big old fish into swallowing the hook.

However, Isaiah was weary unto death of running, and without money he would never get far.

And then, watching the manor house from his place of concealment, a daring idea was born in his mind. It was not only daring, it was foolhardy. But if it worked, he might be made a freed man. It all depended on how much a small girl could remember. Still, he had nothing to lose but his life, and the life he had lived as a slave since childhood had been hardly any life at all.

Somewhat amazed at his own daring, Isaiah took a deep breath and left his hiding place to go to the main house. He had never been inside; field hands were rarely allowed inside a manor house.

He marched boldly to the front door and went in. Once inside, he almost lost his courage. How could he find her? He well knew that if he asked any of the house servants they would not only refuse to take him to the mistress, they would probably call the overseer at once.

The house was strangely quiet. There was no one within sight or hearing. Emboldened, Isaiah strode down the hall. He had been told there was an "office" where the mistress spent much of her time. Like all slaves on a new plantation, he had been curious about the inside of the manor house; on occasion he had peered in the windows, and had once seen Mistress Verner enter a small room just off the hall.

He rapped lightly on the door, holding his breath.

A voice said, "Come in."

He opened the door and went in. The mistress of the house was sitting in the room in dimness, curtains drawn across the one window, with a candle burning. She squinted at him. "Who are you? Oh ... Leon."

"No, Mistress Verner. My birth name be Isaiah."

"Isaiah?" She looked puzzled, rubbing at her eyes. She got up and looked closely at him. "Oh, yes, I remember Malcolm telling me. You're the runaway. You changed your name, I suppose. Isaiah? That strikes a familiar chord...." She rubbed her eyes again. "Whatever it is, can it not wait, Isaiah? I'm rather ... distraught." She passed a trembling hand over her eyes.

"I knows, Mistress Verner. It because of what the white man Quint tell you jest now."

Her gaze sharpened. "What would you know about that? You ... you're the man he was talking about!"

Isaiah nodded. "Yes, mistress. I knew Robert McCambridge."

Hannah sucked in her breath. "Then he *was* of your . . . race?"

"Less'n half, mistress. Your father more than half white." He began to speak swiftly now. "But I be the only one know for sure. All I asks is you make me a freed man and I go. Then the white man, that Quint, won't have no one to back his word. You gives the lie to him, nobody believe what he says. I beg you, mistress, you gives me my freedom and I go. . . ."

Suddenly a door opened in Hannah's mind, and horror flooded in. She saw a shimmering vision of her father's body, covered with blood, lying dead on the floor of the cabin, and she remembered puzzling over why their guest, a man named Isaiah, was no longer there.

With sudden knowledge, she screamed, "You! You killed my father!"

She ran to him, all else gone from her mind. Snatching up a candle holder, she began to beat at him with it. Isaiah backed away, hands up before his face.

"Please, mistress . . . an accident . . . was not meant . . ."

Hannah was beyond listening. She flew at him again, screaming.

Isaiah had backed into the hall now. He was vaguely aware of people running toward them. He dared not fight back. All his years of slavery had taught him that it meant a hanging for a slave to so much as touch a plantation white woman. Terror ruled him, and he took to his heels, Hannah right behind him, still screaming, flailing at him with the candle holder. Isaiah fumbled with the front door, got it open, and ran outside.

André and Bess caught Hannah just outside the door and held her. She struggled and fought them. She screamed after the fleeing Isaiah, "I'll kill you, I'll kill you!"

André said, "Dear Hannah, calm yourself! What in heaven's name did the man do to you? *Mon Dieu!*"

And Bess said, "Child, remember your condition. You behave yo'self, now!"

Gradually Hannah gained a measure of calm. It was only then that she noticed a horse tethered to the hitching post, and a man standing at the bottom of the steps, agape at the ruckus.

Hannah was sobbing now, incapable of speech. Dimly she saw the man approach her, clearing his throat. "You are Hannah Verner?"

"Yes, she's Hannah Verner," André said irritably. "What is it, man? Can you not see . . . ?"

"A letter, I have a letter for Hannah Verner."

"Here, give it to me." André took the letter, gave the man a coin, and said, "Now be off with you."

Bess was leading the sobbing Hannah inside.

"Hannah, wait!" André said excitedly. "Here— here is something I wager you have been waiting for."

She tried to focus on him. "What is it?"

" 'Tis a letter from Michael!"

Michael! Michael had written her a letter!

She snatched the letter out of André's hand, ran into the study, and tore it open with trembling fingers.

8 February, 1719: My Dearest Hannah: I hope you will grant me the privilege of calling

369

you dearest. Since I took my leave of Williamsburg, you have been constantly in my thoughts —and my heart. I now know that it is to my sorrow that I left you. Mayhap you have hardened your heart against me for the manner of my leave-taking. At the time I believed it best. I now know that I was sorely mistaken.

These months past that I have spent in New Orleans, I have come to know my own heart. I love you. I have loved no other woman, and will never love another. I am filled with anguish at the thought that I might never see you again, or at the thought that you may not *wish* to see me ever again.

I will not bore you, dearest Hannah, with details of my life here. Suffice it to say that it holds no fascination for me. I yearn to return to Malvern, and to you. But I will return only if it is your desire, if you can search your heart and find it in you to return my love.

This missive was sent aboard a merchant vessel sailing around the tip of Florida and up the Carolina coast. I dared not risk sending it overland. I know it will require a lengthy time for it to reach your hands, and for your reply to reach me in turn.

I am asking you to be my love, dearest, begging you to be my wife. I will await your reply in an agony of impatience, praying daily that it is the reply I hope with all my heart it will be.

Hannah's heart was beating wildly, and she was crying, crying from happiness, all her harbored resentment toward Michael melted away by these few words on paper.

She got up and started toward the desk, already composing in her mind the answer she would send to Michael this very day!

Then she stopped short, remembering. She clutched at her belly. Dear God—if he came back and learned that she had a strain of black blood, that his *son* would have black blood! How would he react? Her mind leaped to the only conclusion possible. He would turn away from her in revulsion. No matter how much he might love her, his reaction would be that of any other member of the southern gentry.

She had to do something before it was too late!

Hannah ran to the door and flung it open. Jenny lurked just outside. At the sight of Hannah her face got a look of fright, and she turned to hurry away.

"Jenny! Don't be silly, I'm not going to hurt you. Go find Henry and tell him to come to me at once!"

Hannah left the door open and paced, waiting for the overseer's arrival, her thoughts racing, discarding one plan after another. She had two people to deal with. First, she had to deal with Isaiah, as repugnant as it might be. Then she could turn her thoughts to Silas Quint.

Henry came in before she realized it. "Yes, mistress?"

"Find the slave, Leon, and bring him to see me at once. Hurry, Henry! He may be planning to run away. Reassure him that I do not wish to do him harm."

After Henry left, Hannah continued to pace,

371

waiting impatiently, but taking time to read Michael's letter twice more.

She gave a sigh of relief when Henry finally appeared with an obviously frightened Isaiah. She nodded to Henry. "Leave us, Henry."

Henry gave her a dubious glance, then looked doubtfully at Isaiah. Hannah gestured, and Henry went out, closing the door.

"Isaiah . . ." She drew a deep breath. "I'm sorry about before. I . . . well, never mind. You say you . . . killed my father by accident?"

Isaiah hesitated before answering. He *had* been intending to run away, but he knew his chances would be much better after nightfall. Now he took some hope from this white woman's question. Clearly she didn't know the whole truth; her mother must never have told her that Robert McCambridge had caught him about to mount his woman.

He said, "Yes, Mistress Verner. I was a runaway slave and as you knows, Robert McCambridge harbored me. I be learning that hunters and dogs was after me, not far distant. I taken a carving knife from the kitchen and was gon' run. Robert McCambridge tried to stop me. Addled with fright, I struggled with him. He fell on the knife and was killed. I sore saddened over that, and be so ever since."

Hannah stared at him hard, trying to read truth in his words. She remembered her own fright on the night she ran away from Stritch, remembering that she had resolved to die before being taken back, and she believed him. At least, she told herself she did.

She nodded, turning away. "All right. Even if

you are lying, it's past and done. But I want you off the plantation!" She wheeled on him. "Do you understand?"

"I understands, mistress. But I needs money, and to be a freed man. If I'm not a freed man with papers, I be hunted down and . . ."

"Yes, yes." Hannah cut him off with a gesture. "We'll get to that. First, tell me everything you told Silas Quint, every word." She motioned him to sit at the desk, and she took Malcolm's chair. She listened intently as Isaiah talked haltingly, groping for the right words with which to relate his conversations with Quint.

At the end Hannah was silent for a little, gnawing her lip in thought. When she finally spoke, it was as though to herself. "Then it will only be Quint's word, and his word is nothing. Without you to back him up . . ." She broke off, looking directly at Isaiah. "I will give you money, enough to take you far. And in the morning I will go into Williamsburg and have legal papers drawn up, so no one will question them, making you a freed man. You will no longer be a slave. Stay in your quarters until I return from the village. I will come for you after dark. Be prepared to leave Malvern. Traveling at night, you will be far enough away by daylight to be out of danger."

Isaiah, scarcely able to believe his good fortune, said, "I thanks you, Mistress Verner."

Hannah was already starting for the door. She opened it, staring at him. She said sternly, "Listen to me now. If you do not live up to our agreement, if you do not leave Virginia, you will sorely regret it! Is that understood?"

Isaiah bobbed his head, his glance sliding past her.

She looked around and saw that Henry had lingered by the door. His face wore a look of astonishment, his mouth open. Apparently he had overheard her remark. "I will explain it all later, Henry. I am too weary now."

Henry made a sound of protest. Hannah motioned him silent. "See that Isaiah ... see that Leon returns to his quarters, and he is to be excused from field work tomorrow. As I said, I will explain later."

A baffled Henry led Isaiah away, shaking his head.

Hannah was indeed weary. Somehow, now, even the fact of Michael's letter did little to lift her spirits. Her belly felt heavy, and there seemed to be a huge weight on her shoulders. Her eyes were gritty, her skin felt feverish, and her throat was raw from screaming.

She looked about. There was no one within her sight. The house servants, even Bess and André, had deserted her. Hannah opened her mouth to scream for someone.

Then she stopped, laughing weakly at herself. No wonder they were avoiding her. Not long before she had been acting like a madwoman. If she screamed again, they would all probably flee into the woods.

She managed to drag herself up the stairs to her room, partially undress, and fall across the bed. Soon she sank into a troubled slumber.

Her dreams were jumbled, nightmares compounded of flashing knives and spouting blood, black horses rearing, and always Michael's sneering face in the background, his lips forming the same words over and over: "Black bastard! Black bastard!"

A time or two she half awoke to the sound of soothing voices and the welcome touch of cool, wet cloths sponging her feverish flesh.

When Hannah finally came fully awake, the room was flooded with sunlight. She moaned, struggling to sit up.

Bess loomed over her. "Lay back, honey. Don't try to get up. You been one sick child, Miss Hannah. The fever was in you all the night long. You screamed and tossed and spoke mad things. You sweated like a horse."

"What's wrong with me?"

"You overdid yo'self, honey. All that screaming and carrying on yesterday, then the letter from Michael. It all be too much."

"But I have to get up, I have to take the coach into Williamsburg! It's very important!"

Again she struggled to sit up, and Bess pushed her gently back down. It took very little effort, and Hannah finally realized how weak she was.

In a panic Hannah felt her belly. "The baby . . . is he all right?"

Bess gave her a weary smile. "Far's I can tell, he be fine. He won't be, you go running about. Now, the fever done broken, so you'll be fit again after some rest. Here . . ." She turned to a covered bowl on the table beside the bed. "Jenny brought hot broth in a bit ago. It good for you."

Hannah lay back with a sigh while Bess spooned broth into her. Hannah's thoughts moved very slowly. She had promised to have the papers freeing Isaiah made out today. Yet the baby's welfare was more important. What difference would one more day matter?

Hannah knew that she could simply pen a letter granting Isaiah his freedom. That was the manner in which it was most often done. But that wasn't good enough for her purposes. She'd heard of slaves being caught carrying letters from former masters granting their freedom. Sometimes, the person who caught such a slave just destroyed the letter and made him a slave again. But if she had a letter drawn up by a lawyer, properly legal and witnessed, no one would dare question it. She was fearful that if Isaiah was enslaved again, he might try to regain his freedom by telling what he knew of Hannah Verner. . . .

Bess broke into her thoughts. "Child, what troubling you? You look so distraught. It have to do with what went on between you and that Leon yesterday?"

"It's not your affair, Bess!" Hannah spoke without thinking. "Oftentimes you go too far, forgetting who you are!"

Bess drew back, a hurt look on her face. She started to turn away.

"Bess . . ." Hannah caught the woman's hand. "Forgive me. I didn't mean to speak so harshly. You know I wouldn't hurt you for the world! But it's something to do with me alone. It's something I cannot talk about!"

Gazing down at her, Bess's broad face softened. "All right, honey. I reckon you know what's best for you. But that Leon," she added darkly. "I know he be nothing but trouble the minute I laid eyes on him. He a troublemaker, that I purely knows in my bones!" Then she sighed. "I bone tired, honey, setting up with you most the night. Old Bess ain't so young anymore. I think I go lay down for a spell. You needs anything, ring the bell. Jenny'll come running."

"Bess ..." Hannah didn't let go of her hand. "I don't know what I would have done all this time without you. I love you."

"And I loves you, too, honey. You like my own child. You knows that." Bess's eyes filled with tears, and she leaned down to kiss Hannah on the forehead.

Straightening up, she tried to laugh. "Look at me, leaking all over you like a . . ."

She swiped a hand over her eyes and quickly left the room.

Hannah smiled fondly after her for a little. She was still very tired, and weak. She found herself drifting off to sleep, and she dozed off and on all afternoon. Jenny came and went quietly. Finally she brought a tray in with Hannah's supper on it. Hannah was feeling considerably better, much stronger, and she ate with a good appetite.

But she was worried about Isaiah. He probably knew she hadn't gone into Williamsburg. He probably thought she had lied to him. Thinking that, would he run away tonight? She couldn't send anyone for him. Having a field slave brought into her bedroom and left alone with her would raise too many questions. She dared not trust anyone with her secret, not even Bess or André. Yet she was filled with a sense of foreboding. She needed to talk to Isaiah, to quiet his fears.

She tinkled the bell. When Jenny came in, she said, "You may take the tray now, Jenny. And I know you've had a hard day, so you take yourself off to bed. I'll be all right. I'm feeling much better now. I'm going to sleep the night away, and I won't need you again."

Hannah waited another hour, until all sounds of activity belowstairs had ceased. Then she got up and quickly dressed. Throwing a shawl around her shoulders, she left the bedroom. She made it downstairs and out the door without being seen by anyone.

Outside, a melon-slice moon threw a faint glow over the plantation.

Orienting herself, Hannah struck out for the slave quarters.

It was true that Isaiah had watched all day for the coach to leave for Williamsburg. When it hadn't left by noon, he had been convinced that the mistress had lied to him and had some other plan in mind. He thought of fleeing, even if it was broad daylight, but every time he left the cabin he shared with the other field slaves, he saw Henry watching from nearby, eyeing him balefully.

Finally, he strolled boldly toward the manor house. He saw Henry still watching him, but Isaiah figured that so long as he made no move toward the road or the forest, he wouldn't be bothered. He was right. Henry stood watching, glowering, hands on hips, but he made no move toward him.

As Isaiah neared the cookhouse, he saw the old woman, Bess, waddling along the walkway. He hurried to intercept her.

"Mistress Verner ... is somethun amiss? I ain't seen her 'bout all day."

Bess stopped, glaring at him. "What right you got to ask about the mistress, you Leon?"

Isaiah felt anger rise in him. He almost strangled on it. He could gladly choke this old woman for her sass. Just because she was a house nigger, she thought that gave her the right to lord it over a lowly field slave. But he swallowed his ire and said evenly, "I thought she might be ailing."

"Whether she be ailing or not is none of your concern!" Bess snapped. "Now go on about your business and stop bothering me. I be too busy."

Bess swept on, and Isaiah swung around to stare at her broad back until she went into the cookhouse. Then he returned to the slave quarters, where he squatted down, his back against the wall, and idled the rest of the afternoon away. The coach did not leave the plantation.

He thought ahead to the rendezvous with Silas Quint. He was of two minds about it. He knew he was leaving this night, after all were asleep. But he needed money, and Quint had promised him his share tonight. He saw no choice but to meet with the man.

Since it had been a work day, the field slaves were asleep early. Isaiah waited until all was quiet, then crept out of the slave quarters, making his way toward the grove of trees near the main road where he was to meet Quint.

Quint was there, pacing impatiently. "Ye be late, Leon! I thought ye weren't coming!"

"I'se had to wait until all were asleep before sneaking out."

"Well, long's as ye are here." Quint expelled his breath. There was only a faint odor of rum about him tonight; he was near to being sober. He jingled some coins in his hand. "Here be the share I promised ye. 'Tain't much. The wench said 'twas all she had to hand. But we'll get more, me word on it."

He gave the coins to Isaiah, who put them into his pocket without bothering to count them.

"Now, to more pressing matters," Quint said briskly. He took several sheets of paper from his pocket. "I've writ down all ye told me about yon fine lady, Hannah Verner. Having little schooling, I ain't much for writing, but 'twill do." Quint chuckled. "'Course I know ye can't sign your name, but I writ it down. Leon. All ye have to do is make your mark alongside . . ."

"No!" Isaiah began backing away. "I'll not be making my mark on such. . . ."

"Here now!" Quint seized Isaiah by the arm. "Likely nobody'll ever lay eyes on it but me. But I have to have somethun to back up me word, should somethun happen to ye. Surely ye can see that!"

"No, I put my mark on nothing!" Isaiah said firmly.

"Ye will do as I say, hear me good! I'll swallow no back talk from a black buck!" In the moonlight Isaiah could see his sneer. "Ye think I believe ye told me the whole truth? Old Quint ain't a fool. I know ye murdered Robert McCambridge. Me spouse told me about a runaway slave killing her husband. What do ye think will happen should I let word out about that? They'll hang ye, boy, me word on *that*! So put your mark to this document and no more sass!"

Terror drove Isaiah past any fear of harming a white man. His huge hands reached out to wrap around Quint's scrawny throat, and he began to squeeze. Quint kicked and fought, but to no avail.

Isaiah applied more pressure, and suddenly Quint went limp in his grasp. Taken by surprise, Isaiah slackened his grip a trifle. Then he felt something ice-cold slice into his belly. In a moment's time it turned from cold to burning hot, and pain blazed through him. He grunted, and started to slump.

Falling, Isaiah's thoughts flashed back to those moments in the cabin in North Carolina when Robert McCambridge had died from the knife in his hand. And then all thought ceased.

Silas Quint stood over the inert body of the slave, fighting for breath. His head came up, and he sniffed like an animal for danger. There was no sound, no outcry, and he breathed more easily. The slave wasn't dead yet, but he soon would be, his belly slit open, blood pouring from him, his intestines spilling out like giant worms.

Quint's first thought was pride in himself for having the courage to do this thing. He had never lifted a finger to another person in his life, always slinking away from any hint of danger to himself. The thing with Mary had been different, an accident, and she'd been a woman besides. But knowing that Leon had once before killed, Quint had armed himself with the dagger for this meeting. He hadn't really been frightened; a slave wouldn't dare attack a white man. Still, he had come prepared, and now he congratulated himself on his foresight.

Next, his thoughts jumped to what it would mean to him personally. There was no peril of his being suspected. No one knew of his meetings with

Leon. Plantation slaves were always fighting amongst themselves, so it would be laid to the work of another slave.

And Leon's death changed nothing regarding Hannah. She had no knowledge of who on the plantation had supplied Quint with his information, so he was still in the saddle there. The letter with Leon's mark on it would have been confirmation if needed, but Quint was convinced that her ladyship, Mistress Hannah Verner, was too cowed to demand further proof.

Now what he had to do was get away from here. He stooped down for a handful of dry leaves and wiped the dagger clean of blood. He started to turn away toward his horse tethered to a tree, then hesitated, remembering the coins in Leon's pocket. Enough to buy a bottle or two of rum ...

No, better not risk it. The longer he lingered, the greater peril of his being discovered.

He mounted the old nag and drummed his heels into the beast's starved flanks, trying to get a little more speed out of it.

Quint chortled. Soon, now, he would be able to buy a fine horse, mayhap even a coach of his very own, with a slave to drive it. Her ladyship had plenty of slaves; she could spare at least one for her poor old stepfather.

Hannah, on her way to the slave quarters, was having second thoughts about what she had in mind. She really couldn't just barge alone into a building housing a large number of sleeping males and demand to see one of them for a private word. Her step slowed, and she finally stopped altogether, undecided. She glanced toward Henry's cabin; he lived in private quarters with his wife and three children. His cabin was dark. Should she rouse him, ask him to fetch Isaiah to her? But how could she do that without taking Henry into her confidence? He was already puzzled enough by her attitude toward the slave he knew as Leon.

She sighed and turned back toward the house. Then she heard the thud of a horse's hooves up by the main road, moving away. After a moment's thought, wondering who could be riding away from Malvern at this time of night, she started up the drive toward the main road. She heard the hoofbeats for a while longer, but the sound had faded away into the night by the time she came up opposite the small grove of trees near the road.

A sound came from the trees. Hannah stopped, listening. A prowling night animal? The sound came again—a moaning sound.

She took a deep breath and moved in that direction, stepping into the shadows of the trees. The spaces in between were illuminated by moonlight. She stopped for a moment, but could hear nothing more, and moved on. Then, in a splash of moonlight, she saw something lying on the ground. It looked like a body.

Hannah hurried forward. It *was* a body, a man! She dropped to one knee beside him before she saw the blood on his belly, and the coiling spill of intestines. She cried out. It was Isaiah—and he was dead! He must have been alive a moment ago, but all life had drained from him now.

She lurched to her feet and stumbled away to lean against the nearest tree trunk. Her belly heaved, and she vomited. After a long while her mind began to function again.

Her first impulse was to run for help. She even took two steps away, but then halted as her mind cleared.

Who had killed Isaiah? She suspected it had been Silas Quint. Yet how could she prove that? She had only Isaiah's word that he had been meeting with Quint, and now he was dead.

And stark and clear came the memory of the threats she had voiced against Isaiah. Twice, and each time before witnesses. The first time she had been hysterical and threatening to kill him. Those on the plantation, at least Bess and André, she could trust to keep quiet. But the man who had delivered Michael's letter, a stranger, he had overheard as well, and undoubtedly would be most eager to talk if the need arose. And then, coming out of the study later, she had again threatened Isaiah, and Henry had inadvertently overheard. Damn! Under the present circumstances, she could easily be charged with murder. After the events of the previous afternoon, she couldn't very well claim that he had tried to rape her and she had killed him for that. Had she been able to do this, her word would never have been questioned. But now—and then there was the matter of Silas Quint ...

Undoubtedly Quint had all the story by now, including the knowledge that Isaiah had killed her father, and that would serve to give her a motive— if Quint told the story. But, of course, she didn't *want* him to tell the story.

Silas Quint. He would come around now, time and again, and she would have no recourse but to give him money—give and give until she was sucked dry. And if Michael returned and she married him, how could she explain where the money was going? Should she refuse Quint, the man would eventually go to Michael with his story, and it would be all over.

Hannah knew then what she had to do. She had probably known it was the only solution the moment Quint had revealed what he knew, but she hadn't wanted to face up to it. She had long ago resolved to protect herself at all costs. And now she also had the baby to consider.

Her mind firmly made up, Hannah returned to the manor house. She roused Bess, André, and Dickie, and told Dickie to fetch John.

Half an hour later, they were all gathered in the dining room. Hannah told Bess to prepare tea laced with brandy. She smiled tightly. "You will all need it."

She waited until everyone was served, took a sip of her steaming, pungent tea, and said, "I will be leaving Malvern for good at first light."

André reared back in astonishment. "*Mon Dieu!* Dear lady, what is this about?"

"Honey, you can't do that," Bess said worriedly. "Not in yo' condition!"

"I'll manage, Bess. I must."

John sat impassively, saying nothing. Dickie, who had been half asleep, leaned forward, face lighting up.

"It will be useless to question me," Hannah continued. "I cannot reveal my reasons, at least not at the present time, but believe me, please. . . . It is imperative that I leave Malvern at once, much as it grieves me. Now, I want to know who wishes to leave with me. If any one of you do not wish to do so, I won't order you, and I promise not to harbor any ill feelings. And Bess, Dickie, and you, John, I promise to grant your freedom if you choose to remain behind."

"What is your destination, dear lady?"

"I don't know as yet, André," she said simply. "Will *you* go with me?"

Andre shrugged, spreading his hands. *"Naturellement.* So long as I am forced to abide in this wretched country, it matters little to me where." His smile was turned inward. "And I confess that I have become attached to you, dear Hannah. *Oui,* I will accompany you."

"Bess?"

"Honey, honey, you are a worriment to an old woman. And I be an old woman." Bess sighed heavily, and then said in a grumbling voice, "But of course I goes where you goes. Somebody have to tend you in your condition, and birth the child when it's time."

"Thank you, Bess. Dickie?"

"If you want me with you, m'lady, I will go where you go."

Although he spoke with a sober countenance, Hannah could feel him straining to go. He was already looking upon it as a new adventure. She smiled at him fondly, resisting an impulse to ruffle his hair. He was too old for such a gesture of affection now.

"John ..." She faced him squarely. "I dislike asking you most of all, for I know Malvern has been your home these many years. But I am taking the coach, and I do need you."

John said gravely, "I will go with you, Mistress Hannah."

Hannah felt a knot of tension dissolve inside

her, and tears misted her eyes. "Thank you all. I don't deserve . . ." She cleared her throat. "We have much to do before daybreak. Each of you pack only those things you will need. We shall be laden enough as it is."

Bess lingered behind as the others trooped out. She came close to say in a low voice, "I think I know what this about. Some of it, anyways."

"Perhaps you do, Bess." Hannah reached out to squeeze her hand. "But I don't wish to . . . I *cannot* discuss it now! Later, I will tell you everything. You have my promise."

She got up and hurried from the dining room, carrying a candle down the hall to the study.

She got a sheet of paper, dipped the quill into the inkpot, and began to write:

Sir: It is best that you return to Virginia post-haste. I am leaving Malvern this day. But do not worry. Henry will continue to oversee the plantation, so you will know that Malvern is in good hands.

There is no need for me to give you reasons for my leave-taking, sir. You will learn quickly enough on your return. I . . .

Hannah hesitated, face bent over the paper. She was crying, and a single tear dropped unnoticed onto the paper.

She continued writing, quickly now:

I take only a small amount of money and the jewels dear Malcolm gave me on my wedding day. The small sum of money I am taking I consider, as you once remarked to me, my compensation for overseeing the plantation during your absence. Only these things, and the coach, am I taking. The remainder of money in the strongbox I leave intact.

The forgiveness you beg in your letter . . . I grant that, sir, if indeed there is anything to forgive. I know not where I travel, and I would not inform you, in any case.

Hannah signed her name, sealed the letter with wax, and scrawled Michael's name and "New Orleans" on the outside.

She got up, brushing away the residue of tears, and went out, leaving the letter in the center of the desk. She trudged upstairs to pack what few clothes she could get into one chest. Then she changed into a costume for traveling. Dressed, she went to the window and glanced out. There was a faint blush of dawn in the east. They had to hurry; she wanted to be away before the house servants woke and commenced their morning duties.

Carrying the jewel casket Malcolm had given her, Hannah went downstairs. She found them all waiting for her.

John said, "The coach is ready and waiting, Mistress Hannah, and the belongings are all aboard."

"Thank you, John. I have one chest upstairs. Will you and André put it in the coach, please? Dickie, run and fetch Henry. Try not to waken anyone else. I will await him in the study—and tell him to come quickly."

In the study she opened the strongbox in the bottom drawer and carefully counted out fifty pounds, which she then put into the jewel casket.

She was locking the strongbox when Henry, looking alarmed and confused, came hurrying in.

Leaving the drawer open, she straightened up. "Henry, I am leaving Malvern within the hour."

"But Mistress Hannah, I don' understand . . ." Henry began.

"You do not need to understand, and I have no time for explanations," she said as gently as she could. "Here is a letter to Michael Verner. Ride to Williamsburg this day with it. He will return on receipt of it, I am sure. Meanwhile, the plantation will be in your good hands. Malcolm was proud of your ability. Often he told me you could manage Malvern on your own. Now is the time to show that his pride and trust in you were not misplaced. In this strongbox . . ." She motioned to the open drawer. "There is money inside, in case you have need of it before Michael returns. And letters of credit, made out to the bearer. Whatever you use you may account for to Michael. Here is the key. Keep it on your person at all times."

She thrust the key into his palm, closed his fingers around it, and squeezed. She gave him a melancholy smile. "Dear Henry, I know you find this all difficult to understand. But by Michael's return, all will be made clear . . . if not before."

She left then, left a dazed and uncomprehending Henry behind her. The coach was drawn up outside the door. Bess and Dickie were already inside, and John was up on the driver's seat. André stood waiting for her.

"Dear lady . . ." He smiled quizzically. "We have all taken you on faith and agreed to accompany you on this wild flight. But you have yet to inform us where we are going."

389

Hannah gave him a confused look. "Why, I ... I haven't thought ..."

"Then perhaps it is time you do. John must know in which direction to go."

"There is only one thing I know how to do. I will find a tavern somewhere to purchase." Her mouth had a wry twist. "That, and operating a plantation, is all the knowledge I have gained. And I am sure that a plantation is beyond my means." She looked at André intently. "What village can you think of, André, that is known for its taverns? Somewhere far distant from Williamsburg."

He mused a moment, then gave a shrug. "Boston, so I have heard, has taverns in abundance. Boston, Massachusetts. And it is distant enough, *certainement!*"

"Boston it is, then." She called up to John. "On the main road turn north, John."

André helped her into the coach, John clucked softly to the team, and the coach began to move.

She was leaving Malvern, and in all likelihood she would not see it again.

As they swung onto the main road, Hannah turned for a last look. The manor house was bathed in soft morning light. She looked until it was etched forever in her memory, holding back the tears with an effort.

Then she turned her face resolutely forward, and looked back no more.

Silas Quint waited two days after he had killed the slave before venturing out again to Malvern. He had been a little apprehensive during the waiting, but since no hue and cry had been raised, he assumed that he was not suspected.

He still rode the sorry nag, but he had spent the last of the twenty pounds Hannah had given him to outfit himself with new clothing. And he fully intended to get enough from her today to purchase a decent mount.

He rode boldly up to the hitching post, got off, and tethered the horse. He noticed, in passing, that the plantation was strangely quiet, but he was too intent on the coming meeting with Hannah to give it much thought.

Quint stood a moment at the door, smoothing the sleeves of his new scarlet coat. His breeches were velvet, his new hose white, and his shoes red with brass buckles. Never in his life had Quint spent so much on clothing for himself, and he would not have now, of course, except that he expected to leave here today with pockets bulging.

He hoped her ladyship appreciated the finery that her pound notes had paid for. He straightened his shoulders, put a superior sneer on his face, and rapped commandingly on the door. He was sure he heard the scamper of feet inside, but the door did not open. He knocked again. Still no response. Quint thought of opening the door and striding boldly in, but that might be pushing matters a little far.

He knocked yet a third time. When the door didn't open, he muttered an oath and started down the side of the house. Before he reached the end of the building, a black man came around the corner and met him halfway.

The Negro met his gaze levelly, eyes showing thinly veiled hostility.

"I am here to call on Hannah Verner," Quint said arrogantly.

"The mistress not here. She gone."

"Gone? Gone where? Into Williamsburg?"

"She gone away, gone away for good. Where, she don' tell me."

Quint gaped at the man. "Gone for good! I don't believe ye! Ye be lying! That bitch told ye to lie for her. But 'twon't work. I know she's here!"

"Mistress Verner don't tell Henry to lie. She leave in the coach before sunrise two days past."

Quint's thoughts were spinning. He was so stunned he had to lean against the wall for support. "Why should I be taking the word of a field slave?"

"I be no field slave. I be a freed man. My name Henry." Henry drew himself up proudly. "The mistress left me in charge until Master Michael return. You go now, Silas Quint. You not welcome at Malvern."

Henry turned his back and walked around the corner out of sight.

In his rage and frustration, Quint beat on the wall with his fists until he drew blood. Cursing vilely, he turned away and stumbled like a drunken man to his horse. And what he would give for a tot of rum this moment, and he with nary a coin in his pocket!

What was he going to *do*?

The future had looked so grand, and now he was worse off than ever. With that bitch gone for good, he would never get his due!

Quint mounted up and let the nag set its own plodding pace. He rode sunk in gloom, head down.

As the horse went through the gates, Quint

glanced back at the manor house. Then he was struck with an idea.

The strongbox! The box she had taken the twenty pounds from. There had to be money left behind for that uppity black bastard to operate the plantation with.

Quint made up his mind. He was going into that house tonight and steal the strongbox. No, not steal. He was entitled to whatever it contained; it was his due.

He went along the road toward Williamsburg until he was out of sight of the manor house, until he saw a grove of trees off the road. He turned the horse into them and got off.

He settled down with his back against a tree trunk. It would be a long wait. He would have to wait until long after dark, until everyone was abed. If he only had a bottle of rum to keep him company!

He set his mind to dreaming on all the rum he would buy when he had that strongbox.

Chapter Twenty

New Orleans in 1719 made Michael Verner think of a bawling baby born of a mating between a convict and a whore.

In truth, this was not far off the mark. Settled only one year before, New Orleans had a population of some few thousand souls—mostly criminals banished from France to the new world, and whores sent along to service them.

It was a raw, primitive village, the narrow streets stinking of offal, both human and animal. It was prey to every imaginable kind of insect, and prone to flooding from the nearby Mississippi River. In Williamsburg Michael had read an enthusiastic letter in a French newspaper from one Father Duval in which he stated that New Orleans was "a charming land which is beginning to be peopled

... built of simple but fine houses ... the town is one league around ... the country is full of mines of gold, silver, copper, and lead in different places..."

This story of the rapturous delights of New Orleans and of the wealth to be found there was what had drawn Michael. He didn't know where the good father had received his information about the riches, for none were in evidence. There wasn't a mine anywhere around.

And the heat ... Michael was accustomed to hot summers in Virginia, yet he had never before experienced the humid heat of New Orleans.

Most of the people lived in crude huts. What few decent dwellings there were had steeply pitched, hipped roofs that extended beyond the walls to form galleries. Ceilings in the rooms were high, the window openings reaching from floor to ceiling for better ventilation. And most of the better houses were elevated off the ground on piers, to provide better exposure to what little breeze might exist, and to escape the periodic overflowing of the Mississippi and the invasion of vermin.

The houses were built right up against their neighbors and crowded the narrow, muddy streets so that a person on foot had to walk in the street itself. The only good feature of the houses was that most of them had walled gardens in the rear.

Michael stood at the upstairs window of such a house now, smoking a cigar and staring down into the street, which was empty at this early hour.

It was just past dawn, yet Michael's naked body was sheathed in sweat. The air coming in the window was muggy, close, so heavy it pushed against him with an almost palpable force.

Michael laughed shortly. It was for this that he had ridden for weeks through swamp and pestilence, through almost impenetrable forests, through several near-fatal encounters with Indians and renegade whites.

He had always looked upon the French as a civilized, sophisticated people, and, before coming here, he had expected to find at least a reasonable facsimile of Paris. How wrong he had been!

Perhaps some day, when the village was inhabited by other than the dregs, the outcasts, and the criminals of France ...

He made a face and tossed the smouldering cigar into the street. He couldn't even buy decent cheroots in this place. He saw the cigar land in a mud puddle, and he laughed again. At least there was little danger of fire here; it was too damp. Flood, yes. He had been told that the Mississippi had risen over its banks a year back and swept away most of the village.

A sleepy voice behind him said, "Michael?"

Michael turned and looked at the bed. Marie Corbeil was one of the few women of substance in New Orleans—substantial both in flesh and in economic status. She owned this building, and provided lodgings and food for the better class of men in New Orleans.

Physically, she was a voluptuous female, heavy of breast and buttocks. She was some years older than Michael, but those years had given her valuable experience in bed. She was a sensual woman, and Michael had found much pleasure with her, even though he often cursed himself for his lustful nature.

She lay now in the nude, long black hair fanned

397

out on the pillow, knees drawn up, the rise of white, columnar thighs like portals guarding a secret garden of erotic delights.

Her black eyes twinkled at him, full lips curving in a lazy smile. "Come, sweet. Come here." She beckoned to him with outstretched arms.

Michael sighed and went to her. The heat of her welcoming body was humid as the air, but the sweetness of her yielding flesh drove all else from Michael's mind as he penetrated her.

"Ah, yes! Yes, sweet, yes!"

As he thrust to meet her arching body, Michael thought fleetingly, and with a certain sadness, of Hannah. But it was not in his nature to be celibate.

In the mornings, when she awoke in his bed, Marie needed no preparations for love. She was always ready for him. In his embrace now her body thrashed in her frantic drive for the ultimate peak of sensation.

And when it was finally over, as they lay side by side, she caressed the damp hairs on his chest. "I know not what I would do in this pigsty of a village if it weren't for you, sweet," she murmured. "And when you go, I will be left saddened."

"What gave you the idea that I might be leaving?" Michael stroked her long hair, smiling.

She raised her head to look at him with grave eyes. "You think me a fool? I have asked nothing of your past, as you have not of mine, but I know you linger here only until you receive word from someone. A woman, naturally. And when that word comes, you will be gone."

Michael was silent, not too surprised. She was an amazingly perceptive woman. It was true that he knew nothing of whence she had come, nor why she was here in this place. Her origins were French, that much he knew, although she always spoke perfect English. He suspected she had been a high-class whore at one time or another; certainly she was a woman of some education. But she asked nothing of him, no commitments, no protestations of love; she asked only that he give her pleasure in bed, and that he was happy to do.

Marie sat up with a huge yawn. She kissed her fingers at him. "It's time I went down to supervise the preparation of the morning meal."

Drowsy, Michael lay watching her dress. She came to the bed to kiss him lightly, then left the room.

Michael remained in bed a while longer, hands under his head, staring at the high ceiling. His thoughts were on Hannah. Would she reply to his letter? It was now May. If she had answered promptly, a letter should be arriving soon. He hoped so. He didn't wish to linger here through the summer. The heat now, he knew, was nothing to what it would be in a month or so.

But what if she didn't answer? What if she did not love him, nor wish to ever see him again? Then what would he do?

He muttered an oath and got out of bed. He refused to let himself think beyond that. When it became evident that she had no intention of replying to his declaration of love—then would be the time to reach a decision about his life.

That afternoon found Michael riding Black Star north to the outskirts of New Orleans.

He had been fortunate in one respect. There

had been no problem with earning a livelihood. To the citizens of New Orleans, gambling was a passion, a way of life. They would gamble on anything. They even wagered on how high the river would rise when it became swollen following the spring thaw of snow in the north.

So Michael had found it easy to win enough to live well. Yet there was an ironic twist to it. He had fled Williamsburg so he would not have to kill a man. In the brief time he had abided here, however, he had been forced to kill two men. The riffraff of New Orleans were not of the gentry, challenging those who angered them to duels, and they were apt to take their gambling losses badly.

Many were prone to think that a man who won heavily at cards was a cheat, and were not hesitant about saying so. On several occasions Michael had been forced to defend himself against such charges, and on two of those occasions men had drawn pistols from their belts. He had been given no choice but to kill them in self-defense. It seemed that no matter where he went, he was forced into killing. Was there some sort of curse on him? Perhaps because of his treatment of his father?

Michael dismissed such speculations as fanciful, of no value to him, and rode on.

Gambling was the reason he rode out today. Michael had attended a number of cock fights, which were popular in New Orleans, and had found cock fighting to be a cruel and bloody sport. He supposed today's event would be even more so. But curiosity combined with boredom had driven him to attend.

Michael sighted a crowd of some fifty people up ahead. He found a place well back from the crowd

were he could tie off Black Star. He had learned
that the horse spooked at the smell of blood, and
this match held promise of much blood being
spilled.

Today's event was an unusual one, even for New
Orleans. It was a match between a bull and a bear.

Michael walked toward the gathering. Booths
had been set up, and they were now serving all
manner of food and drink. He made his way
through the throng until he was near the center.
He stopped to stare.

It was indeed a strange sight!

A large, square arena had been crudely constructed of high logs driven into the ground, about
a foot apart, so that the spectators could see within.
Inside the arena, one at each end, stood two strong
wooden cages about thirty feet square and twelve
feet high. In one cage was a large, powerful, slate-
colored bull. In the other cage was a big, fear-
some-looking grizzly bear.

As Michael watched, several men entered the
arena with sharpened poles, and began poking at
the animals through the bars of the cages. The
bull roared and tossed wicked-looking horns. The
grizzly growled and tried to knock aside the tor-
menting sticks. Soon, blood flecked the hides of
both animals.

Men wandered through the crowd, carrying
money in their hands, offering wagers on either animal. The bear seemed to be slightly favored in the
wagering. Michael thought differently, but he re-
frained from making a wager, already regretting
coming here.

He sighed. He was here, and it was a long ride

back into the village, so he might as well watch it through to the finish.

Before long both animals were enraged, the bull frothing at the mouth, shaking the bars of his cage by butting his head.

All the men but two quickly left the arena. The other two climbed atop the cages, one to each. At a given signal, slide gates were hoisted. The bull charged out first. Head down, he charged across the arena, fetching up against the sturdy log fence with force enough to shake the ground. The crowd on that side shrank back in fright.

The bear came out more slowly. The bull saw him and snorted, pawing the ground. Then suddenly he charged. The grizzly reared up on his hind legs, jaws agape, roaring. The bull came straight at him. The bear gave a mighty swipe with one paw, grazing the bull alongside the head with enough power to deflect the hooking horns at the last instant.

The spectators roared, surging close to the logs again, watching avidly.

The bull plowed to a stop, shaking his head in bewilderment. Then he bellowed, head swiveling until he spotted the bear, and charged once more. The grizzly, lumbering awkwardly, couldn't escape the horns this time. The point of one hooked him in the side, and blood spurted.

As the bull charged on past, the grizzly, bellowing with pain and anger, galloped after him. He caught up to the bull halfway across the arena, raised up on his hind legs again, and swiped with a paw. This time his paw connected with the bull's back, claws raking. The power of the blow sent the bull to his knees, runnels of blood flowing down his side.

Bellowing, he surged to his feet and retreated backward. He eyed the upright bear for just a moment. And then, with an ear-splitting roar, he was in full charge once more. This time his aim was truer, and both horns went into the bear's belly, impaling him. The bull shook his head, and the bear fell free.

The grizzly backed into a corner, cowering, licking his wounds. Men poked at his back through the log fence with the pointed sticks, but he refused to budge from the corner.

The bull, as though knowing victory was his, strutted proudly back and forth, bellowing, while the crowd cheered and the winners went around collecting their wagers.

Michael, sickened by what he had observed and thoroughly disgusted with himself for being present at such a brutal, bloody spectacle, made his way through the crowd to Black Star and rode back to New Orleans.

Marie Corbeil was waiting for him with a letter. Giving it to him, she said plaintively. " 'Tis the letter you've been awaiting, sweet, I'm sure. And I expect New Orleans has seen the last of Michael Verner."

It was a warm, drowsy afternoon in late June when Michael Verner returned to Malvern. He had not wished to encounter anyone he knew, and gone straight to the plantation.

He let Black Star set his own pace. The animal was weary; both man and horse were weary and gaunt from the hard weeks of riding through the daylight hours, resting only when it became too dark to find their way. Once again, it had been a trip fraught with peril.

There was one disadvantage to riding through hostile country astride a magnificent animal such as Black Star—everyone coveted him. Still, there was an advantage to balance it off; Black Star could easily outdistance pursuers.

But now Black Star's usually glossy hide was dull, shrouded with road dust. Michael was dusty, too, and he wore a stubble of beard as well, for he had not shaved since saying good-bye to Marie Corbeil in New Orleans.

The animal's pace quickened as they came into view of Malvern.

"That's right, beauty." Michael caressed his mane. " 'Tis home. A welcome sight indeed. Pray we do not ever have to leave it again."

The plantation seemed normal, everything in order. Smoke poured from the cookhouse chimney, and Michael saw that the fields were green with growing tobacco. He rode directly to the stable. Children at play stopped to stare at him.

As he guided Black Star into the stable, a man emerged from the dimness. It wasn't John; it was no one Michael knew.

Dismounting, he asked, "Where's John?"

"He left, massa. Left with the mistress."

"I'm Michael Verner. Unsaddle the horse, water and feed him, then curry and rub him down."

"Yes, Master Verner."

Striding toward the house, Michael's thoughts were amused. He was acting like the master of Malvern already. Maybe his father had been right; maybe he should have taken to it long ago.

He'd been gone so long, he doubted that he knew the names of half a dozen of the people at Malvern. He was met just inside the front door by a nervous young girl. "Let's see ... you're Jenny, am I right?"

She bobbed her head. "Yes, Master Verner."

Michael drew a deep breath. He was home!

He said, "Would you please heat me a tub of water, Jenny? I am sorely in need of a bath. And when Henry comes in from the fields, will you send him to me?" His gaze sharpened. "Henry *is* still here?"

"Oh, yes, Henry be here. He been managing the plantation since the mistress left."

Michael took a long bath, scrubbing the accumulation of grime from his body, and then shaved closely. His clothes were torn and filthy, and he had none with him except what he had worn on the long ride. In his old room, he found clothes packed away that he had worn before he'd left Malvern. Trying them on, he found them to be a tight fit, but they would have to serve until he could purchase more.

It was dark when he went downstairs. He found the brandy bottle in the dining room and took it and a glass into the study. He had eaten little all day and was famished, yet he wanted to talk to Henry before he ate. He poured a glass of brandy and drank. In the desk he discovered a box of his father's cigars, and lit one from the candle. The cigar was old and crumbly, but it was still better than what he had been able to buy in New Orleans.

He also found something else that wrung a grunt from him. He knew his father had kept valuables and money on hand in a strongbox in the bottom drawer of the desk. Opening the drawer, he found the strongbox gone.

Had Hannah taken it?

Michael took out her letter and read it, although he knew it by heart now, word for word. If she had taken the strongbox, why would she have lied in the letter? Once again, he looked closely at the round, wrinkled spot on the paper. When he had read the letter in New Orleans and seen the spot, he at first had thought she'd spilled a drop of water. Then it had occurred to him that she had been crying when she'd penned the letter, and a single teardrop had fallen. He desperately wanted to believe the latter.

At a sound in the doorway, he quickly returned the letter to his pocket and looked around. Henry stood in the doorway, twisting his hat in his hands.

At the sight of Michael, his face blazed with relief. "Praise the Lawd, Master Michael, I be happy you back!"

"Yes, Henry. I am happy to be back," Michael said absently. He motioned. "Father's strongbox . . . did Hannah take it with her?"

"Oh, no, master. Mistress Hannah left it behind, in my trust. She gave me the key." From his pocket Henry took the strongbox key.

Michael sighed with relief. "Good! Then you moved it somewhere else."

"No, master, it gone," Henry said wretchedly.

"Gone! Gone where?"

"Some'um steal it. Three days after Mistress Hannah left, I comes in here to check. It be gone. The window there . . . the latch been busted."

"A slave then, here on the plantation?"

"I not think so. They be fearful of stealing."

Henry seemed strangely hesitant. Michael studied him with narrowed eyes. "You suspect someone. Come on, man, out with it!"

"I . . . it be a white man, I thinks. Silas Quint."

"Who's Silas Quint?"

"He Mistress Hannah's stepfather. No-account white trash. Ever since she come to Malvern, he sneak around begging for her money. She allus turn him away . . . till that last day. She talk to him then, right in here. Black Bess toll me so. Must have given him money. He come back two days after the mistress leaves, wearing much finery. Before he allus wears clothes like a beggar. He mad when I tells him Mistress Hannah gone. Next morning, when I comes in here, the box gone."

"I'll have a word with Master Quint, you may be sure," Michael said grimly. He paced to the window to stare out. At a sudden thought he turned. "How on earth have you managed, Henry, without money all this time?"

"I . . ." Henry drew himself up proudly. "I talks to the shopkeepers in the village and gets credit against this year's tobacco crop. Gon' be a good crop, Master Michael."

"You're a good man, Henry. And you've managed well." He crossed to grip the man's shoulder. "Now . . ." He motioned to the chair by the desk. "Tell me what you know about this." Henry sat gingerly, and Michael took his father's old chair. He leaned forward. "First, do you have any idea why Hannah ran away in such a fashion? I received a letter from her, but nothing in it made much sense."

Haltingly, Henry related what he knew of Hannah's abrupt departure with Bess, Dickie, John, and André Leclaire. For the moment, he avoided mentioning Hannah's pregnancy. He was not sure how to break the news.

"And that's all?" Michael said at the end. He threw up his hands in exasperation. "Henry, that doesn't tell me a damned thing about *why* she took flight like that!"

Unless, he thought suddenly, she doesn't love me, doesn't want to see me ever again. But there was the teardrop on the letter. Or perhaps it *had* been a drop of water, after all.

Henry was speaking. ". . . One thing a puzzlement, Master Michael."

Michael snapped out of his pensive musings. "What's that, Henry?"

"The night afore she leave, Mistress Hannah, she tol' me I soon know *why* she leave. The day afore she had a ruckus with a field hand, a slave Master Verner bought afore his death. Name of Leon. But Mistress Hannah call him Isaiah, and she chase him out'n the house with a candle holder, screaming she gon' kill him."

Michael frowned. "And so?"

Henry drew a deep breath. "'Bout an hour after the mistress leave, Leon, he found dead up near the main road, his belly ripped open. . . ."

"And you think that's the reason she left? Because people would believe she killed a slave?" Michael said explosively. "If that's the reason . . . damnation, that would be a fool thing to do! Who would ever hold a plantation mistress responsible for killing a . . ." He bit his words off, and got up to pace back and forth. "Besides, it isn't in Han-

408

nah to kill. She's exasperating, willful, God knows. But to kill, no. I don't believe it. Nobody would!"

"That what I think, too, master."

"Could she perchance have stumbled upon the body and feared that she might be accused of murdering this Leon?"

"It possible."

"If so, fleeing was the worst possible thing she could have done." Smacking a fist into the palm of his hand, Michael strode to the window to stare out at nothing. "What did they think in Williamsburg when you reported it?"

"I tell no one, Master Michael. Leon, he buried here on Malvern. Nobody knows. I buries him myself."

"You did *what*?" Michael spun around. "That was taking a hell of a risk, Henry!"

"Who miss just another slave, Master Michael?"

Henry's glance was level, and despite himself, Michael had to look away. "You're right, of course. Still, you were taking a risk." He forced his gaze around. "I think I understand ... this way, you thought no one would ever know, or have a chance to suspect Hannah of wrongdoing."

"I ... it in my mind." Henry looked down at the hat he was twisting in his hands. "Leon, he a bad 'un. And it my fault, he being here. I talk the old master into buying him."

Again, Michael crossed over to clasp his shoulder. "And I am grateful, Henry. For everything you have done ..." Then he burst out, "But that damned foolish girl! Why, for the love of God? Do you have any idea at all where she went?"

"None, master." Henry shook his head. "She not

409

tell me. All I knows is, the coach turn north on the main road."

"And that means she could be almost anywhere. No hope in hell of finding her! I wonder if this Silas Quint has any idea?"

"I don't know."

Michael said harshly, "I'll ride into Williamsburg on the morrow and have a few words with Master Quint." He sighed. "Now I'm bone weary, and also famished. You may go, Henry. On your way through the pantry, tell whoever is in charge that I will be wanting my supper soon."

"Yes, master."

Still Henry hesitated. Michael glanced at him sharply. The overseer was staring down at his hat, turning it furiously in his big hands.

"Well, Henry?"

Henry looked at him, clearly reluctant to speak.

"Come on, man, what's on your mind?"

"There 'nother thing, Master Michael . . . Mistress Hannah, she with child."

"My God, man, what are you saying? Are you sure?"

"I sure. She already showing."

Michael's thoughts were racing, his mind going back. When had it been? Late November? Could it be *his* child? "You don't know how far along . . . no, of course you wouldn't. Thank you, Henry. You may take your leave now."

When Henry was gone, Michael poured more brandy and drank it in a gulp. He fired another of his father's cigars from the candle, and sank down into the old chair. Dazed, he tried to understand this new development. Hannah pregnant? But if that were true, and if the child was his, why in the devil had she run away.

Of course there was one simple answer—one Michael didn't wish to accept.

The child wasn't his. It belonged to another man.

Silas Quint had been living these past months in a style he would never have imagined for himself. When he had brought the strongbox home from Malvern that night and broken it open, the contents had been rich beyond his wildest dream. He was a wealthy man.

He had finally gotten his just due!

And who would ever suspect he had spirited the strongbox away? Hannah was the only one would have suspicioned him, and she was gone away for good.

He had bought fine clothes and a good mount for himself. And the best of food and drink. When questioned about the source of his sudden good fortune, he had declaimed, "'Tis an inheritance from a relative in faraway England, a relative old Quint never even knew he had!"

And since he usually bought drinks for those who questioned him, they accepted his explanation without quibble. He was even welcome at the Raleigh now, where before he would have been thrown out on his tail had he ventured even to stick his nose inside.

It had been at the Raleigh last eve that he had guzzled rum until he was barely able to stagger home. He had spent none of the riches on improving the hovel. Quint had little interest in the place where he slept. It was a place to bed down, and that was enough for him.

He had expanded on his lie to some of his drinking companions, telling them he was thinking of taking a sea voyage to England to visit the grave of the uncle who had thought so kindly of his poor nephew that he had left him his estate. Or perhaps it was his aunt; he had trouble keeping the sex of his rich relative straight from one telling to the next.

Consequently, when his bed began to shake the morning after his grand time at the Raleigh, Quint thought he was dreaming of just such a sea voyage.

Then a thumping sound, followed by a jarring of the bed, jolted him awake, and he realized that he wasn't dreaming. The bed *had* been moved, moved several feet.

Fully clothed, even to his shoes, Quint sat up, trying to blink away the rum fog. There was something he should remember ...

Then a voice said triumphantly, "There it is! Henry was right!"

The figure of a man reared up from where he had been kneeling beside the bed.

And terror struck at Quint as he remembered. The strongbox! He had been keeping it hidden under the bed.

The shock cleared the last of the rum from his brain. "How dare ye come into my abode uninvited! Who are ye, and what do ye want?"

"I'm Michael Verner, and what I want is this strongbox you stole from Malvern, Silas Quint," the intruder said coldly. He was a tall man with black hair and dark eyes that blazed fiercely down at Quint. "I prayed that you would be stupid enough to keep it near you. I knocked loudly enough to wake the dead. When I received no answer, I came in as you came to Malvern—uninvited. Failing to wake you from your rum-soaked slumber, I started to search. Under the bed was the first place I looked. You're not only a thief, but stupid as well. I can have you in gaol for this. Men have been hanged for less!"

"Not stealing, I wasn't," Quint whined. "Just getting me due."

Michael frowned. He found this man as contemptible as Henry had claimed. Filthy, a sot, living in a pig sty. But he also found him puzzling. He didn't act as frightened as a man being caught out as a thief normally would. He said curtly, "What do you mean, your due?"

"I had it coming to me, I did! That wench, Hannah, was indentured to Amos Stritch. Then she up and ran away, and old Stritch wouldn't serve me no more. I went to Malvern, but her ladyship wouldn't give me my due." A sly smile crept over his lips. "Till the last time. Then she came across, she did!"

"You're a despicable man, indenturing your own daughter as a tavern serving wench!"

"Not me daughter. Not me blood," Quint said indignantly. "Mary already had the brat when I wed her."

"That's a quibble, man. She was still of your family." Michael gestured. "No matter. Do you know where Hannah went?"

"She daren't tell me, not Mistress Hannah!"

"Why not?" Michael said quickly. "Was it because of you that she left Malvern?"

"Could well be." Again that sly look came over his face. "Could be Mistress Hannah feared to face old Quint again."

413

"And why should that be?"

"'Cause of what I know about her!" Quint raised his voice and thrust his red face at Michael. "About her and the man who sired her!"

"How do you know about her father?"

"I know what that black buck Leon told me. . . ." Quint bit off his words.

And the true course of events immediately became clear to Michael. "Leon is dead, Quint. And you killed him! Didn't you?" Michael reached down, closed his hand on the man's shirt, and hauled him up off the bed. "You murdered the man!"

"No, no, 'tis a lie!" For the first time Quint showed fear. He pushed ineffectually against Michael's chest. "My word on it! Old Quint ain't killed no 'un! She—Hannah probably did it to quiet his clapper!"

"You lie, you scum!" Michael shook him hard. "Now I want the truth from you!"

Quint swallowed. "I need a tot, just a tot, young Verner, to straighten me up."

Michael let him go and stood back. "All right, have your drink. Mayhap it'll bring some sense to you."

Quint scurried to the head of the bed and scooped up the rum bottle sitting on the floor. He tilted the bottle up and drank greedily from it, paused to take a breath, and drank again. He was steadier when he finally faced about.

"So ye want the truth, do ye?" he said with a sneer.

"If the truth is in you, yes."

"Ye may not like it when ye hear it."

"You let me be the judge of that. And if I learn

414

you're lying to me, it's the gaol with you for thievery. Maybe even the hangman's noose for murder."

Quint smiled nastily, his confidence growing with the rum in his belly. "When ye hear what I have to tell ye, ye won't send me to gaol. Ye will be glad to pay to keep me clapper quiet."

Michael just stared at him, face cold.

"Did ye know that Mistress Hannah was with child?"

"So I understand."

"But did ye know 'tis your brat?"

Michael tensed. "How do you know that?"

"Because the wench as much as admitted it to me!" Quint said gloatingly.

Michael, careful to hide his reaction from Quint, felt a glow of happiness spread through him. Hannah was bearing his child! But on the heels of that came a thought that dampened his gladness. Why, then, had she fled?

Quint had tilted the rum bottle up and was taking another swig. He wiped his mouth. As an afterthought, he held out the bottle. "Care for a tot, young Verner?"

"I don't drink with gutter trash!"

"Ye will be needing it when ye hear . . ."

"Just get on with it, man!" Michael said impatiently.

"Gladly, young Verner." Quint perched on the edge of the bed. "I will now tell ye the truth about Hannah McCambridge and her father. When ye learn the truth, no longer will ye want the name of Verner connected to the wench who was once Hannah McCambridge. . . ."

PART FOUR

Hannah

Chapter Twenty-one

"Oh, I've been told that true love brings joy,
That warms the heart like the sun.
And so I loved, and I gave my heart,
As many a young maid has done.

"But oh, they lied, for 'twas naught but pain,
And oh, I cried for my love, in vain.
I found a love that I could not hold,
My tears are warm, but my heart is cold."

Hannah finished singing the song to the sound of
thunderous applause and shouts from the throng
of men, and a few women, on benches and chairs
taking up more than two-thirds of the public room
of her tavern, The Four Alls.

The song was new, played and sung for the first

time tonight. As André's supple fingers stopped on the keys of the harpsichord and the applause subsided, Hannah bowed slightly to the audience.

"Thank you, ladies and gentlemen, for your kind applause. Now I should like to introduce my accompanist, André Leclaire, the composer of the piece you granted me the pleasure of singing for you. . . ."

She beckoned, and André, elegant in gold and white, wearing a snow-white peruke of his own making, rose from the bench and crossed to join her. "My very dear friend, and your gracious host for the rest of the evening, André Leclaire!"

André took her hand. The applause rose. Hannah bowed again, and André made a graceful knee.

Under the sound of the applause, he said, "As always, dear lady, you honor my poor words and music."

"Honor!" She snorted softly. "You are a fraud, André! And you know you admire your own compositions inordinately."

"Perhaps that is true, madam," he murmured, laughing. "But a . . . well, a *pleasant* voice does not detract from their enchantment. And do not forget who has taught you to sing, dear Hannah."

Smiling behind her hand, Hannah dug an elbow into his ribs.

As the applause died, shouts came from the audience. "More, more!"

"I am sorry." Hannah held up her hands. "Only one performance an evening. That is the rule of the inn. Now, by your leave, ladies and gentlemen . . ."

She bowed yet a third time, this time much lower,

so that men in the audience craned their necks, some even standing, in order to get a better view of the daring décolletage of her gown, especially designed for her by André.

Then she said, "But I am sure you can prevail upon Monsieur Leclaire to play for you."

Quickly, then, she moved off the small stage and took the narrow stairs, hidden by the curtains, up to the second floor. The inn did not offer overnight accommodations; all of the second floor had been converted into sleeping quarters for Hannah and her entourage.

She was smiling as she mounted the stairs, remembering André's advice when she'd first begun to sing and the audience had demanded more from her. "Always leave them wanting more, dear lady. You must treat them as you would a lover, teasing and tantalizing. If they receive their fill, they may not return. But leave them longing for more and they will return. *Certainement!*"

As usual, André had been right. Hannah laughed aloud. He wasn't *always* right. He had added one innovation to their first tavern in Boston that had come near to bringing disaster down on their heads before they'd really gotten started. . . .

At the head of the stairs she saw that the door to Michele's room stood partly open. Hannah carefully opened the door farther and tiptoed into the room. There was one candle burning low, and Bess dozed in a rocking chair alongside the crib.

Bess awoke with a start. "Be quiet, honey. She sleeping."

Hannah tiptoed to the crib and stood looking down at the sleeping child. *Her* child, hers and Michael's. It had not been a son, as she had hoped,

419

yet she was content. The girl had Hannah's copper hair and long lashes, but she much resembled Michael in her dark eyes and features. She slept now, long lashes curled like feathers over her eyes.

Hannah had asked André what the French equivalent of Michael was.

"Michele—but I do not believe I have heard of a *girl* named such."

"Michele it shall be. I wanted Michael's child to be a son, but since that is not to be. . . ."

Gazing down, Hannah's heart filled with love. If only Michael could see her! Hannah tried to shield herself from the thoughts of Michael. The year was 1721, the month March. In Virginia it would be spring now, but not here in this raw, New England climate. More than two years had passed since last she had seen Michael Verner; it was beyond reason to think that she should still love him after that passage of time. But in moments such as this, gazing down at their sleeping daughter, thoughts of Michael intruded into her mind.

With a sigh she reached down to tenderly brush a strand of hair out of the sleeping girl's eyes, resisting an urge to kiss her, fearful of waking her.

Turning, she whispered, "You'd better go to bed, Bess. It grows late. She'll sleep through the night."

"You right, honey." Yawning, Bess stood up. She had a bed in the room on which she slept; at even the smallest sound from Michele, she would be wide awake.

"Good night, Bess."

"Night, honey."

Hannah went out, closing the door softly, and continued on to the next room down the hall, her own. Removing her dress, she sat at her dressing table, brushing her hair.

The brush strokes slowed after a little, and her thoughts traveled back over the time that had passed since that dawn she had last seen Malvern. . . .

It was far from easy in the beginning. First, there was the birth of Michele, which came not long after they found lodgings in Boston. Fortunately they had arrived in Boston in spring, not in the middle of one of those harsh, bitter, New England winters of which Bess complained constantly. But Hannah had been able to do little about opening a tavern until after the birth of Michele. The fifty pounds she had taken along with her were almost gone by the time she was prepared to go into business.

She was fortunate in having André's advice and assistance, fortunate in more ways than one. He sold the jewels for her, and he turned out to be a shrewd bargainer, getting far more than she would have dreamed possible.

"And all the time I thought you were a terrible businessman."

"But I am, dear lady," he said with that wicked grin. "When I do business with honest folk, I am, alas, too soft at heart. But these people who bought your jewels . . ." He made a contemptuous face. "They are scavengers, feeding on the misfortune and misdeeds of others. They well knew the value of your jewels, but were convinced they were stolen property—thus, they thought they could purchase them for a mere pittance. Which they likely would have had you bargained with them.

421

But when it comes to dealing with low, cunning minds, I can be just as devious."

Hannah ran her fingers through the pile of coins and pound notes on the table. "You are amazing, André, a source of constant wonderment to me." She smiled up at him. "And I thank God for you at least once a day."

André got more than enough from the sale of the jewels for Hannah to take over a tavern in Boston from a proprietor who was so far sunk in debt that he was willing to sell for just enough to pay his debts. When the tavern, which André named The Pilgrim's Rest, was purchased, Hannah had ample funds to stock it, with several hundred pounds left over.

She put everything in André's name, even having him pose as the proprietor. She still was fearful of having her name made public. Suppose it was learned back in Virginia that a Hannah Verner resided in Boston? She had yet to explain to the others, and they had been considerate enough not to press her for an explanation.

But, from the very beginning, they didn't prosper. There were too many taverns already doing business in Boston, and the majority of those who frequented taverns remained faithful to their regular inns.

The duties of Bess, John, and Dickie were well defined. John handled the coaches or horses when that chore was required; Bess ran the kitchen; and Dickie, having now attained his full growth, was in charge of the bar. Hannah and André saw to the books and other duties necessary to the management of a tavern.

Still, André was left largely at loose ends, and he

soon became restless. Finally, when two months had passed and it was clear they were slowly failing, he made a proposal.

"Dear lady, we must do something to attract trade. And I have had one of my brilliant ideas. We shall provide entertainment for the customers whilst they eat and drink. I do not know why someone has not done this before!"

"Entertainment? What sort of entertainment, André?"

"A playlet—I shall pen a playlet! A slightly ribald entertainment requiring only a few players, so the expense will not be heavy. I will even play a role myself!"

"I don't know, André," Hannah said dubiously. "It has never been done before. . . ."

"Only the more reason why it should be!" André said triumphantly. "You will see. We shall attract them in droves!"

Hannah finally gave her consent.

"But not even you will view it until the night we reveal it first to an audience," André insisted. "I wish you to be surprised, and entertained, as well as they."

André used two of the tavern people to play roles, Dickie and a barmaid named Merry. He played the third role himself.

The trio worked in secret for two weeks, and on the night the playlet had its first performance, Hannah realized why.

Watching from the front of the dimmed public room, she was shocked, appalled, and amused. For it *was* witty, and the large crowd attracted by a sign André had nailed out front—"An Entertainment! A Divertissement to Amuse All!"—was con-

423

vulsed with laughter. The playlet *was* bawdy and amusing—but it held up to ridicule one of Boston's most prominent, magistrates, a big-bellied, pompous individual given to wearing extravagant wigs. This particular magistrate was married to a woman half his age, and rumor had it that he was being made a cuckold. In the playlet André portrayed an outrageous caricature of the man called Squire Bigwig. The audience at once identified the character, and their laughter increased.

Hannah, knowing they courted disaster, was sorely tempted to stop the performance. But it was too late. The damage was already done. She watched it through, helpless with laughter....

André had cleared a space in the back of the public room. Before the performance, he came out and made an introductory speech. "Imagine, if you will, the parlor of a great townhouse! The townhouse of Squire Bigwig ..." André made graceful motions with his hands, as though conjuring up furnishings. "Our apologies for the lack of stage furniture. You must exercise your imagination. Squire Bigwig has a lovely young wife, Merry, mayhap none too bright. And young Tom Daring, catching a glimpse of her, is immediately smitten. He is, uh, determined to have her. Learning that Squire Bigwig is in dire need of the services of a butler, Tom Daring applies for the position...."

André retired, and the playlet began. The barmaid, Merry, played Mistress Bigwig, and Dickie was Tom Daring. After two nonsense scenes of Tom Daring being employed as the butler, he finds himself in the house alone with Merry, Squire Bigwig being out on business. Merry, complaining of an aching head, asks Tom, the new butler, to fetch her a glass of wine.

The final scene began:

TOM DARING: Ah, madam. It grieves me, humble servant though I am, to see your lovely face contorted with pain.

MERRY: (showing sudden interest) Oh, you think my face lovely, then?

TOM DARING: (with great fervor) Yes, indeed, madam. I have never beheld a face so fair. If it were not beyond my station to do so, I should offer to ease your pain.

MERRY: You know how to ease pain?

TOM DARING: (with mock humbleness) I have some small knowledge, madam. You see, ere I fell upon hard times, I had some training as a physician.

MERRY: (looking coy) Well then, I suppose it would not be at all amiss should you try your art to ease my pain. I mean, it is not as if you were a *common* butler, is it?

TOM DARING: No, madam, not at all. (He walks around behind her and places his hands on her shoulders. She is wearing a décolleté gown.) First, madam, I must bring stimulation to your shoulders.

MERRY: (still coy) But the pain is in my head, sir.

TOM DARING: Ah, but we must bring the blood upward. That is the first rule. (While he is talking, he is massaging her shoulders, his hands going lower and lower.)

MERRY: (smiling) Yes, I do feel the blood

moving. (Squirming ever so little) I am sure of it.

Tom Daring: (breathing heavily) Yes, yes, madam. I feel it, too! (His hands are now down into the décolletage of the dress, and he is massaging her breasts. Both he and Merry are showing signs of sexual excitement.)

Merry: (excitedly) Oh, yes, I feel it! I feel it!

(Tom removes his hands, and, kneeling down, takes her into his arms. At that instant, there is a tremendous crash as the door is flung open, and Squire Bigwig storms in.)

Squire Bigwig: (apoplectically) What is this? What is this? What are you doing? What is going on?

Tom Daring: (leaping to his feet) Oh, nothing, sir, nothing at all! The mistress felt faint. I was merely trying to support her, to keep her from falling to the floor. I had just fetched her a glass of wine. (He points to the wine, untouched, on the tray.)

Merry: (fanning herself with her hand, and quickly arranging her gown) Oh, my dear! I thought I should faint. It was fortunate that Tom was just on his way into the room with a glass of wine for the pain in my head.

Squire Bigwig: (looks suspicious, but allows himself to be mollified) Well then, that casts a different light . . .

(Tom Daring quickly picks up the tray, presents the wine to Mistress Bigwig and leaves the room, trying to walk so that the bulge in his breeches, a false one, is not visible. But of course it is, and the audience roars with laughter. Squire Bigwig seems oblivious to this.⌡

SQUIRE BIGWIG: Well then, is the ache in your head gone, my love?

MERRY: (a pause) Why, so it is. (She looks thoughtful, then sad.) But I am afraid, sir, that I now have an ache of a quite different sort!

One of the things that surprised Hannah was the assurance with which Dickie carried off his role.

Later, André confided in her. "I think the lad has been tumbling Merry. And what is wrong with that? He is long past the age."

André was right in one respect. The playlet was an immediate success. All of Boston was agog with news of it, and for a week the tavern had to turn away customers.

Then the model for "Squire Bigwig" learned of it and descended on The Pilgrim's Rest in full wrath, along with a number of other prominent Bostonians, all with Puritan ancestors not too far distant. They decreed that if the "entertainment" did not cease forthwith, all those connected with the tavern would end up in gaol.

Word quickly spread, and tavern-goers were fearful of being seen even near The Pilgrim's Rest. Their business became a trickle, and within a week Hannah was forced to close the doors.

"Barbarians!" André raged. "Pursy-nosed hypocrites! They all like their slap and tickle, but behind closed doors and beneath thick quilts. When it is mentioned in public, even in the spirit of fun, their noses turn blue as if from the cold of their damnable winters!"

427

Hannah let him storm, scarcely listening, busy with her own thoughts. She had to do something, she realized, and quickly, before all her money was gone.

"If we locate out of Boston a way, on a well-traveled road, they probably will not bother us there. And we can still offer entertainment, but of a different kind," she said.

André looked at her suspiciously. "A different kind? What is in your mind, madam? When you get that look on your face, mischief is soon afoot!"

"Why, all I meant," she said artlessly, "was that we should provide the entertainment ourselves."

"We?" He waved his hands in agitation. "Exactly how shall *we* do that, pray?"

"You will play the harpsichord, and I will sing."

He stared at her in horror. "Sing? Before an audience mostly of men?"

"Now who's playing the prude?" she said mockingly.

"But dear lady . . ."

"At Malvern you told me I had a true voice. You taught me much. I think we do well together. And with some more teaching from you . . . of course," she added slyly, "if you think yourself not capable of teaching me well enough so I may amuse our customers . . ."

"Dear Hannah, André can teach a crow to sing as sweetly as a canary!" he said with much aplomb.

So it was settled.

They found an inn three miles out on the post road running south and west from Boston. The tavern had been closed for more than a year, and Hannah was able to purchase it for very little, again in André's name. It needed much work. But as soon as the upstairs rooms were suitable for habitation, the seven of them (including Merry) moved in. Hannah bought a harpsichord, and for three months they labored long and hard. André wrote several songs for her, and attempted to give her the professionalism and poise necessary for public performances. Of self-assurance, he told her, she had an ample supply.

By the time they were ready to open the tavern, he said with a sigh, "I have heard better singers. Not in this backward country," he amended hastily, "but in my own. However, perhaps you will suffice. After all, what do these uncivilized folk know of singing?"

"I thank you for your generous compliment," Hannah said sarcastically. "But I must insist on one thing. My name will not be made public."

"Not made known?" he said in dismay. *"Mon Dieu*, Hannah! Are you not carrying this mystery of yours beyond reason?"

"I'm sorry, André," she said, tight-lipped. "That is the way it is to be."

"Ah, well." He sighed, raising and lowering his hands. Then he brightened. "But that might add a nice touch. The lady of mystery! You come on unannounced, you leave unnamed!" His smile was roguish. "I am delighted I thought of such an idea!"

The inn's name, The Four Alls, was André's idea. He had seen a tavern with such a name on their weary journey from Williamsburg. Being André, of course, he had added his own touch. He had had a very large sign made; it now hung over the front door of the tavern. On the sign was the name, "The Four Alls," along with a painting.

The painting represented a palace, on the steps of which stood a king, an officer in military uniform, a clergyman in gown and bands, and a common laborer in plain dress. At the bottom of the sign was the satirical inscription:

1. General — I fight for All.
2. Minister — I pray for All.
3. King — I govern All.
4. Laborer — And I pay for All.

When asked which king was thereupon depicted, André would reply with an innocent look, "Why, your English king, *naturellement*. Certainly not the king of France!"

Hannah thought of another innovation. She determined to serve Southern-style cooking, with Bess supervising the kitchen help.

"If nothing else," she told André, "we'll have decent food to eat ourselves. Aside from the severe winters, I think the thing I most dislike about New England is the atrocious food!"

There was some difficulty getting many of the ingredients. In the end she sent an order aboard a merchant vessel sailing up and down the coast; certain foods and condiments were to be brought up from the colony of Virginia. The shipment arrived just in time, a few days before they were ready to open.

The week before the scheduled opening Hannah placed a notice in the almanac published by Dr. Nathaniel Ames, who also operated a tavern some miles farther south on the post road. The notice read:

Advertisement! This is to signify to all Persons who travel the great post road southwest from Boston that a house of Public Entertainment, THE FOUR ALLS, is now open three miles from Boston. If such Persons see Cause to be Guests at the aforementioned Inn, they shall receive Refreshment and shall be well Entertained at reasonable rates. The kitchen will serve Southern-style victuals, such as are not to be found elsewhere in all of New England!

The inn was a success almost from the day of its opening. The advertisement itself aroused enough interest to attract the curious, and it was located close enough to Boston so that it was within an easy drive by coach or ride by horse. The twin attractions. Bess's southern cooking and Hannah's singing, were soon the talk of all Boston. Ther? were some scandalized whispers over the sign poking fun at the king, and Hannah feared that some legal action would be taken. But as the days passed and nothing untoward happened, her fears lessened.

André graciously gave her credit for part of their success. "The fact of your playing the lady of mystery has added considerable spice to our entertainment."

Naturally everyone connected with the tavern was besieged by queries concerning Hannah. Who was she? Where had she come from? What was her name?

All such queries were referred to André. André, with his usual charm and wicked smile, handled everyone adroitly. He told a different story to each

431

questioner—one time Hannah would be of royal family from the continent, banished from her homeland because of some great scandal, the details of which he dared not reveal for fear of her life; another time she might be a famous courtesan who had decided to leave her life of sin and give of her beauty and great talent to an appreciative audience. Yet another time she might be the illegitimate daughter of a renowned governor of a southern colony, who had thrown her out of his home.

Hannah was highly amused by his stories. Occasionally she was accosted by some curious male from the audience, but John, whose duties now consisted in the main of guarding her privacy, would immediately send such individuals on their way.

And so The Four Alls flourished. It was true that when the New England area was ice-bound with the advent of bitter winter, they often shut down the inn for days at a time, for such was the onslaught of snow and ice that the post road was closed to all traffic. But since it was the main traffic artery going south, it was open to travel except during extremes of weather.

During the times when the inn was closed, Hannah was content to remain inside, warm and cozy for days on end, practicing with André, perfecting her art—at least what André called her art—and spending a lot of time with Michele.

Her warm beauty caused her to be the recipient of many gifts and notes from admiring males; but she spurned them all, sending the gifts back with gracious notes, unsigned.

For well over a year after coming to Boston,

Hannah was rarely in the presence of a man—except for those of her entourage. André could not understand her actions. One evening he took her aside and said, "Dear, dear Hannah, I do not understand you! We are successful. You need not spend all your time working. Now you may relax and enjoy yourself. It is not natural for a woman as lovely, as young, as you to be without the companionship of a man. What is your intention—to remain closeted unto yourself for the remainder of your life? You might as well hie thee to a nunnery!"

Admittedly, her body did cry out for love. Since Michael had awakened her slumbering passions, Hannah had known that hers was a sensual nature.

Finally André's urgings, and her own feelings, caused her to venture far enough out of her shell to invite one of her admirers for a late supper in her living quarters. She had been impressed by the evident feeling in the note he'd sent to her:

Madam: I adore you! Night after night I have observed your beauty across the public room, listened to the sweetness of your voice. It strikes my imaginings that you are singing for me alone. Please find it in your heart to grant me a word with you. All I ask is to be near you, to bask in the warmth of your beauty. I will not ask more unless it is your desire. Your adoring servant, Grant Endicott.

During what little contact she had had with the men of Boston, Hannah had formed the opinion that in New England men were cold and distant, with hearts as icy and harsh as their New England winters, and about as articulate as carriage horses.

Intrigued by Grant Endicott's note, she penned an answer:

Sir: Thank you for your kind missive and your flattering compliments. Would you do me the honor of supping with me in my quarters this Friday eve, following my performance?

As usual, she did not sign her name.

André was delighted when he was told of the assignation. Bess was openly scandalized, but secretly pleased to see the child letting a man approach her again. She grumbled, "A caution it is, being alone in yo' room with a man! I be careful to keep the door closed so that child won't see her mama's carryings-on!"

When Friday evening came, Hannah was amused to notice that the food that was to be sent up from the kitchen was of the best—mostly cooked by Bess, she was sure.

When they'd renovated the old tavern, two bedrooms upstairs had been turned into Hannah's living quarters. One was still a bedroom, but the other was now a sitting room, with a dining area. It was there that she and Grant Endicott would sup.

Hannah was further amused to learn that Grant Endicott, a tall, thin man of some thirty years, was after all a Southern gentleman, born and raised on the coast of South Carolina. His family was in shipping and had recently opened an office in Boston; he, the eldest Endicott son, had been put in charge.

After making a graceful knee and raising her hand to his lips, he said, "Do you realize, madam, that I do not know your name?"

"It is Hannah."

"Hannah?" He waited, one eyebrow raised. "Just Hannah?"

"That is all you need to know."

"As you wish, madam. Ah ..." He smiled in open delight. "You are of the South. Singing, I could not be sure, but now I know. That soft voice, nothing like the harsh, clipped tones of these New England women! Am I not correct?"

"I will say no more, sir." Then she smiled. "Much of my appeal here is the mystery surrounding me. Would you wish to tear away that veil of mystery?"

"Not in the least, madam!" His eyes were a warm brown, and they now took on a serious, intent look. "But to know you as woman ... that is indeed different!"

"We shall see," Hannah said a touch coyly. She turned away, nodding. "Will you share a glass of wine with me, sir?"

"Thank you. It will be my pleasure."

Hannah poured wine for them, and they sat before the hearth. It was a chill autumn evening, and the heat was welcome.

Grant raised his glass. "To your health, milady."

They drank. Hannah had been a little nervous about this meeting, but the wine relaxed her inner tension, and she found herself looking forward with enjoyment to the evening ahead.

"These New England women you mentioned, sir ... have you perchance known many of them?" she asked coquettishly.

"Ah, not so many, I fear." He sighed. "They are cold, difficult to approach."

"But you do not find Southern women so?"

"Our Southern ladies are warm and generous of nature. At least, I have always found this to be." Now his glance turned bold, ardent.

There was a light knock on the door. Hannah called out, and the two barmaids from the public room came in carrying trays steaming with food. They placed the food on the small, linen-draped table in one corner.

Hannah and her guest sat across from each other at the candle-lit table. The food was all Southern-style—cured ham, sweet potatoes, black-eyed peas, cornpone Hannah suspected Bess had baked with her own hands. And at the finish, a delicious pudding.

Grant ate with relish. "Ah, down-home cooking." He sighed. "I so miss that in Boston. They *boil* everything to death up here. I must confess that the victuals you serve in your dining room, madam, were what drew me here in the beginning. Then, of course . . ." He stopped eating to look across at her. "Then I heard your sweet voice and observed your beauty, and I was lost."

"You flatter me outrageously, sir," Hannah said with lowered eyes.

"Not flattery, madam. The truth, I swear." He reached across the small table to squeeze her hand briefly.

After the meal was finished and the table cleared away, Hannah followed the two barmaids to the door and unobtrusively locked it after them.

She turned to Grant, who was sprawled before the fire, replete with food and wine. "A tot of brandy, sir?"

He stirred, looking around at her somewhat dubiously. "It does grow late, madam."

"Pooh! Not at all. I am seldom abed before the stroke of midnight."

"Then I shall accept your offer."

Pouring two glasses of brandy, Hannah felt warm and content, aglow with anticipation of the evening's coming pleasure. Grant's eyebrows rose when he saw that Hannah also had a glass of brandy, but he made no comment.

This time Hannah sat close to him. He squirmed uneasily, but did not move away. It was the most Hannah had drunk since those grand balls at Malvern, and she felt slightly giddy.

The drink loosened Grant's tongue somewhat, and he was loquacious about South Carolina; he was clearly suffering from homesickness. Hannah scarcely listened, her gaze on the leaping flames, making an expected response now and then.

Suddenly Grant sat up with an exclamation, his glance on the ticking clock in the corner. "Madam, a thousand pardons! It grows late, very late. I have imposed on your hospitality long enough. . . ."

"But why should you go?" she murmured. "You are my guest, and I have not asked you to take your leave." She allowed her hand to rest lightly against his thigh, and turned her head on the back of the seat, her parted lips invitingly close.

He stared hard into her eyes, so near, swallowing. Then he uttered a sound like a groan, and embraced her, mouth descending on hers. It was a tentative kiss, and Hannah could feel the tenseness in his body, as if he expected her to rebuff him. Instead, she returned the kiss ardently, her hands stroking his back. Grant wasn't wearing a wig. She tangled her fingers in his long brown hair, and forced his mouth closer to hers.

437

Finally she turned her face aside to murmur in his ear, "Why do we not go into the bedroom, Grant? It is much more comfortable there."

"But madam, I do not wish to take advantage of such a short acquaintance...." His protest was weak. He spoke as though in a daze, his tongue thickened with passion.

Hannah stood, pulling him up with her. "Come, Grant."

He followed her blindly into the bedroom. He was shy and bold by turn, and Hannah had to undress herself and help him undress as well.

It wasn't until later that Hannah realized that, enclosed in her own rosy haze of need, she had manipulated him almost at will.

Once on the bed, coupled, Grant performed satisfactorily enough, his own physical need enabling him to leave her sated. She fell into a deep sleep.

When she awoke, he had dressed and gone.

And neither Hannah nor The Four Alls ever saw Grant Endicott again.

When she told André of this, he roared with laughter. "Were you perhaps a little, uh, aggressive, dear lady?"

"Possibly," she said with downcast eyes. Then she looked up with a flash of spirit. "But I am my own woman now! No man beckons and commands me! I am no longer Hannah McCambridge, indentured serving wench and tavern whore, nor Hannah Verner, plaything of a plantation master! I am Hannah, damn it! *Hannah!*"

"Perhaps so, madam, perhaps so." André sobered, choking off his laughter. "But I doubt that the males of the Southern gentry will take kindly to that. Nor, for that matter, the New England males either."

About the latter, André had been mistaken. One Joshua Hawkes, Captain Joshua Hawkes, had proven him wrong about at least one New England male. Captain Hawkes was a born and bred New Englander.

And it was Josh Hawkes Hannah awaited now, as she sat brushing her hair.

Her head came up as there was a thunderous knock on the door, and she smiled in delight. Captain Joshua Hawkes always announced his presence with gusto. In fact, he did everything with gusto.

She hurried to the door and threw it open to the tall, broad-shouldered, black-bearded man who towered in the doorway.

"Josh! I didn't even know your ship was in Boston until I received your message!"

Roaring with laughter, he stepped inside, slammed the door with a booted foot, and scooped her up in his arms, tossing her high.

"Didn't know myself, lass. Two days out of Boston harbor, we developed a bad leak in the hold, and I had to turn back for repairs. Else Josh Hawkes might be feeding the fishes about now. Now you wouldn't want that, would you, lass?"

Laughing, she said, "No, Josh dear, I would never want that. Although I must say ..." She ran her hands down the broad, muscular length of his back. "You would make a tasty meal for the fishes!"

"Aye, that I would." He sat her down and rubbed his hands together briskly. "Where's the

439

brandy, Hannah, lass? 'Tis chill as a witch's tit without!"

"It's where it always is."

She watched him with great fondness as he crossed the room to the sideboard, sea boots thumping the floor. He picked up the brandy bottle, poured a generous dollop into a glass, and drank it down.

Sometimes, in Josh's presence, Hannah thought of Michael. There was certainly nothing elegant about him; she had never seen Josh in anything but rough seaman's clothes and sea boots, and he drank and ate and made love with a great appetite. Yet there was the black beard, there were the snapping black eyes—enough to cause her to think of Michael when first she'd seen him, when he'd been masquerading as a pirate named Dancer.

Josh had tumbled her into bed within the hour the first time he'd set foot in her private quarters. His was the ship that transported foodstuffs for The Four Alls from Virginia and the Carolinas. Hannah had seen him twice before on board his ship when she'd been there to order things she wanted brought up from the South.

The third time, he had come to the tavern to collect money due him. He'd had his fill of brandy downstairs in the public room and watched her performance before sending word up that he wished to see her. She had told John to send him up, thinking it was merely a business matter.

But almost as soon as their business had been completed, Josh had swept her up into his arms and carried her into the bedroom. He'd put her down on the bed, tossed up her skirts, and proceeded to take her. At first Hannah had fought

440

him. But the struggle had excited her, and when he'd gotten on the bed with her, she had arched to meet him with her passions fully aroused.

Later, in the drowsy aftermath, he had confessed that such had been his intention all along. "My business wasn't all that pressing," he had said with that roaring laugh. "But when I watched you sing below, lass, you roused the old scratch in me!"

"What if I'd screamed?"

He'd looked astonished. "I don't know. It never occurred to me that you would." Hannah had had to laugh. That was Josh Hawkes—direct, uncomplicated, unsubtle as a bull.

There was no great love between them, only a mutual respect and affection, and the infrequent tumblings in bed, which Hannah could enjoy with the same gusto as Josh—no emotional entanglements asked or promised.

Finished with the brandy, he came striding to her now. "Well, lass?"

Hands on hips, she retorted, "Well, Josh?"

His laughter rumbled. He cupped her face gently between his hands and kissed her. His hands were hard with rope calluses, yet as tender as the touch of a kitten. He smelled and tasted of the sea, and Hannah felt her leaping response to his kiss.

"No need to carry you this time, is there, lass?"

"Aye, Josh. No need at all."

Holding hands, they went into the bedroom. In bed, Hannah watched him undress with her usual awe. Aside from the beard, his body was practically hairless, but the massiveness of it reminded her of a great oak, and in her imagination she could see him on the deck of his ship in a storm, feet planted solidly, roaring his defiance into the screaming wind.

He came to her and took her—with great tenderness, yet with a fierce and very demanding passion, engendering in her an answering need. At the very height of their passion, he lowered his face to kiss her, and Hannah thought fleetingly of Michael, wondering how it would be to be kissed by him in full beard. Then pleasure took her, and all thought of Michael Verner fled from her mind.

After the last seizure of ecstasy had passed, Hannah said breathlessly, "How long will you be in port, Josh?"

"The shipfitters promised to have the ship caulked by day's end, so I sail with the morning tide."

She rolled toward him, one hand coming to rest on his chest. "Then we should make the best use of the time we have, shouldn't we?"

He shouted laughter. "Greedy wench, aren't you?"

"A captain's lady must needs take advantage of the little time made available to her," she said demurely.

"Aye, that she should, lass! She should indeed!"

Still laughing, he took her into his arms again.

Chapter Twenty-two

Amos Stritch had made his way very well in Boston. In the two years since his abrupt departure from Williamsburg, he had prospered; his purse had grown fat. Of course his figure had grown fat again along with his purse, and he was cursed with attacks of the gout. The damnable New England winters only served to aggravate this condition. However, Stritch did not consider the discomfort a bad price to pay for his prosperity.

Upon his arrival in Boston, he had discovered a fortuitous circumstance. The pirate ships had been frightened away from the Carolina and Virginia coasts by the sudden demise of Blackbeard and his crew, but they were still finding a profitable market for their stolen liquor cargoes farther north.

443

Within a few weeks, Stritch had made valuable connections with pirate shipmasters with liquor to sell. They'd been eager to have him act as their agent—they'd been a trifle fearful of approaching tavern owners directly, now that the news of Blackbeard's fate had spread.

Stritch had had little difficulty striking bargains with the tavern owners of Boston. Their inborn New England instincts told them what a canny bargain was, and few had suffered any strong qualms of conscience about the possible source of the liquor they bought, so long as it was plentiful and well below legitimate prices.

Within a little more than a year Stritch had prospered to such an extent that he had saved enough funds to purchase a tavern of his own. It was located on the south edge of Boston, on the post road going south. There, he had retired from being an agent between pirate and tavern owner, and had set about leading the life of a gentleman innkeeper. . . .

He immediately renamed the tavern the Cup and Horn and opened for business. There were no slaves to be purchased here, and the few indentured servants had too high a price on them, so he had to make do with what people he could hire. This galled him considerably, but there was no help for it. The ones he hired usually didn't last long. When Stritch flew into one of his rages and threatened them with his cane, they usually quit at once. And since he was always convinced they were stealing from him, he was always angry. Luckily the kitchens in this cold climate were located inside. Since he tried to be everywhere at once, seeing to it that the help didn't lollygag on his time, that was convenient. Needless to say, he was not a popular man to his employees. But since he did know the tavern business—better than any other innkeeper in Boston, he was sure—he prospered.

He heard about the new tavern, The Four Alls, opening south of Boston, but he paid the stories little heed. After all, it was some miles distant, so how could it possibly affect his trade? He ignored as well the stories about entertainment being offered there, some wench singing. He thought it a foolish thing to do. In his opinion, a man came into a tavern to drink, mayhap have a bite of food, gossip with his drinking companions, and perhaps play a game of cards. Listening to some wench caterwauling would take the customers' attention away from what they had come there to do. Stritch dismissed it from his mind, assured there was nothing for him to worry about.

Yet he soon began to notice that his trade was falling off. Every night, it seemed, fewer men came into his tavern.

One chill May evening Stritch was standing before the fireplace warming his backside when a man named Fry, one of his regulars, came in. A man in his forties, almost as rotund as Stritch, Fry came across to him, grinning.

"A good evening to you, Squire Stritch!"

Stritch grunted. "Ain't seen you in my tavern for these two evenings past. Been ailing, have you?"

"Naw. I been out to that new tavern on the post road, The Four Alls, the past two evenings."

"Why in the devil's name would you ride all that way for your evening's tot of rum?"

"Heard about the lady they got entertaining out there."

"How could a wench in any tavern be called a lady?"

. . "This one is. Besides, nothing else to call her. Nobody knows her name. Leastways, those that do ain't telling. And a comely one she is! Sings like a bird, she does. And that bosom of hers! Makes a man want to get right up there with her and make a grab for them. Indeed it does!"

Stritch was frowning. "Has no name, you say? Seems queer."

"Might seem so to you, but not to them that comes to listen," Fry said cheerfully. "And they're coming in droves. Both nights I was there, a man couldn't find a place to sit his arse down. Had to stand."

"I find it hard to fathom why a man would go to a tavern to listen to some wench warble," Stritch grumbled. "Interferes with his drinking."

"That's because you ain't seen her." Fry's grin broadened. "Aside from that, they serve different food out there. Southern cooking they call it."

Something like a chill passed over Stritch. "Southern cooking? Here in Boston?"

"Yup. Not bad, either, for a change. Right tasty. And folks seem to take to it like a bear to a honey-tree. 'Course, well could be that all this talk of the pox has made folks happy to get out of town a ways."

Stritch fretted for another two weeks, watching worriedly as his trade dropped off more and more. Often he stood in the doorway and watched those who had been his regular patrons pass the Cup and Horn by on their way south.

Of course, Fry's comment about a smallpox epidemic in Boston *could* have something to do with it. Rumors of a plague grew daily. Stritch paid scant heed; an innkeeper heard all sorts of rumors.

Finally, Stritch knew that he had to see this new tavern for himself. He was still convinced that it was all a passing fancy, that tavern frequenters would soon grow weary of listening to some wench sing. But something nagged at his mind, something he couldn't put a name to.

He hated to leave the Cup and Horn without his supervision for even an evening. But there was nothing for it; he had to go.

Stritch owned no horse; he was too heavy to mount one without assistance. So, in addition to all else, he had to go to the expense of hiring a carriage for the evening. He thought of asking a ride with someone he knew, but he wanted no one to know he was sneaking into this new tavern for a look.

He was both astounded and dismayed at the number of horses, carriages, and coaches outside The Four Alls when he arrived. He sat a moment, reading the elaborate sign with a faint sneer. The signs favored by innkeepers in and around Boston were too fancy for Stritch's liking. But he had adopted one of their customs—having all the letters in the sign of his new Cup and Horn inscribed in capital letters.

It was early June now, and the weather had started to warm. But not wanting to risk being recognized and laughed at, Stritch had come wearing a long wig, a tricornered hat pulled down low over his eyes, and a great cloak. Getting down

447

from the carriage, he pulled the cloak up around his chin; then he limped inside.

At the sight of the crowded public room, his gout gave a painful twinge.

At the far end of the long room was something Stritch had never seen before. A sort of platform had been constructed, rising some two feet off the floor. At the moment the platform was empty except for a harpsichord. At each end of the platform, hanging from ceiling to floor, were two muslin curtains, extending out about six feet from the walls.

All a waste of valuable space, Stritch thought with a sneer. That space could well be filled with tables, chairs, and benches. And yet, he couldn't deny that the large crowd in the room filled him with dismay.

He forced his way through to the bar, using his cane as a prod. The young man behind the bar looked vaguely familiar to Stritch. He was very busy, his head down, as he poured drinks for customers clamoring for service. The two serving wenches in the room were hard put to keep up with the demand for service.

Stritch finally got a tankard of ale and paid for it, all without the young man behind the bar ever looking up at him.

Holding the tankard high over his head and using his cane again to clear the way ahead of him, Stritch made it to a bench by the front door. He found a place for himself and sat down. He sipped at the ale, intending to make it last.

Within a short time the bar was closed down temporarily, and the two barmaids and the youth from behind the bar went around the room blowing out some of the candles, leaving the tavern dim. Then the youth disappeared behind the curtains for a moment before coming out with a crystal candelabra ablaze with lighted candles, which he placed atop the harpsichord.

He held up his hands, and the crowd fell quiet. "Monsieur André Leclair!" he announced.

An elegantly dressed man wearing a snow-white wig came out onto the platform, bowing to a scattering of applause, and sat down at the harpsichord. He played a light, airy melody. Stritch snorted contemptuously into his ale. He knew nothing of music; it was a waste of time, in his opinion.

Before the end of the piece, someone slipped into the empty space on the bench beside Stritch. Glancing at him, Stritch saw a big man with a full black beard, dressed in seaman's clothing.

The melody ended, and Stritch looked again at the platform. The man in the white peruke was stepping out of sight to the right, behind the curtain. An expectant hush fell over the audience. Then the man came back, leading a tall, full-bodied woman with copper hair. She wore a red velvet dress with a low-cut bodice. Loud applause greeted her.

Stritch's breath left him in a hiss, and he leaned forward. He blinked his eyes rapidly, scarcely able to credit his senses. If he had consumed much drink, he would have thought himself besotted, imagining things. But only part of a tankard of ale . . .

Then she began to sing, and Stritch knew he wasn't imagining things. The wench up there was Hannah. Hannah McCambridge! He sat stunned, dazed in his disbelief. Then a rage slowly consumed him. A pain wrenched at his heart, and he thought he was in danger of apoplexy.

It was all he could do to keep from rushing headlong up there, grabbing her by the neck, and squeezing, squeezing that white throat until she was dead.

Would this damnable woman out of his past dog his footsteps for the rest of his life?

Blood drummed in his ears, and his vision blurred. Her voice came to him as from a great distance:

"My love is like the vi-o-let
That bloometh in a hidden place,
And only I know where she lies,
And only I may see her face.
The bold rose in the garden grows,
And many men may find her there,
But I alone my true love know,
My vi-o-let, so sweet and fair."

As the song ended, to applause and voices shouted in praise, the man beside Stritch nudged him with an elbow.

". . . Lass is grand, would you not say, sir?"

"What?" Stritch blinked around at him.

The man with the beard was grinning. He bobbed his head toward the platform. "I said the lass is grand, is she not?"

"Yes, yes," Stritch mumbled. Then he roused himself from his stupor enough to ask, "Would her name be Hannah, perchance?"

The bearded man's gaze sharpened. "Aye, that it is. But how did you know?" Then he gave vent to

450

rumbling laughter. "I told the lass her secret would be out ere long."

Saved an answer, Stritch turned his burning gaze back on Hannah, who was singing another song. He heard not a word. His gaze, his whole world, was narrowed down to that hated face framed by the coppery hair. Never in his life had such hatred coursed through his veins!

She sang one more song, then made a pretty bow to wild applause. Ignoring the shouted demands of "More, more!" she ran off behind the curtain. Stritch dimly took note of the fact that the bearded seaman had left his seat and was casually strolling along the right wall. At the curtain he paused for a look around, then quickly ducked behind the curtain and out of sight.

Stritch sat on, his ale tankard empty now, his thoughts crawling and writhing like a nest of poisonous reptiles.

Upstairs, Hannah sat at her dressing table, brushing her hair, ears tuned for the expected knock.

And then it came, the thunderous pounding.

She got up and hurried to open the door. As Josh stepped in, she stood on tiptoe to kiss him. "Hello, Josh dear. It's good to see you."

"And me you, lass, indeed it is! Aye, the voyages seem to get longer and longer toward the end now, looking forward as I am to seeing you again."

"You could always leave the sea," she said gravely, "and find employment on shore."

"Aye, you'd like that, would you? Take a man who's known little but the sea since he was a little tyke and chain him to the land!"

"No, Josh, no! Never that! I spoke only in jest!"

"I know, lass, I know."

His big hands caught her under the armpits, and he lifted her high, swinging her around twice; on the second swing swiping at the door with his boot, slamming it shut.

"Your secret is finally out, you know." He set her down and strode toward the brandy bottle to pour a glass.

"And which of my many secrets might that be?"

Josh took a deep draught of brandy. "Your name. Whilst I listened to you warble in the public room below, a man asked if your name was Hannah."

"Well, I knew it couldn't be kept a secret forever." Hannah shrugged, not really caring. As time had passed and nothing untoward happened, she had begun to believe that the wall of secrecy she had gone to such pains to erect around her was as foolish as André implied.

Josh finished the brandy and came toward her, smiling softly. "I haven't much time tonight, Hannah. I have only a short time to while away."

"Always in a rush," she said mockingly. "I never saw such a man for hurry."

"Oh, not always, lass. I think you can attest to that."

And, as though to prove this to Hannah, he made tender, agonizingly slow love to her. Yet there seemed a new, a greater intensity about his lovemaking tonight that puzzled Hannah.

When their mutual pleasure peaked and they lay close in a snug embrace, Hannah with her head in the cradle of Josh's shoulder, the puzzle was solved for her.

452

"I have bad news to convey, lass." He laughed softly. "Or perhaps good news to you—who knows?"

She raised her head. "What news is that, Josh?"

"Soon, you will not be blessed with my presence for a long time. I'll be gone six months, perhaps even a longer time."

"Six months!" she exclaimed in dismay. "Why, Josh? What is wrong?"

"Nothing's wrong. It's just something I've been hankering toward for some time." He pulled her back into his arms. "I have signed on as the master of a ship sailing for Liverpool. That's why I'm leaving you early this night—I'm seeing the owners of the ship and signing the necessary papers tonight. Soon as she's provisioned properly, I'll be sailing."

"But why, Josh? Liverpool! To me, it seems half-way across the world!"

"Aye, it's a far piece. But not quite that far." A pensive note came into his voice. "I've grown weary of sailing up and down the coast like a fisherman. I feel drawn to the high seas, where I can match wits with Old Man Neptune once again."

"But you once told me that you'd had your fill of sailing across oceans. You've been doing it most of your life."

"I know I said such. I lied, both to myself and to you, lass. Once a man sails on the high seas, he never loses his desire for it. It's his home, do you see?"

"Six months!" Hannah sighed. "It's a long time."

She took his shaggy head between her hands. What would she do without Josh? He had come to be a comfortable part of her life, as important to her as Bess, André, and Dickie, although for a different reason.

She smiled. "Well, we made no promises, did we?"

"That's right, lass, no promises." He laughed softly. "We swore in the beginning, no promises. Come, lass. I don't have to leave for a little time yet."

He swept her up into his arms again and kissed her ardently. Laughing together like children at play, they tumbled back and forth across the bed.

Amos Stritch had found that he could always rely on his instinct for queer business afoot. He harbored a strong suspicion that the black-bearded seaman had slipped upstairs to bed the copper-haired bitch. So Stritch didn't dare sneak up until the man was gone.

He remained on the bench, holding the empty tankard, his rage smouldering in him, bitterness filling his mouth like the taste of gall. The crowd had slowly dispersed, and an hour later there were only a few men left in the public room, but Stritch sat on, his gaze fastened on the curtain against the wall. Once, a barmaid approached to ask if his tankard needed refilling. Stritch sent her scurrying away with a snarl.

Finally his vigil was rewarded. He saw the man with the black beard slip out from behind the curtain and quickly make his way to the front door and out, strutting like a rooster.

Tumbled her good, had he? Good! Likely then she would still be abed. That would make it all go easier.

Stritch got up and sidled along the right wall,

leaning on his stick, exaggerating his limp. At the curtain he looked quickly around, saw he was unobserved, and stepped behind the curtain. And there, as Stritch had reasoned out, was a narrow staircase leading up.

But also there, standing at the bottom step, arms folded, stood a huge black man.

"Nobody allowed back here."

"I must have an audience with your Mistress Hannah. It is most urgent."

John shook his head. There was something hauntingly familiar about this fat man. "Nobody allowed upstairs unless Mistress Hannah gives the word."

"She'll wish to see me. 'Tis about a shipment of liquor. Tell your mistress ..." Stritch frantically groped for a name, any name. "Tell her Ben Fry wishes a word with her. She will see me. By my oath, she will!"

"I'll go ask," John said reluctantly. "You stay here till I return."

John started up the stairs, then paused, the memory coming to him. "You lie! Your name is ..."

He started to turn back, and Amos Stritch brought the heavy stick down atop his head.

John crumpled without a sound and lay still. Stritch glanced quickly around. No alarm was raised. He worked his mouth, spat on the prone figure, and stepped over it. He labored up the steep stairs, wheezing.

When he reached the top, he saw only closed doors. Carefully he cracked the first one enough to peer in. All he saw was a dim candle burning and a child asleep in a crib. He eased the door shut and proceeded down the hall to the next one.

He opened it enough to see that it was a sitting room, dimly lit by one candle. A fire was dying in the hearth. The room was empty, but it had the smell of female, and to his left Stritch saw the dark rectangle of an open door. He knew instinctively that these were Hannah's quarters.

He entered as quietly as he could, closing the door behind him. He had no key with which to lock the door, but there was no help for that. He took a step, lurched, and had to come down hard on the floor with the cane.

At the thumping sound it made, a sleepy voice issued from the dark doorway. "Josh, dear? Is that you? Did you forget something?"

Stritch stood very still, trying to quiet his wheezing breath.

In the bedroom, Hannah, struggling up from sleep, was puzzled. She was sure she'd heard something.

Once again she said, "Josh?"

When there was no answer, she got out of bed and started toward the door, clad only in a nightgown, trying to knuckle the sleep from her eyes.

In the other room she came to an abrupt halt, staring at the stranger in her rooms. "Who are you, sir? What are you doing in my rooms?"

"Don't recognize old Stritch, wench? It ain't been that long. Or maybe your lover left you with addled wits?"

Hannah recoiled with a gasp. "Amos Stritch! Dear God! How did you find me?"

"I came here to see what was luring customers away from my tavern! 'Twas your singing, they said. Not that at all." He sneered, his gaze licking at the outlines of her figure through the thin

456

nightgown. "You're servicing them up here. I saw the seaman slip in and out. You've found your true calling, you damnable bitch! A tavern whore you were, and a tavern whore you are now!"

Hannah didn't bother to answer the accusation. She was over the first shock of seeing Stritch again, and her old hatred of him returned to her full force. "The man who visited my quarters is an old friend, naught else. Now you leave, Amos Stritch, before I have John take your cane to you!"

"Friend, was he? You think I believe that?" Stritch's rage was mounting. "And to think, with me you played the coy maid." Remembrance of the times she had fought and sore wounded him came back to Stritch, and he now knew what he was going to do. When he had ventured up the stairs, his purpose had been dimly formed. But now he knew he was going to cane her within an inch of her life! Never again would she be attractive to any man!

Hannah snapped, "I want you out of my rooms, Amos Stritch! If you do not take your leave at once, I shall call John!"

Stritch gave vent to a sneering laugh. "Who will come to your calling? Your black man lies dead at the bottom of yon stairs. I used this on him!" He raised the thick cane in both hands and took a lurching step toward her.

Hannah backed up. From the mad glitter in his eyes she realized belatedly that she was in mortal peril.

He took another step, and the cane whistled down. Hannah tried to duck aside, and was too late. The cane struck her a cruel blow on the shoulder, and her arm immediately went numb.

Truly frightened now, she darted around him toward the door. As her hands fastened on the knob, Stritch caught her by the hair and jerked her back, throwing her across the room. She skidded and fell to her hands and knees. As she started to get up, the cane descended across her back. Pain blazed through her like a train of fire, and she screamed.

"Scream, you bitch, scream! Little good 'twill do you!" Whap! Again the cane lashed her brutally across the bare shoulders. "You ruined me once, now you're doing it again! When I'm done with you this night, you'll not be able to ruin me ever again!"

This time the cane came down with such force it left a bloody streak across one shoulder. Hannah screamed again.

At the same time, the door crashed open, and André charged in. His eyes flashed fire as he took in the scene.

"It's Amos Stritch, André!" Hannah shouted. "Be careful of him—I think he's gone mad!"

"Ah, the villain Stritch, is it?"

Stritch turned, lashing out with the cane. André danced nimbly aside.

Stritch roared, "Stay out of this! It's between me and her. 'Tis none of your affair!"

"Oh, but it is, you blackguard!"

From the fireplace André snatched up the poker. He advanced on Stritch, the poker held like a sword. "Let us have at it, then!" He jabbed Stritch in the belly with the poker. "*En garde!*"

Stritch flailed away with the cane. Each time André parried with a thrust of the poker, knocking the stick aside and jabbing the end of the poker into Stritch's protruding belly. Spots of blood produced by the sharp end of the poker appeared on Stritch's shirt front like bright red flowers.

Hannah got slowly to her feet, watching in fascination. André had assumed the classic dueling position, one hand resting lightly on his left hip, the other holding the poker. He was graceful, still elegant in the clothes he had worn for their performance, but this was an André different from any she had ever seen. His face wore a look of deadly intent, his eyes mere slits, and she knew intuitively that he was no stranger to the art of dealing death.

He was too much for Amos Stritch. The older man was tiring rapidly, his breath coming in wheezing grunts, and the swipes with the cane were weakening. André was slowly forcing him back against the far wall, constantly dancing in and out, jabbing him in the belly and the chest with the poker.

Now Stritch had lost all room to maneuver. His back was against the room's one window. With a hoarse cry he threw the cane from him. "No more! No more, I pray you! Enough!"

"No, not enough, you wretch!" André shouted. "Now I run you through!"

He drove the point of the poker at Stritch's heart, and had it been a sword he would indeed have run him through. Hannah was sure that in that moment André truly had forgotten that the poker was not a sword.

The jab threw Stritch off balance. He cried out shrilly, arms flailing the air in an attempt to recover his balance. Then he fell, straight back, crashing through the window. André gave a start

459

and made a desperate grab for him. He did get a
hand on one ankle. But Stritch's weight was too
much. André lost his grip, and Stritch fell from
sight, a despairing cry coming from him.

Hannah rushed to the window. Together, they
looked down. There was enough moonlight to
show them Amos Stritch lying still on the ground
below.

"Mon Dieu!" André said in a stricken voice. "It
has happened again. . . ."

"No, André." Hannah took his hand. "You are
not to blame yourself. It was an accident."

"Not so. I ran him through. . . ." André shook
his head dazedly, staring at where the poker had
fallen to the floor, then up at Hannah. He sighed,
and gave a fatalistic shrug. *"Oui,* an accident." He
became brisk. "I should hurry down and learn his
condition." As Hannah started out with him, he
said, "No, you remain here, Hannah."

Her step slowed, and she stopped. Then she
remembered with a gasp. "John! Stritch said he
killed John!"

Hannah hurried along behind André down the
staircase. She gave vent to a sigh of relief when
they reached the bottom and she saw John sitting
up, gingerly feeling the back of his head. Blood
had matted his hair and was running down his
neck. Attracted by the commotion, Merry and
Dickie stood gawking down at him.

As André hurried on out, Hannah said sharply,
"Merry, fetch a basin of water and a washcloth.
Hurry!"

She was gently washing the blood from the gash
on John's head when André came back.

At her glance, he raised and lowered his shoulders, and said soberly, "Amos Stritch is no more. The fall snapped his neck like a twig."

Hannah stood up, squared her shoulders, and said in crisp tones, "Dickie, ride at once into Boston and fetch the sheriff. When he comes, I shall tell him the truth—at least as much of the truth as he need know. The villainous Amos Stritch felled John with a cowardly blow, then crept up the stairs to my rooms and attacked me. I fought him, and in the struggle he fell by accident through the window and was killed."

Chapter Twenty-three

Captain Joshua Hawkes was not to make his sea voyage to Liverpool.

A few days after his last visit with Hannah, she received word that he was ill with the smallpox, and lay near death in the house of a seaman friend near the waterfront of Boston harbor.

"I must go to him at once!" Hannah said to André.

André protested strenuously. "Dear lady, you do so at great peril. I have experienced these damnable pox plagues on the Continent."

"But I owe Josh that much!"

"He did not send for you, did he?"

"He is too proud to ask. Or perhaps he is too ill."

"Then what earthly good would a visit by you do him?"

Hannah paced, thinking hard. Since they were located a good way out of Boston, they had heard only a few rumors of the smallpox in the city. At the time, it had not seemed very serious. But now it appeared that the plague had become virulent and was spreading rapidly. Fearful of Michele's welfare, as well as for the others, Hannah had closed the tavern to all customers until such time as they could reopen safely.

"What is this inoculation for the smallpox I have read about in the Boston *Gazette*? Perhaps if I go to this Dr. Zabdiel Boylston and have it done to me, it will be safe for me to travel the streets of Boston. Do you think so, André?"

"I know only what I have read of it. Experiments have been undertaken in Europe, for some years, I understand, by inoculating healthy people with mild doses of the pox, thereby building up an immunity to the disease. These experiments have been a subject of a raging controversy amongst physicians for some years now."

"Exactly what do they do?"

"The procedure is not too pleasant, madam." André grimaced. "The physician, I understand, opens a vein, and fills the incision with pus taken from a smallpox victim."

"Ugh!" Hannah covered her mouth with her hand. "Sounds dreadful. But does it work?"

André shrugged. "As I say, there is much controversy. The good Dr. Boylston claims that it does work, at least in a certain percentage of cases. I have heard rumors that he has inoculated his own child, so his faith must be strong."

"Then I shall try it." Hannah lifted her chin. "I shall visit Dr. Boylston this very day."

"Very well. If you insist. I know well not to debate with you when your mind is made up. I shall go with you, and drive the coach. We dare not take John or Dickie."

"But you, André, how about you?" she said in some alarm. "Will you not be in danger?"

"No, madam. I had the damned pox years ago. And those who have once suffered through it, and are fortunate enough to survive, are forever after immune."

Hannah studied the smooth skin of his face with surprise. "But I thought . . . ?"

"Why do I not have the pockmarks, then?" He smiled ruefully, running his fingers caressingly over his smooth cheeks. "Again, I was fortunate, as so very few are. For it is true that most of those who live through the pox remain forever after pitted about the face."

Hannah shuddered. "I have seen them. Horrible!"

"Then perhaps you should not venture out?"

"No!" she said stoutly. "I am going to this Dr. Boylston for his inoculation!"

At any other time, Hannah would have thought it humorous, the elegantly attired André Leclaire up on the driver's seat driving the coach into Boston to Dock Square, where Dr. Zabdiel Boylston resided. It was not one of the things André was good at, and she did have to smile at the string of French oaths floating back to her inside the coach. André had little affinity for animals.

But the things she saw on the streets of Boston

were not conducive to laughter. The streets were strangely empty, for one thing, and she noticed that many of the shops were closed up tight. The only activity she saw was a group of Negroes cleaning the streets. Some houses they passed had red flags on their doors. Hannah later learned that this was to warn anyone approaching that the house contained someone infected with the pox. She also learned that guards had been posted outside the infected houses in the beginning to keep everyone away. But the epidemic had spread now to the point where there were not enough guards available.

At Dr. Boylston's house. André went in with her. Dr. Boylston looked terribly drawn and weary, so weary that he stumbled as he came forward to greet them.

"I have been working as much as twenty hours a day, treating the afflicted and trying to convince the selectmen that they should immediately inoculate those still of good health," he told them.

The doctor led them into his small office off the foyer. It was the first time Hannah had ever been inside a physician's office, and she was frightened by the strange instruments she saw. As her eyes became accustomed to the dimness, she saw a skeleton dangling in one corner. She recoiled with a gasp, clutching André's hand.

André smiled. "That one is far beyond harming you, dear lady."

Dr. Boylston eyed her keenly. "Are you convinced you wish to go through with this, Mistress, us . . . ?"

"Hannah Verner." Hannah was past the point of hiding her name. "Does it prevent the pox?"

"In my opinion, it does. In some cases. Not a majority, I am afraid. It is far from perfected." He sighed. "And if you were to consult my medical colleagues here in Boston, they would one and all assure you that I am a madman."

"It is my understanding that you inoculated your own child?"

"That is true, madam."

"Then I must show no less faith than you, Dr. Boylston," Hannah said steadily.

As Dr. Boylston prepared her for the inoculation, he kept up a steady conversation—to take her mind off what he was doing, Hannah was sure.

"The plague was brought aboard His Majesty's ship *Seahorse* back in April. A seaman came down with the pox and was unfortunately allowed ashore. That was the beginning. Boston has suffered through these plagues before, in 1689 and 1690, again in 1702. Those who survived the illness then possess immunity—that is perhaps half of Boston's present population. But no child born these nineteen years past is immune. And those same nineteen years of freedom from the pox mean that a large portion of the adult population is totally unfamiliar with what few precautions and safeguards they should take. They were unready, ill-prepared for this, and must learn anew. Unfortunately, most Boston people are still Puritans at heart, and they believe the pestilence is a punishment from God, visited on them for their sins, past and present. And therefore . . ." Dr. Boylston smiled grimly. "They believe me some kind of devil's consort for offering to inflict on them even a mild form of the disease. . . ."

Hannah turned her head away, closing her eyes to what he was doing.

"So there is much opposition to me and those few who believe in my inoculations," Dr. Boylston continued, "opposition from clergymen and selectmen alike. Each time we have brought the matter up before the selectmen, they have rebuffed us. Feeling is running high. Why, even my neighbor, Cotton Mather, had an explosive device tossed through his window. Fortunately, no one was injured."

"Cotton Mather, the infamous witch hunter?" André asked in astonishment.

Dr. Boylston laughed. "Yes, Friend Mather is an overly pious man, perhaps even fanatical. Strange, is it not? I thought Friend Mather mad when he conducted the hunt for witches. But in this matter he is strongly on my side.

"I am finished, madam." Dr. Boylston stepped back. "I would advise you to proceed straight home and get abed. You will suffer some mild symptoms—fever, aching, perhaps prostration—for several days. But do not be alarmed. If the inoculation is successful, you should recover ere long and be immune thereafter." He turned to André. "And you, sir, do you possess the courage of Madam Verner?"

André smiled tightly. "I have suffered through the pox, Dr. Boylston."

"Ah, one of the fortunate ones!"

"Dr. Boylston," Hannah said, "I have a daughter, two years old. . . ."

Dr. Boylston frowned. "Do not go near her until you are up from bed and around again. Do you have someone to care for her?"

"Oh, yes. Bess does that for me."

468

"Then do not come in contact with this Bess either."

As the doctor ushered them out, André asked, "Would you hazard an estimate as to how long this damned plague will linger?"

"It will probably remain with us for some time—mayhap the rest of the year." Dr. Boylston's face was shadowed with melancholy. "And many—a great many, I fear—will perish."

(Dr. Boylston's prediction was to prove remarkably accurate. The smallpox lasted well into the year 1722, the months of February and March being the first free of death since it had struck. All together, over six thousand people were infected, and the deaths were estimated at one in six.)

Outside the doctor's house, as Hannah was helped into the coach by André, she said, "Now drive me to the house where Josh lies ill."

"But dear lady," André said in disapproval, "the doctor said you were to return home at once and go to bed!"

"*After* I have seen Josh. If I wait overlong, he may be dead and buried before I have a chance to see him."

"But the man has the pox, Hannah! This recent inoculation will not save you. . . ." He sighed, staring into her set features. "You, Hannah Verner, are the most stubborn, most exasperating female it has ever been my misfortune to encounter!"

"If you will not drive me, I will handle the coach myself."

"Oh, hell and damnation!"

Muttering under his breath, he climbed up onto the seat and shouted imprecations at the horses.

At the house near the harbor where Joshua Hawkes lay ill, Hannah found the same red flag flying. Sulking, André refused to accompany her inside.

"If you intend to play the fool, I'll have no hand in it!"

At her knock the door was inched open, and through the crack she glimpsed a pale, gray-bearded face.

"This is a house of pestilence, madam," said the man barring her way. "No visitors are welcome."

"Is Joshua Hawkes here?"

"He is, and sorely ill."

"I demand to see him, sir!"

"Madam . . ."

In a sudden burst of anger, Hannah slammed her foot against the door. It flew open, the man staggering back, and Hannah swept in.

"Where is he?" she demanded. "Where is Josh?"

The gray-bearded man shrugged resignedly and indicated a closed door down the hall. Hannah strode to the door and opened it to a dim room; only a candle stub was burning. An odor assailed her nostrils—the cloying, sweet odor of decay and death.

She took a tentative step inside. She could make out one bed against the far wall. "Josh? It's Hannah."

There was a stirring sound from the bed, followed by a groan. Hannah ventured a few steps closer.

Then the figure on the bed turned, and Hannah gasped with horror. Josh's eyes burned like fire with fever. But his face . . . dear God, his face! His beard had been shaved off, and his face was cov-

470

ered with what she thought at first were freckles. But as her vision grew more accustomed to the dimness, she saw that the freckles were tiny blisters—pus-filled blisters.

His feverish gaze cleared a little, and he moaned in anguish. "Hannah! Lord in Heaven, what are you doing here? Don't look, don't look at me!" He turned his face away. "Go, lass. Leave now, before it's too late!"

Hannah stood frozen, her mind recoiling at what she had seen.

His voice rose, harsh now in anger. "Go, damn you! I'm pox-infected, and I'm dying! Don't come nearer to me. I don't want you to look upon me. I don't want you here, you understand?"

Then the spell gripping her broke, and she fled in fear and horror. Eyes filling with tears, she stumbled out of the house and to the coach.

André straightened up from where he leaned against the coach. He caught her in his arms. "What is it, Hannah?"

"Oh, André! His face, dear Josh's face! It's horrible!"

"I need not say I warned you." He helped her into the coach, and headed it out of Boston.

Hannah wept most of the way back to the inn. But her tears had dried by the time they reached it, and she was consumed by guilt. She should have remained with Josh, nursed him, taken care of him. She owed him that.

At the inn André took her upstairs at once and gave her a glass of brandy. Hannah drank some of it, then told him of her guilt about Josh.

"No, no!" André shook his head. "It would have been a foolish and dangerous thing for you to do.

471

And 'twould have accomplished naught. He is, I'm sure, receiving the best of care. He is with friends. And he did not want you there. He told you that!"

Hannah was silent. She was exhausted and sick at heart. André paced restlessly, hands behind his back. Finally he stopped before her. He said firmly, "I think you should take Michele, and Bess of course, and leave this damned place until the plague is over. I understand many people from Boston are fleeing. So should you."

"But I have nowhere to go." Hannah made a helpless gesture.

He studied her for a moment. "You could return to Malvern."

"No!" She sat up, shaking her head violently. "I could not go there. I wouldn't be welcome!"

"Why not?" he said challengingly. "Hannah, it is past time you talked of what drove you to leave Malvern."

She thought for a moment, then shrugged. "All right. It is your due. You are entitled to know.

So Hannah told him all of it.

He listened closely, interrupting her once, when she told of finding Isaiah murdered. *"Mon Dieu,* Hannah! You fled because of that? Foolish girl!"

"No, not *only* because of that. That was only an additional . . . fear. Wait until I've finished."

When she was finally done, André stared at her thoughtfully for a long moment, took a turn around the room, and came back to her. "This black blood in you, and Michele, that you are so fearful of . . . from what you have told me of your father, I wonder that you've never thought he might have been descended from a king in Africa.

472

Many slaves brought over are, you know. You might have royal blood in your veins, dear lady!"

"What does that matter?" she said. "Anyway, it's not what *I* think, but what . . . others might think."

"You mean young Verner, I presume?"

"Yes! Michael!"

"In this letter you penned to him, did you make mention of this, of Michele?"

"No, but I'm sure he knows all by now. My stepfather has told him, you may be sure!"

"Did you ever think that you are doing young Verner an injustice, making assumptions about how he will take the news?"

"You have been in the South long enough, André." She leaned forward. "How do *you* think the gentry in Virginia . . . how do you think the son of a planter who has owned slaves would feel about learning that a daughter of his is part Black— even a small part?"

"Yes, I suppose so. Still, you could have waited, told him of it face to face."

"I couldn't bring myself to do that." She shuddered. "I could only think of the loathing on his face when he learned!"

André sighed, then motioned in anger. "In France, we think little of such things, but in this country . . . "*Mon Dieu!* I suppose it will be many years before they become civilized enough to . . ."

He broke off. "Then you will not consider returning to Malvern?"

"Never!"

"Nor somewhere else, out of harm's way, until this plague is past?"

"Where? And for how long? You heard Dr. Boylston. The plague could linger for months. No, I shall remain here."

A few days later André came to Hannah with the news that Joshua Hawkes was dead of the pox.

But by that time Hannah was abed herself, afire with fever, her body aching all over, slipping in and out of delirium, and she had little heart to grieve for Josh.

André was the only one allowed in her rooms, except for one brief visit by Dr. Boylston. André fed her—mostly broth and other liquids—changed her bed linen daily, and seemed to always be there with a soothing word and a wet cloth with which to sponge her fevered face and body.

In her nightmares, born of the fever, Hannah dreamed that her face was being turned into a horror by the pus blisters she had glimpsed on Josh's face, and every time she was clear-headed for a few minutes she demanded of André a mirror in which to examine her face. André indulged her vanity. Each time she examined her face, she could find no pustules or pockmarks, only a complexion made rosy by the fever.

Dr. Boylston's visit was during the last days of her confinement, and she was rational enough to hear his pronouncement: "Madam Verner will be up and about within a few days, André. Her symptoms were mild. I must compliment you on your nursing, sir."

Hannah, who had been feigning sleep in the hope she might overhear bad news if such the doctor had to impart, sat up when the door closed behind him.

The good news had buoyed her considerably. "Nurse," she said weakly. "Water, please."

474

"A nurse now," André said grumpily, approaching her bed. "Many things I have been named, but never nurse!"

Hannah could contain her laughter no longer.

"You damned witch!" He stood over her, with a mock scowl. "You heard every word!"

"I did, and I'm going to be fine!" She caught his hand. "Dear, dear André, thank you. Whatever would I do without you?"

"That, of course, is the question. Poorly, I suspect. Very poorly indeed."

He went to fetch her a glass of water.

Dr. Boylston's prediction was proven true. Two days later, Hannah was up and about. She was weak and a bit wobbly in the limbs, but the fever was gone, and she was starving. She had lost several pounds during the days she had been abed.

"Tell Bess to send me up some solid food before I waste away." And then, for the first time in days, she thought of someone other than herself. "How *is* Bess? And Michele, and the others?"

"They are all splendid, madam. Except for the good doctor, I haven't opened the door to a soul. So how could the pox get in here, unless it be carried by a spirit?"

"I was thinking ... since Dr. Boylston's inoculation worked with me ..."

"*Seemed* to work, dear Hannah. Even the good doctor is not all that positive."

"It worked with me," she continued steadily. "Should not the others also be inoculated?"

André sighed heavily. "Since I had anticipated this from you, I have talked with them. John and Bess absolutely refuse. And Dickie ... well, the idea

475

holds little appeal for him. . . ." He started. "Madam, you are not thinking of Michele?"

"I am. It worked with me, and Dr. Boylston inoculated his own child. Michele is of my blood. I am confident it will achieve the same result with her."

"I wish I were as confident."

"Take the coach into Boston and fetch Dr. Boylston. Tell him what I have in mind."

Reluctantly, André did her bidding.

On his arrival, Dr. Boylston was much gaunter, and his stooped figure seemed to have aged years.

"Madam, I will inoculate your daughter if you desire. But I must again warn you that it only achieves results in some cases."

"I wish you to go ahead."

Later, Hannah and André served Dr. Boylston a glass of brandy and a meal in the deserted dining room. The brandy and the food brought some color to his gray cheeks.

Finished, he leaned back with a sigh. "I believe that is the first time in weeks that I have sat down and eaten a full meal."

"You look overworked, Dr. Boylston," Hannah said.

"I am, madam. But there is no help for it. All the physicians in Boston are overworked, but the sick and dying need our poor services. We suffer most from lack of nurses. Most able-bodied women have fled the city, and those still here not yet afflicted with the pox are fearful of venturing out of their homes. The few women who are immune and willing to help are pitifully few. All too few."

"What exactly does this nursing consist of? Does a person need some training in medicine?"

"No, no, not at all." Dr. Boylston shook his head. "The only things that can be done for those afflicted are to keep them clean—bathe them once or twice a day—feed them a quantity of liquids, and see that their bed linen is burned regularly."

"Why, I am capable of doing those chores!"

"Dear lady!" André said in quick dismay. "Surely you're not thinking of doing such?"

"Why not?" she said defiantly. "Dr. Boylston is in sore need. I owe him a debt of gratitude for what he has done for me and mine."

"Madam, your assistance would be deeply appreciated," the doctor said fervently. "And you will earn *my* undying gratitude."

"It's settled, then. The moment Michele is sufficiently recovered from your inoculation, I will come to you."

A week later, Hannah was a familiar figure on the streets of Boston. She had learned to handle the coach and horses herself, leaving André to see after those at the tavern. Michele had come through the inoculation splendidly.

A room was prepared for Hannah downstairs at *The Four Alls,* and she remained completely isolated from all but André. At the end of each day's nursing, she removed her nursing garments at Dr. Boylston's house, took a very hot bath, and then changed into uncontaminated clothing before returning to the inn.

Hannah was depressed by what she saw on the streets of Boston. The number of red-flagged houses increased daily. Families were decimated by the pox. The streets were empty except for groups of mourners on their way to meeting houses to hold services for the recently dead. Almost all the shops were closed now, and business was at a standstill. Often, on her way home at night, Hannah met the "dead cart" rumbling over the cobbled streets. Sometimes it was piled high with bodies, like sticks of firewood.

Aside from the fact that her own efforts at nursing seemed to be of little avail, the thing that depressed Hannah the most was the tolling of the funeral bells. All day long they tolled; each and every time a new death was announced.

When Hannah returned to The Four Alls, often as late as midnight, to sink into an exhausted slumber, the bells would toll their dirge in her dreams, and she would awaken with a stricken cry.

Boston had truly become, as Dr. Boylston quoted to Hannah from the writings of Cotton Mather, "A dismal Picture and Emblem of Hell; Fire and Darkness filling of it, and a lying spirit reigning there...."

It was well into the month of July now; the plague was raging, at its height. It was a very hot July, and the houses Hannah went into, shuttered and closed tightly, were like ovens. She drove herself relentlessly, bathing the smallpox victims, burning everything they came into contact with, and feeding them broth. And time and again, she watched them die before her very eyes. When one did manage to survive, it struck her as a miracle.

She left the inn in early morning and labored all the day long, usually until long after dark. And except from Dr. Boylston, and those close to the few survivors, she received little thanks. Somehow it had become known that she had been inoculated by Dr. Boylston, and the other Boston physicians would not let her near their patients. But this was of little consequence, since Hannah had all the work she could handle anyway.

She lost weight, she had difficulty sleeping, and she came back to the inn many nights, after a death, weeping.

André threw up his hands and said in despair, "Why do you continue with this, madam? *Why?*"

It was a question Hannah had asked herself many times, and she was unsure of the answer. She finally concluded that it was a combination of gratitude for Dr. Boylston's inoculations and guilt over the fact that she had fled from Josh in horror while he was dying. She told André none of this, although she imagined he was shrewd enough to divine her reasons; he knew her well enough by now.

The inoculation controversy was truly heated now that the plague had Boston in its grip. Time after time, Dr. Boylston and Cotton Mather went before the selectmen pleading to be given authority for a city-wide program of inoculations. Despite the fact that Dr. Boylston could now point to over a dozen people saved from the pox by his inoculations, the opposition from clergymen and other physicians in Boston was too violent, and the selectmen refused to act. And now vicious rumors were abroad that Dr. Boylston's inoculations were responsible for the plague's continuing and growing worse.

Hannah, with her usual partisanship for those she liked, began talking to anyone who would listen about the merits of Dr. Boylston's inoculations. A few listened with some sympathy, and others in grim silence. But in most cases she encountered open hostility. Undaunted, she continued to praise

Dr. Boylston and his inoculations, urging people to take advantage of the opportunity available to them.

A week later her efforts bore fruit, but not in the manner she had expected.

Her day's nursing finished a little earlier than usual one afternoon, she had taken her bath and changed into her going-home clothes. In the hall she met Dr. Boylston, and he invited her into his office for a cup of tea.

Dr. Boylston was concerned about her. "Madam, you look drawn and exhausted. You have lost much weight. Mayhap you have been doing too much. My advice is to take a few days' bed rest. 'Twould be good for you."

"With people dying every day? You don't take even so much as an hour off—I am astonished you find this much time to spend with me. No, I am young and strong. I will not slacken my efforts in behalf of your good work!"

The doctor smiled, shaking his head. "Your André informed me that you were a stubborn wench. Very well, Madam Verner." He got to his feet. "At least, I insist you go home now. Come, I'll escort you to your coach."

Outside the house, they found a crowd gathered. At their appearance a murmur swept through the gathering, and then an ominous, sullen silence fell.

"I like this not at all," Dr. Boylston murmured in her ear. "Perhaps you should remain here for the night. I can send a message to the inn."

"No!" Her head held high, Hannah extended her arm to him. "I will not show them fear!"

Dr. Boylston hesitated momentarily, then

shrugged and took her arm. They started toward the coach a few feet away.

Shouts came from the crowd:

"There they are! The devil and his witch!"

"The devil and his handmaiden!"

"'Tis they bringing the pox down on us!"

"Devil! Witch!"

"Should put them to the stake!"

"The irony of it," Dr. Boylston muttered. "Friend Mather should be here."

Suddenly, out of the crowd, came a rain of rotten fruit and vegetables, pelting them with stench and splatters of filth.

Dr. Boylston urged Hannah into a run. Striking out at their tormentors with one arm, his other around her shoulders, he forced a way through to the coach. He opened the door. "Inside, madam! I will drive!"

Hannah ducked inside; the doctor slammed the door and climbed up on the driver's seat. He took the whip from its holder and flailed about him with it. The crowd edged back. He shouted at the horses. The coach began to move, and soon they were rattling over the cobblestones at a reckless speed.

Inside the coach, Hannah wiped ineffectually at the splatters of rotten fruit on herself. Then reaction set in, and she gave way to tears. It seemed she cried so easily nowadays.

André hurried out to meet them at the inn. Hannah ran past him and toward the side door of her temporary room.

Dr. Boylston called after her, "You remain here for several days, until their venom is spilled. I *command* you to remain here, madam!"

481

Dr. Boylston's command to Hannah was unnecessary.

The next morning she awoke to chills and fever and an aching body. Delirium seized her again, conjuring up demons.

Her nightmares were peopled with the dead and the dying, the sounds of bells tolling, and Josh's shaven, blistered head severed from his body, mouth open in soundless accusation. And then Michael's face was there, lips forming scathing words: "Whore, black whore!"

In the nightmare she lay spread-eagled on the four-poster bed in Amos Stritch's room in the Cup and Horn, arms and legs tethered to the corner posts, and Stritch's heavy body was falling toward her, revolving slowly, mouth open, shouting, "Murderess! Murderess!"

And his falling weight descended on her, crushing her, smothering her.

Crying out, Hannah sat up in bed, clutching at an arm. In a moment of clarity she saw that the arm belonged to André.

Squeezing it, she whispered, "I'm going to die, aren't I? Dr. Boylston was wrong. I have the pox!"

"Hush, dear Hannah, hush," André said gently. He passed a cool, wet cloth over her fevered forehead. "Rest. Sleep and rest is what you need."

No longer caring, Hannah sank back, welcoming sleep, as though it were death coming to claim her.

For days she lay thrashing and moaning on the bed, André in attendance. She drifted in and out of delirium. At some time during that period of delirium she was moved upstairs to her bedroom.

Once, during a clear period, she saw Bess in the room with her, changing her nightgown.

"Bess," she said, "you shouldn't be here! You'll catch the pox from me!"

"Hush, honey. Yo' have to save yo' strength."

"But you . . ." She subsided and let Bess finish. Then, as the woman started out of the room, she raised her head to ask, "Michele . . . is she all right?"

"That child just fine, honey. Yo' hurry and get well so's she can see her momma again."

In another dream Hannah saw Michael in the room, standing over her, his face both sad and solemn. Strangely enough, she saw no censure on his face this time.

Twice, she dimly realized that Dr. Boylston was with her. He gave her a spoonful of vile-tasting liquid. Angry at him for having lied to her, she spat it out. And then André was holding her in firm hands, her mouth forced open, and she had to swallow the foul-tasting medicine.

Then one day she awoke clear-headed. She was weak, so weak she could scarcely move. She looked down at herself and saw that she had wasted away during the bout of illness. She started to feel her face, then let her hand fall away, dreading what she might discover. Listlessly, she turned her head toward the window. Sunlight streamed into the room.

She heard the door open. Too weak to raise her head, she lay without moving.

In a moment André loomed over her. "Hannah?"

"What is it, André?"

A smile of delight blossomed on his face. "Ah, thank the gods!" He placed a hand on her forehead. "It's cool. Your fever has broken. You have been quite ill, dear lady, but the doctor said that

483

when your fever broke, your recovery would be swift."

With some spirit she said, "How can I trust his word? All of Boston was right about him!"

"Now that's more like the Hannah I know," he said cheerfully. "But you shouldn't say such about the good doctor. He has been here on numerous occasions, hovering over you like a hen over her chick! Without him, you might well have left us."

He stood back, chin resting on one hand, a secretive smile on his face. "It strikes me you are well enough to receive a visitor."

"I have no wish to receive visitors."

"Ah, but this one you will want to see, I wager!"

She looked at him with little interest. "Why this particular one?"

"Because it is young Verner, my dear! Michael Verner is waiting to see you!"

Chapter Twenty-four

"Michael!" Hannah lifted her head. "Michael is *here?*"

"He is indeed. And chafing at the bit. He paces the hall outside, and has for days now."

"Then it was not a dream," she said softly.

André shook his head. "No, dear lady. It was no dream. He was in once to look at you."

Suddenly agitated, Hannah said, "Fetch me a mirror, André. At once!"

Sighing, André went into the other room and returned with a hand mirror. Hannah snatched it from him and, holding her breath, she looked at her face. She was very pale, her face thinned, yet there were no pockmarks. In wonder she ran her fingers over her cheeks, uttering a small cry of delight at their smoothness.

"Dear Hannah." André shrugged elaborately. "I tried to assure you that you did not have the pox. Dr. Boylston said you suffered from exhaustion, perhaps a touch of influenza, and even a small recurrence of the effects of your inoculation. But it has now all run its course."

A sudden thought struck her. She lowered the mirror to her lap and looked at André. "How did Michael find me? How did he know I was here?"

"I penned him a letter, telling him of your whereabouts, nigh two months back, the very day you told me the circumstances of your flight from Malvern. He left immediately on the receipt of my letter, sailing up the coast on the first ship available. He has been here three days now."

She stared at him thoughtfully. "You took a great deal upon yourself to do this without my consent!"

"Should I have awaited your consent, it would never have happened, dear lady."

Hannah was silent, knowing what he said was true. She lowered her gaze to the mirror. There was still one important question to be asked and answered.

"Does he know . . . ? Did he ask . . . ?" She stopped herself. André was not the one to ask.

André was observing her amusedly, chin propped on his hand again. "Young Verner has asked naught of me, my dear Hannah. He has seemed mostly concerned by . . ." It was his turn to stop short. He started to turn away. "I will allow him in, and the two of you may decide who is to ask and who is to answer questions."

"No, André!" she said in a panic. "Please! Not yet! I cannot have him see me like this. Help me, please! I must at least look once more like a living person, not like someone freshly risen from the grave, or Michael will take one look and hurry back to Malvern posthaste!"

He laughed aloud. "Ah, the vanity of women! Very well, we shall see what we can accomplish."

André helped her wash and put on a clean nightgown. Then he powdered her face and touched her lips with faint color. Lastly, he brushed her hair. During her illness, it had lost much of its natural luster, but at least André was able to brush out all the tangles.

He stood back, hand on hip, and looked at her. He nodded. "Yes, that will be perfect."

He went to the large chest and took out a soft green silk shawl that Josh had given her upon returning from one of his trips. The green silk brought out the color of her hair, and gave brilliance to her eyes and the pale translucence of her skin, André thought.

Studying her with his head to one side, he smiled impishly. "I have done all within my power. Sometimes, even someone as talented as André can only do so much."

"Go! Send Michael to me!"

"Yes, milady." He made a mocking knee, and left the room.

But now that the moment was at hand, Hannah, sitting propped up in the bed with a wildly beating heart, found that she could scarcely breathe.

Then the door opened, and Michael stood there. For a long moment, neither spoke. Michael seemed older than Hannah remembered him, and his face was very grave.

He advanced toward the bed, dark eyes searching hers. "Hannah, my dearest Hannah! I feared that I would never set eyes on you again!"

"And I ..." Her breath caught. "I feared you would not wish to see me, sir."

.."Foolish, foolish woman!" He shook his head. "I love you, dear heart."

Tears came to her eyes, and she held out her arms. "Ah, Michael! And I love you!"

He sat on the side of the bed and took her into his arms. Cradling her face against his chest, he stroked her hair, murmuring words of endearment.

Finally she sat back, tears drying. "There are things I must tell you before ..."

"Hush, dearest." Gently, he placed his palm over her mouth. "There is nothing you must tell me. I know all."

"All?" Eyes huge, she stared at him. "You know about my father?"

"Yes. Silas Quint told me all. ..."

He told her then of the theft of the strongbox, and of his finding it in Quint's hovel. "'Twas then he told me of your father." He laughed curtly. "The wretch seemed to think that his news would force me to keep quiet about his theft. He even admitted to me that he killed the slave, Isaiah."

"But will he not tell others about me?" Hannah held her breath.

"Silas Quint will tell no one anything, dearest. He is dead. Your stepfather is dead, Hannah."

"What happened?"

"I had him put in gaol for his thievery and the murder of the slave. It seems that Quint himself was such a slave to drink that being deprived of it threw him into delirium. Four days after he was placed in gaol, the gaolkeeper found him hanging by the neck from his own belt."

Hannah thought, briefly, of Amos Stritch, and his way of dying. It would seem that just ends had come to both men, and in much the same manner.

She looked at Michael again, her breath bated. "You know that my father was of mixed blood, yet you still have love for me, and come to me?"

"That knowledge did not affect my love for you, Hannah. I loved you before I knew, and I love you still. Many a night these two years past I have lain awake all night at Malvern, aching for your embrace."

"And Michele . . . you know about Michele?"

"I do indeed!" His face lit up. "A beautiful child." A note of pride crept into his voice. "I think she much resembles her father."

"Oh, you do, do you?" Hannah had to laugh.

As though this were a signal, the door opened, and Bess came in, carrying Michele in her arms.

Michael started to his feet and crossed toward them.

"Michael!"

He stopped, looking back in question.

"The pox, were you exposed to it? Did you come through Boston?"

He shook his head. "No. Forewarned by André's letter. I disembarked at New York and purchased a horse to make the rest of my journey. Your inn is the nearest I have been to the afflicted city."

Hannah breathed a sigh of relief, and smiled as Michael took the child from Bess's arms. He held her as gingerly as he would an egg, a look of great tenderness on his features as he gazed down at his daughter.

"She a powerful strong child, Master Michael." Bess's laughter rumbled. "Have no fear of breaking her."

Michael returned her to Bess's arms. "Having a daughter will take some growing accustomed to. You had better handle her, Bess."

Bess brought Michele to Hannah, who kissed the girl and tickled her under the chin. Michele laughed happily.

"Now honey," Bess said sternly. "I be going down to the kitchen and whip up some victuals. We have to fatten you up some, don't we, Master Michael?"

"Indeed we do, Bess."

As Bess left the room, Hannah said, "I wanted a son for you, Michael. I'm sorry."

"We have much time before us, dear heart. A son you'll bear me in time, I am sure."

Hannah simply stared at him.

Again he sat on the bed beside her. "Why else do you think I am here? To take you back to Malvern as my bride. We shall leave soon as your health permits. We will be wed while passing through Maryland. There, it can be done quickly. Back in Virginia, it would take much time—a posting of banns and such. This way, we arrive at Malvern as man and wife." He arched an eyebrow. "Unless you wish a wedding ball and the like."

"And shock the whole colony of Virginia?" Hannah laughed. "You taking to wife a wench who bore your child two years past? No, what you suggest fits my wishes well."

He nodded in satisfaction. "So shall it be, then."

"Oh, Michael!" She wrapped her arms around

490

him. "I never dreamed I would experience such happiness!"

The Four Alls was a place of joy during the days that followed.

Hannah's strength slowly returned. She gained weight. Bess plied her with so much food that Hannah had to fend her off. When finally she could venture downstairs and outside, Hannah took much delight in sitting in the shade of the big tree behind the inn and watching Michael romp with Michele.

Dr. Boylston paid one more visit, and pronounced her fit. Having already been apprised of the situation by André, he said, "You have my gratitude, madam, for your efforts in my behalf, and my best wishes for your future happiness. Fortunately for us all, the plague seems to have reached its zenith. It undoubtedly will linger with us for some time yet, but I have a feeling that the worst has passed."

The following day Hannah gathered everyone in the dining room. Except for the presence of Michael, she thought, it was much like that midnight meeting at Malvern.

She said, "Within a few days, Michael and I ..." She squeezed Michael's hand. "We are departing New England for good and returning to Malvern."

"Praise the Lawd for that!" Bess muttered.

"I have gathered you all here to learn if you wish to return with us or remain here. Bess, I gather from your remark that you would prefer to return to Virginia?"

"Lawd, yes, honey! I have my fill of the winters here. The coldness here gets into my bones!"

491

"John?"

"I will return to Malvern, Mistress Hannah." John's solemn face cracked in a rare smile. "You will need a driver for the coach. Both horses and coach have seen hard usage of late, and will need a proper hand at the reins."

"Thank you, Bess ... John. I promised both of you your freedom if you came with me. It is yours now, if you wish. Michael, is that all right with you?" Looking at Michael, she received a nod. "So when we reach Malvern, you may go your own ways, if you like."

"Malvern is my home," John said simply.

"Honey, what an old woman like me do out in the world on her own?" Bess said. The rumble of her laughter sounded. "'Sides, som'un have to see to that child. Strikes me yo' ain't gon' be spending much time at doing that for a spell, once we'uns get back to Malvern."

Hannah, feeling a blush stain her cheeks, refused to look at Michael. Instead she glanced at André. "André?"

He looked thoughtful. "What are your intentions as to The Four Alls?"

"I haven't quite yet decided." She watched him closely. "Have you any suggestions?"

He smiled, and made a mock bow. "I thought that perhaps your humble servant might stay and operate it, with your permission, madam." He looked slightly embarrassed. "I know, dear lady, you will think it strange of me, but I have taken to innkeeping. Especially the entertainment part. I am sure I could find another lady of mystery to take your place. Or ..." That wicked smile flashed. "Failing that, I could always pen another playlet."

"Not as wicked as the first, I hope!"

492

He gave that Gallic shrug. "Methinks Boston will be too concerned with recovering from the plague to bother overmuch with bawdiness in the outskirts."

Hannah said, "And you, Dickie ... what are your wishes?"

"I, too, take to tavern life, m'lady," Dickie said shyly. "I am more content here than on a plantation. I hope you will not think ill of me for that."

"Not at all. It's your choice. You are your own man now. You have served out your term of indenture."

Since Hannah now knew how robustly Dickie tumbled Merry, she had little fear that he might fall under André's influence. She said, "I will make a bargain, then, André. The tavern is already in your name. If you will agree to accepting Dickie as partner, I will give The Four Alls to both of you as a gift."

"I would be most happy to accept Dickie as my partner. I have little liking for the more practical side of innkeeping. But you are far too generous, dear lady," he protested. "I am overwhelmed!"

Hannah went to him, kissed his cheek, and took his hand in hers. "You have not only been a true friend, André, but much, much more. Without you, I probably would not have survived. Perhaps we all would not have survived. It is settled, then. The inn now belongs to you and Dickie."

André turned away. Hannah could have sworn there were tears in his eyes. It was one of the few times she had seen André Leclaire at a loss for words.

She then took Michael's hand and led him upstairs to her rooms. "I hope you don't think I was too forward, taking it upon myself to settle matters about the tavern without seeking your counsel."

"My dear, it is entirely your affair. I know nothing of taverns. I think you did wonderfully well, and are most kind and generous. As well as most beautiful."

He took her into his arms and kissed her. It was the first ardent kiss that had passed between them since their reunion.

A sleeping hunger awoke in Hannah, and she returned the kiss passionately. She felt his manhood beginning to grow against her.

"Ah, Michael! My darling!"

It was he who broke the kiss and stepped back. "No, now is not the time!"

Somewhat dazedly she said, "If you are concerned about my health, you need not be. I am fine now."

"It is not that, dearest. We shall not be together in love until we are man and wife. There will be no more bastards in the Verner family." His lazy grin took the sting from his words. "I want my son, if I should be so blessed, to be legal in every sense."

A week later they were ready to leave for Virginia. The coach was loaded, Bess and Michele inside, and John on the driver's seat.

Michael took Dickie's hand, then André's. He said warmly, "You have my gratitude, sir, for seeing to Hannah's welfare."

"It was my pleasure, young Verner." André aimed his wicked grin at her. "She at times can be a most exasperating wench, but at other times most delightful in her mischief."

Hannah kissed Dickie good-bye with tears in her

eyes, and then kissed André full on the mouth. "Dear André! How I will miss you! I wish you all the best."

"And I you, dear lady. May the gods be kind to you in all things."

"Someday I may learn that André Leclaire is a famous playwright . . . if you do not instead end up in gaol."

"Ah, well." He sighed. "As the great Bard said, 'The play's the thing.'" He raised her hand to his lips, then looked into her eyes with sadness. He said softly, "*Au revoir*, dear lady."

Hannah did not look back as the coach sped away. Except for the two dear friends from whom she was departing, there was nothing left behind she would grieve for.

Michael and Hannah became man and wife late one afternoon in a small hamlet in Maryland.

The clergyman, a middle-aged man with the look of a startled horse, looked even more startled when he discovered that the only witnesses were to be two black people, one carrying a white child.

Hannah hid a smile behind her hand when the clergyman was informed that the man and woman he was marrying both had the last name of Verner. The poor man would probably never recover from the shock!

But he gamely ploughed ahead with the ceremony, and Michael finally turned to her to claim the bridal kiss. In that moment, Hannah felt that she had everything she had ever wished for.

The hamlet had only one inn, and that had only one room they could have all to their own for the night. It was a tiny, dark room, and smelled of mouldering linens, and was none too clean.

"My apologies, madam. 'Tis indeed a poor bed-chamber for your wedding night."

"It will serve, dear Michael. To me, it is as splendid as the bridal chamber of a princess!"

Laughing, Michael caught her in his arms. "It strikes me you were of a different nature last time we shared a bedchamber."

"And you too, sir!"

She kissed him, and their laughter quickly turned to passion. He squeezed her in such an excess of ardor that her breasts began to ache, both from want and the pressure of his chest muscles.

She arched her head back to stare up into his eyes. She said saucily, "Would this not be better between the sheets?"

"It would, dearest."

They undressed hurriedly. Hannah was finished first, and she lay looking at his fine body. The years had added no fat to it. If anything, he was slimmer, more muscular than ever.

It was a warm night. Hannah kicked back the quilt and held the sheet up for Michael to slide under. He turned to her, one muscular thigh across hers. Tenderly his lips touched her breasts, until the nipples rose like thimbles. And his hands roamed over her body, teasing, exploring, caressing, until she tossed in a fever of need and passion.

"Michael! Ah, Michael!"

He rose to take her, and Hannah welcomed him with an openness and ardor that took his breath away. She arched high with a cry as he thrust into her.

496

Hannah felt consumed by the fierce passion raging through her. This was a combination of love and pleasure that carried her to a height of pure ecstasy she knew she had never experienced with anyone else, and never would.

At the peak of sensation she rose and clung to him, arms locked around his back. She shuddered, moaning, and then fell away.

But as Michael started to move from her, she tightened her grip, murmuring, "No, darling. Stay."

After a time he moved again, and she let him go, but only to stretch out beside her. She immediately rolled toward him, an arm and a leg thrown across his body.

"Darling Hannah ... I must confess to curiosity about something. But if you wish not to speak of it, I will not press you."

"Anything, dearest," she murmured drowsily. "Never again will there be secrets between us."

"When you ..." He cleared his throat. "When you, well, learned of the heritage passed down by your father, what were your feelings?"

"My feelings?" Her mind came fully awake. She lay for a moment without speaking. "My first thoughts were of you and what *you* might think." She rose on one elbow and looked down at him. "One thing you must understand ... I never felt ashamed of my father! And I never will. He was a wonderful man, and I loved him with all my heart. I've done much thinking on the subject, and have come to one conclusion, at least. I am still the same person that I was before I learned of my father's Negro blood. I feel no different, I look no different. Two of the people I love and respect most in all the world are black, and they are the equal of any white man or woman, and better than most. In my own mind, I cannot feel that my black blood is any great disadvantage. Besides, I think that being an indentured servant isn't a great deal different from being a slave, except for the color of one's skin. And André told me that white people have been made slaves in times past."

"True, that is true," Michael said in a low voice.

"And you, Michael? What are your feelings?"

"My feelings? *Touché*, Hannah dear." He laughed shortly. "To be frank, as a lad and later, at Malvern, I never thought much about it. The slaves were *there*, they were a fact of life. My father, I know, did not wholly approve of slavery. He told me so many times. But he said it was necessary for plantation economy. And then ..." Now his laughter was fuller. "You will find this hard to believe, but the first true thought I gave to the fact of slavery was when I was a pirate with Blackbeard!"

"With Blackbeard?" Hannah said in astonishment.

"Yes, my dear. Incredible as it may seem, many of his men were blacks, mainly escaped slaves, I should imagine. I asked him once why that should be, and he said ... I will try to remember his exact words. He said, 'Ever' man should be free to do as he wishes, bucko. Color and race, they don't matter. Aye, a black man to Teach is just another man, be he able to do what I ask of him. What do ye think a life of piracy is? A free life, a life where ever' man is equal. . . .'" That from Captain Teach, the blackest of villains! It did give me pause. And something else he said: 'I know that ye,

498

at least Malcolm Verner, keep slaves on your fine plantation. Ye think that makes ye any better than old Teach?' And you know, I could think of no response to that. But if a man such as Blackbeard could consider a black man his equal, why should I feel any different? From that day I have looked at black people, slaves and free alike, with new eyes. Oh, I don't suppose I'm going to make every slave a freed man when I return to Malvern. Two years have passed and I have not. But it is something to think upon. And speaking of the two years past . . ."

He turned toward her, and Hannah found that he was ready for her again.

"Ah, aren't you the ardent one, sir!"

"I will make a further confession to you, dear heart. I am a man of great passions. My blood runs hot. Yet I have been celibate since I returned to Malvern from New Orleans."

He paused, as though expecting some response from her, and Hannah tensed inside. Was he anticipating a similar confession from her? She recalled her remark of a moment back, avowing no more secrets between them. It was on her lips to speak of Josh, and then the ageless instinct of womankind, warning when to speak and when not to speak, kept her lips sealed.

"If such be the case then, sir, it appears we have much to make up for. And I, dear Michael, am much a wanton when with you. I hope that does not shock you."

"Shock me? Not at all, dearest. It delights me!" He shouted laughter. "Never would I wish a cold stick in my bed!"

She murmured, "Cold stick I am not, sir."

Hannah opened her arms and her body to his embrace.

The coach approached Malvern at dusk on a cool September afternoon. In an effort to reach Malvern this day, John had driven the coach hard since dawn that morning.

Travel-weary as she was, Hannah sat up and peered eagerly out the window as the coach turned into the familiar drive.

"There, there is Malvern!" She took Michele from Bess's arms, and held the girl out the window so she could catch her first glimpse of the manor house. "That will be our home henceforth, Michele."

As though their approach had been heralded far in advance, all the slaves were gathered before the house as the coach drew up.

Henry stepped forward to open the coach door and help Hannah down. "Welcome back to Malvern, Mistress Hannah."

"It's grand to be back, Henry."

Michael was next. He clasped Henry's shoulder. "How are matters here at Malvern, man?"

"Malvern be fine, master," Henry said. "It good you be back in time to see to the harvest."

Hannah took Michele from Bess again and ran ahead toward the door held open by Jenny. She wanted to be the first to carry her daughter across the threshold of Malvern. Michael lingered behind to talk with Henry. Carrying Michele, Hannah ran from room to room.

She was exultant. She whispered to the child, "Baby darling, I am finally, once and for all, the true mistress of Malvern!"

Then she heard Michael's bellow. "Hannah! Where are you, wench?"

She went running into the hallway. Breathless, she said, "What is it?"

He gestured to the wide staircase. "Do you recall the last time we went up those stairs together?"

"Indeed I do, sir! You used me ..." Then, remembering, she glanced around with a start at all the grinning faces.

"And so I shall again!" He took Michele from her and gave the child to Bess. Then, before Hannah realized his intention, he scooped her up into his arms and started with her up the staircase.

Face scarlet, she said in his ear, "Michael, I am home, at long last."

"You are indeed, from this time forward."

Michael bounded on up the stairs. Face still flaming, yet laughing for all her embarrassment, Hannah put her arms around his neck, hid her face in his shoulder, and let a warm tide of contentment sweep over her.

In her mind she said again, *Mistress of Malvern!*

ED MCBAIN'S MYSTERIES

JACK AND THE BEANSTALK   (17-083, $3.95)
Jack's dead, stabbed fourteen times. And thirty-six thousand's missing in cash. Matthew's questions are turning up some long-buried pasts, a second dead body, and some beautiful suspects. Like Sunny, Jack's sister, a surfer boy's fantasy, a delicious girl with some unsavory secrets.

BEAUTY AND THE BEAST   (17-134, $3.95)
She was spectacular—an unforgettable beauty with exquisite features. On Monday, the same woman appeared in Hope's law office to file a complaint. She had been badly beaten—a mass of purple bruises with one eye swollen completely shut. And she wanted her husband put away before something worse happened. Her body was discovered on Tuesday, bound with wire coat hangers and burned to a crisp. But her husband—big, and monstrously ugly—denies the charge.

Available wherever paperbacks are sold, or order direct from the Publisher. Send cover price plus 50¢ per copy for mailing and handling to Pinnacle Books, Dept.17-302, 475 Park Avenue South, New York, N.Y. 10016. Residents of New York, New Jersey and Pennsylvania must include sales tax. DO NOT SEND CASH.

BLOCKBUSTER FICTION FROM PINNACLE BOOKS!

THE FINAL VOYAGE OF THE S.S.N. SKATE   (17-157, $3.95)
by Stephen Cassell
The "leper" of the U.S. Pacific Fleet, SSN 578 nuclear attack sub SKATE, has one final mission to perform—an impossible act of piracy that will pit the underwater deathtrap and its inexperienced crew against the combined might of the Soviet Navy's finest!

QUEENS GATE RECKONING   (17-164, $3.95)
by Lewis Purdue
Only a wounded CIA operative and a defecting Soviet ballerina stand in the way of a vast consortium of treason that speeds toward the hour of mankind's ultimate reckoning! From the bestselling author of THE LINZ TESTAMENT.

FAREWELL TO RUSSIA   (17-165, $4.50)
by Richard Hugo
A KGB agent must race against time to infiltrate the confines of U.S. nuclear technology after a terrifying accident threatens to unleash unmitigated devastation!

THE NICODEMUS CODE   (17-133, $3.95)
by Graham N. Smith and Donna Smith
A two-thousand-year-old parchment has been unearthed, unleashing a terrifying conspiracy unlike any the world has previously known, one that threatens the life of the Pope himself, and the ultimate destruction of Christianity!

Available wherever paperbacks are sold, or order direct from the Publisher. Send cover price plus 50¢ per copy for mailing and handling to Pinnacle Books, Dept.17-302, 475 Park Avenue South, New York, N.Y. 10016. Residents of New York, New Jersey and Pennsylvania must include sales tax. DO NOT SEND CASH.